Praise for *A Song at Twilight*

"Written with a lyrical grace reminiscent of Rosamunde Pilcher, Pamela Sherwood's *A Song at Twilight* spins a powerfully romantic tale of two honorable, star-crossed lovers trying to find their way back to each other's arms."

—Mary Jo Putney, *New York Times* bestselling author of *Sometimes a Rogue*

"Rich with drama and mystery, Robin and Sophie's love story is a sweeping tale filled with the drama of the Cornish landscape and lyrical yearning of the music Sophie sings."

—Teresa Grant, author of *The Paris Affair*

Praise for *Waltz with a Stranger*

"Sherwood effortlessly evokes the world of Edith Wharton and Henry James, and her exquisite character development, memorable secondary characters, and impeccably researched historical setting infuse this elegantly written debut with a richness and depth worth savoring."

—*Booklist* Starred Review

"Readers will be enchanted."

—*RT Book Reviews*

"Sympathetic protago   *ely*

A Song at Twilight

PAMELA SHERWOOD

sourcebooks
casablanca

Published by Sourcebooks Casablanca, an imprint of Sourcebooks, Inc.
P.O. Box 4410, Naperville, Illinois 60567-4410
(630) 961-3900
Fax: (630) 961-2168
www.sourcebooks.com

Printed and bound in the United States of America.
VP 10 9 8 7 6 5 4 3 2 1

In memory of my father

"If music be the food of love, play on."

—William Shakespeare, *Twelfth Night*

One

O, call back yesterday! Bid time return.

—Shakespeare, *Richard II*

London, July 1896

HE'D BEEN A FOOL TO COME, BUT HE COULDN'T HAVE stayed away if his life depended on it.

All around him, Robin could hear the rustle of programmes, the faint coughs and murmurs as the audience settled in before the performance. Down in the pit, violins lilted and cellos thrummed as the orchestra tuned up its instruments. The concert had sold out quickly—he'd been fortunate to secure a prime seat in one of the lower tiers with a clear view of the stage. But even the galleries and balconies were full tonight.

He smoothed out his programme with hands that shook only slightly, then read the lines of print over and over until the words ran together in a meaningless blur. David Cherwell, the promising Welsh tenor, and Sophia Tresilian—one of the finest young sopranos in recent memory—performing together for one night only at the prestigious Albert Hall.

Sophia. The name seemed to belong to some glamorous

stranger. In Cornwall, among those who knew her best, she was just Sophie. Sometimes "Snip" to her brother Harry. "Lark" to her sister Cecily. And to Robin himself... He pushed the thought away, reminding himself that he'd lost the right to call her anything at all four years ago. Lost it, renounced it, thrown it away... and for the best. What could he have offered her then but heartache and ruin?

And now here she was—celebrated, adored, at the start of a brilliant career. And here *he* was, watching and waiting. To see all that radiant promise fulfilled. To comfort himself with the knowledge that he'd done the right thing. And for one more reason that he could not, dared not, put into words yet.

One way or another, tonight would tell the tale.

The house lights dimmed and the orchestra launched into a brisk overture that Robin barely heeded because his attention was fixed on the stage. As the last flourish sounded, he saw the slender figure walk out to take her place before them all.

Not tall, Sophie, but she carried herself with a poise that made her appear so. Stage lights caught the coppery glints in her dark hair, shone on the smooth ivory heart of her face, the slim column of her throat, rising from the décolleté neckline of her gown—a gown the color of midnight, almost void of ornament, severe but becoming. She'd worn white the first time he saw her—a young girl's dress, artless and unsophisticated, but even then the woman had begun to emerge. And here she stood now, the blossom to the bud, so beautiful it made him ache.

And not just him. He sensed the heightened awareness around him, the way so many of the men in his vicinity seemed to come to a point. Like hounds catching the first whiff of game, or orchid hunters sighting a rare, elusive bloom.

Unseen, the piano rippled out an introduction, the somber chords echoing through the hall, now hushed and reverent as a church. Onstage, Sophie raised her head and began to sing.

"Music for a while, Shall all your cares beguile…"

Purcell—she'd always had a fondness for that composer's songs. Her voice held the same purity he remembered, but with an added richness, the patina of training and experience. Caught between pride and pain, Robin sat motionless and listened, absorbing every note.

How long had it been since he'd first heard her sing?

Five years ago, this past December. A lifetime ago…

Two

So smooth, so sweet, so silvery is thy voice,
As, could they hear, the damned would make no noise,
But listen to thee (walking in thy chamber)
Melting melodious words, to lutes of amber.

—Robert Herrick, "Upon Julia's Voice"

31 December 1890

ACCORDING TO THE COMMON WISDOM, WINTER DID
not truly begin in Cornwall until the middle of January. But
Robin fancied he felt a tang of frost in the air even now,
a harbinger of the season to come. And night had fallen
quickly, as it always did at this time of year.

He urged his horse forward as Roswarne rose up before
him, dignified and Georgian, but imbued with a mellow, even
welcoming, charm. The manor's lighted windows shone like
beacons in the darkness, golden and glowing. He was glad,
suddenly, that he'd accepted Sir Harry Tresilian's invitation,
rather than returning to London or seeing out the old year at
Pendarvis Hall with Great-Uncle Simon, who scarce took heed
of his presence. But then the past was far more real to the old
man than the present, so Robin tried not to take it personally.

"The more the merrier," Sir Harry had told him. "We Tresilians always have a full house at year's end, and you'll not have a better chance to meet your future neighbors."

His neighbors. He recognized perhaps a handful by sight—most were pleasant enough upon meeting, but he sensed an element of reserve on their parts, a reminder that he was yet something of an outsider, despite his name and heritage.

Robin was accustomed to that. How could he not be, given the pattern of so much of his life? But now he wondered if an outsider could *make* himself belong, set down roots deep enough, strong enough, in a place that he became a part of it. If he spent the rest of his life here, would he eventually find acceptance, or would he forever remain on the periphery?

Pushing those bleak thoughts aside, he rode up the drive to Roswarne. A groom waited to take the reins of his horse as he dismounted, and he made his way up the steps to the front door.

Parsons, the Tresilians' butler, admitted him, but his host, immaculate in black and white evening dress, came striding into the foyer to greet him. Though not yet thirty, Sir Harry carried himself with the confidence and assurance that only a man wholly comfortable with himself and his place in the world could muster.

"Pendarvis!" The baronet clasped Robin's hand, smiling. "Welcome to Roswarne. Come in and let me introduce you to the family. We've some light refreshments set up in the ballroom, and the dancing's to begin soon. After the music, of course."

"Of course." Robin smiled back. They were mad for music, these Cornish, and when in London, he himself enjoyed the occasional concert or night at the opera. While he doubted any of the performers here would rival what one heard at Covent Garden or the Albert Hall, music seemed a fitting way to celebrate the season.

He followed his host into the ballroom, a handsome salon hung with cream silk, bright with candles, and redolent with the spicy fragrance of evergreens. Numerous guests were already present, helping themselves to refreshments or admiring the tall, lavishly decorated Christmas tree that graced one corner of the room. Some looked around as Sir Harry entered with Robin, and several even smiled.

Robin returned their smiles and began to relax. Most people, even strangers, were friendly enough if you were willing to meet them halfway.

"We keep the Christmas tree up through Twelfth Night," Sir Harry told him. "It brightens things up, don't you think? And there's my mother, standing beside it." He led Robin over to where a comely woman of late middle age was talking to a handsome dark-haired young man.

"My mother, Isobel, Lady Tresilian," Sir Harry began. "And my cousin, James Trelawney. Mother, James, this is Robin Pendarvis."

Lady Tresilian inclined her head. Her coloring was fairer than her son's, but Sir Harry had inherited her brilliant green eyes. "So pleased you could join us this evening, Mr. Pendarvis. I understand you've come down from London to visit your great-uncle?"

"Yes, for a time," Robin replied, sketching a bow. "Great-Uncle Simon is not in the best of health at present, and I plan to remain in Cornwall until he is somewhat recovered."

Lady Tresilian's smile grew warmer. "Very commendable. I do not know your great-uncle well, but I should be sorry to hear of anyone being poorly, with no family on hand to help. I hope you are enjoying your time here."

"I am indeed, Lady Tresilian. Cornwall makes a pleasant respite from London."

"I could not agree more," Trelawney said, exchanging a wry smile with Sir Harry.

And there it was, that sense of shared history and common

tastes that marked them as family, even more than their physical resemblance. How long had it been since Robin had had that feeling himself? Since his parents' death, or earlier, before his brother Will had died?

He banished those melancholy thoughts as several more Tresilians came up to join them and be introduced in turn: brothers, a brother-in-law, nieces, and nephews. Robin smiled and shook hands, doing his best to keep all the names straight.

"So, where are Sophie and Cecily?" Sir Harry inquired.

"Setting up in the music room," his mother informed him. "You know how nervous Sophie gets before a performance."

"My youngest sister, Sophie, is perhaps the most talented of us," Sir Harry explained to Robin. "She sings *and* plays the violin."

"She sounds very accomplished," Robin said politely, hoping that his host wasn't just speaking as a fond brother and the girl would be at least tolerable to listen to.

Sir Harry checked his pocket watch. "I should see how things are going in the music room too. The performance will be starting in about ten minutes. Have some refreshments, Pendarvis—the ginger biscuits are especially good."

Making his way over to the refreshment table, Robin helped himself to a few ginger biscuits and a damson tart, along with a glass of light wine. The biscuits were as delicious as Sir Harry had promised, spicy and rich, and the tart even better. Lady Tresilian smiled at his praise and informed him that a lavish supper would be served after the dancing.

The musicale started at its appointed time, and Robin followed the other guests into the music room, a spacious salon done in soft greens, inviting as a breath of spring on this cold winter's night. Holly and ivy festooned the mantelpiece and the frame of the bay window, through which one could glimpse the impenetrable darkness of the evening sky, now black as jet. But a fire burned cheerily in the grate, and in the center of the room stood a gleaming grand piano, flanked by several other instruments, including a harp and a cello. Mindful of the Tresilians' hospitality, Robin took a seat in one of the front rows of chairs, determined to show interest and enjoyment even if the performers should turn out to be not quite up to par.

A trim, brown-haired young woman—introduced as Sir Harry's sister, Cecily Penhallow—sat down at the piano and launched into Beethoven's "Moonlight Sonata," playing with skill, assurance, and expression. So much for preconceived notions, Robin thought, and serve him right for being a snob, if unconsciously so. He relaxed in his chair, letting the rippling, lucent chords wash over him. When Cecily had finished, he applauded with genuine enthusiasm, as did the other listeners, and she obliged with a sprightly Chopin étude for the encore.

Others followed: two men played a duet on violin and cello, then a woman sang two songs, one in Cornish, while accompanying herself on the harp. The level of skill was remarkably high, and the performers' obvious love for what they did more than compensated for any technical shortcomings. Not that there were many; indeed, each performer seemed to have brought his or her best to this evening.

After John Tresilian had performed a lively flute solo from Mendelssohn's "A Midsummer Night's Dream," Cecily returned to the piano, followed by a dark-haired girl in white, who appeared no older than seventeen. Sophie Tresilian, Robin supposed—a guess confirmed by her introduction. An air of pleased expectancy pervaded the room as she took her place by the piano, which seemed to augur well for her abilities. That she was also quite pretty, with a dimpled smile that transformed her rather serious face, did not hurt her cause either.

Robin half expected her to perform something light-hearted and sweet, the sort of song deemed suitable for one of her tender years, about flowers, birds, or a girl's first love.

Instead, Cecily played an almost somber opening, stately and grave. Sophie stood as still as a statue, seeming to absorb every note into her blood and bones, then began to sing:

> *"Tomorrow shall be my dancing day*
> *I would my true love did so chance*
> *To see the legend of my play*
> *To call my true love to my dance*
> *Sing O my love, O my love, my love, my love*
> *This have I done for my true love."*

Pure as a choirboy's, her voice lilted along the high ceiling of the music room. Robin had heard this ancient Cornish carol sung before, but never with such haunting beauty and clarity. Or with such an inherent understanding of both the joy and solemnity surrounding the occasion of Christ's birth. Transfixed, Robin listened as Sophie's silver-clear soprano led all of them through the next steps of the sacred "dance." She sang less than half the carol, focusing on the verses most relevant to the Christmas season, but she held her listeners spellbound from first to last.

Although every performer had received generous applause, the audience paid Sophie the added tribute of a moment's silence first. Robin surprised himself by clapping until his hands tingled, and was further charmed when he saw the faint blush mantle Sophie's cheeks. Modest as well as talented: an enchanting combination.

She smiled and nodded acknowledgment, then gestured to Cecily to resume playing the piano. Her encore, Purcell's "Fairest Isle," was exquisitely performed as well, with a simplicity that let the song's loveliness speak for itself. Oh, she had something, this girl—it *hadn't* just been brotherly love speaking when Sir Harry mentioned her talents.

Somewhat to Robin's disappointment, Sophie did not produce a violin after finishing her second song. Instead, she made way for the other performers who gathered about the piano for a rousing rendition of "The Sans Day Carol," inviting the audience to join in the choruses. Although not familiar with the song, Robin listened attentively and soon added his voice to the others, doing his best to help bring the musicale to a triumphant close.

"And the first tree in the greenwood, it was the holly!"

❧

The musicale finished, the guests adjourned again to the ballroom, where the orchestra was tuning up its instruments for the quadrille, traditionally the first dance of the evening.

Almost without realizing it, Robin looked around for Sophie Tresilian and located her in a corner of the ballroom, talking animatedly to several young men close to her own age. The sight sent a sharp twinge of envy through him. Envy he knew he'd no right to feel, for what was *he* to her?

Youth calls to youth, Robin reminded himself. A girl of seventeen, barely out of the schoolroom. He was eight—nearly nine—years her senior, and felt far older. And that wasn't even taking into consideration the... unique position in which he found himself. Even if it were possible, even if his circumstances were different, he should not be looking at her like this.

Except that he couldn't seem to look away. And somewhere deep inside of him, a spark of rebellion flared to life. Must he spend every waking moment doing penance for his folly? Denying himself even the most fleeting and innocent of pleasures? Pretending that he no longer felt desire, attraction, or even a simple wish for companionship?

The spark grew into a flame—glowing fierce, bright, and hot. What harm, he thought, could one dance do?

Rebellion hardened into resolve. Just for tonight, he

would behave like a man with no history—and nothing to regret. Just for tonight, he would allow himself a dance with a lovely young woman whose bright smile and even brighter talent had touched him in ways he'd no longer thought possible. On the last day of the old year, surely he could be permitted one indulgence?

Quickly, before he could talk himself out of it, he strode toward Sophie's corner.

&

She'd never been the belle of the ball before, Sophie reflected bemusedly, and while it certainly was gratifying, it was unsettling too. Young men who wouldn't have spared her a glance last year crowded around her now, all lavish in their praise of her performance and eager to claim her dances.

Summoning a smile, she set down their names on her dance card, secretly astonished at how fast her waltzes, polkas, and even quadrilles were going. She sensed rather than saw a slight opening in the throng and turned toward it with relief, only to come face to face with…

Oh, my.

A man she'd never seen before stood watching her with an intensity that unsettled her more than the most fulsome compliments she'd received tonight. A tall, lean man, with dark hair and the bluest eyes she'd ever seen. Eyes that made her think of sapphires or midnight skies…

"Good evening, Mr.—?" Sophie let the last word trail off questioningly, hoping she didn't sound as flustered as his unwavering regard made her feel.

"Pendarvis." His deep voice held only a trace of a Cornish accent. "Robin Pendarvis. Your brother invited me here tonight."

Recognition sparked at the name. "Oh, then you must be related to Simon Pendarvis?"

"His grandnephew," he confirmed with a slight bow.

"May I compliment you on how well you sang tonight, Miss Tresilian?"

She felt herself flushing as she had *not* done after far more extravagant praise. "Thank you, Mr. Pendarvis. I was in good company—there are some wonderfully talented musicians in the county."

"So I've discovered." He paused. "I was wondering if I might have the pleasure of a dance with you? The first waltz, perhaps?"

Sophie glanced at her card, experiencing a pang of regret when she saw the name already beside it. "I'm afraid the first waltz is claimed. But the supper dance is free, and it is also a waltz—if you're still interested." *Please be interested*, she thought with an urgency that surprised her. But this mysterious man with his unquiet eyes drew her as irresistibly as the moon drew the tides. If he would just partner her in this dance, take her in to supper afterward...

He smiled, the expression transforming his angular face, and for just a moment, she forgot how to breathe. "I am indeed. Please put me down for that, Miss Tresilian."

"Miss Sophie." A new voice—cool and cultured—interrupted them.

Looking up from her card again, Sophie saw that Sir Lucas Nankivell—one of their neighbors—had appeared just at Mr. Pendarvis's shoulder and was regarding her fixedly.

"Good evening, Sir Lucas," Sophie greeted him politely, wondering why his gaze should affect her so differently than Mr. Pendarvis's. The baronet was pleasant enough to look at, after all: tall and athletically built, even if—as Harry said—he would never see thirty again.

"I wanted to tell you how exquisite your performance was," Sir Lucas went on, his gaze still intent on her. "The equal of any singer I have heard in Covent Garden."

"You flatter me, Sir Lucas," Sophie said lightly. "But thank you all the same."

"I assure you, Miss Sophie—I do not offer empty compliments," Sir Lucas persisted. "Now, might I have the pleasure of partnering you for the supper dance?"

"Forgive me, Sir Lucas," Sophie began, feeling insensibly relieved, "but I have already promised that dance to Mr. Pendarvis." She nodded toward the man in question.

Sir Lucas turned his head and, much to Sophie's astonishment, subjected Mr. Pendarvis to a prolonged and not particularly friendly scrutiny. Mr. Pendarvis stared coolly back, but Sophie thought she saw a tiny muscle tighten in the corner of his jaw.

Suddenly uneasy, she resumed, "I should introduce you. Mr. Pendarvis, this is Sir Lucas Nankivell, Baronet, one of our neighbors. Sir Lucas, Mr. Robin Pendarvis."

"Pendarvis," Sir Lucas echoed, his gaze still on the other man. "Of Pendarvis Hall?"

"Indeed." Mr. Pendarvis inclined his head in acknowledgment.

"A fine old establishment."

"Thank you."

"It must take some… work to maintain it." Was that a faint sneer in Sir Lucas's voice?

"Most properties do." The chill in Mr. Pendarvis's eyes belied his calm tone.

"Indeed." A wealth of condescension infused that single word.

Sophie glanced from one to the other, her uneasiness growing. *Dear life, what ailed these men?* Despite the polite, even innocuous words, they reminded her of nothing so much as a pair of strange dogs sizing each other up; only the raised hackles were missing. She'd never seen such a blatant case of—if not hate, then strong dislike at first sight.

She was wondering how to defuse things when Sir Lucas turned back to her. "Perhaps another dance then, Miss Sophie?" he suggested. "The first one *after* supper?"

"Yes, of course." Sophie penciled his name in, then tried

to smile impartially at both men. "I shall see you, by and by.
But I can hear the music starting for the quadrille, and here
comes my brother to dance it with me!" she added with
relief. "If you'll excuse me, gentlemen?"

Fortunately, they both stepped aside at once. Gathering
up her skirts, Sophie hurried to meet John—brothers were a
godsend at times like this! But she couldn't help glancing back
over her shoulder. Much to her relief, Mr. Pendarvis and Sir
Lucas were now heading in opposite directions. But then
surely neither man was foolish or ill-bred enough to make a
scene—not over a dance, of all things!

Even the supper dance… Sophie found herself smiling
at the prospect as she and John joined the couples lining up
for the quadrille. Robin Pendarvis, with his brilliant blue
eyes and air of mystery—a man, not a callow youth—would
be sharing a waltz *and* supper with her! What had begun as
an evening of simple pleasures—music, good food, good
company—suddenly promised far more.

✑

The dances came and went in quick succession: waltz, polka,
galop… Sophie was astonished to find herself in demand for
so many of them. But it was pure delight to be considered
"out" now, and thus able to dance as often as she liked. Not
even having her toes and hem stepped on by her less graceful
partners could dim her pleasure in that.

Talking of partners… now and again, her glance strayed
to Mr. Pendarvis. Far from hiding in corners or taking refuge
in the library or some other masculine enclave, he remained
in the ballroom, dancing with ladies of varying ages—from
girls just emerged from the schoolroom to middle-aged
matrons who still clearly loved to take a turn about the floor.
The discovery pleased her, even though she couldn't help
envying his partners, a feeling that intensified when she saw
the satisfied, even smug smile sported by one of them—a pert

redhead slightly older than herself—as Mr. Pendarvis led her through a spirited polka.

That supper dance couldn't come fast enough after that. Watching Mr. Pendarvis's approach, Sophie only wished she were wearing something a bit more sophisticated tonight, crimson, perhaps—or green, to complement her eyes. But Mama had been quite firm about what was suitable for a girl Sophie's age at her first adult party. So, white it had to be.

Fortunately, if the light in his eyes was any indication, Mr. Pendarvis didn't appear to find Sophie's appearance lacking. "As promised, Miss Tresilian." He sketched a bow. "Though I've noticed you've been much in demand this evening. You are not too weary, I trust?"

"Not at all. I love to dance." Sophie took his proffered hand, her pulse quickening pleasurably at his warm, firm clasp. "My sister, Cecily, warns me I won't always be able to keep up like this, so I might as well enjoy it while I can."

"Wise counsel, if somewhat dampening," Mr. Pendarvis agreed, leading her out onto the floor. "But I feel I should apologize in advance. I'm not the most exciting of dancers."

Sophie smiled at him. "That's quite all right, Mr. Pendarvis. I've had some partners this evening who afforded me rather more excitement than I desired. I should be glad of a nice, uneventful waltz at this time."

"Then I shall do my best to make it thoroughly sedate," he said, smiling back. "As long as you don't fall asleep in the middle of the set."

She laughed. "Oh, I've yet to experience that with any partner."

And as they stepped into position, her right hand clasped in his left, his right hand settling at the small of her back, Sophie felt a thrill of anticipation that gave the lie to her previous words. However this waltz proceeded, she was certain it would prove anything but uneventful.

~❦~

Her head just topped his shoulder, and for a moment, Robin felt a shock of familiarity that was not entirely pleasant. He pushed it away, made himself concentrate on the young lady in his arms—who could not be more different.

Dark rather than fair, slender without being ethereal, with those lively green eyes that looked straight into his own, without artifice or dissembling. Sophie might be young, but she was by no means gauche or awkward. Indeed, she had a poise and self-possession that any woman of any age would envy. Like the rest of her family, she exuded the sense of being comfortable with herself and her place in the world. Not complacent, and certainly not smug, but... secure. Confident, as few girls of seventeen were.

The music began, a lilting Strauss confection, and Robin led Sophie a trifle hesitantly into the dance. But then, who wouldn't feel self-conscious taking the floor with one's host's youngest sister and the apple of her family's eye? He just managed to avoid looking around to see if Sir Harry or any of the Tresilians were watching them, telling himself he was being ridiculous.

So, a gentle waltz—just as he'd promised her. He held her the prescribed distance away, aware of the heat of her body, warm from previous dances, through the thin silk muslin of her gown. And the scent that drifted from her skin—a simple essence of violet, delicate but haunting.

Once, many years ago, he'd been beguiled by what he thought was innocence. But this girl, with her open face and shining smile, was a true innocent, someone to be cherished and protected. That she also happened to arouse feelings in him that were rather less innocent was his problem entirely. If only he hadn't been such a credulous fool *then*, perhaps he could let himself acknowledge those feelings *now*, without guilt or regret...

But that sort of thinking availed him nothing. The past

was the past, and he had to live with that. Closing the door on all the "might have beens," Robin concentrated on the dance. Much to his relief, he seemed to be doing passably well—Sophie's hem and toes were intact, so far. And Sophie herself waltzed beautifully, her steps light and graceful. Little wonder that so many young men sought her out as a partner.

Her voice broke in on his thoughts. "Mr. Pendarvis, are you quite all right? You were looking so—forbidding just now."

"Was I?" He summoned a smile and guided her into a turn. "A moment's distraction, Miss Tresilian, that I hope you'll forgive. I am not usually so inattentive when dancing with a charming young lady."

"Are you sure there isn't something troubling you?" she persisted, her gaze intent on his face. "Your great-uncle, perhaps? I'd heard he was unwell."

"He's a little under the weather, but I suspect it's mostly age that ails him," Robin replied. "That, and having outlived so many of his old friends and companions. I offered to stay with him tonight, but he seemed indifferent to the idea."

Sympathy warmed her eyes and voice. "My Grandmother Tresilian became like that toward the end of her life. She turned inward and hardly seemed to know any of us anymore. All we could do was see that she had all she needed and make her as comfortable as possible."

"That's what I am trying to do. It's at times like this I wish we were closer, though—I did not meet my great-uncle until I was sixteen, and we've met only sporadically since then."

"You did not grow up in Cornwall then, Mr. Pendarvis?"

"I did not have that pleasure, Miss Tresilian. My father was a captain in the army—we followed wherever the regiment took him. I never set foot in Cornwall until after his death, but he'd told me all about spending his childhood summers here. When I saw it for myself, I could not believe how *green* everything was, and how mild the climate. My father's last posting was in India—sadly, he died there, of fever—so you could scarce imagine two places more different." The only similarity was how alien he'd felt in both. Aloud, he said, "I beg your pardon, Miss Tresilian. This conversation has turned far more serious than I intended it to."

"No need to apologize, Mr. Pendarvis," she assured him. "I'm sorry about your father—I've heard that living conditions are very rigorous in India."

"You've heard rightly. It's a country that holds much beauty but much danger as well, especially for unwary foreigners," he added, remembering some close calls during his boyhood; a poisonous snake had figured prominently in at least one of them. "It took me some time to accustom myself to how much calmer England seemed, by comparison."

Sophie's brows arched. "Calm but not boring, I hope?"

Robin looked down into her piquant young face. "No, not boring at all. Especially now."

Her eyes widened as she absorbed the compliment, and a faint flush rose in her cheeks, but he thought she did not look at all displeased. Encouraged, he executed a successful twirl, and they danced on.

❧

The break for supper came, and he escorted her into the dining room, which in size and shape reminded him of a lord's medieval great hall. A long table decked in snowy linen dominated the room, and the food had been laid out on huge serving platters for diners to help themselves.

As Lady Tresilian had promised, supper was lavish, as befitted the season: roast joints of beef and mutton, ham, goose, lobster, and salmon. Savory and sweet pies of all description—Robin had heard the joke that the devil himself avoided Cornwall for fear of being baked in a pie—along with hothouse fruits, puddings, jellies, and pitchers filled to the brim with rich Cornish cream. Cider, champagne, and wine were also available in abundance; Sir Harry prided himself on his cellar, Sophie informed him.

Once they were seated, Robin served them both from the various laden platters. Sophie ate lightly, but with the eager appetite of seventeen, whetted no doubt by her performances in the music room and on the dance floor. He liked that she did not peck or nibble at her food, as too many fashionable young ladies did.

"Would you like anything more?" he asked, as she polished off the last delectable bite, then eyed her empty plate a touch wistfully.

She shook her head. "I mustn't gorge myself, not when there's more dancing to follow. But I will take a little more champagne, if you please."

He reached for the bottle and poured out half a glass of the pale sparkling wine for her.

Sophie sipped it delicately. "Wonderful," she said on a sigh. "They don't usually let me drink anything stronger than tea, or occasionally cider, unless it's a very special occasion."

Robin glanced involuntarily toward the end of the table, where Sir Harry was sitting; fortunately, his host was not looking in their direction. "Oh, dear. Will your brother be displeased by my plying you with strong drink?"

She gave a gurgle of laughter, as irresistibly bubbly as the champagne. "Only if we're foolish enough to tell him! But you needn't worry, Mr. Pendarvis. I'm enjoying this evening far too much to spoil it by getting tiddly."

Her frank admission made him smile as well. Nothing of the coquette about Sophie, he thought, nothing calculating or artful. Her face, her manners, and her conversation were open, candid, and unaffected, and all the more endearing for that.

Did she have any idea of her own appeal? She'd a host of admirers, but he'd seen no evidence that she'd been flirting with any of them. Or with him for that matter.

Which was all to the good, Robin reminded himself. In London, at some of the parties he'd attended, he'd had to discourage a few young ladies inclined to set their caps at him, once they heard of his expectations as Great-Uncle Simon's heir. Nothing so stark as the truth, but enough to let them know he was not a likely candidate for matrimony at this time.

Not until tonight had he found himself wishing he were. But he had no business hoping for—if not the impossible, then the deeply improbable, and no right to cry for the moon. Life was in the moment, and at this moment, seated beside this lovely, enchanting girl-woman, he felt he had all he could want. Let that be enough, for now.

"It has been—a very pleasant evening," he said aloud.

"Hasn't it?" Sophie smiled at him over the rim of her glass, her eyes glowing like jade. "I am so glad you've enjoyed yourself, Mr. Pendarvis. And even gladder that you accepted my brother's invitation."

"As am I, Miss Tresilian." Robin picked up his own wineglass to touch it lightly to hers. "To the New Year."

"To the New Year," she echoed, and they drank the toast together.

❧

As expected, Sir Lucas Nankivell claimed Sophie for the dance after supper. Robin yielded her with a smile that concealed his mounting irritation. It was rare for him to feel such instant antipathy toward a person he'd just met, but something about the man rubbed him the wrong way—whether it was his too-perfect appearance, his supercilious manner toward Robin himself, or his rather proprietary air toward Sophie, though at least she'd shown no sign of encouraging the fellow. Indeed, she seemed genuinely regretful to part from *him*, which afforded Robin considerable comfort. He was further consoled by the knowledge that the dance was a Lancers

Quadrille—lengthy, but providing far fewer opportunities for intimacy than the waltz he and Sophie had shared.

Robin shook his head, deliberately putting all thoughts of Nankivell out of his head. This was one of the most enjoyable parties he'd attended, and he wasn't about to spoil it by dwelling on the one unfriendly person he'd encountered tonight. Instead, he found himself a partner for the Lancers in Cecily Penhallow, even though she spent most of it talking about her husband and children. A pleasant, good-tempered woman, Robin thought as he escorted her back to the side of her adored Arthur, but lacking some of Sophie's sparkle and fire.

The evening hummed along agreeably. He participated in several more dances, including a polka with Sophie, as all her waltzes were now taken. The lively pace allowed little time for intimate conversation, but he enjoyed watching her romp, light as thistledown, through the set.

Sometime later, he found himself beside the Christmas tree, nursing a glass of cider as he watched the couples on the floor. Sophie was in the midst of a schottische, twirling upon her toes with the grace of a ballerina. Robin sipped his cider and tried not to envy her partner too much.

A voice spoke up from the other side of the Christmas tree, startling him.

"—only seventeen. Not ready for marriage, by any means."

"Young ladies her age marry every day in London."

Robin stiffened. He recognized both voices: Sir Harry's and that cool, cultured one that held no trace of a Cornish burr. And he knew, without a doubt, of whom they were speaking.

"Well, this isn't London, Nankivell." Sir Harry sounded just a bit testy. "Although since you have raised the subject, my sister has not yet made her debut in town society."

"You mean to bring her to London?" A hint of triumph in the baronet's voice had Robin's hand tightening about his glass.

"Perhaps." Sir Harry sounded guarded.

"I would say she's assured of a successful Season," Nankivell declared, with the air of one who considers himself an authority on such things. "Looks, charm, breeding—and I know you mean to dower her handsomely. But take care that she doesn't attract the wrong kind of suitor; fortune hunters are thick on the ground in London."

Sir Harry's response was cool. "Fortune hunters may be found anywhere, Nankivell. Including right here in Cornwall."

Robin tensed at the implication, but Nankivell did not appear to take umbrage. "Just so," he replied in a tone as smooth as Cornish cream.

"In any case, I believe I can be trusted to protect my sister *and* whatever fortune the family chooses to bestow on her," Sir Harry continued. "As for suitors, much will depend on what Sophie herself thinks."

"Your sister does not strike me as someone who would refuse an offer that would be so much to her advantage," Nankivell persisted.

"I would hope my sister would take the time to be sure of what she wanted before making her choice." Sir Harry's voice had taken on a decided edge. "And we are situated well enough that she need not decide in haste, or to accept the first offer she receives—unless she herself is convinced it's the right one. I trust I have made myself clear?"

"Entirely." And this time, that cultured voice held a note of pique, even displeasure.

"Then we need discuss this no further." Sir Harry's voice turned brisk. "It lacks just a quarter hour to midnight, and I have the most excellent tawny port on hand that I've been saving for just this occasion. Would you care to partake of a glass with me?"

After a moment's pause, Nankivell replied in the affirmative, and they moved off together in seeming amity. And on his side of the Christmas tree, Robin exhaled slowly, the taste of cider bitter in his mouth.

So, Sophie was an heiress. He should have guessed as much, but he'd been too beguiled by everything else she was to consider how she was fixed financially. He'd wager that detail was never far from Nankivell's mind, however.

Sophie, all youth, beauty, and bright promise. And Nankivell with those too-knowing eyes that seemed to calculate everyone's monetary worth, doubtless hoping to secure her and her fortune for himself. Robin felt an almost visceral surge of revulsion at the thought.

And what right had he to feel anything of the kind? His own past mocked him for his hypocrisy. Because if Sir Lucas Nankivell had no business thinking of Sophie Tresilian's many charms, Robin himself had far less.

He edged away from the Christmas tree, trying to forget what he'd heard, along with his own reaction to it. Best to go now, before he did someone—namely Nankivell— a violence.

He located Lady Tresilian in a far corner of the ballroom, talking to several other women, including her elder daughter. "Ah, Mr. Pendarvis, must you leave us now?" she inquired, once he'd offered his farewells. "Can we not persuade you to stay and see the old year out with us?"

"Thank you, Lady Tresilian, but I really must be going," he replied. "Great-Uncle Simon will be expecting to see me tomorrow morning."

She gave him her hand. "Very well then, I wish you a happy New Year, and I hope that you will call upon us in future."

Robin bowed over her hand. "Thank you, Lady Tresilian. I may at that."

He headed for the entrance hall, deliberately not looking back toward the dance floor, where he'd last seen Sophie embarking on a waltz with another of her many admirers.

No right to think of her that way. No right at all.

But her face was still before him, even after he'd left the

house and was mounted on his horse, riding slowly back toward Pendarvis Hall in the darkness and cold.

The spell had been cast, and he did not know how to break it. Nor, if he were being wholly honest with himself, was he sure he wanted to.

Three

I attempt from love's sickness to fly in vain,
For I am myself my own fever
For I am myself my own fever and pain.

—Henry Purcell, *The Indian Queen*

London, 1896

THE APPLAUSE ROARED IN HER EARS, THUNDEROUS AS the sea at high tide as it rushed into the mouths of the caves. Sophie bowed her head in acknowledgment of the audience's appreciation, feeling the triumph and euphoria fizzing through her veins like champagne. This was what it was all about: the joy that came from making music, and nothing, not the most grueling rehearsal, not the most exhausting schedule, ever diminished that joy. She prayed that nothing ever would.

Beside her, David took her gloved hand, raising it to his lips in a gesture of mingled gallantry and solidarity. Sophie could feel his own exhilaration in the quiver of his fingers twined in hers. They exchanged a smile and bowed again, drawing renewed applause for their final piece, a soaring duet from Verdi's *La Traviata*.

Then they were making their exits, heading for the performers' green room and the inevitable rush of admirers and aficionados that would follow.

Not for the first time, Sophie found herself wishing she could just slip away unnoticed, surround herself with the stillness and quiet while she reveled in tonight's achievement and the simple satisfaction that came of doing what one loved best. But her years on the concert circuit had taught her the impossibility of that following a performance. Not to mention the supper party afterward—to be held tonight at the Savoy Hotel—where there would be still more people to contend with. She stifled a sigh; while music could lift you to unimagined heights, inevitably you had to come back down to earth, and the descent always left her feeling rather flat. And for her, the glory seemed to dim all the faster the more people she had to talk to and the more questions she had to answer.

She caught David's eye and he sent her a commiserating shrug. Though more gregarious than she, he knew her humor in this but also understood its futility. They were professional singers at the start of their careers and could not afford to snub their audience. Temperamental prima donnas might think otherwise, but neither she nor David was that foolish.

A dresser standing backstage handed them each a warm wrap. David, in full evening kit, accepted his only for form's sake, but Sophie was glad enough to drape hers over her shoulders. It never failed to surprise her how quickly one cooled off after leaving the stage.

They had a few minutes' privacy and solitude in the green room, which Sophie put to good use, patting her face dry with a clean handkerchief and refreshing herself with a draught of cooled, lightly sweetened tea, brewed especially for her. Then, suddenly, voices and footsteps sounded in the passage, and the room filled up in what seemed to be the blink of an eye. All the best people, or so she'd been told repeatedly: elegant, fashionable people, some of whom wielded considerable influence in the music world.

Sophie had just enough time to assume a bright social smile before the first visitors engulfed her: two splendidly dressed couples, one young, one of late middle age. A family, by the looks of it, and her guess was borne out when they introduced themselves to her as Viscount and Viscountess Ashby, their daughter Harriet, and her husband, Mr. Sutcliffe.

"You were wonderful, Miss Tresilian," Lady Ashby said warmly. "This concert has been one of the highlights of the Season."

"Thank you—I'm so flattered that you think so." Sophie felt her smile becoming more relaxed and genuine.

"I have always loved Mozart," the viscountess continued. "Especially *The Magic Flute*. I so enjoyed your rendition of Pamina's lament."

"I'm partial to *The Marriage of Figaro*," Mrs. Sutcliffe chimed in. "I saw you in it last spring and thought you were simply divine as Cherubino. I'm so glad your 'Voi che sapete' was on the programme tonight. Was it very difficult, playing a breeches part?"

She seemed genuinely interested in the answer, so Sophie obliged her. "Oh, it was a bit of a challenge, but marvelously liberating too. Trousers do give one much more freedom of movement than skirts. I have three brothers, and I've often envied them their greater independence. And they do have a far easier time of things when it comes to clothes."

"I have two brothers, both older, and I feel much the same," Mrs. Sutcliffe confessed with a smile.

"Shall you be singing in any more operas?" Lady Ashby inquired.

"Oh, I couldn't say at this point," Sophie replied. "Now that the tour's finished, I mean to take a short holiday. But my manager will let me know of any offers that seem appropriate."

"Well, we all hope to see you again soon," the viscountess

said graciously. "Our congratulations on a wonderful performance tonight."

The gentlemen offered their compliments as well, and the Ashby party moved on, leaving Sophie to bask in a warm glow of achievement. It was always enjoyable to receive the accolades of those who actually seemed to care about music.

Feeling more cheerful, she braced herself for the next rush, which came almost at once. Strangers continued to pour into the green room, some as grand as the Ashbys, others humbler, but all of them congratulatory, even friendly. Nonetheless, the sheer number of well-wishers was overwhelming, the individual faces and voices all swallowed up in a churning sea of humanity.

Taking advantage of an all too brief respite, Sophie gulped a lungful of air and glanced over at David, only to find he was surrounded as well. But he could at least claim familiarity with his present admirers; although she had met them only once before, she recognized his mother, brother, and sister-in-law.

"Well done, *bach*, well done!" Llewelyn, the brother, was saying as he pumped David's hand. "Practically in tears, the ladies were."

They lapsed into a mixture of English and Welsh that Sophie didn't even try to follow, because by now more people had come up to surround her. She felt a brief pang that no one from her own family was here tonight, but most of them had seen her earlier performance at the Alexandra Palace before she'd left on her European tour in March.

Still, it would have been lovely to know that there was someone familiar in the audience watching her. This *was* her first time performing at the Albert Hall, and she couldn't help but feel that the achievement lacked a certain savor without someone special to share it with.

"Sophie, darling!" A familiar voice—with a familiar accent—caught her ear.

Sophie felt her heart and spirits lift as the crowd parted and two people came toward her: a beautiful, golden-haired woman and a lanky but elegant man with brown hair and piercing green eyes, both dressed in the height of fashion.

Thomas and Amy Sheridan, her closest friends in London. All but family, really—Amy's twin sister Aurelia had married Sophie's cousin James, now the Earl of Trevenan.

"You were wonderful!" Amy said warmly, her blue eyes glowing as she embraced Sophie. "Even better than the last time I saw you."

"A triumph, my dear," Sheridan said, smiling down at Sophie in turn.

Sophie smiled back without constraint. "Thank you—I'm so glad both of you came!"

"Wild horses couldn't have kept us away," Amy assured her. "Especially since your next engagement is singing at my soiree two evenings from now! Are you sure you won't be too tired, after tonight?"

"Oh, I will be in top form by then, I assure you." She would always be willing to sing for the Sheridans. After all their kindness and hospitality over the years, it seemed the very least she could do.

"Come for luncheon tomorrow," Amy invited. "We've got Mrs. Herbert to accompany you, and the two of you can work out your programme for the evening. You haven't yet seen the new house, in any case. Our salon is almost twice the size of the old one."

"I'd be delighted to come," Sophie said. "And to see your Isabella too."

Amy's face lit up at the mention of her infant daughter, born the previous autumn while Sophie had been touring America in *The Marriage of Figaro*. "I can't wait for you to meet her! Shall we say, one o'clock—if that's not too early for you?"

Sophie assured her that one o'clock was fine, and after a

last exchange of congratulations, the Sheridans stepped aside to let the other well-wishers approach.

Sophie soon lost track of the number of people she spoke to. David's family came over to offer their compliments, but most of the others were unfamiliar. Not for the first time, she was conscious of the irony: thousands might come to see her perform, admire her phrasings, and hang rapturously upon her every note, but she was destined to remain a stranger to them, just as they were strangers to her. They could have no inkling of the person behind the performer and very likely no interest, either.

Which was how it should be, she reminded herself sternly, or how could she have any sort of privacy worth the name? There'd be time enough, now that her concert engagements were almost finished for the Season, for her to go away and be just Sophie for a while. She'd promised herself at least a week's holiday—leasing a lovely cottage in the Cotswolds—and then there was John's wedding later this summer. She'd be home for that, no question.

Home. The sudden longing for it struck her with an almost physical force. Because, even after all this time and all her successes, Cornwall was still home. A home from which she'd exiled herself for the better part of four years, but home nonetheless.

Her eyes stung, shamefully, and she looked down, blinking hard and berating herself all the while. Not since her first tour had she allowed herself to succumb to homesickness; she would not do so now, not when she'd enjoyed such a singular success tonight.

Vision now clear, she quickly summoned a smile for her next guests—only to feel the smile freeze on her face and the words die in her throat when she looked up at last.

For a moment she thought her eyes were deceiving her, that fatigue and excitement were making her hallucinate. Because the man coming toward her, his face formal and unsmiling, was the last one she'd expected to see tonight. Or any other night, for that matter.

Robin Pendarvis. Here. In London.

Like one in a trance, she watched him approach, cutting through the crowd with the swift, purposeful stride she had loved in him. A few of the fashionably dressed throng glanced at him in mingled curiosity and irritation, but none attempted to deter him. And then he was before her, close enough to touch if she stretched out her hand... as she must *not* do, lest she lose herself once more. *Someone of her own*, a voice half-wry, half-mocking whispered in her head. Except that he hadn't been—or only for a little while.

"Miss Tresilian."

His voice was the same, deep and resonant, its slight Cornish burr more of an intonation than an accent and much fainter than her own when she'd first come to London as a wide-eyed debutante. Nor did he look so different from the way he had four years ago. Thirty-one now, and no longer in his first youth. Perhaps a little leaner, with some faint lines about his eyes and mouth. But his dark-brown hair was still thick, his eyes still blue and piercing. A visionary's eyes that saw how things might be and strove to transmute them into reality.

And how she'd loved that in him.

The only thing he hadn't been able to envision, at the last, was a future for them, together. But that had been her decision as much as his. No rancor between them, ever— she'd been determined on that score—but regrets enough to last a lifetime, aching continually, like an old wound in inclement weather.

She was still staring, tongue-tied and transfixed. *Remember who you are*, Sophie told herself. If not a diva, she was still a professional singer of some note, no longer a schoolroom miss to be thrown into confusion by a chance encounter. Shaking off the paralysis, she swallowed dryly and managed to summon a response. "Mr. Pendarvis. Good evening. You are looking very well."

The angular planes of his face seemed to relax at her words. "As are you, Miss Tresilian, and sounding even better. Magnificent, in fact. I congratulate you."

Sophie found she could smile, though the expression felt strange and unfamiliar on her face. "Thank you."

His eyes warmed, their cool blue brightening to a hue that reminded her of a sunlit summer sky. "I can't say that I'm surprised, however. I knew you were destined for a great future from the moment I first heard you sing."

Memory stirred, seductive and dangerous as a siren's song. "Thank you again," Sophie said hurriedly, "but I still have so much to learn. I am... glad to see you here tonight. It's always good to see a familiar face. What brings you to London?"

His face grew remote again. "Some business, of a personal nature."

"I see." Sophie tried to sound neutral. "Well, I am honored that you found the time to attend this concert."

A smile softened his features. "I would not have missed it for the world." He paused, his eyes intent on her face. "Miss Tresilian, I wondered if we might have a private word."

Sophie felt her pulse quicken, along with a strange flutter of what was either excitement or apprehension just behind her midriff. "A private word?" she echoed faintly.

Robin nodded. "About something that may concern us both—"

He broke off, glancing over his shoulder as the hum of conversation around them suddenly intensified. Following the direction of his gaze, Sophie saw more visitors coming in. Soon it would be impossible for that private word, if it weren't already. And from the look she saw on Robin's face, he'd come to the same realization.

Turning back to her, he asked almost abruptly, "Miss Tresilian, do you still ride in the mornings?"

She moistened her lips. "I do. When I can, that is."

"In Hyde Park?"

She nodded confirmation, aware of the press of people around them, the escalating buzz of countless voices praising, exclaiming, criticizing…

He leaned in, his voice pitched for her ears alone. "The Rotten Row, then? Between the hours of nine and ten o'clock?"

"Yes." The lone syllable emerged more as a breath than as a word, but he appeared to have no difficulty hearing it.

He drew back, spoke in the same low tone. "Until then, Miss Tresilian."

A sketch of a bow, then he was gone, threading his way through the crowd. Hemmed in by the throng, Sophie could only watch as he attained the doorway and disappeared through it.

As completely as he'd disappeared from her life four years ago.

❧

The dining room at the Savoy shone with the steady, even radiance that only electrical lighting could give. Tables shrouded in pale damask all but groaned under the weight of platters heaped high with delicacies concocted by the hotel's many French chefs. Champagne, claret, and other wines flowed freely. Crystal sparkled, china gleamed, and silver chimed, while the near-constant murmur of conversation filled the air.

Standing in the thick of it all, her nerves already at full stretch, Sophie wondered just what would happen if she threw back her head and screamed at the top of her lungs. Given her training, it would be a scream of truly operatic proportions. Waiters would drop their trays, diners stop with forks halfway to their mouths, and all would turn to stare at the mad soprano in their midst. The prospect alone was almost enough to tempt her to such a breach of decorum, but inherent good sense restrained her.

"*Bachgen*. Are you all right?" David's voice, low and solicitous, spoke at her ear.

Sophie took a breath before turning her head to smile at him. "I'm fine, David. Simply weary, that's all. And perhaps I have a bit of a headache coming on."

"No wonder, that, given the racket we endured tonight." He gave his engaging lopsided smile. "It's exaggerating I thought they were, about the echo in the Albert Hall."

A little laugh escaped Sophie; they were both familiar with the old joke: that the Albert Hall was the one place where every composer could be assured of hearing his work twice. "It could have been worse, I suppose. Imagine if we'd been singing Wagner!"

David pulled a face. "Nobody should have to endure 'The Ride of the Valkyries' more than once."

"My sentiments exactly, so I hope they find a way to fix the sound problem someday." Sophie glanced about the dining room. "People seem to be leaving. Do you think anyone would mind if I slipped away myself?"

"Not if you're discreet about it," he replied. "And I'd say most of the ones still remaining are more intent on their supper than on us."

"Well, it was a very good supper, and a splendid party too," Sophie conceded, feeling a little guilty that she hadn't enjoyed it more. "But I can barely keep my eyes open. Would you help me find a carriage to take me home?"

"I'll do better than that. I'll ride back and see you home personally."

"You don't have to do that!" she protested. "Truly, I don't wish to drag you away from all this."

"From my adoring public, you mean? I think we'll both survive it." David took her lightly by the elbow. "Now, no argument, my girl. It's white as a sheet you've gone, and no mistake. You don't want to keel over in front of half of London, do you?"

She managed a smile. "No, no, you're quite right. Thank you, David."

Within minutes, he'd managed to get both their cloaks and summon a carriage. They climbed in together, heading back to Mayfair. Blessedly, David made no attempt to engage her in conversation, but leaned back against the seat and maintained a companionable silence.

Grateful for his understanding, Sophie stole a glance at him. Brown hair, brown eyes, just a finger above average height—pleasantly ordinary in looks, but he grew in stature and presence the moment he set foot on the concert stage and that golden tenor rang out.

He'd been a good friend to her, David—ever since her first tour in the autumn of '92. London gossip conjectured he was more than that, but they'd never crossed that line between being friends and being lovers. Sometimes she wished they had, because the prospect of a love affair with David seemed so straightforward: they were both singers, they understood and respected each other's work, and they'd built up a strong mutual trust from their shared years on the concert circuit. Sophie had known of many romances that were based on far less.

Except that she'd never felt that sort of love for David, nor he for her. But they still had that unbreakable trust. If she were to confide in him about... what had happened tonight—or four years ago, for that matter—she knew he would be sympathetic and discreet.

But she wasn't quite ready to share this latest occurrence in her life, with him or anyone else. How could she, when she could scarce believe it herself? Sitting here in this quiet carriage, as it bowled along the gaslit streets, she found it easy to believe that she had imagined the whole encounter. She'd been under so much pressure these last few months—first those concerts abroad, and now her first appearance at the Albert Hall. Perhaps in the furor and excitement following the concert, she'd only *thought* she'd seen Robin Pendarvis, much less spoken to him and agreed to meet tomorrow in Hyde Park. A fantasy brought on by overwork and loneliness, nostalgia for times past...

The carriage came to a stop, jolting her back to the present.

"We're here," David announced. "19 Curzon Street."

Sophie roused, blinking like an owl in sunlight as she gathered the folds of her cloak around her. "Yes, yes, of course."

They alighted from the carriage, David going first and offering Sophie a hand down to the pavement.

"You look half-asleep already," he observed, eyeing her with concern. "Best go straight up to bed, then."

Sophie shook her head, knowing just how elusive sleep was likely to prove that night. "Not yet. I've so much going round and round in my head. Do you want to come in for a bit?"

He shook his head. "Thanks, but I'm bound for my brother's house now—all the family's staying there. An age it's been since we've had time to talk."

"Then go—enjoy your time with them. I'll be fine."

He searched her face. "If you're sure, then?"

Sophie nodded. "I am. Good night, David—and thank you."

He gave her hand a light squeeze, then climbed back into the carriage, which rolled off into the night.

Sophie turned toward the house, a tall terraced shape in the shadows, made her way slowly up the walk, and let herself in. The house received her in its silent embrace, so comforting after the noise and bustle of the Albert Hall and the Savoy.

Not for the first time, she was glad to have this refuge. While she'd come into her inheritance two years ago, she still thought living in hotels while not on tour would be far too extravagant. During her first years as a professional singer, she'd taken rooms at a respectable boardinghouse, not wanting to impose too much the Sheridans or other friends in London. But since her coming of age *and* the success of the *Figaro* tour, she found herself with the means to move into something better, where she could have more independence and a greater degree of privacy: a flat, perhaps, or even a small house, if she could afford the rent.

The Sheridans had approved her scheme, and after some hesitation, so had Sophie's own family. Thomas Sheridan had located the house on Curzon Street last autumn, while Sophie had been in America, and managed to negotiate quite a reasonable rate with the landlord. Sophie suspected that, as a duke's grandson, Sheridan had been able to pull a number of strings to secure such a price, but she wasn't about to look a gift horse in the mouth. Meanwhile, with Sophie's blessing, Amy had interviewed and engaged the staff just before the Season began. The small household ran with clockwork smoothness, and the unflappable servants appeared untroubled by a mistress who spent her mornings on musical technique and her evenings at theatres and concert halls—when she was even in London, that was. Likewise, no one had yet handed in his or her notice on hearing the piano or violin at all hours, even on nights when Sophie found herself unable to sleep.

The servants had long since retired, as she'd expected them to, given the lateness of the hour. But the hall lamps had been left on to show her the way. Like one in a dream, she slowly mounted the stairs, gripping the banister to keep herself moored to her bearings. The thick carpeting muffled her footsteps; she felt almost as if she were entering a tomb.

A foolish fancy, she chided herself, for the Curzon Street house was nothing like a tomb. While she hadn't been in residence long, she'd taken considerable pains to make it both comfortable and tasteful: a real home, not a showplace. And for the most part, she felt she had succeeded, even if, at times, she found herself... lonely.

Sophie shook her head to dislodge that most unwelcome thought, and quickened her pace until she reached her chamber on the second floor. The lamps were on there as well, and her maid, Letty, was waiting up for her, looking sleepy but determined. Feeling a little guilty, Sophie let the girl divest her of her evening gown, help her don her nightdress of fine cotton batiste, and brush out her hair before dismissing her for the night.

Alone, she sat at her dressing table, carefully removing the last traces of powder and rouge with a clean linen facecloth. After inspecting the results in the glass, she leaned back in her chair, idly toying with a bottle of perfume, a custom blend of rose, lavender, and neroli. From Paris—she could afford such luxuries now. Indeed, there were precious few that were beyond her means. She glanced down, noticing as though for the first time the array of cosmetics laid out for her particular use: more bottles of scent, jars of face cream and delicately tinted face powder, pots of rouge, and a rose-colored salve for her lips. *Painted lady*—her mouth quirked at the thought. How astonished, even scandalized, Mama and Cecily would be to see all this!

The drawers of her dressing table held a similar treasure trove: a silver-backed hairbrush and tortoiseshell comb, a rainbow of silk ribbons, sprays of artificial flowers, velvet snoods, feather aigrettes, fans of lace or painted silk, even a few brooches. All the accoutrements of a lady of fashion.

Bemused, she turned to study her chamber, a cocoon of comfort and elegance around her. A selection of watercolors and tasteful prints adorned the pale aquamarine walls, and the bedspread and curtains were the same sea-blue twilled silk. A cheval glass set in a polished walnut frame stood in the corner opposite the bed beside an enormous wardrobe hung with more gowns than she'd ever dreamed of owning, even as a debutante newly come to London for her first—and only—Season. The chest of drawers was likewise laden, filled with dainty lace-trimmed undergarments, embroidered handkerchiefs, and countless pairs of stockings and gloves, the latter fashioned of every material from silk to kid.

Other niceties as well: a glass-fronted bookcase holding a selection of volumes—novels, poetry, even plays—to beguile the time not spent in music; a music stand for her violin, which she still practiced regularly, although her voice was her main instrument now; a Sheraton escritoire in one window alcove, and a wing chair upholstered in dark blue brocade in the other. And in the corner nearest the bed, her Russian Blue cat, Tatiana—a recent present from an admirer—lay slumbering, curled up like a velvety grey question mark, in a sumptuous basket lined with blue silk.

The bedchamber of a successful, sophisticated woman. The woman she'd made herself become, first as a defense against everything that had happened four years ago—and then because she'd grown comfortable in that armor. A carapace constructed of training, poise, and yes, carefully honed talent. She did have that, had taken care of it, and it had repaid her effort and taken care of her. She was lauded as an *artiste* now, one poised on the brink of greatness, or so some of her critics claimed, though she tried not to let their praise go to her head. Today's sensation was tomorrow's has-been in the music world, and she still had much to learn. But it was encouraging nonetheless to know she'd come this far in a fairly short time.

She gazed into the glass again, seeing a poised, reasonably pretty young woman of twenty-three. Even without the aid of cosmetics, her complexion was good, her color healthy, and her skin presently free of blemishes. In the last couple of years, she'd lost the last traces of childish roundness about her cheeks and chin, and the faint widow's peak at her hairline had become more pronounced. The resulting shape was more elegant, a heart tapering to a slightly pointed chin. But it was her eyes that held her attention now: if experience could be traced in one's face at all, surely it must appear in the eyes.

But the eyes that stared back at her, though heavy-lidded and slightly shadowed with fatigue, were the same ones she remembered from four years ago.

The eyes of the girl who had loved Robin Pendarvis.

And still did?

She looked away, unwilling to answer that question, and rose from her chair, taking a quick turn about the room in an effort to compose herself. Her pulse had quickened, a light but rapid beat of blood in her veins, and she swallowed convulsively, feeling as if her heart had literally risen in her throat.

Her gaze darted about her chamber again. The life she'd built these last four years was all around her. A busy, fulfilling life that included new and fascinating places to visit, exciting friendships with like-minded people, and music, always music. Her calling—and her comfort.

Was it truly worth it, to risk that life, that hard-won peace, by opening old wounds?

Something that may concern us both.

His words echoed in her memory, and for a moment, she almost hated them—and him—for the dormant hope they roused in her. Hope, that most dangerous of emotions, seductive and treacherous at once.

Her wanderings had brought her to the alcove where her favorite chair stood. Sinking into it, she stared unseeingly out the window at the night sky. Her thoughts still swirled and seethed inside her head like a troubled sea.

A faint tug at her hem and a questioning mew made her look down. Tatiana, awakened by her mistress's restlessness, sat at her feet, gazing up at her with unwinking green eyes. Sophie smiled and lifted the little cat onto her lap. Tatiana turned about a few times, kneaded Sophie's knees with her tiny needle-sharp claws, then settled down at last, purring.

There was something inherently soothing about stroking

a cat. Tatiana's grey fur was as dense and thick as velvet, and her warm little body vibrated with her purring—as good as a hot water bottle any day. Sophie continued to stroke, her whirling thoughts finally achieving some semblance of order and coherence.

Robin.

She remembered when they'd first met, at Roswarne, during that party for New Year's Eve. How he'd fascinated her, that tall, spare young man with the arresting blue eyes, who'd stared at her as though she was the only woman in the world. How eagerly she'd anticipated their first dance, their shared supper after—and how disappointed she'd been later to learn he'd slipped away without saying good-bye to her.

A girlish infatuation, she'd told herself at the time. A passing attraction to a handsome newcomer that would fade with subsequent meetings and increased familiarity.

If only it had been so... for both their sakes.

To go or not to go. To keep tomorrow's tryst—or stay away, sparing herself and Robin the pain of their countless "might-have-beens."

Sophie breathed out a long sigh, set Tatiana on the floor, and rose slowly from her chair. Impossible to decide now, with her thoughts and feelings in such turmoil. She should sleep—or try to. Perhaps tomorrow she would see her course more clearly.

But when morning came, she was no closer to a decision.

Four

She is coming, my dove, my dear;
She is coming, my life, my fate.
The red rose cries, "She is near, she is near;"
And the white rose weeps, "She is late."

—Alfred, Lord Tennyson, "Maud"

HE WOULD *NOT* LOOK AT HIS WATCH AGAIN, ROBIN told himself sternly.

He knew already that a good twenty minutes had passed since his arrival at Hyde Park. He also knew there were several possible reasons why Sophie had not yet come, including the lateness of last night's concert and the earliness of this proposed meeting. Those weren't the reasons that gnawed at him, of course, but he did his best not to dwell on *those*.

Beneath him, the horse—a serviceable chestnut gelding—sidled and snorted, his breath forming a faint cloud on the misty air. A cool morning for July, fog hovering like a veil over the trees lining either side of Rotten Row.

He gentled his restless mount, patted its gleaming neck, and murmured absentminded nonsense in a soothing voice. Of their own volition, his thoughts drifted back to that spring in

Cornwall five years before. All the mornings when he'd waited
for Sophie—first by chance, then by design. To see her riding
up to him on her dapple-grey gelding, her green eyes alight,
that dimpled smile he adored shining forth like a sunrise.

And other memories, slightly less chaste, as what had
begun between them—despite his better judgment—gathered
force and momentum. The pure curve of her cheek, the
tender nape of her neck. The delicate scent of violets—her
favorite—that always seemed to cling to her skin and even
her hair. And the way her riding habit—plain and dark
though it was—limned her developing form, hinting at high,
sweetly rounded breasts and surprisingly long, slim legs.
God, he'd have had to be stone-blind not to notice how the
enchanting girl was becoming a woman, and afflicted with
ice water in his veins not to desire her. Clandestine meetings,
low voices—she knew the side paths where they could ride
or walk undisturbed. Sitting with her on the rocks, watching
the sea race to the shore…

A soft coo, followed by a rapid flutter of wings, broke the
silence, and he glanced up to see a brace of wood pigeons
flying overhead to nest in the trees. Sobered, he looked down
again. The surroundings might be different now, but the feelings of anticipation were all too familiar. And the feelings of
dread—the unspoken fear that one day Sophie would wake
up, realize the folly of her girlish fantasies about him, and
leave him waiting in the lane.

If she hadn't known then what a poor bargain he was,
she certainly knew now. The thought chilled him to the
marrow, even as he acknowledged the very real possibility
that she had changed her mind about meeting him. Some
might think he deserved no better—and Robin included
himself among them.

And if she did not come… well, he would live with
that. Just as he'd had to live every day of the last four years
without her.

He glanced up, without any real hope, toward Hyde Park Corner—and his breath caught.

Like a figure out of memory, slim and straight in a dark green habit, she rode toward him through the morning mist.

❦

Hardly anyone was stirring in Hyde Park at this hour, Sophie observed as she urged her horse, a dependable bay riding hack, onto the sandy track commonly known as Rotten Row. Most of the fashionable would not make their appearance until the afternoon, when their horses and equipages would crowd the Row and the carriage track running alongside it.

Peering through the mist, she saw him, astride a chestnut hack. His dark head was uncovered, but even without that, she'd have recognized him. No other man had that tension to him, that restless energy simmering below the surface.

Her mouth dried and her heart pounded as though it would leap from her chest, but she made herself ride onward, reining in when they were just a few feet apart.

His eyes, blue and brilliant, met hers. "You came."

"I did." Her voice sounded clipped and curt in her own ears. "I gave my word, I believe?"

His lips curved in that faint, wry smile she remembered so well. "I wouldn't have blamed you if you'd chosen to break it."

The ghost of other broken promises hovered between them. "Let's not... speak of that just yet." Sophie glanced back over her shoulder. "We appear to be the only ones awake just now."

"I've heard Society won't be stirring until noon at least. Shall we ride?"

Sophie nodded, and they set off together at a slow walk toward the west end of the Row, unwilling or perhaps afraid to break the silence. For a time, they could sustain the illusion that they were no more than any other lady and gentleman—polite acquaintances—taking the air together. Not thwarted lovers with years of carefully maintained distance between them.

Off to their right, the Serpentine rippled, its waters grey and sluggish beneath the overcast sky. If Sophie strained her ears, she could even hear the slow rush of the current.

Impossible not to remember other mornings, other rides. Meetings like these—only then she'd gone forth with eager anticipation, wanting only to see him again, whereas today… Her palms were damp inside her gloves and the hollow feeling in the pit of her stomach had nothing to do with what little breakfast she'd managed to choke down.

She stole a glance at Robin; his own face was somber to the point of stoniness. She knew that look of old, from Cornwall—the starkness in his eyes, the grim set of his mouth, closed tight against the secrets he'd guarded from all of them, even her. Perhaps especially her.

How hard she'd tried to breach his defenses, battering herself against them with the persistence of the sea dashing itself against solid rock! And how ridiculously, foolishly pleased she'd been by every morsel she'd managed to extract from him, how certain she'd been that someday there would be no secrets between them—only the trust and confidence that should exist between two people who loved each other as they did.

Seventeen could be an appallingly stupid age, she reflected mordantly. There were times when she could cheerfully have drowned her younger self and thus spared the world and posterity her adolescent folly.

Robin finally broke the silence. "You were splendid last night," he said. "A credit to your training."

"Thank you." Her response was automatic, even mechanical, but she felt an eddy of warmth about her heart all the same.

"I was lucky to be in time to purchase a ticket," he continued. "I understand your concert sold out quickly."

She nodded. "My manager was pleased by that development. He thinks it's because *The Marriage of Figaro* was such a success last year."

"I wish I had seen you in *Figaro*. But I read your notices in the London papers—I am pleased that you enjoyed such a triumph." He smiled again, more easily this time. "Cherubino is a delightful role. I am sure you would make an enchanting Susanna too someday."

"Well, as to that—I've had the chance to play Susanna," Sophie confessed.

His brows arched. "Did you indeed?"

"It was while we were touring in America—New York. The soprano playing Susanna caught the grippe and was off for three nights. I was her cover, so I took over." She found herself smiling too, reliving the mingled delight and terror of her first evening in the role. "It was frightening, but thrilling too. There are so many wonderful parts for women in that opera."

"Perhaps one day you'll sing them all," he suggested.

"Perhaps." Sophie changed the subject. "But there's nothing duller or more insufferable than someone who talks of nothing but her aspirations. How is the hotel?"

"Prospering," he replied, with evident satisfaction. "Your brother is relieved—and James too, I might add. The last few seasons we've sold out all summer. And I've been able to modernize further—there's electrical light in the Grand Salon now, and I had a telephone put in last year."

"I am pleased to hear it. I know how hard you've worked to make it a success." All those plans and dreams. She had tried hard not to think of Pendarvis Hall these last four years, not to remember the exciting days after he'd first hatched the scheme, the private tour he'd given her, the garden where they'd kissed for the first time… and never the last night she'd been there. The night everything had come crashing down around them.

Robin was still speaking. "I think the staff is finally reconciled to what the Hall has become. It helps, I think, that we are so much in demand and our clientele no less sought after. Even in the off-season we have guests. We were nearly full at Easter, and we held a ball on Easter Monday."

How strange this was, their exchanging these polite formalities: her career, his hotel. But what other subjects were safe?

She manufactured a smile. "You see? I knew that ballroom would be ideal for such an occasion."

"So you said," he acknowledged. "And we've held a few concerts there as well. Along with some smaller entertainments in the garden. The pavilion, to be exact."

Another suggestion she'd made. The memory set a dull ache just below her breastbone.

She swallowed gamely, willing herself not to dwell on that halcyon afternoon five years ago. "Of course. I hope the weather did not turn inclement. You were always concerned about that, as I recall."

"So far, our luck has held in that regard. Though our garden concerts are held only in spring and summer."

"Very prudent." Sophie's hands twisted in her horse's reins.

They were talking about the *weather* now, of all things. More of these polite inanities and she would go stark, staring mad. She glanced ahead, seeing the crossroads that divided Hyde Park from Kensington Gardens, and further on, the spired Gothic canopy of the Albert Memorial. Nearly to the end of their path... and the end of things they could discuss safely.

But it had to be said. There was no way to avoid the subject any longer.

Bracing herself, Sophie prepared to tear off the emotional bandage she had worn for the last four years. "And how is Nathalie?" She felt obscurely pleased when her voice did not waver. "How is—your wife?"

And saw by the way Robin's eyes darkened and his mouth drew taut that the memory—of all they'd shared and all they'd lost—was burned as deeply into him as it was into her.

Five

O, how this spring of love resembleth
The uncertain glory of an April day;
Which now shows all the beauty of the sun,
And by and by a cloud takes all away.

—William Shakespeare, *Two Gentlemen of Verona*

Cornwall, April 1891

OF ALL THE SEASONS IN CORNWALL, SOPHIE THOUGHT she loved spring the most. Almost May now, and the weather was, as always, changeable, but the temperatures were warmer, the breeze mild and carrying the most delicious scents of green, growing things. Gorse bloomed in bright golden profusion on the moors and along the cliff tops, and Sophie thought she'd seen some heather starting to put forth white and purple blossoms. There were fewer primroses and daffodils than earlier in the season, but the bluebells were now out in the woods and on the hillsides, transforming the ground underfoot into a shimmering carpet of lavender blue.

The gardens were also looking their best, in Sophie's opinion. Her mother had always spent hours in the gardens at Roswarne, fussing over the flowers that prospered in

Cornwall's light, warm soil—lupines, hollyhocks, roses—and so far, they were generously repaying her attentions with a splendid show of color and bloom.

Sophie herself was in the grip of spring fever, rising early in the morning so as not to waste a moment of precious sunlight and going out to ride immediately after breakfast, as she had today. Even her beloved violin could wait a few hours until she had the fidgets worked out of her horse's legs, as well as her own.

She patted Tregony's dapple-grey neck as they rode along, wholly in accord with each other that such a morning should not be wasted indoors, whether in a stall or a parlor. Today would be perfect for a gallop or even a brisk canter along the beach, she mused. Intent on her plans, she didn't notice the rider coming toward her along the lane, not until her horse tossed his head and whickered a greeting.

Startled, she looked up. "Mr. Pendarvis. Good morning."

He reined in his horse—a fine-looking bay with black stockings—and touched his hat to her. "Good morning to you, Miss Tresilian. You're abroad early today."

"Well, it was so lovely when I awoke this morning that I simply had to take advantage." Sophie paused, feeling just a little shy. Oh, they'd met several times since that New Year's Eve party, for he and Harry had become good friends, but it had been a while since she had spoken to him without anyone else about. She couldn't help but remember how congenial a companion he'd been that night, how easy to talk to, and wishing… But that was neither here nor there, she told herself hastily. Aloud she said, "You're up quite early yourself, Mr. Pendarvis."

"Indeed. I'm trying to get into the habit of riding every day," he explained. "It's been years since my great-uncle rode, and the horses need the exercise. So do I, for that matter. I should soon become as fat as an alderman if I took a carriage everywhere."

Sophie stifled a giggle. It was hard to imagine anyone as lean and spare as Mr. Pendarvis putting on that much weight. "Do you often come this way?"

"Well, I don't know St. Perran well enough to say I ride here often, but this seemed a promising track." He patted his horse's neck. "At least Gorlois seems to like it."

Sophie smiled. "Never fear. If you ride out often enough, you'll come to know the whole county like the back of your hand. We'll make a proper Cornishman of you yet."

He smiled back, a softening of those severe lips that made him look quite a bit younger. "Your brother has promised something similar, so I am resigning myself to my fate."

She raised her brows. "Willingly, I trust?"

"Willingly and happily, I assure you." He patted his horse's neck again, his expression growing serious once more. "Still, there's much to think of, especially now that my life has changed so much these last few weeks."

"Of course." A touch guiltily, Sophie noticed the black band encircling his upper arm. "We were all sorry to hear about your great-uncle," she added quickly.

The funeral had taken place in early April. A rather quiet affair, as most of Simon Pendarvis's friends and contemporaries had predeceased him, but the Tresilians had attended. So had several other notable families in the county, if only to meet the new owner of Pendarvis Hall. Sophie had noticed several young ladies eyeing Mr. Pendarvis speculatively during the funeral service and at the reception that followed. Calculating little things… Sophie had experienced a secret twinge of relief when he'd showed no particular interest in any of them.

"Thank you." Mr. Pendarvis inclined his head. "Although I suspect death might have come as a release to him, in some respects. And at least it was a peaceful passing."

"What will you do now? Settle permanently in Cornwall or go back to London?"

He did not reply at once. "I've been considering the former, but I still have a number of decisions to make—none of them easy. I thought a ride might clear my head."

"Have you tried riding down to the shore? It's not far from here, and I go there sometimes when *I* need to think. Something about the wind and the water always helps to blow the cobwebs away. I was heading there now actually." Sophie hesitated, wondering if he would think her bold for asking, but ventured all the same, "Would you care to accompany me?"

"Thank you, Miss Tresilian," he replied after a moment. "I should like that very much."

Sophie smiled. "Right this way, then," she said, and kneed Tregony forward, as Mr. Pendarvis and Gorlois fell into step beside them.

∼⊷∽

Riding at a brisk trot, they soon neared their destination. Mr. Pendarvis kept pace without any sort of problem, Sophie observed with approval. His position in the saddle was good, his back straight without being stiff as a poker, and his hands were light on the reins. Gorlois appeared to respect his mastery too, perhaps the ultimate testament to his rider's skill.

They reached the margin of the beach, stony and covered with marram grass, then yielding to softer, finer sand after the first few yards. Catching the salty scent of the wind off the sea, Tregony tossed his head and snorted with pleasure, while Gorlois flicked his ears and stood staring at the great expanse of bounding water in the distance.

Mr. Pendarvis stroked his horse's neck as they ventured onto the sand. "I'll wager it's been a while since he's been near the sea. I hope it doesn't make him nervous."

"Oh, I daresay he'll remember, by and by," Sophie assured him. "Especially if you start riding him here more often. Our horses all love the beach."

She glanced at the wide stretch of pale gold sand now before them, and bit back the temptation to say "Race you," as she might have to one of her brothers. "Shall we canter?"

Mr. Pendarvis was willing and they urged their horses forward to a brisker pace, speeding up to a canter once they reached the water's edge. And suddenly, without a word exchanged between them, they *were* racing, breaking into a full gallop, side by side along the shore. The stiff ocean breeze whistled in Sophie's ears, stung the blood into her cheeks, as Tregony's hooves thundered beneath her. Breathless and half laughing in sheer pleasure, she glanced at her companion and was surprised by a grin, wide, brilliant, and utterly unguarded, that transformed that too-serious face into something almost boyish—and devastatingly attractive.

It wasn't just the race that had her short of breath now. Flushing, she concentrated on pulling ahead, but he kept pace with her, Gorlois matching Tregony stride for stride.

They pulled up at last, panting and laughing. And Mr. Pendarvis's laughter was every bit as potent as his grin, Sophie discovered.

"I'd say we call that even, wouldn't you, Miss Tresilian?" he remarked, patting Gorlois's gleaming neck. The bay gelding snorted, his earlier misgivings about the water gone, clearly keen to go on racing.

"A draw, I confess it," Sophie gasped, holding up a hand as Tregony sidled and danced beneath her. "Oh, dear—I think I've got a stitch in my side!"

"Then we'll stop at once," he said with instant solicitude. "Do you need some help down from the saddle?"

Sophie felt her heart give a curious sort of flutter that had nothing to do with the race they'd just run. She took an extra moment to reply, letting her breathlessness mask her confusion. "Thank you. I would be glad of some assistance."

He swung down from the saddle—very smoothly, a part of her mind noted—and then came around to her side.

Sophie slipped her leg from around the pommel, then turned
to descend into his waiting arms.

His hands caught her about the waist and lifted her down
as if she weighed nothing at all. Strong hands, with a firm
grip; she felt their warmth even through his leather gauntlets
and her woolen habit, and an answering warmth flooded
through her from head to toe. Flushing again, she looked
down as he set her lightly on the sand.

"All right then, Miss Tresilian?" he asked, stepping back
a pace.

"Yes, thank you." Sophie wondered if she still sounded
breathless. His body was mere inches from hers: lean and
hard-muscled—sparer than those of her brothers', whose
frames tended to the compact, even solid. Mr. Pendarvis
was built more like her cousin James, though James had
never affected her in this way, never set every cell in her
body tingling with this heightened awareness. Nor had
any other man of her acquaintance, however attractive,
and despite her youth, Sophie had experienced her share
of girlish infatuations. This was something else entirely:
headier, and subtly dangerous.

And she was being exceedingly foolish, almost as silly
as those girls who'd made eyes at Mr. Pendarvis at his
great-uncle's funeral, though she had some consolation in
knowing she wasn't anywhere near as mercenary. It was the
man himself who compelled her: the sinewy strength of his
body that moved with such loose-limbed grace, those strong,
angular features, framed by thick dark-brown hair and enliv-
ened by those intense blue eyes. And that element of mystery,
of hidden depths below the surface of his rather infrequent
smile. But however attractive she found him, Mr. Pendarvis
was a friend and a neighbor, nothing more—certainly not
someone to encourage the idle fancies of a girl barely out
of the schoolroom. She stepped back, summoning what she
hoped was a bright, friendly smile.

"Why don't," her voice husked slightly, so she cleared her throat and tried again, "why don't we sit down on those rocks over there until we're recovered our breath? The horses could probably use the rest as well."

He agreed, and they made their way up the beach to where a cluster of large rocks stood, gathering warmth in the sun. Sophie sat down on one with an obligingly flat top, twitching the skirts of her habit into place. Mr. Pendarvis leaned against the rock beside hers, and they watched the sea in companionable silence while their horses stood nearby, nosing at heaps of beached kelp and other sea-borne flotsam.

The sea was a clear blue today, laced with green—like a piece of shot silk Sophie had once seen in a shop window. Gulls wheeled overhead, crying raucously, and cresting waves raced toward the shore, sending up columns of spray as they dashed themselves upon the sand.

Sophie stole a glance at Mr. Pendarvis. He looked such a different man out here in the open, relaxed and at ease as he seldom was in public. Just now, his expression conveyed only contentment, which sharpened into pleasure, even awe, as a towering wave struck the shore and flung a volley of foam into the air.

"I think the sea is putting on quite the show for us today," she observed, smiling.

"Is it always so fine here, on the coast?" he asked.

"On the north coast," Sophie told him. "It's gentler on the south shore. Still lovely, but less dramatic. My mother grew up on the south shore, and we've gone to visit her family there, but I know in my heart I'll always be a north coast girl. This beach is one of my favorite spots—of course, there are so many beautiful places to be found in Cornwall, especially in the spring."

His smile warmed her, set her heart fluttering again. "And I'll wager you know them all."

"A good many of them," she confessed. "But then I've

lived here all my life. It would be very strange if I didn't know my own county."

"Have you ever thought you might live elsewhere someday? Most young ladies dream about going to London for their Season. Or even further abroad, to Paris."

"Well, I am to have a London Season," Sophie replied. "Next spring, Harry says. And I wouldn't mind visiting Paris, and perhaps Italy as well—Florence and Milan. I should love to attend an opera at La Scala one day. But as for where I'd choose to live"—she made a gesture encompassing the sea, the sky, and the distant cliffs—"my heart is here, and always will be."

"*This is mine own, my native land,*" Mr. Pendarvis quoted with a faint half smile.

"Yes, that's it." Sophie tried not to sound self-conscious, or worse, defensive. "Perhaps that makes me a bit provincial, but—"

"Not at all. I think it must be very reassuring to know exactly where you belong."

"I suppose it is," Sophie said, after a moment's reflection. "It goes back for generations, you see. There have always been Tresilians in St. Perran, and even further afield in Cornwall. You might come to feel that way yourself, eventually," she added. "I understand that the Pendarvis name is a very old and respected one in the county."

"So Great-Uncle Simon told me, any number of times." His smile turned rueful. "I couldn't help feeling that he disapproved of me a bit, for not growing up in Cornwall."

"Well, that wasn't anything *you* could control. Wasn't your father a younger son?"

"A son of a younger son, and destined for the army, like his father," he clarified. "But they were both born in Cornwall, and I swear, it must have got into their bones."

"Cornwall has a way of doing that—getting into your bones *and* your blood."

"So I understand. However far they traveled or wherever

they served, my father and grandfather thought of Cornwall, and even Pendarvis Hall, as home." He glanced wistfully toward the tumbling sea. "I hope someday I can say the same."

Sophie restrained the impulse to touch his hand, so close to hers on the rock—a friendly touch, but still something of a liberty to take with a gentleman she was just beginning to know. "Give it time, Mr. Pendarvis. I am certain you'll come to feel at home here."

"I hope you're right. I would very much like to feel at home *somewhere*." Still gazing out to sea, he hitched a hip onto the rock he'd been leaning against. "I must have lived in nearly half a dozen places by the time I was twelve."

"So many?" she asked, amazed.

"Everywhere from Ireland to India," he confirmed. "And my mother, God rest her, did her best to make a home for us in every place we lived. And not to let my father see her weep when his postings changed and we had to leave it all behind."

Sophie winced. Imagine putting down roots, only to have them torn up and having to start all over again somewhere else—and half a dozen times! She was not sure she could have endured such a life. "Your mother sounds like a remarkable woman, and so resilient."

"She was. It takes courage to live as she lived, to adapt to all kinds of conditions." His face grew pensive. "In the end, the only condition she couldn't seem to survive was living without my father. They met at a ball in London when he was on leave. According to them both, it was love at first sight. She outlived him by only two years."

"I am so sorry," Sophie said at once. "My parents were devoted to each other as well. Papa died when I was eleven—a sudden illness. We still miss him, but we have so many good memories. I don't know what any of us would have done if we'd lost Mama as well. Was that when you first came to Cornwall—after your mother's death?"

"Actually, I'd visited the previous summer. Mother

thought I should get to know my father's family. I spent a few summers here, but Great-Uncle Simon wasn't used to young boys. My mother's relations were the ones who took me in after she died."

"Were they a military family?"

"No, actually. My maternal grandfather was an industrialist—a very successful one—from Yorkshire. My mother was raised as a considerable heiress, a much more sheltered existence than the one she led after marrying my father." Mr. Pendarvis shook his head reminiscently. "After life following the regiment, it was like landing in the lap of luxury: a large house, an army of servants, a private tutor, *and* my own bedchamber. I couldn't quite get accustomed to it, even though my uncle and his family did their best to make me feel at home."

"But you didn't wish to follow in your father's footsteps and join the army yourself?"

He shook his head again. "My younger brother Will was the army-mad one, but he died at ten years old. He was never very hardy. Nor did I wish to become an industrialist like my uncle and grandfather. I have the greatest respect for their efforts and I'm grateful for what business acumen they've worked to instill in me, but I had no particular genius in that sphere."

"So, what did you want to do instead?" Because he *would* have done something, of that she was certain; he'd far too much drive and intensity to live complacently on his expectations. Which was, she admitted with an inner sigh, one of the reasons she found him so intriguing.

"Oh, I tried on a number of dreams for size," he replied. "I went up to Oxford when I was eighteen and considered the law or even taking Holy Orders. Then, one summer, I went abroad to France and fell head over ears in love with Norman cathedrals." His expression grew abstracted, even dreamy, and she knew his thoughts had flown back to that time. "I don't exaggerate, Miss Tresilian—it was a passion as sudden and blinding as any schoolboy's. I abandoned Oxford and apprenticed myself to an architect in Rouen for the next four years."

Sophie's eyes widened. "Good heavens! Were your mother's family very upset by this?"

"Well, they weren't pleased, at any rate. I wasn't disinherited or cut off in any other way, but my uncle did tell me he thought I was being quixotic and impractical, and that I'd rue the day I embarked on such a course." His mouth quirked. "And as it turns out—he was right."

"He was?" Sophie felt obscurely disappointed. The look on his face when he mentioned the cathedrals had been so rapt, almost exalted; he'd clearly loved his time in France. How sad that his dream hadn't lived up to its promise!

"More than he knew. Oh, I won't say those years were entirely wasted, or that I learned nothing of use, but much of that time is—best forgotten, I think."

Sophie eyed him more closely; his face had grown shuttered, even remote, during those last words, and his voice was similarly neutral. Something must have happened in Rouen. A professional setback, perhaps? She knew little beyond general details of what an architect's career might entail, but she imagined it must be a demanding and competitive profession. "So, you returned to England?"

"In time. And I found some work as an architect in London—mostly doing the sort of thing I'd done in France, helping restore homes and the occasional parish church. I even resigned myself to not being the next Christopher Wren," he added with a wry smile. "There's not much call for building cathedrals in England these days, but everyone needs a place to call home."

And home would hold a special meaning for him, when he'd spent so much of his childhood moving from place to place. "They're building a cathedral right now in Truro,"

Sophie told him. "It's not complete yet, but it looks to be a handsome building. And there must be churches all over the West Country in need of renovation or restoration. You could find plenty of work here—that is, if you mean to continue as an architect, now that you've inherited," she added hastily, remembering that many landed gentry considered it a comedown to have to work at all.

His brows drew together in a faint, abstracted frown. "It's strange, but I never imagined myself *not* working, not even when I found out I was the heir three years ago. I don't think I'm made for idleness—the prospect of doing nothing day in, day out holds no appeal for me. Nor do the usual fashionable pursuits—I'm no sportsman, and I have no aspirations to join the Marlborough House set, or any other such circle."

"You sound like James. My cousin, James Trelawney," she explained at his blank look. "You might have met at New Year's. He inherited an earldom in January, most unexpectedly. Before, he was just a partner in the family mine and an investor in some local industries. Now he's a peer, with an estate to maintain, and he's having the same problem adjusting that you are."

"Ah, yes. Now I remember. His accession was quite the nine days' wonder, I hear."

"No one was more surprised than James himself. His cousin was only thirty, and robust."

"I know. We met briefly—the previous earl and I. Great-Uncle Simon was his godfather." Mr. Pendarvis's gaze had gone cool at the memory. "I can't say I was much impressed by him."

"Harry knew him a little and thought poorly of him too. All the same, it's a shock that he should have died so young, and so suddenly. And on the very night we were celebrating at Roswarne, just a few miles away." Sophie suppressed a shudder. The late Earl of Trevenan had been discovered dead at the foot of a cliff on New Year's Day.

"Tragedies usually happen that way, while everyone else is going about his business," Mr. Pendarvis observed. "Still, it's an ill wind that blows no good, and your cousin will probably do more credit to the position than his predecessor."

"*I* think he will," Sophie said with confidence. "But, like you, James has all sorts of new responsibilities now, to say nothing of expenses. He's up in London now, talking to his solicitor and trying to find ways to keep Pentreath—that's his estate—going."

He sighed. "A grand inheritance can be a curse as much as a blessing, at times."

"Which would you call yours?" Sophie risked a sympathetic touch of his sleeve. To her relief, Mr. Pendarvis did not withdraw his arm, though she supposed it was also possible that he simply hadn't noticed, in his current brown study.

"I'm still trying to decide. No," he amended, "that's not entirely fair. Great-Uncle did his best to maintain the Hall. He was never a great spendthrift, even in his youth, *and* he married a woman with a large dowry, though they'd no children to inherit."

"Or to spend what money they had," she pointed out. "The late Lord Trevenan was very extravagant and ran up all sorts of debts—that's one of the difficulties James is facing."

"A small mercy," he conceded. "Nonetheless, it will likely take every penny I possess to keep Pendarvis Hall fit to be lived in."

"Is it in such poor condition as that?" Sophie asked. "I noticed nothing amiss when I was there for the funeral, and it's always looked splendid from the outside."

"Things could be worse," he admitted. "But it's still going to need substantial work in some areas. The roof, for example, and the damp has got into some of the upstairs rooms."

"Have you ever thought of letting the Hall, or selling it outright?" she ventured, trying to ignore the swift, sharp pang that went through her at the thought of him leaving Cornwall.

Fortunately, his next words reassured her on that score. "Strangely enough, I find I don't care to do either. For one thing, breaking the entail would be a difficult and costly business. For another... call it folly or family pride, but Pendarvises have lived at the Hall since Queen Elizabeth's time. It seems... wrong to abandon it to strangers."

Because the Hall was home, Sophie thought. Home to his great-uncle, his grandfather, and now himself, the man who'd known no true home as a boy. "I should feel the same way as you," she said warmly. "Harry is only a baronet, and Roswarne's tiny in comparison to your Hall, but he regards our estate—our home—as something to be safeguarded for the next generation of Tresilians. Perhaps that makes us hopelessly old-fashioned, but there it is."

"I suppose that makes me old-fashioned as well," he said with a wry smile. "But there's more than just the property to consider. I wouldn't feel right about turning off the staff. They've earned their places through years of loyal service. Who am I to come sweeping in and deprive them of their livelihood? Even if I just let the Hall, a tenant could still dismiss them and hire new servants, and my great-uncle's people would be no better off than before." He shook his head. "The life of a landed gentleman may not be what it used to be, but that doesn't cancel out our responsibilities to those who depend on us."

Our. Us. Sophie hid a smile. He was talking like a landowner already—better yet, a conscientious, responsible landowner, who valued loyalty and had a care for his servants. Mr. Pendarvis might not realize it, but he was more than suited to his new position and, she suspected, equal to its challenges.

"There's another possibility," she suggested, a bit diffidently. "Have you considered following your great-uncle's example and taking a wealthy bride?"

His face closed off at once, as it had when he'd been talking about his time in Rouen. "Out of the question. I have no desire to turn fortune hunter."

Sophie winced at his clipped, curt tone and cursed her own tactlessness. "Naturally, one shouldn't wed for money alone," she said placatingly. "And I certainly don't see *you* as a fortune hunter. But if you should happen to meet and form an attachment to a lady of means…" She broke off as her thoughts sped to her own fortune, which would come under her control on either her majority or her marriage, and she flushed, feeling suddenly and horribly self-conscious.

Much to her relief, Mr. Pendarvis had turned his gaze seaward again. "I am relieved that you do not think me mercenary, Miss Tresilian." His tone was neutral to the point of colorlessness. "But even if I had the inclination to marry, I am in no position to take a wife."

Sophie took a composing breath and set about extricating her foot from her mouth. "Of course. I understand why you might feel that way, with—so much unsettled in your life. Pray forgive me, and forget that I ever made such an ill-timed suggestion."

The hard line of his mouth softened, much to her relief. "Forgiven and forgotten, Miss Tresilian." He relaxed on his rock, his expression now thoughtful rather than aloof. "So, things being as they are, I need to find a way to keep the Hall going without bankrupting myself in the process. And since letting the place, breaking the entail, and marrying a fortune are all out of the question, I'll have to come up with something else."

"Is there any unentailed property you could part with?"

"I think Great-Uncle Simon has already sold off most of that. But my uncle might have some ideas about worthwhile investments. I've written to him already, asking for suggestions. I'll be inviting him, his wife, and their children down to stay in any case. There's enough room at the Hall to house that entire branch of the family."

"The Hall looks like it could accommodate *several* families," Sophie observed. "I know you don't wish to let the place, but it's a pity you can't have temporary lodgers, or offer guided tours or fishing weekends. There's a distant cousin of ours with a castle in Scotland who takes in paying guests during the shooting season—"

She broke off when she saw Mr. Pendarvis was staring at her, an arrested expression on his face. "I'm sorry. Have I said something wrong?"

"No. Not at all, Miss Tresilian. In fact," he continued, his eyes taking on a speculative gleam that turned them a startling, almost electric blue, "you may have given me an idea."

"What sort of idea?" she asked, intrigued at once.

He gave her a slow, contemplative smile. "A brilliant one, or a completely mad one."

Sophie fixed him with an exasperated stare. "Would you care to elaborate on that?"

"Not until I have a chance to weigh the evidence and decide which it is! But mad or brilliant, it's an idea I didn't have before, for which I owe you my deepest thanks."

"You're welcome, I suppose," Sophie said a bit dubiously. "I'm—glad to have helped, though I just wish I knew what you were thanking me for."

His smile widened into that engaging, boyish grin. "All in good time, my dear Miss Tresilian! And now we should be starting back," he added, almost springing up from his rock. "Before your family starts to worry about you."

Sophie stifled a sigh. He was right, of course—she had been gone far longer than she'd intended. But she could not regret a moment of this interval, or the strange intimacy she had sensed growing between them. The way he had opened up to her... she felt oddly privileged that he should have chosen her, of all people, with whom to share the story of his childhood. And a childhood more different from her own she could scarce imagine.

But he seemed to want another kind of life for himself now: a life with roots, and a definite purpose. And she was more than willing to help him achieve that—as his friend, of course, she amended hastily. The same simple, uncomplicated way that Harry was his friend.

Except that she had to admit, if only to herself, that the frisson that went through her as she took his hand to help her to her feet felt *nothing* like simple, uncomplicated friendship.

❧

They were riding back toward Roswarne at a more sedate pace, talking of this and that, when Sophie heard someone call her name. Reining in her horse, she glanced toward the sound to see Sir Lucas Nankivell approaching on his showy chestnut hack.

"Good morning, Miss Sophie." The baronet touched his hat to her.

"Good morning, Sir Lucas," Sophie returned politely. In fact, it was nearly noon, but Sophie had heard the baronet was accustomed to town hours, so no doubt this *was* early for him.

"I see you're up with the dawn, as usual," he observed. "And might I add, looking every bit as lovely?"

"Thank you." Sophie offered a small smile, not wholly certain of how to respond to the compliment. She suspected she might be more flattered if the baronet's gallantry didn't have such a… practiced quality about it. Well, that didn't mean he *wasn't* being sincere, in his own way, she reminded herself.

Sir Lucas's gaze had flicked over to Sophie's companion. "Pendarvis."

"Nankivell." Mr. Pendarvis inclined his head.

"I see that you're abroad early as well."

"Indeed."

Sophie glanced from one to the other, reminded afresh of the strange antipathy between them, which had apparently abated not one jot since their first meeting. Sir Lucas's eyes were slightly narrowed, his nostrils flared, and his expression indecipherable. Mr. Pendarvis's face was likewise hard to read, but his mouth had set like stone and his posture, relaxed a few moments ago, was stiff, almost rigid. *Oh, dear.*

"Well, I really should be going, Sir Lucas," she said brightly. "I've stayed out later than I intended to, and I mustn't keep the family waiting too long for luncheon. Good day to you."

For a moment, he looked as though he would detain her, then he inclined his head and moved his horse to one side so they could pass. "Good day, Miss Sophie. Pendarvis."

"Nankivell."

Just as chilly as before, Sophie noted ruefully as she urged Tregony forward. She darted a glance at Mr. Pendarvis, who had drawn level with her, but his face was still impassive. She avoided looking back at Sir Lucas, though she was conscious of a growing relief as the distance widened between them.

Not that she disliked Sir Lucas. He was one of their neighbors, after all, with whom they'd always been on fairly good terms. But she'd been taken aback when Harry had informed her that the baronet had recently approached him with a formal offer of marriage for her. While she supposed Sir Lucas was handsome enough and his home, Nankivell Park, was accounted both large and grand, the thought of him as a suitor inspired no great longing. She'd actually felt relieved rather than indignant on hearing that Harry had dismissed his suit on the grounds of her age and inexperience.

There was another, more private reason to be thankful as well. *Swans and Tresilians mate for life.* No denying that the family motto had shaped Sophie's perceptions of love. Call it foolish or fanciful, but she'd always believed that she'd know in an instant when she met the man she was meant to love for the rest of her life. If that was true in any way, then Sir Lucas Nankivell was certainly *not* that man.

She glanced at Mr. Pendarvis again, relieved to note that he no longer seemed as stiff or forbidding. His face had gone abstracted instead, the way it had on the beach. Mulling over that idea of his, she suspected—the one he was presently refusing to share. Still, she'd rather he was concentrating on that than on his ill feelings toward Sir Lucas. Though *why* the two men should dislike each other so… Well, it was none of her business. Some people were just oil and water, and that was all there was to that.

A little further on, they came to their earlier meeting place, a crossroads marked by a hawthorn tree, just beginning to put forth its white flowers.

"Here's where I must leave you, Mr. Pendarvis." Sophie did her best to sound cheery. "But I hope you'll call on us soon. I know Harry would be glad to see you."

As would she, but it would be too forward for a proper young lady to say so. *And what a sad bore being a proper young lady was at times*, she reflected.

His demeanor thawed noticeably. "Thank you, Miss Tresilian. I hope to do so. And thank you for your company on the ride as well. I hope you can forgive my abstraction," he added with a rueful smile. "I realize I've been poor company this last mile or so."

Sophie couldn't help but return his smile. "You are forgiven, Mr. Pendarvis. May I one day hope to learn the cause of such abstraction?"

"If this latest brainstorm turns out to have any merit, you'll be among the first to know," he promised.

"I mean to hold you to that, sir." Bidding him farewell, Sophie turned Tregony down the left-hand path that led to Roswarne.

Six

Sweeter than roses, or cool evening breeze
On a warm flowery shore, was the dear kiss,
First trembling made me freeze,
Then shot like fire all o'er.

—Henry Purcell, *Pausanius*

Cornwall, May 1891

PUTTING DOWN HER VIOLIN AND BOW, SOPHIE
frowned over her music. While she thought her performance of Vivaldi's "Spring" had improved significantly,
her rendition of "Winter" still seemed to lack the necessary
speed or excitement. Perhaps the musical demands of that
piece weren't within her compass yet. Her own teacher
had called her a proficient violinist, who'd improve further
with practice, but no virtuoso, which was lowering but
not untrue.

She looked up at a light cough from the doorway to find
Parsons standing there.

"Forgive the interruption, Miss Sophie," he began. "But
Mr. Pendarvis has called, hoping to speak to you or Sir Harry.
I've put him in the library."

"Oh! Thank you, Parsons." Sophie rose from her chair. "I'll go in to him at once."

"Very good, Miss Sophie." The butler bowed and withdrew.

Sophie glanced at herself in the mirror above the mantel, hastily smoothing her hair and her skirts. She wore a day dress of sea green muslin today, which deepened the color of her eyes, and a pretty string of Italian glass beads about her throat. Not *too* young or girlish—she was eighteen next month, after all. Telling herself not to be flustered, she made for the library.

Mr. Pendarvis was standing by the desk, but he turned around at her entrance. Sophie hoped she was not imagining the welcoming light in his eyes—even if it signified nothing more than friendship.

She came forward, smiling. "Mr. Pendarvis, good morning. What brings you here today?"

He smiled as well. "Good morning, Miss Tresilian. I'd hoped I might find your brother at home, but your butler tells me he's gone out?"

"I'm afraid so. Harry had business in Truro and probably won't be back before dinner."

"Serve me right for not sending word beforehand," he said ruefully. "But I was so eager to discuss something with him that I didn't think ahead." He held up what looked like an artist's portfolio. "Perhaps I could prevail upon you to have a look? As I recall, I promised you'd be among the first people I told."

"Is this about that idea you had?" she asked eagerly. Over a week had passed since their conversation on the beach. "The one you said was either brilliant or completely mad?"

"The very same." He laid the portfolio on the desk. "And I'm still trying to decide which, so I thought I'd ask your opinion—or Harry's."

Intrigued, Sophie watched as he opened the portfolio and took out two large drawings, which he laid out side by side upon the desk. One she recognized at once as a sketch of the exterior of Pendarvis Hall. The other...

"What is this exactly?" she ventured, stealing an uncertain glance at him.

He took a breath—composing himself, she realized. "This, with work, capital, and a good deal of luck, will be the Pendarvis Hotel in the not too distant future."

"A hotel?" Astonished, she looked down at the second drawing again, belatedly recognizing it as a floor plan: a painstaking recreation of the Hall's interior. Rooms, passages, stairwells—one could get lost trying to keep track of them all. "You mean, like an inn?"

"Yes—only on a grander scale. It was what you told me about your cousin, and how he earned enough to maintain his castle. Since I don't wish to let or sell the Hall, I thought the best solution would be to make it pay its way, and convert it into a resort hotel."

"Like the ones in Newquay?"

"Very similar. I understand that the resorts in Newquay did not begin as private residences, but I'm thinking that could be used to work in the Hall's favor." His mouth quirked in the faintest of smiles. "If guests are willing to pay to lodge in a Scottish castle, perhaps they'd be equally as willing to do so in a Cornish country estate. There's certainly no lack of space—the Hall has three wings and more than twenty bedchambers!"

Twenty bedchambers! Sophie shook her head, more than slightly dazed by the thought. The Tresilians had done well for themselves over the years, but their prosperity didn't extend to a house built on the scale of Pendarvis Hall. It was on the tip of her tongue to say she couldn't begin to fathom how this place could ever be converted into a hotel, but a glance at Mr. Pendarvis silenced her. He looked as she'd never seen him before: his eyes alight, his spare frame almost vibrating with barely contained energy. Was this how he'd looked in Rouen, dreaming of Norman cathedrals? Intense, inspired, even fanatical… in the way that artists or visionaries could be. The transformation in him was at once disconcerting and, she had to confess, undeniably attractive. He had a passion for this work, as keen as hers for music. Well, far be it from her to play the wet blanket, especially before hearing the whole of his scheme.

"It's certainly an ambitious plan, Mr. Pendarvis," she ventured. "Why don't you tell me a little more about how you'd go about it?"

❧

Some twenty minutes later, Sophie looked up from the floor plan, excitement kindling within her like a stoked fire. "And you truly believe this could work?"

"I do, yes." His voice rang with complete conviction.

She studied him with the same attention she'd given his plans. During their discussion, he'd removed his coat and flung it over a nearby chair; his waistcoat was now undone, his shirtsleeves pushed back to the elbows, and his dark hair tousled from running his fingers through it. But that was as nothing compared to the other changes she saw in him. The slight diffidence and hesitance from their earliest meetings was gone. In its place was a crackling confidence, an authority that informed his every word and motion as he explained just what was involved in constructing the Pendarvis Hotel and how he meant to accomplish it. The way his eyes sharpened, the way his hands gestured, trying to conjure up the image so vivid in his own mind.

Sophie had followed along as best she could, asking questions whenever she felt lost or uncertain. For the most part, she had understood the gist of his plans: the bedchambers would be refurbished, freshly painted, or repapered, and private *en suite* bathrooms would be added to most of the rooms not already furnished with one.

"But what about—?" Sophie had started to ask, then paused, blushing a little and wondering how to broach a possibly indelicate subject.

"I plan to install more water closets," Mr. Pendarvis had replied, with no trace of embarrassment. "The very latest kind, of course. And there will be central heating too. Great-Aunt Martha already had it put into the main wing—one of her last improvements before she died. I'll make sure the rest of the Hall has it as well."

That would solve two major difficulties with country houses right there, Sophie mused: inadequate plumbing and insufficient heat. She spared a moment to be thankful that her family had always kept Roswarne up-to-date in that regard, then asked, "And gaslights?"

"Also already installed, even before the central heating." He paused, then added, accurately gauging the drift of her thoughts, "I am under no illusion that I can recreate a place like Claridge's or the Savoy in the heart of Cornwall. There certainly won't be a pneumatic lift, or electrical lighting— yet—but I can promise guests the basic amenities at the very least, and I hope some luxuries as well."

"How does your staff feel about this plan?" Sophie asked. "It would be quite an adjustment for them to make, to go from serving a family in a private home to waiting on guests in a hotel. Have you discussed it with them yet?"

"Not just yet," he admitted. "I'm still working out all the details. But I hope to make a good argument for the hotel, when the time comes. And their positions at the Hall wouldn't really change—they'd be doing much the same work as they are now. And I could hire other people as needed, not just more domestics, but porters and waiters too."

"Not all of them will see things as you do," she warned. "Or be willing to accept such a big change. Some might even give notice."

"That would be their choice," he conceded. "Although

I'd hope to convince everyone to stay on. It's not as if the Hall has ceased to become a country home. It's merely that the unused parts of it could be put to better purpose than standing empty all year round."

"Would you still live there yourself?"

"I shall be the innkeeper, so I could hardly live elsewhere. I thought I might reserve one wing for my personal apartments. This one, perhaps." He touched the west wing on the floor plan. "More than adequate for a bachelor establishment. Great-Uncle Simon was living mainly in a solitary suite toward the end of his life."

"But would that be enough for you? What if—" She broke off, just in time, before she could ask what he'd do if he did decide to marry and have a family, after all. But he'd been so adamant the last time the subject had arisen that it seemed foolish to persist. "What if you find you need more room?" she amended.

He shrugged. "I can't imagine needing much more space than an entire wing. But I suppose I could move to another part of the Hall—or redesign the wing to suit my needs. I'd be a poor architect indeed if I couldn't manage that."

"Of course. But are you sure you wouldn't mind having strangers occupying your house, at all hours, in every season?"

He considered her question, then shook his head. "I don't think so. Perhaps if I'd grown up at the Hall and had a deeper sentimental attachment to it, I'd feel differently. Or if I had a title to uphold, like your cousin, and was expected to keep the estate intact to every last brick for whoever succeeded me. As it is… well, I'd rather have a guest in every chamber than rattle about like a pebble in a shoe in a house that's too large for me alone. And I'd still have to pay to maintain the Hall, whether there was one person or twenty living there."

"That's a good point," Sophie acknowledged.

"So, do you think my plan has any merit?"

His tone was casual, but Sophie could sense how

important the answer was to him. And so he deserved an honest response.

"I think your plan has considerable potential, Mr. Pendarvis," she said at last. "You've obviously thought the matter through, and I don't doubt that you've a good grasp of what's involved here, as an architect. But it's a risky venture, all the same. It *could* succeed, especially if you can persuade others in the county to invest." She glanced down at the floor plan. "I wish I could picture this as clearly as you do. I can't quite visualize it from just a drawing."

"Would it help if you saw the place for yourself?"

Sophie looked up, startled, but Mr. Pendarvis appeared to be in earnest. "It might. At least, it would do no harm to see it."

"Well, then, Miss Tresilian, would you care to visit the Hall?" he inquired. "If your family doesn't object to my stealing you for a few hours, that is."

"There's no one here to object. Harry's in Truro, John's at the mine, and Mama's in the village helping to organize a flower show. So I'm completely at liberty to accept your invitation," she concluded, smiling at him. "Just give me a few minutes to change into my habit."

"No need for that—we can drive over in my gig. And besides"—he paused, studying her with those intense blue eyes—"I find that dress far too becoming to wish you to change it."

"Thank you, sir," Sophie said lightly, though she could feel herself flushing with pleasure at the compliment. "Then just let me get my hat and coat, and we'll be on our way."

❧

Fortunately, it wasn't considered *too* improper for a lady to drive in the country with a friend, Sophie told herself. And Mr. Pendarvis had become a friend to Harry, and thus to the whole family, these last few months. All the same, she experienced a faint tingle of excitement when he handed her into the gig, and then climbed in beside her and took the reins.

Sitting in such close quarters, she could feel the warmth of his near thigh through her skirt, and even breathe in his scent, a pleasant mingling of clean linen and shaving soap. Bay rum—her father had favored that scent as well. As a child, she'd come to associate it with the comfort and security she always felt in her father's company, but it had a rather different effect on her when she smelled it on Mr. Pendarvis.

She glanced covertly at him as he drove—adroitly, though with understandable caution, as he was still getting used to the roads in Cornwall. It helped that the horse was such a placid, unexcitable beast, trotting along at an easy pace and obeying its driver's lightest command.

"I heard a violin playing when Parsons showed me in," Mr. Pendarvis remarked, once they were underway. "Was that you practicing?"

"Yes—I hope it didn't sound too terrible. I haven't got the knack of that concerto yet."

"I'm no expert, but it sounded fine to me," he asserted. "Indeed, I should like to hear it again sometime, once you're satisfied with your progress."

"Perhaps the next time you dine with us at Roswarne we can have music afterward," she suggested. "I don't know if I'll have mastered Vivaldi's 'Winter' by then, but I can give you a decent rendering of his 'Spring.'"

"Your favorite season." There was a smile in his voice.

"Just so," Sophie acknowledged, smiling back.

They chatted lightly of music and seasons for a good quarter hour, then Mr. Pendarvis turned a corner, passed through a gate—and there, at the end of a curving drive, stood the Hall.

Despite having visited the estate before, Sophie still caught her breath when she looked up at the great facade. Was this how Elizabeth Bennet had felt, looking at Pemberley the first time? She'd heard that the Hall had begun life as a medieval manor house of modest proportions. While various changes had been made to it over the centuries, it had been extensively rebuilt during Queen Anne's reign on a far grander scale. The owner of that time had commissioned an Inigo Jones–like Palladian front, and the landscape was said to be Capability Brown, and carefully preserved over generations.

Generations that had got successively smaller, Sophie reminded herself. Ancient as the Pendarvis name might be, their numbers had dwindled nonetheless. Grand or humble, a house only lived if there were people who cared for and maintained it. Sobering to think that Robin Pendarvis might be the last, or among the last, to do so.

She felt even more somber once they'd entered the house, admitted by the butler, a tall, stern-faced Cornishman with an air of general imperturbability.

"Ah, Praed," Mr. Pendarvis began, "this is Miss Sophie Tresilian, Sir Harry Tresilian's sister. She's visiting the Hall this afternoon."

"Very good, sir. Miss Tresilian." Praed inclined his head and withdrew, leaving the master to escort his awestruck guest.

Awestruck *and* tongue-tied, Sophie acknowledged ruefully, as she took in her new surroundings. Even the entrance hall was impressive, and beyond that lay a house the size of a small palace. Roswarne could probably fit into one wing of it.

"Any part of the Hall you particularly wish to see?" Mr. Pendarvis inquired.

"Oh, I'm prepared to be guided entirely by you," Sophie assured him. "I'd get hopelessly lost if I even tried to explore this place on my own!"

"I felt much the same on my first visit," he observed. "*And* I kept wondering how many regiments could have been quartered here." A corner of his mouth lifted in a wry smile. "Pendarvis Hall as a barracks—Great-Uncle would have been horrified."

Sophie stifled a giggle. "Only if you actually *planned* to garrison soldiers here one day!"

"It's not likely to come to that. Although he'd no doubt take a dim view of my plans for the Hall, if he knew." A shadow flickered across his face. "Well, one cannot be a slave to the past forever. Let's start with the main wing. I promise in advance not to run you off your feet."

❧

True to his promise, Robin avoided running Sophie off her feet, but he rather suspected she'd have run him off his if their positions were reversed. Nearly two hours later, she showed no sign of flagging, her interest and enthusiasm in his project undimmed. What a partner *she'd* make, he mused, and quickly suppressed the pang that arose in him at the thought.

Now he watched as she moved about the chamber they were currently viewing, her expression thoughtful, even admiring, as she surveyed the daisy-patterned wallpaper and the canopied bed with its matching coverlet and curtains of spring green brocade.

"A woman's touch," she said at last, so emphatically that Robin had to smile. "And not just here—all through the house! Who decorated the Hall most recently?"

"My Great-Aunt Martha, I believe. Sadly, I never knew her," he added. "Great-Uncle was a widower when I first came to Cornwall, but I've heard that she had a kind heart and quite good taste, for a merchant's daughter."

"Well, good taste isn't solely the provenance of the aristocracy. I'm sure there are duchesses and even queens with the most hideous taste imaginable." Sophie glanced about the chamber again. "This is—restful and elegant, rather than magnificent."

Robin raised skeptical brows. "And that's an advantage?"

"Absolutely—magnificence can be oppressive. If I were a guest, I'd very much enjoy staying in such a room. Any lady would." She smiled, her eyes aglow. "Oh, I can imagine your hotel so much more clearly now that I've seen the house again!"

Robin studied her closely, but saw no sign of dissembling. "Can you really?"

"I do—honor bright!" Sophie assured him, crossing her heart for good measure. "But you'll need some help if you're to realize all this."

"Investors," he interpreted without difficulty, stifling a sigh. "I know my best chance is to find some people willing to back this scheme."

"Would your family help? The ones in Yorkshire, I mean?"

"It's possible. My uncle Richard owns a part-share in a few London hotels." He smiled wryly. "No doubt he'd consider this far more practical than designing cathedrals in France. I'll write to him tonight and ask his opinion. If he approves, he might be willing to advance me some capital, if only for the sake of family. But I suspect it would help even more if I could interest some of the local gentry in this venture. Do you think—Harry would be open to it?"

"He *might*," Sophie replied, after a moment. "*If* he felt it benefited the county—and the rest of Cornwall. He thinks hard times are coming. Mines have been closing down, workers emigrating—a hotel could give them a reason to stay. Steady work *and* safer than going down a mine or out to sea. *And* you'd be offering employment to women as well, wouldn't you?"

The practicality of her argument impressed him, but then, Sophie came from a practical family, Robin reflected. The Tresilians owned not only a tin mine, but also shares in local fisheries. "I'd planned to."

"Well, then, I'm sure Harry would be willing to hear you out at the very least." Sophie fretted her lower lip, a sight that Robin found more endearing—and distracting—than he cared to admit. "And maybe the Prideauxes. I know Roger Prideaux likes to have a finger in different pies. And the Tregarths, the Polwheles, and maybe the Nankivells—"

"No." He hardly recognized the cold, clipped monosyllable as his own voice.

Sophie's eyes widened. "I—beg your pardon?" she ventured, after a moment.

Robin surreptitiously unclenched his fists, willing himself back to calm. "If you were referring to Sir Lucas Nankivell, then—no. I would prefer not to do business with him."

"Oh." To his chagrin, Sophie was still eyeing him warily, as if he were a bomb about to explode. "Well, I suppose you may be right to feel so. Sir Lucas has never been known for having much of a head for business. It's just that his family has such an old name in the county, and I know that can lend a bit more credibility to a project."

Robin exhaled. "Forgive me. I did not mean to bite your head off. I'm aware that the Nankivells are a long-established family in St. Perran, but I feel there's a certain—conflict of interest that would prevent any sort of profitable partnership between Nankivell and myself."

"Conflict of interest?" she echoed blankly. "Over what?"

Over more things than you can imagine, Robin thought, looking into her lovely, uncomprehending face. Aloud he said, "I mentioned before that I'd inherited some railway shares from my grandfather. Nankivell recently approached me about acquiring them, but I am disinclined to sell."

"I see. Well, then, what about James—as a possible investor, I mean?"

"Your cousin—the new earl? I thought he was having financial difficulties of his own."

"Oh, he is, but that doesn't necessarily rule him out as a potential backer. In fact, he might be even more receptive to your scheme because of his own situation." Sophie paused, then added significantly, "He wrote in his last letter that he was courting a Miss Newbold from New York. We *think* she may be an heiress. And if they marry, he might be in a better position to invest in your hotel, especially if she supports the idea too. I've heard that Americans are great admirers of industry and entrepreneurship."

"A possibility," Robin conceded, "but let's not count our chickens just yet. The lady might choose another. I've heard some heiresses won't consider anyone lower than a duke."

"Miss Newbold would be lucky to have James, even without a title!" Sophie declared staunchly. "Besides, he described her as lovely and charming, so she *must* be both. And there's no harm, is there, in being just a *little* ambitious?"

"I suppose not, provided one isn't burdened with unrealistic expectations." A memory from a less pleasant time tugged at him and he forced it back. "Well, I hope your cousin's suit prospers, and if it does, perhaps I'll approach him then. Now, as we've seen most of the first and second floors, would you care to stop and have some refreshment? The first time *I* toured the Hall as Great-Uncle's heir, I had to fortify myself with a whiskey and soda," he added wryly, "but you might prefer tea."

Her dimpled smile flashed out at him. "Tea would be welcome, but there's something I should like to see first, downstairs."

"Downstairs? On the ground floor?"

She nodded. "Would you show me the ballroom, Mr. Pendarvis?"

❦

"Dear life," Sophie breathed, gazing about the salon. "It must be *twice* the size of ours!"

"I shouldn't be at all surprised." Mr. Pendarvis sounded less than enthusiastic about that circumstance. "Pendarvis Hall used to entertain on a lavish scale—house parties, pheasant shoots, hunt balls, and the like. But there hasn't been anything like that here for a good five years. Maybe even ten."

"At least your staff keeps this room swept and dusted," Sophie pointed out. The ballroom floor still held a gleam of polish, and the walls—tinted a pale blue-green—showed no sign of mildew or peeling paint. The wall sconces were free of rust, and the panes of the French doors were likewise spotless. The draperies might be a little faded, but they were oyster brocade, and pale enough for their age not to show too obviously.

She glanced up at the high arched ceiling and the huge chandelier, its crystal prisms swaddled in Holland cloth. "Mr. Pendarvis, you want guests of a certain—quality, don't you?"

"I'd take anyone who could pay, but I suppose I *am* hoping to attract a particular clientele," he admitted.

"What Society calls 'the best people,'" Sophie supplied, without difficulty. "No shame in that. But if you're trying to entice them down here, fresh from London and the Season, you'll need to offer more than food and lodging. They'll expect to be entertained as well—to enjoy at least some of the pleasures they enjoy in town."

He stared at her, clearly appalled. "Oh, God." The words came out half-strangled. "Will you think me a complete dunce if I tell you that had never crossed my mind?"

"Not at all. You're an architect—naturally you're more intent on getting the house in order. But there's plenty of time to learn how to plan activities for your guests. Or you could simply hire someone to direct your entertainments instead," she added as he blanched visibly.

"There is that." He exhaled, some of the panic receding, and summoned a sheepish smile. "You're quite right—I've been focusing on the hotel as a building to be renovated, rather than as a place where actual people will be staying. Thank you for pointing that out to me."

"Well, I've never stayed at a hotel, but I have attended a

few house parties *and* helped Mama plan some at Roswarne. The comfort of one's guests is always the most important thing to consider. Even in the country, people want to be amused and entertained." She glanced around the salon again. "Fortunately, with a room this size, you can hold all sorts of grand events. And it would be something, wouldn't it, to see this place come alive again?"

"It is a bit like a tomb, isn't it?" he observed dryly.

"That's not what I meant." She looked up once more at the swaddled chandelier. "Can't you imagine it? Everything lit and blazing. The floor polished and shining. Flowers everywhere. The musicians up there in the gallery, and the guests all dancing. You could probably fit most of the county in this ballroom."

"Good Lord, really?" Mr. Pendarvis eyed the salon with distinct unease. "I've never hosted as much as a dinner party, let alone a ball!"

"It isn't *easy*, planning something of that size," Sophie admitted. "But neither is it impossible. Your staff would know what to do, and you could ask your friends and family for advice as well. Hotels do hold formal balls on occasion—there was one at the Newquay resort this past Easter Monday."

"Yes, I heard something about that myself." He paused, studying the room with new interest. "And that they have dances some afternoons, at teatime."

"Good thinking," Sophie approved. "And don't forget receptions, concerts—maybe even plays!" Excitement began to kindle inside of her as she considered the possibilities. "You could mount a stage over there." She gestured toward the far wall. "Nothing too huge, just a raised platform, and put down a carpet and rows of seats in front."

He narrowed his eyes, trying to see as she saw. "Perhaps. The concert idea may have some merit. I don't know about plays—the theatre in Truro would be better equipped for that."

"Dramatic recitals, then," Sophie suggested. "Some of your guests might even be persuaded to take part themselves. You'd be amazed at how many frustrated thespians there are." She struck a dramatic pose and declaimed with great fervor, "*A soldier of the Legion lay dying in Algiers, / There was lack of women's nursing, there was dearth of women's tears—*"

"Stop." Mr. Pendarvis held up a hand. "My dear, I would much rather hear you sing."

My dear. The words took her by surprise, and she glanced at him, suddenly hesitant. "What, now?"

He raised his brows. "Don't tell me you've grown self-conscious about your voice, Miss Tresilian! I remember how poised you were at New Year's. And I should like to hear just how your voice sounds in this great cavern. How else should I know if it's suitable for those concerts you've suggested?"

"Well, if you're certain—" Sophie wandered toward the center of the room and positioned herself below the highest point of the ceiling. The soft light of early afternoon rippled along the pale green walls, casting a watery pattern that made her think of undersea caves and grottos. Inspired, she cleared her throat, took a breath or two to steady herself and pitch her voice properly, then launched into "The Mermaid's Song," a Haydn canzonetta she had always loved:

> *"Now the dancing sunbeams play*
> *On the green and glassy sea,*
> *Come, and I will lead the way*
> *Where the pearly treasures be."*

Her voice rose, gratifyingly clear even in this vast space. A faint echo resounded from the walls and ceiling, but not strongly enough to distort the sound. Encouraged, she sang on:

> *"Come with me, and we will go*
> *Where the rocks of coral grow.*

Follow, follow, follow me!
Follow, follow, follow me!"

She lowered her voice just a fraction, let it become confiding, even enticing. Mermaids were sirens, after all, eager to lure unsuspecting mortals beneath the waves. Enchanting creatures, but dangerous too—she added a note of cajolery as she embarked on the next verse:

> *"Come, behold what treasures lie*
> *Far below the rolling waves,*
> *Riches, hid from human eye,*
> *Dimly shine in ocean's caves.*
> *Ebbing tides bear no delay,*
> *Stormy winds are far away.*
>
> *Come with me, and we will go*
> *Where the rocks of coral grow.*
> *Follow, follow, follow me!*
> *Follow, follow, follow me!"*

She let her voice rise triumphantly on the last chorus and fell silent—only to find Mr. Pendarvis staring at her so intently that she began to feel self-conscious after all.

"Do you not care for the song, Mr. Pendarvis?" she ventured. "Or was I a trifle off-key?" She didn't think she had been, but perhaps he had heard otherwise.

He shook his head almost absentmindedly, his gaze still upon her. "No, no—you were note-perfect, as far as I could tell. And the song was—quite pleasing. Fitting, actually." A faint smile crooked his lips. "You look like a Nereid in that dress. My idea of one, anyway."

Sophie felt herself flushing at the compliment. "Thank you," she said, striving for a light tone. "I love that song; it's been one of my favorites since I first heard it. Whenever

I sing it, I try to pretend I *am* a mermaid. Haydn wrote so many charming songs, didn't he?"

"Charming, indeed." He continued to study her, a faint crease etching itself between his brows. "You should really do something with that voice of yours," he said, almost abruptly. "If your family would just let you go and have some proper training in London—"

"It's not as if they're stopping me!" Sophie protested loyally. "And I *am* going to London next spring. Mama and Harry have even suggested that I study at a conservatory— someplace like the Royal College of Music."

The crease smoothed out. "Have they indeed? Good. Because you're wasted here, performing at musicales and evenings at home. As a professional singer, you could have the world at your feet, if you chose."

"At my feet?" The thought seemed incredible. *She*, the daughter of a provincial Cornish baronet, singing on the stage? Holding audiences in the palm of her hand?

"I mean it." His voice was gentle, but his gaze held an intensity that took her breath away. "Let's have no false modesty, my dear. You have a rare talent, and a fair amount of stage presence as well. Cultivate both, and you could go far indeed—concerts, recitals, even the opera. *If* that's what you want, of course."

"I'm not sure what I want, exactly," Sophie confessed, feeling suddenly very young and uncertain. "I dearly love music—singing and playing. I always have. But I've never considered making a career of it!"

"Understandable. Young ladies aren't generally encouraged to seek careers, or any other outlet, save a good marriage. And perhaps I am taking great liberties even to suggest such a thing. Your family probably wouldn't thank me for it," he added with a rueful grimace. "But I'm afraid that I have a deep-seated aversion at seeing talents go to waste. Would you think me unforgivably impertinent if I ask you to consider what I've said?"

"Not at all. I'm flattered that you think my abilities worth the trouble," Sophie replied. "And who knows? Perhaps someday I *will* be a famous singer and give a concert at the Royal Albert Hall." For a moment, an image of herself—splendidly gowned and bejeweled—standing upon a stage rose in her mind. She forced it back at once, sternly telling herself to concentrate on the matter at hand. "But we're discussing *your* dreams today, Mr. Pendarvis. Namely, how you can turn the Hall into the best, most popular, most sought-after resort hotel in Cornwall!"

He relaxed, smiling. "Point taken, Miss Tresilian. Have you any further suggestions regarding this gargantuan ball-room of mine?"

Sophie pursed her lips. "Well… I did hear a bit of an echo while I was singing, but a carpet and perhaps some heavier curtains should take care of that, I think. And the advantage of a salon this size is that you needn't limit the number of performers here. You could invite a whole choir or even an orchestra!"

Mr. Pendarvis looked slightly daunted at the prospect, but to his credit, he nodded. "I'll bear that in mind, although I think it may be prudent to start small. A few singers, perhaps a string quartet."

"Or an elocutionist…"

They spoke a while longer, suggesting various acts and possible alterations to the room to make it more comfortable for performers, then, by mutual consent, they strayed out through the French windows and onto the terrace.

Leaning against the marble balustrade, Sophie breathed in the fragrance of countless flowers, borne toward them on the mild spring breeze. "It's coming alive, all around us. Your dream—can't you feel it?"

He rested his folded arms on the stone coping. "If it is, then I know entirely whom to thank for it, Miss Sophie."

His compliment pleased her, but she shook her head.

"*You're* the visionary, Mr. Pendarvis. I'm just adding a few embellishments."

"Without embellishments, this vision would still be bare bones. Whereas now"—he glanced toward the house rising tall and stately behind him—"it has some *allure* to it."

Sophie gazed out at what she could see of the gardens, a softly undulating sea of flowers, shrubs, and blossoming trees. "I take it you have plans for the grounds as well?"

"That is the easiest part, by far. The grounds and gardens need little alteration to appeal to guests. They can wander wherever they like. There's a rose garden, an herb garden—not to be confused with the kitchen garden—a formal garden, boxwood hedges, and a fountain."

"A fountain?" Sophie echoed, charmed. She was fond of fountains and rather regretted that Roswarne did not have one. The sight of water leaping into the air, the dancing droplets sparkling in the sun, lifted her spirits in the same way that watching the tide come in did.

"And a reflecting pool—too shallow to drown in, fortunately," he added. "And a small maze that's simple enough to avoid getting lost in."

"Children would enjoy that," Sophie said with conviction. "And they'll need to be entertained too, if their families come here. Have you a tennis court?"

"Yes, actually. And lawns for croquet or bowling," he added, much struck by the thought.

"What about sport? Is there a trout stream on the estate? James has one at Pentreath."

"There's a lake. Great-Uncle used to keep it stocked with trout and perch, but he lost interest in fishing during his last years. I could start things up again there."

"Shooting?"

He shook his head. "Great-Aunt Martha didn't care for it, and I must confess I don't either. Besides, I'd be worried for my guests' safety with all those guns about. I don't know that we even have much in the way of game birds on the property anymore. But whatever there are may continue to thrive unmolested. Same for foxes—I'm not about to have the Four Burrow Hunt riding hell for leather through the grounds either."

"I've heard the best hunting is south of here, in any case."

"Good—I don't wish to ruffle too many feathers among my new neighbors." He paused, his gaze turning reminiscent. "I don't know if Great-Uncle ever rode to hounds, but some Pendarvis ancestors might have. There's a hunting lodge across the park—a good ten minutes away on horseback. It hasn't been used in years and is probably in poor repair. I may have it razed and build something else. Perhaps a holiday cottage for guests who want more privacy."

Sophie glanced over in the direction of the gardens again, frowned as something caught her eye. "What's that over there? It looks like—a cupola?"

Mr. Pendarvis followed the direction of her gaze. "There's a pavilion, just beyond the rose garden. Not large, but rather pretty nonetheless. It's not too far. Should you like to see it?"

"Oh, yes, please!"

Together they descended the short flight of stairs leading from the terrace to the gardens.

❧

Enclosed by boxwood hedges, the rose garden was an oasis of color and fragrance. The flowers were just beginning their first exuberant bloom: a riot of rich reds, soft pinks, and creamy whites all unfurling in the spring sunshine. Sophie inhaled deeply—the rose garden at Roswarne was her mother's pride and joy, but this one appeared no less lovely. At any other time she would have been pleased to stop and explore further, but at the moment, her attention was fixed on the structure just visible beyond the last hedge.

It was worth the walk, she decided as she and Mr.

Pendarvis emerged from the rose garden, and the pavilion came into view. She'd pictured a marble rotunda, solid and perhaps a little squat, but this was more graceful, even dainty. Slender, white-painted columns upheld the tiered roof, the pinnacle of which was formed by the tiny cupola she'd first spied, and delicate latticework framed the arching windows and ornamented the walls, which rose no higher than one's waist. Honeysuckle twined about the pillars and festooned the roof, their creamy trumpets giving off a perfume that was enticing now and would be downright seductive by evening.

"It's lovely," Sophie declared without reserve, and her host smiled.

"This is a new part of the Hall," he told her. "Well, new as in within the last twenty years or so. Great-Aunt Martha wanted a gazebo where she could take tea alone or with friends. Mama liked it too, and I remember coming here a few times, when I felt I needed a bit of privacy. The grounds-keeper maintains it well—it's needed only a few repairs over the years. Shall we?" He gestured for her to precede him up the steps into the pavilion itself.

The teak floor felt reassuringly solid beneath Sophie's feet. She drifted from archway to archway—eight of them, making the building an octagon—and admired the view from each one. Smooth green lawn stretched away on all sides, ideal for picnics or suppers *al fresco*, she pointed out to Mr. Pendarvis, who stood leaning against the archway closest to the steps.

"A possibility," he acknowledged. "Or afternoon tea on the lawn."

"And the pavilion isn't too tiny," Sophie mused aloud. "I was thinking—a string quartet could fit in here comfortably enough. And with those open walls, you could place rows of chairs on almost all sides of the pavilion, except behind the performers, of course."

"You're proposing outdoor concerts as well?"

"Why not? Doesn't London hold concerts in the park on occasion? You could do something similar here."

"Wouldn't that be tempting fate? I know how often it rains here."

"True," she conceded. "But one could say that about nearly every place in England. And we do have fairly mild springs and summers. You could put up an awning over the seats for cooler afternoons and evenings, or move things indoors if rain *should* come on." She looked up at the underside of the roof. "And this would be a lovely place to perform. Less formal than the ballroom, and romantic too, especially in the evenings. Can't you imagine it? A summer evening, with all the stars out and perhaps a full moon, and the honeysuckle in bloom…"

"As long as no one complains of the ague afterward."

Sophie shook her head. "Men! You haven't an atom of true romance in you!"

A corner of his mouth quirked up. "I'm content to leave the romance to women, my dear. But forgive me—I don't mean to be a spoilsport. And the idea has its charms… summer concerts at the hotel. Perhaps you'll become a great singer one day and perform here as a guest artist. All the best people will come flocking down to Cornwall just to hear you."

"Now who's being a romantic?" Sophie scoffed lightly. "But, I admit, I should be delighted to sing here someday." She drifted to the center of the pavilion floor and gazed out across the lawn, imagining it all: a balmy summer evening, graced by a silvery crescent moon, the air fragrant with honeysuckle and roses, the lilt of violins, and a sea of faces gazing expectantly up at the stage.

Holding the picture in her mind, she began to sing, her voice lower and more intimate than in the ballroom: "*Once in the dear dead days beyond recall, / When on the world the mists began to fall—*"

She broke off at the expression on Mr. Pendarvis's face; the canted brow gave him a wry, quizzical look. "What?"

"What do you know of *days beyond recall*? You're seventeen."

He sounded bemused rather than condescending, but Sophie flushed defensively. "Eighteen, nearly. And perhaps I understand more than you think."

She glanced up at the roof above her and continued with the chorus, still singing at half pitch but with a springwater clarity that filled the whole pavilion:

> *"Just a song at twilight, when the lights are low*
> *And the flickering shadows softly come and go,*
> *Though the heart be weary, sad the day and long,*
> *Yet still to us at twilight comes Love's old song,*
> *Comes Love's old sweet song…"*

As the last notes faded into silence, Sophie stole a glance at Mr. Pendarvis to find him staring at her, his face unguarded in a way she had never seen it. The firm line of his mouth was relaxed, almost soft, and his eyes…

She caught her breath as the air flashed electric between them. Then, in the next instant, he shouldered away from the pavilion entrance and closed the distance between them in two strides.

Sophie did not know whether his mouth came down on hers or whether hers rose to meet his, but the end result was the same. Here, in this sun-warmed pavilion fragrant with honeysuckle, Robin Pendarvis was kissing her, his mouth tender but assured, his arms enfolding her and drawing her close to his heart. Marveling, she closed her eyes and kissed him back.

She'd dreamed of this moment, of her first kiss, as many young girls do. And there had been attempts here and there—shy, awkward, inexpert busses from boys as young and inexperienced as she. But this was a man's kiss, and the woman within her awoke beneath the touch of his lips and strove to match him, passion for passion. And love for love.

Because she *knew* it at last for love: these feelings that had been developing ever since New Year's, only far more intense—purified now into something she could not have denied, even had she wished it.

Here you are. Here we are.

The rightness of it sang through her like an aria composed just for her. *This was he.* The man she was meant to love all her days.

The knowledge rolled over her like a great wave, terrifying and exhilarating at once. Breathless and exultant, she clung to him, savoring the lean hardness of his body so close to hers and the mingled scents of clean linen, bay rum, and warm male skin.

He drew back, gazed down at her with hazed, almost slumberous eyes. "My God, Sophie." His voice sounded thick, almost slurred. "You are lovely. So lovely."

"Robin." His name emerged as a whisper. She freed a hand, reached up to touch his face… and saw awareness flash back into his eyes, followed swiftly by panic: a portcullis descending to repel invaders.

"My God!" His tone was wholly different now as he pulled away from her, his eyes wide and slightly wild. "Forgive me, Sophie—Miss Tresilian! I should not have taken such liberties."

Sophie swallowed. "On the contrary, perhaps you should have taken them long before."

He turned from her, raked a hand through his hair, took a few agitated strides about the pavilion. Strange how she should feel so much calmer than he at this moment. "I didn't intend—I never meant—"

"I know." Feeling oddly composed, she summoned a faint smile. "You are the last man I could ever imagine *planning* something like this."

He stared at her, the crease prominent between his knotted brows, then said abruptly, "As a gentleman, I know what should follow from—*this*. But as I told you before, I am not in a position to marry, or even to court a lady such as yourself."

"I remember." Sophie cleared her throat. "But you do not strike me as the sort of man to trifle with a lady's affections. Or to engage in dalliance, when your intentions are not— what they should be."

"Honorable, you mean." He smiled without humor. "I am flattered that you hold me in such high regard. But in this case, you are correct. I did not intend seduction when I brought you here, either to the Hall or the gardens."

"Of course you didn't." She kept her voice low and soothing, as though gentling a restless horse.

He exhaled gustily. "Might I prevail upon you to accept my deepest apologies and my assurances that this won't happen again?"

Sophie fixed him with a level gaze. "With regard to your apologies, I see no reason for them, as I was a willing partici- pant in this kiss. And as for your assurances, I for one will hope they are incorrect, because I should like very much for this to happen again—when you *are* in a position to marry, or at least court."

"Sophie…" The sound of her name on his tongue was sweetness itself, and it told her all she needed to know. She was not the only one affected by what had passed between them.

He turned away again—trying to compose himself, she realized. "Perhaps one day," he began, then broke off, shaking his head. "I cannot expect you to wait. Not when I don't know how long it will be before I can make any promises. You have all your life, all your *youth*, before you, and I have no right to interfere with that! No right to bind you to—to something you might regret, in time."

It was on the tip of Sophie's tongue to protest, but the

tension she saw in the set of his shoulders silenced her. So close to the breaking point, and if she pushed—as she longed to do—she might drive him away completely.

"Very well," she said at last. "I confess, I do not see things exactly as you do, but I will respect your wishes in this. May we agree to be friends—special friends—for now? Surely no one could find anything wrong in that."

He drew a ragged breath, then "Friends," he echoed, with obvious relief. But she thought she heard a trace of regret in his acceptance as well, which eased the smart somewhat for her.

"And I *will* be discreet, Mr. Pendarvis. Robin." She permitted herself the luxury of using his Christian name and took renewed heart from what she saw in his eyes: hunger and longing, headier than the finest French champagne. This *wasn't* finished, whatever he might say.

"Thank you," he said, with clear gratitude. "I'll take you inside now. And perhaps we should start back to Roswarne soon, before your family misses you."

Young though she was, Sophie recognized the signs of a man in full retreat, trying to deny what had just occurred. Like trying to put a genie back in the bottle, and about as likely to prove successful.

But this was progress of a sort. He was at least admitting the *possibility* of marriage. Not cutting it off altogether and refusing to consider it. All she had to do was be patient—and all would come right at the end. She was sure of it, sure enough for both of them.

But because he'd looked so conscience-stricken, so determined to do the right thing, whatever it cost him, she held her tongue, assumed a demure expression, and allowed him to escort her back to the house.

Seven

I told my love, I told my love
I told her all my heart...

—William Blake, "Love's Secret"

Cornwall, June 1891

SO THIS WAS WHAT IT CAME DOWN TO IN THE END: lies, deceit, and an implacable enmity that could no longer be concealed behind a mask of good manners.

Gripped by an icy rage, Robin stared into the face of the man whose vicious slanders had almost cost him his reputation among his new neighbors—and so much more. Nankivell stared back with equal loathing and no trace of remorse. Not even the disgust of Harry and James, whom he had also traduced, had cowed him. Clearly he regretted nothing about his scheme, except its failure.

"This upstart," the baronet sneered, gesturing at Robin. "This Johnny-come-lately. Just what do you know about this fellow, Miss Sophie?" His voice dropped, became low and insinuating. "I could tell you things."

He was bluffing, Robin knew. There was no way this man could know his history, but the words sent a jolt of alarm through him all the same. If Nankivell—or someone like him—ever found out...

A sudden presence beside him: Sophie, head held high, eyes flashing, as she confronted her former suitor. "I know that *he's* a gentleman, Sir Lucas. That's all I need to know."

Oh, God. Her faith in him, so solid and unshakable, was at once a wound and a balm. *Oh, my dear, if you but knew...*

Startlingly, Sophie's declaration took the wind right out of Nankivell's sails. He flushed and turned away. In other circumstances, Robin might have enjoyed his adversary's discomfiture, but now all he wanted was to get out, fast, before his control disintegrated and his last defenses crumbled.

Which way I fly is Hell; myself am Hell...

Major Henshawe, the magistrate whose assistance they'd requested for tonight, was discussing defamation and recompense. Somehow, Robin summoned the composure to excuse himself. He'd abide by whatever Harry and James decided. He thought he saw pity in Harry's eyes as they shook hands—Christ, how much had he suspected about Robin's feelings for his sister?—and turned away from it as from a blow.

"Robin!" Sophie pleaded, stretching out her hand, but he stepped away from that too.

"Good night, Miss Sophie." Such simple words, so hard to say. "And to all of you."

He strode from the library, not looking back. Each step seemed to tear the heart from his body—he knew he'd already torn out *hers*—but he kept walking, not stopping until he was standing on the front terrace, surrounded by darkness, waiting for his horse to be brought up.

Such a fragile thing, hope—but ever since that kiss in the pavilion, he'd let himself indulge in it. Let himself believe there might be a future for them, someday... until Nankivell's words had reminded him of how impossible that was.

The door flew open behind him, and she was there, breathless and urgent at his shoulder. "Mr. Pendarvis! Robin! Don't go!"

Robin swallowed dryly, feeling her entreaty pull at him like a chain about his heart. "I've already overstayed my welcome, Miss Tresilian. Pray excuse me."

She caught his sleeve as he turned away. "There's no reason for *you* to leave! You, Harry, James—none of you killed Lord Trevenan!"

"That's not why—"

She made an impatient gesture. "And forget what Sir Lucas said! He was talking out of spite—just as he was when he slandered you!"

"Perhaps," he conceded with a taut nod. "But the essence of what he said is true enough. I do have secrets that I have kept from you and everyone else in Cornwall."

"I don't care about your secrets, Robin! I've never cared!" Passion—and tears—thickened her voice. He risked a glance at her, then wished he hadn't. The moonlight bleached her upturned face to marble, showed her brimming eyes, the faint quiver of her lips. Sophie, who never cried, who was made for laughter and music...

"But *I* do." He forced himself to remain calm, even distant. Not to take her in his arms as he burned to do. Not even to wipe away—or kiss away—her tears. Behind them came the sound of distant music that seemed to mock their shared pain.

"You should find someone else," he continued doggedly, looking away from her and into the gloom. Through the darkness, he glimpsed the shadowy shape of an approaching groom leading his equally shadowy horse up to the terrace. "Someone with no secrets and no past to regret. You deserve—that kind of happiness, that security."

"I'd rather have love!" she choked out. "*Your* love!"

He swallowed again, feeling as if his heart were lodged in

his throat. "You say that now, but you'll see that I am right. Good-bye, Miss Tresilian."

Her breath caught in a sob that tore at his heart. Hating himself, Robin strode down the steps and all but sprang into the saddle, riding off as though the devil was at his heels.

❧

Two days later

"Mr. Pendarvis is here to see you, Sir Harry," Parsons announced from the doorway of the breakfast room.

Sophie froze with her teacup halfway to her mouth. *Robin.* After the way they'd parted two nights ago, she'd begun to fear he'd never return. That hope was lost, but now...

She set down her cup carefully, caught Aurelia Newbold's sympathetic eye, and managed a smile. Then Parsons was showing him in, at Harry's behest, and she could see no one else.

Her first thought was that he looked tired and anxious, and, in spite of everything, her heart went out to him—even more when she heard his first words. "Forgive the intrusion, Harry, but I've just heard there was some trouble here yesterday, and someone was injured?"

Sophie felt herself flushing as his gaze met hers, and a wild elation surged through her. He'd come because he thought *she* might have been hurt! Hope was alive, after all.

"That would be me," James was saying. "But not seriously—a graze on the arm, nothing more. And I'm glad to say the trouble's been resolved."

As we all are, Sophie thought, repressing a shiver at the thought of the danger he and Aurelia had faced.

Robin relaxed visibly. "I'm relieved to hear it, Trevenan. Might I know the details?"

James directed him to Harry, as he and Aurelia were about to leave for Pentreath. The American girl thanked them for their hospitality as she rose from her chair. Sophie wondered if yesterday's ordeal had resolved things between her and James; she liked Aurelia and her twin, Amy, but of the two, Aurelia seemed better suited to her cousin. But that was their business, she reminded herself, turning back to Robin. "Would you care for some tea, Mr. Pendarvis? Or a bite of breakfast, perhaps?"

"Yes, take a plate and join us, Rob," Harry chimed in. "I'll tell you what happened, once I've seen James and Miss Aurelia on their way."

Alone with Robin—and how rare and fortuitous that was!— Sophie poured him a cup of tea. "Come and have something to eat now," she urged. "You'll be the better for it."

"Thank you." But instead of going over to the sideboard, he sat down beside her. "I am… very glad that you were not hurt yesterday."

"I was never in any danger," she assured him. "Indeed, I was safe at home at the time. But it was good of you to come and inquire."

"I'd have come in any case."

The admission startled them both. Sophie bit back an exclamation of triumph and saw that Robin was frowning. Not in anger, she thought—rather, he seemed to be wrestling with himself over something. "Sophie… do you mean to ride this morning?"

"I was considering it," she ventured.

"Then may I accompany you?" His eyes, almost midnight-dark, were intent on hers. "There is—something I need to tell you, and in all conscience I cannot remain silent any longer."

From any other man, the words would have sounded like the prelude to a proposal. Because it was Robin, she knew otherwise, but her heart still gave a little bound. At least he seemed willing to confide in her again; surely that was a good sign. Hearing Harry's returning footsteps in the passage, she said quickly, "Yes, of course. I can be ready right after breakfast."

❧

"*Married?*"

"Four years ago, in Rouen." Robin's face was expression-less, but the tautness of his body revealed more than those terse words ever could.

Sophie turned away, struggling to remain or at least *appear* calm, even as her thoughts fluttered and flapped wildly through her head, like a flock of birds unable to settle.

Married. The confession rocked her to the core. And at the same time, it explained *so much*. Robin's repeated assertions that he was in no position to marry. His careful discouragement of the hopeful young ladies' desires of attaching the Pendarvis heir. And his continued attempts to keep *her* at arm's length.

Sophie felt her face flame at the realization. For a moment, she wanted to do nothing more than fling herself onto Tregony's back and gallop away before mortification consumed her. Only the knowledge of how difficult *that* would be while hampered by a riding habit and a sidesaddle kept her rooted where she stood. That—and the growing conviction that, whatever secrets lay in his past, Robin Pendarvis truly *cared* for her. Indeed, she would stake her life on the belief that what he felt for her was real. That was precisely what she was doing *now*.

She stole a glance at him. Perhaps it was wishful thinking on her part, but… he did not look to her like a man who still felt a strong attachment to his wife. But whatever his feelings for this unknown woman he'd married, Sophie wasn't going to behave like a hysterical ninny and ride off in a storm of tears and recriminations. Not after he'd finally confessed the whole truth, at *her* urging, no less. The least she could do was to stay and hear him out.

She turned back to him, doing her best to speak calmly. "So, your wife was—is—a Frenchwoman?"

Gratitude flashed in his eyes, and for that, she was glad she was staying.

"Half-French, on her mother's side," he replied. "Her father was English, but died before she was born, and her mother died when Nathalie was four years old. Her uncle, Paul Gerard, was her guardian and my mentor, the architect I studied under. But he died suddenly—a fall from a roof—two years into my apprenticeship, and left her virtually penniless."

"Did you marry her to protect her, then?" Knowing Robin, she could easily imagine how he might do something of that nature.

He hesitated for a fraction of a second. "In part, perhaps. I did feel some obligation to my late mentor. But it wasn't quite that simple."

Sophie grew very still. "Did you love her?"

"I—thought I did. It was a boy's passion, on my side. I don't know what it was on hers."

Sophie swallowed. "What did she look like?"

He did not answer at once, and when he did, the words came out jerkily, as though forced from him. "She was tiny. *Mignonne.* Fair-haired—very fair, with light eyes. Almost silvery." His mouth twisted, half-wry, half-wistful. "I used to call her *La Belle sans Merci*. She could be… enchanting, at times—willful, a little spoiled, but charming too. More than half the young men in the village were smitten with her." He looked down, pulling distractedly at a loose thread on one of his riding gloves. "I was barely past my majority when we wed, and she was just nineteen."

Nineteen, only a year older than Sophie herself. And Robin had been twenty-one—surely not as guarded and secretive as he was now. And an early, ill-starred marriage *was* a secret of some magnitude. She could understand why he hadn't wished it to become public knowledge—or a weapon in the hands of someone like Sir Lucas Nankivell.

"She had no other kin," Robin continued. "Her father had broken with his relations to marry her mother, and she did not wish to go to England. I was determined to take care of her, to earn a good living for us both. We weren't married a year before she became restless, discontented. I worked too long, she said. Left her alone too much. And she did not like where we were living, in Rouen. She hoped we might go to Paris, to be closer to the heart of things. But it was beyond my means to relocate there."

So lack of money had been one bone of contention. Sophie wondered if... *Nathalie* had known of Robin's expectations as the Pendarvis heir, and whether the girl had set out to captivate him for that very reason. She forced herself not to voice that suspicion; it would be petty and unworthy of her to cast aspersions on a woman she'd never met. Moreover, she suspected the thought might have occurred to Robin as well.

"Before we'd been married two years, she left me. With one of her lovers."

"*One* of—"

Robin's blue eyes had gone starkly grey, and the faint stretch of his lips was no smile at all. "She had several to choose from, or so I understand."

"I'm—sorry," Sophie faltered, aware of how pale and inadequate that sounded.

"After she'd gone, I went rather off the rails at first. Drinking, mostly. And—other things." He did not look at her when he said the last.

Other women, Sophie deduced. Well, that did not surprise her, under the circumstances. Robin might consider her sheltered, but a girl with three brothers could not grow up wholly ignorant of the ways in which men could... misbehave.

He exhaled, glanced up again. "Work saved me. After several months, I put down the bottle, crawled out of the gutter I was wallowing in, and took up the tools of my trade again."

"I'm glad," Sophie said at once. "At least she couldn't destroy that for you."

The ghost of a smile hovered around his mouth. "Well, it was better for my liver, certainly. I moved into cheaper accommodations, continued my apprenticeship with one of my mentor's colleagues, and got on with my life in general."

"Did you think Nathalie would come back?" she asked gently. "Did you *want* her back?"

Again Robin hesitated before replying. "I don't know," he said at last. "Perhaps I did at first—but in time, I realized how ill-suited we'd been. We were too young to know that when we married, of course. Too young—and on my side, too infatuated."

There was a wealth of self-condemnation in his voice—far too much, when only half the blame was his, and by far the smaller half, in Sophie's view. She said in her most bracing tone, "Well, you wouldn't have been the first young man to make that sort of mistake. What happened after you finished your apprenticeship? Clearly you chose not to stay in France."

"No. In time, I concluded there wasn't anything left for me in Rouen. Besides which"—his smile was faint but genuine—"I actually began to feel homesick, so I came back to England. Found work in London, assisting another architect, consulting, and designing. And—I resolved to find a way to end my marriage, as soon as I had the means."

Relief flooded through Sophie, along with a sharp twinge of satisfaction. So he *didn't* wish to remain married to—that woman, after all. She hadn't realized until that moment just how afraid she was that he might still care for his wife. Or still desire her, if she was as beautiful as he described. *La Belle Dame Sans Merci...* No one would ever think to bestow such a sobriquet on Sophie. Fortunately, Robin seemed to like her just as she was.

"Of course, divorces take time and money to obtain," he continued. "I didn't have a great deal of the second, but I had plenty of the first. Or so I thought."

"Did you tell your mother's family?"

He shook his head. "They didn't approve of my studying in Rouen. I shudder to think how they would have reacted to my marrying a Frenchwoman, especially one who conducted herself as Nathalie did. Besides, I got into this coil by myself. I wouldn't have felt right using their money to free myself of it."

And if he'd hesitated to tell his own kin about his ill-starred marriage, he certainly wouldn't have divulged it to a county of people who were comparative strangers, Sophie mused. It warmed her, eased a secret worry, that he was telling her of all people. Trust… in spite of everything, they did have that.

"What must you do, then, to free yourself of it?" she asked, deliberately prosaic. Men always seemed more at ease when discussing the practical details on how a problem should be solved, and Robin was no exception. "Have you sufficient means to pursue a divorce now?"

He nodded. "Yes, now that I've come into my inheritance. Although I might be best served by launching the hotel first. If I can make it turn a profit, that should expedite matters. As for the rest…" A shadow crossed his face. "I daresay that can be managed as well."

"Will it be very difficult to bring a suit against," she couldn't quite bring herself to say *your wife*, "Nathalie?"

"She was unfaithful, and she left me, so, no, I don't think it will. But I need to have her found, first. And name her lover as co-respondent. It will take time to track Nathalie down. Even today, I'm not wholly sure which man she fled with, or if they're still together." Robin's face grew even more somber. "It's going to be an ugly business, I'm afraid."

"But at least you'll be free in the end. To begin again." Even to marry again, though she did not dare voice that thought aloud.

But she did not need to. From Robin's expression as he looked at her, she knew his mind had arrived at the same conclusion. "Sophie, divorce—carries a stigma. I would not have you hurt by it."

"A foolish stigma—you and Nathalie were both young and made a mistake. Why should you have to suffer for it for the rest of your life? And why should anyone hold it against you for removing yourself from a miserable situation?" she added with increasing vehemence. "Don't you think plenty of others would do the same, if it were possible? Honestly, as dark secrets go, *yours* could be so much worse!"

For a moment she thought he might smile, but the shadow crossed his face again. "It's bad enough, I assure you. And while I'm deeply grateful for your family's friendship, I can't imagine your mother or Harry would want you to—form an attachment to a divorced man."

"Mother and Harry would know that you're far more than that. You're a friend, a neighbor. You're Harry's business partner. And," she took a breath, then recklessly cast all maidenly reservations aside, "the man I happen to love—and wish to spend my life with!"

The words seemed to echo through the quiet clearing. No turning back now; she'd crossed the Rubicon. Had Caesar himself felt the same mingling of fear, excitement, and *destiny*, she wondered.

His face was ashen but resolute. "I've said it all before. You should go to London, have your Season. Find a young man without this sort of—muddle in his past, and let him court you."

Sophie took a step toward him, holding his gaze with her own. "Tell me you don't want me, Robin. Tell me so I'll believe it—and then I will go."

"Sophie—"

"Make me believe you feel nothing when I do this." She laid her hand on his arm, felt it harden like iron beneath her touch. "Or this." She brought up her other hand to cup his cheek, drew close until their bodies were separated by no more than a whisper. "Look at me, Robin—and then send me away, if you can."

The breath went out of him in a shuddering groan. "Oh, God."

She knew she'd won then. That he would fight her no longer—and she pressed her advantage shamelessly, slipping her arms about his neck and drawing his head down to hers. For a moment longer he resisted, then suddenly his arms closed around her and his mouth fastened on hers with a desperate hunger.

She kissed him back just as ardently, triumph surging through her veins. Hers at last, deny it how he would! And she was *his*, without question, and for all time.

When he raised his head at last, his eyes held the same dazed expression she'd seen that day in the pavilion. "Witchcraft," he murmured, freeing a hand to cup her cheek. "It must be. How else could you override all my scruples and common sense?"

Sophie nestled her cheek into his gloved palm. "I had a great-grandmother who claimed we were directly descended from Morgan Le Fay—*she* was a Cornishwoman, you know. But Great-Granny Trevethan was known to be something of an eccentric so we don't take that claim too seriously. *I* would simply call it love, myself."

Robin exhaled, his breath stirring her hair. "In your case, I have no trouble believing in a Fay ancestress." He dropped his hand and pulled away, studying her with anxious eyes. "My dear, you could do so much better for yourself. Half the cream of Society would be eating out of your hand, especially once they heard you sing."

"Well, that's very flattering, but I think I'm old enough to know my own mind. And my own heart." The certainty of what she felt rang like a bell in the deepest part of her soul. And it was with that certainty that she smiled up at him now.

"I will go to London—that's already in the cards. And I

will have a Season, and possibly study at the Royal College of Music as well. But in the end, I will be coming home. To Cornwall, and to you." She touched his cheek and counted it a victory when he did not refuse the caress. "Swans and Tresilians mate for life, Robin. I'm not about to let you go."

In his face she could see the struggle between longing and stubborn self-denial. Foolish man, she thought fondly.

"Sophie… just think about what I've said."

"As long as you do the same." She glanced at the sky, noting that the sun had climbed higher since they'd stopped to speak of this. "It's getting on toward noon, I think. Shall we ride down to the beach today?"

"I think, perhaps, I should return to the Hall. There is—much work to be done before I can begin to call it a hotel. But pray don't let me spoil your outing."

He was distancing himself from her again, she noted with an inner sigh. Only to be expected, given what he'd told her, but what a relief it would be when he finally accepted the inevitable. Well, she could be patient a while longer. As long as it took, until he was free.

"Fair enough," she said brightly, refusing to show discouragement or disappointment. "I'll be on my way, then. Might I trouble you for a leg up?"

Ever the gentleman, he helped her remount Tregony, and Sophie took care not to cling to him overmuch as he did so. Once in the saddle, she looked down into his troubled face.

"Thank you for confiding in me, Robin." She kept her voice level, calm, and kind, knowing that was what he needed now. "I appreciate knowing what has been haunting you these last few months. But as far as I'm concerned, it changes nothing."

She touched her heel to Tregony's flank and rode away.

Eight

Journeys end in lovers' meeting.

—William Shakespeare, *Twelfth Night*

21 September 1891

Dear Robin,

I understand what a concession I have won by persuading you to let me write to you while I am in London. But I faithfully promise to include nothing that will cause you discomfort or place undue pressure upon you. I value our friendship too highly to risk it by demanding more than you feel you can give, just as I appreciate the encouragement you have always shown me regarding my music. Pray do not feel obliged even to respond to my letters unless you wish to.

So here I am, lodging with James's aunt, Lady Talbot, and studying at the Royal College of Music. It's not as large as might be expected, though there's a fine view of the Albert Hall from the west side—only eighteen practice rooms and no concert hall on the premises. And since there are nearly a hundred of us studying here, you can imagine how crowded things get! I heard there's to be a larger conservatory built, but I shall probably be finished studying here long before it's completed.

Still, it's the teachers who make a school, and mine are all wonderful, though very demanding—even more than my governess or my music master in Cornwall. I have heard that Jenny Lind—the Swedish Nightingale—once taught here, some ten years ago…

❦

1 October 1891

Dear Sophie,

I assure you, I would never be so discourteous as to ignore your letters or fail to reply. As you have said, we are still friends, and I take a keen interest in your progress as a musician, so I would be pleased to hear of your studies at the College. I have had the opportunity of seeing the place while I was working in London. A not unhandsome edifice, but I agree, rather too small for its intended purpose. A larger institution could only benefit the students and the staff.

But I am glad, though not surprised, that you've settled in comfortably and are taking to your training like a duck to water. Given your natural talents and your diligence, you will surely go far. Indeed, I suspect we may be calling you "The Cornish Nightingale" someday…

❦

9 October 1891

The Cornish Nightingale? Flattery will get you every-where, dear friend! I don't know that I'll ever achieve the same success as Miss Lind, but there seems to be a consensus among my teachers that I would make a better singer than a violinist. So I am to concentrate mostly on the singing from now on, though I shan't give up the violin by any means and I will continue to perform with the College orchestra, at least for now. But enough about me. I should love to know how progress is going on the hotel. Harry mentioned something in his last letter about having the plasterers in?

Sophie

❧

20 October 1891

The hotel is gradually taking shape, my dear, though I must emphasize the word "gradually." The plasterers and the plumbers have both been in to clear out the drains and install the additional water closets I mentioned during your tour of the Hall. There were a few minor mishaps in the process, but fortunately, nothing irreparable, and the commodes appear to be in good working order. I hesitate to continue with this topic, which might be considered dull at best and indelicate at worst. Sadly, my epistolary style tends to the practical rather than the poetic. Although you may have cause to be grateful for that, as you might otherwise be subject to my attempts at verse. A sonnet composed to your eyebrow, or more appropriately, to your voice, which I still seem to hear whenever I enter the ballroom now...

Robin

❧

1 November 1891

...A sonnet to my eyebrow? Believe me, sir, I am a small matter curious...

Sophie

✌

7 November 1891

…I fear your curiosity on that score is destined to remain unsatisfied.

Robin

✌

15 November 1891

…Spoilsport. Still, perhaps I should be relieved. I certainly wouldn't want to prove Jane Austen's theory that poetry drives away love, rather than nourishes it…

Sophie

✌

23 November 1891

…Talking of nourishment, Shakespeare claims that music is the food of love. And as of this writing, I find I have come to agree with him…

Robin

✌

28 November 1891

…I have read your latest letter over several times, hoping I have not mistaken your meaning. That it is neither girlish fancy nor wishful thinking that imbues your words with more significance than they actually possess. But dare I hope that you have perhaps grown more receptive to the thought of a future together?

Sophie

✌

6 December 1891

Like you, I have thought over what to say in response to your last letter. My dear, I do not wish to give you false hope. You are aware of my circumstances—I must inform you that they have not altered, although I am exploring possible solutions in order to change that. But if I can offer you no promises, neither will I deny the depth of my attachment to you. I can grant you that much honesty, at least. And yet I do not wish you to feel constrained or bound by such an admission. You have a London Season before you, and may yet meet a worthier man who may lay greater claim to your affections and offer you far more in the way of material advantages than I...

Robin

❧

11 December 1891

I never knew it was possible to receive a letter that could fill me with such deep happiness and profound exasperation at the same time. Have I not said before that I am of an age to know my own mind and my own heart? And I hope I do not number inconstancy among my faults—whatever happens or whomever I meet during my Season, my head is not likely to be turned by these "material advantages" to which you refer!

But I am determined not to quarrel with you, my dearest friend—not when I am to come home for Christmas. We will speak more of this then. Until that time, I am and always shall be

Yours,
Sophie

❧

Cornwall, June 1892

Spring. Sophie's favorite season in Cornwall, when the cliffs were lush and green, the gardens in full bloom, and the woods carpeted in bluebells. Robin had been up with the dawn to pick a sheaf of the flowers, knowing how she loved them.

Because, at long last, Sophie was home. Had been home since yesterday, in fact, and Robin had nearly vaulted onto a horse to ride over and see her at once. But her family had a prior claim on her, so he'd restrained himself with some difficulty and instead sent her a brief note inquiring as to whether she would meet him for a ride the following morning. Her reply had been an equally brief but affirmative "Yes!"

Now he stood in their special clearing beneath the flowering may trees—and waited, shifting the sheaf of bluebells from arm to arm and vainly trying not to fidget. Gorlois cropped the grass beside him, and he found himself envying the horse's unshakable placidity.

Nearly six months since he'd last seen her, when she'd come home for Christmas. Perhaps a finger's width taller than when she'd left for London but still slender, though her form was becoming more womanly. The Tresilians had invited Robin to spend Christmas Day with them, and after only a brief hesitation, he had accepted. Sophie had been at the heart of it all, radiant with the joy of being back with her beloved family and, he dared hope, pleased to see him as well. She had refused the idea of a musicale, saying she did not wish to show off, but she had sung carols with her sister and he could hear the new maturity in her voice, though it had remained as pure as ever.

As the evening wore on, they had gravitated toward each other, taking care to be discreet. Robin had still been shaken about his confession of love, amazed to have made that leap over what had initially seemed an unbridgeable chasm. But

Sophie, smiling and newly soignée, had not let him succumb to panic. She was his, she'd told him, and as far as she was concerned, that was that—even with the London Season ahead of her in the spring.

And somehow, against all expectation, Robin had begun to believe her. Why should they not be happy, after all? He hadn't robbed or murdered anyone—he'd married unwisely and too young. Surely that was no cause for eternal damnation or a lifetime sentence of loneliness. He was trying to obtain a divorce. Perhaps there would be a flutter of gossip and speculation when the news got out, but his neighbors would soon find more salacious fodder elsewhere. Once things had calmed down, after a lengthy engagement—he would insist on that, at least—he and Sophie could marry.

He'd held on to that dream throughout the dreary months of winter and into spring, even as Sophie was making her curtsy to Society, sponsored by Lady Talbot, with some assistance from the fashionable young hostess Mrs. Thomas Sheridan, née Miss Amelia Newbold from New York. A small voice in his head had insinuated from time to time that Sophie was bound to be a great success and attract many eligible suitors, but he'd done his best to ignore that voice. If—knowing what she knew of his life before her—Sophie could have faith in him and their future together, surely he could do no less.

And so hope had taken root and continued to flourish, albeit quietly in the shadows. And Robin had gone on working. As renovations on the hotel had progressed, the Hall had taken on new life, like an aging beauty who had fallen on hard times and was now being revived with loving care, constant attention, and the generous application of money. More than a year after embarking on this mad scheme, Robin would be welcoming his first guests within a month.

Only time would tell whether his venture would succeed on the scale for which he hoped. He would work like a

Trojan, all hours of the day and night, to make sure that it did. But whatever the outcome, nothing could dim the luster of the achievement itself or a future that now seemed bright with promise.

Then he heard his name being called and looked up to see his future riding toward him.

She'd grown still taller in her time away, or perhaps she just carried herself as though she had. And there was a new poise in the set of her head and shoulders, the sort one sees in a woman who has realized she is good to look upon. And her habit of navy blue broadcloth was definitely of a more modish cut than the one he'd seen her wearing before, and an equally stylish hat perched upon her head. But the smile that lit her face when she saw him was the same as it had always been, the smile he'd seen in his mind's eye for the last six months, and the faint chill of apprehension about his heart melted away like the last traces of snow beneath the sun.

She was home. Sophie was home.

Then she was alighting from the horse and coming toward him, catching up her skirts as she went.

Smiling, Robin held out his flowers. "Welcome home, my dear."

"Bluebells!" Sophie cradled the sheaf in her arms and bowed her head to inhale their fragrance. "So beautiful! You can find some lovely blooms in Covent Garden, but nothing like these! But then, some flowers really are best in the wild." She looked up at him, those enchanting dimples flashing into play. "And of course, these flowers just happen to be the color of your eyes."

"Good God, really?" Robin did not know whether to be flattered or appalled by the comparison. "Well, call me old-fashioned, but I think it's the gentleman's place to compare his lady's eyes to flowers. Although"—he gazed into her eyes, still sea green and as gorgeous as ever—"I think jewels might be more appropriate in your case—emeralds, particularly."

"Very pretty. Although I would much rather have had a letter from you than compliments—or jewels, for that matter. Why did you not write to me in the spring?" she reproached. "Since April, I could count the number of letters I received on the fingers of one hand, with digits to spare."

"I wished you to have an—unfettered Season," Robin confessed somewhat sheepishly. "The freedom to meet—other people, without feeling you were under any obligation to me."

Sophie sighed. "Other men, you mean."

He gave her a rueful smile. "I see I've become an open book to you."

She smiled back. "After months of correspondence, surely that does not surprise you."

"Well, I am given to understand that a number of young men found you enchanting. Your mother and sister have been keeping track of your success, and Lady Trevenan as well, since *her* sister was helping to sponsor your debut. I gather you were quite the success in town."

Sophie bent over her flowers again. "Oh, I did well enough."

Robin recognized evasion when he saw it. "No need for false modesty, my dear. I read the London papers. All about how you danced no less than three times with the Earl of K—"

"Kelmswood?" She looked up, her eyes twinkling. "Oh, *he* dances with everyone. Amy told me all about him. Kelmswood devotes himself to one lady per season, then once the season's over—poof! He's away and off to his next conquest. Amy said she was foolish enough herself to believe him halfway in earnest. Fortunately, I knew better—and in any case, I was not his chosen prey this spring."

Robin crossed his arms. "I imagine he wasn't the only peer you met."

"Well, according to Amy, Thomas is related to a great many families in society, either through blood or marriage. So I met a number of his connections this past spring. But no one who particularly impressed me, or upon whom *I* made any great impression either, I suspect."

He eyed her narrowly. "You're not going to convince me that you went an entire Season without attracting at least one offer. Not unless all the men in London—young, old, and middle-aged—were simultaneously struck deaf, blind, and witless."

A dimple quivered at the corner of her mouth. "Very flattering, sir! Well, I'll spare my breath, then—there was indeed an offer. More than one, actually—and some were even suitable. But I can say, in all honesty, that none was exactly to my liking, so I am returned as I left, free of any entanglement."

"And heart-whole?"

She colored, but her gaze was steady on his. "I wouldn't say *that*, as well you know."

"Are you sure you haven't had your head turned, even just a little?" he inquired lightly.

"Well, I did enjoy being in London during the Season," Sophie conceded. "Such an exciting, bustling city! But Cornwall will always be my home. I can't begin to tell you how good it feels to be back! *And* I hear your grand opening's just round the corner—wild horses couldn't have kept me away from that! When is it to be, officially?"

"July—we're already booked solid for the first fortnight of the month, and I think we'll be having more guests once the Season officially ends. Talking of which, are you sure your hosts didn't mind your leaving London early?"

Sophie shook her head. "Lady Talbot wanted to visit her daughter in Gloucestershire, and the Sheridans have been so busy this spring they'll scarcely miss me. Did you know Amy's becoming one of the most popular hostesses in town? And Thomas exhibited two paintings this year at the Royal Academy! Going about with them was tremendously exciting. Amy even had me sing at a musicale of hers, with my teachers' blessing."

Robin eyed her closely. "And how did that go?"

"Rather well, I thought. I wasn't the only performer that evening, and I suspect Amy's guests would have been pleased by anyone—or polite enough to act as if they were. But several of them came up afterward to tell me how much they'd enjoyed my performance." She smiled in obvious pleasure at the memory. "If I was in any danger of having my head turned in London, it would have been then. But I still have so much to learn."

"Don't underestimate your talents," Robin told her. "London audiences can be very discriminating, and I'm sure Amy Sheridan was well aware of that when she asked you to sing. Well done, my dear—your teachers must be delighted with you."

"Well, I *hope* they're pleased," she replied. "I used to think they found fault with me in the early days because I was doing everything wrong, until someone else assured me they do so because they believe me to be worth the trouble. Once I realized that, I became a great deal less thin-skinned and truly began to enjoy my training."

"I hope to hear the benefits of that training soon. I've missed your voice—and the rest of you as well."

"I have missed you too. Which you should most assuredly know by now, since *I* kept up my end of our correspondence!" she added with a hint of asperity.

Robin found himself grinning like a schoolboy. "It appears that I shall be paying for that neglect for some time. Well, then—allow me to *show* you how much I missed you."

He held out his hands to her as he spoke. She gazed up at him searchingly, then her eyes lit with that soft glow he loved, and she took them. Drawing her close, he kissed her over the bluebells still cradled in the crook of her arm, savoring the warmth and sweetness of her lips.

The first time he'd kissed her without any reservations, without the ghost of the past breathing down his neck. He freed a hand to cup her cheek, the skin like warm satin against his palm, and deepened the kiss, licking at the seam of her lips, then letting his tongue just brush against hers. Sophie shivered beneath his ministrations, a low moan breaking from her throat as she strove to return his ardor.

"You've never kissed me like that before!" she exclaimed, once they'd surfaced.

"With good reason," Robin said, wondering if he sounded as breathless as she. "No objection, I trust?"

"None at all. Only…" She studied his face intently. "You seem *different* today. Not as—not as tense as I remember."

He smiled ruefully. "Have I been such a misery to deal with? Forgive me. I know I must have tried your patience sorely these past few months."

"You did rather strain things," she admitted with the candor he loved in her. "Not that I didn't understand why, of course. But you're so much more relaxed now, far more than you were at Christmas. *Freer*—if that makes any sense," she hastened to add.

"More than you know, my love."

Her gaze sharpened at his tone. "Robin, do you mean… is this about that *other* matter?"

He took a breath, nodded. "There has been some progress on that front—thanks in large part to James. We've become good friends since last summer—even more so, now that he's decided to invest in the hotel. So I took him into my confidence a few months ago. Not about everything, of course, but I remembered how he'd begun the investigation into his cousin's death last year. I told him I needed to conduct an investigation as well, on a matter of some sensitivity, and he recommended the inquiry agent he had employed himself. A Mr. John Norris who's proved nothing if not tenacious."

"He's found her, then? Your—wife?" Sophie still had trouble with that word, he noticed.

"Not just yet. But he's sent me some preliminary reports

involving Nathalie's possible activities for the last few years or so." Robin paused, uncertain how much to impart. But this was *Sophie*, the girl—no, woman—with whom he meant to share his life. She had a right to know what they might be facing, although he still meant to shield her from the more sordid details.

"It appears," he resumed cautiously, "that Nathalie has traveled through much of Europe, most notably France, Germany, and Switzerland. At least a woman answering her general description has been seen there—often in the company of a man."

"The same man?" Sophie asked, without even a trace of a blush.

"Apparently not. And she seems to have used different names as well—the better to travel undetected, no doubt." And to avoid paying bills. Nathalie had left a trail of expenses behind her on the rare occasions she'd traveled alone.

"But where is she now?"

"Apparently she came to England about a year ago. And Norris is even now attempting to locate her."

"England?" Sophie seized hold of his sleeve. "Is she still here?"

"He believes so. And"—Robin took another breath—"he believes her most recent lover to have been an Englishman, though his identity hasn't yet been confirmed."

Sophie bit her lip. "I'm sorry, Robin. I know this can't be easy for you to hear."

"Not easy, no," he confessed. "But perhaps less difficult than it might have been. I have not thought of her as my wife for some time now. We've lived apart far longer than we've lived together." He paused, thinking over how he'd felt on first reading Norris's report. Impossible to deny that he *had* experienced anger and even hurt on learning of his estranged wife's repeated infidelities. But, on reading further, he'd found those feelings subsiding—far more quickly than expected—and in their place, something almost like pity. For the callow youth he'd been, for the flighty, light-minded girl he'd married so hastily and ill-advisedly, and for the mess they'd made between them.

"I don't wish Nathalie any ill," he said at last, half-surprised to find that he meant it. "But there's no point in our continuing in this marriage. She may do as she pleases, as long as I can have my divorce and my freedom. And you," he added, laying his hand over Sophie's.

Smiling, she turned her hand palm up and twined her fingers with his. "You will always have me, Robin. I promise. Oh, it will be such bliss when this is over, and we can concentrate on the future!" she added on a sigh.

"It will indeed, my love," Robin agreed, enfolding her and her by-now somewhat crushed sheaf of bluebells in his embrace. Kissing her again, he deliberately pushed all thoughts of the past aside.

Sophie was right: it was the future that mattered now. *Their* future—and he would do his utmost to make sure that they had one, together.

Nine

All night have the roses heard
The flute, violin, bassoon;
All night has the casement jessamine stirr'd
To the dancers dancing in tune;
Till a silence fell with the waking bird,
And a hush with the setting moon.

—Alfred, Lord Tennyson, "Maud"

23 June 1892

THE PEARLS LAY IN THEIR NEST OF BLACK SILK, A SOFTLY gleaming double strand with an ivory sheen just touched with rose. The perfect gift for a girl who'd become a woman.

Nineteen tonight, on Midsummer Eve, Robin thought as he stared down at the luminous spheres. Did the distance between them seem just a little bit less with this birthday? Perhaps nineteen and twenty-seven sounded a fraction closer than seventeen and twenty-five.

He was being absurd, he knew. Eight years was nothing compared to the difference in age between some couples of his acquaintance. And Sophie was mature for her years, far more mature than Nathalie had been, which was one of the many things he loved about her.

When should he give these to her? Given the secret nature of their understanding, it would be unwise to offer them in the presence of her family. In private, then, when they managed to steal a few moments alone. And it would likely be some time before she could actually wear them. When they were in a position to announce their engagement, perhaps?

All the same, he wanted her to have them tonight, somehow. The pearls were a promise of the future they would have someday. When he would be free to shower her with gifts, however extravagant and impractical. When he could call her his love, his future wife, and know it for truth.

"Oh, I have bought the mansion of a love, but not possessed it."

A mansion—well, that was certainly apposite. Pendarvis Hall, his home and someday hers. And wonder of wonders, she did not mind that it was also a business. How many women would choose to be the wife of a country hotelier, rather than the bride of a peer?

One in a thousand, no doubt. But he'd make sure she never regretted her choice. He was a man now, not a bewildered boy fumbling his way through a marriage he and his child-bride had been too immature and ill-suited to handle. And Sophie was nothing like Nathalie—he'd found true gold in her, not fairy gold that would vanish in a trice.

Meanwhile, he was working hard to make the soon-to-open Pendarvis Hotel a fit home for them both. Perhaps in the days ahead, he could show her the wing where they would live after they were married. She could have her choice of chamber, decorate it however she saw fit. She liked cool colors, he remembered—shimmering blues and greens like the sea and sky. Perhaps he'd give her a parure of aquamarines as a wedding gift, if he found some fine enough.

But he'd already begun to furnish a room on the ground floor to accommodate her music: a piano and a harpsichord, just like the ones at Roswarne, and enough space for any other instruments she fancied. They could have musicales there if she liked, or intimate evenings around the piano. Or she could simply use it as a place to practice or even compose. And if, in the fullness of time, they were blessed with children, perhaps some would inherit her talent. The thought made him smile—well, and why shouldn't their whole brood be musical? They'd be Cornish, after all. Perhaps *he* should consider taking up an instrument at his advanced age. Piano, or perhaps the cello—they could play duets.

Robin shook his head over the fanciful drift of his thoughts. *Castles in the air.* But then, what was so wrong with that? How could one *live* without something to look forward to? And it wasn't as though what he dreamed was so impossible, or completely beyond his reach. Indeed, the future for which he and Sophie both longed seemed closer than ever before. Once he'd taken the first steps to dissolve his marriage to Nathalie, he could talk to Harry, let him know he meant honorably by Sophie. Despite their friendship, he knew Harry had had reservations about him as a suitor for his youngest sister. But surely things were different now, or would be soon. And now that Sophie had had her Season and come back still unattached...

Perhaps they'd have to wait a year or so until the divorce decree was finalized. In which case, Sophie could return to the College of Music for another year if she so wished. It was only right that she have the opportunity to develop her gifts further. Perhaps she might even accept some engagements as a professional singer—just to see if she had any liking for a performer's life. But she'd affirmed that she wanted *him* and a life in Cornwall, and if she were truly sure of that—well, he had no real desire to persuade her otherwise.

Hope. It had been so long since he'd allowed himself to indulge in it that the merest taste was like to intoxicate him. It fizzed along his veins like the champagne she loved. If his voice had been better than merely passable, he would have burst into spontaneous song.

If he were only free, he could speak tonight and ask Sophie to be his forever. But that was sheer greed, Robin told himself sternly. At least they had an understanding now—and this would be a night to remember, for both of them.

He'd got the idea just a few days after Sophie's home-coming. The hotel would open for business next week, in time to accommodate the first flood of summer guests fleeing the heat and dust of London for the seaside. James and Harry had told him there were likely to be more in August, after Parliament closed. Granted, much of Society would migrate north to shoot grouse. But for those less inclined to blood sport, a resort hotel in the West Country provided an appealing alternative. And in the meantime, what could be more appropriate than a private party at the hotel that he, Harry, and James had labored to create together? A party to celebrate not only their success but Sophie's birthday as well? Sophie, whose casual suggestion just over a year ago had started him on the path to this, though she refused to accept any credit for it, insisting that the achievement was all his.

The Tresilians and Trevenans had hailed the idea with enthusiasm and delight. So they would all assemble here this evening—the partners and their families—to sample the pleasures the new Pendarvis Hotel had to offer. Monsieur Renard, the hotel's new chef, had prepared a birthday feast fit for Queen Victoria herself, and the dining salon and ballroom had both been suitably decorated, and musicians engaged to play for the evening.

The mantel clock chimed the hour and Robin looked up from his study of the pearls. Seven o'clock—his guests would be arriving any moment now, if they hadn't already. Smiling, he snapped the jewel box closed and slipped it into his breast pocket before heading downstairs.

Sophie had always been secretly pleased that her birthday fell on Midsummer Eve, with its traditional associations of magic and enchantment. Ever since she was a little girl, she'd taken a special delight in all Midsummer festivities, from masquerades to bonfires. Last year, Harry had held a ball at Roswarne in honor of her birthday, and while the evening hadn't ended well, she had enjoyed *some* parts of it—at least until Sir Lucas's slanders against Robin, Harry, and James had come to light.

But that was in the past. Tonight promised to be far more enjoyable. She'd been at once flattered and touched by Robin's suggestion to celebrate her birthday here—and quick to accept, for she hadn't yet seen the Hall since her return. Nor had any of the other women in her family, though that was understandable, given that Cecily lived on another coast and Aurelia had recently borne James a son and been preoc-cupied with motherhood.

But tonight they were all here: Sophie, her mother and brothers—including Peter, home from school and several inches taller than he'd been at Christmas, James and Aurelia, even Cecily and Arthur, up from the south coast just for the occasion. Descending from the carriage, Sophie glanced up at the Palladian facade of the Pendarvis Hotel and felt the same thrill she had the first time she had seen it: imposing as ever, especially since repairs had been made to chimneys, roofing, and other areas of stonework. Minor repairs, according to a relieved Robin—the bulk of the renovations and remodeling had been to the interior of the Hall.

The great front doors stood open to the warm summer night, a tacit invitation and welcome to all comers. Following her family up the steps and into the hotel itself, Sophie caught her breath at her first sight of the entrance hall—the same, and yet arrestingly different. For a start, it seemed so much larger, though that could have been the effect of the freshly painted white walls and the gilt-framed mirror that reflected everything back at them with dazzling clarity. To Sophie's left, a doorway—wider than she remembered—afforded a view of a spacious reception room, converted from what she remembered as being the front parlor: furnished with low tables and comfortably padded armchairs, thickly carpeted, and dominated by a huge desk of gleaming oak, all neat compartments and pigeonholes. No one stood behind it at present, but according to Harry, they had employed a most efficient man, who'd managed hotels in York and London, to take up the position of concierge in three days' time. For the moment, Praed was fulfilling those duties along with his own as butler.

To judge by the reactions of those around her, Sophie wasn't the only one impressed by what she saw. Her mother, Cecily, and Aurelia were all gazing about the foyer with astonishment and growing pleasure.

"It looks wonderful!" Aurelia exclaimed, and as an American heiress who'd surely seen her share of resort hotels, her opinion counted for quite a bit, Sophie thought. "Just as fine as anything I've seen in New York!"

"Thank you, Lady Trevenan."

Robin's voice floated down to them, and they looked up to see him, immaculate in black and white evening kit, descending the stairs. Sophie had never seen him looking so confident—or so handsome.

He paused on the landing and smiled. "Welcome, all of you, to the Pendarvis Hotel."

"Thank you, Mr. Pendarvis," Lady Tresilian replied, smiling back. "You've done wonders with this place. I must confess, I had my doubts at the beginning, but no longer. Pendarvis Hall will make a beautiful hotel."

"Considering how hard we've worked, it had jolly well better!" Harry declared with a theatrical grimace, and they all laughed, the formality of the evening yielding to something more relaxed and congenial.

Robin descended the rest of the stairs. "Dinner is about

to be served in the Grand Salon. May I have the privilege of escorting the guest of honor?"

Sophie felt herself flush, her cheeks doubtless the same shade as the rose-pink gown she had donned for the occasion. Flattering and disconcerting to be the focus of attention tonight, *his* attention in particular. She slanted a hopeful glance at her mother, and could barely contain her delight when Lady Tresilian replied in a warm, even indulgent tone, "You may indeed."

Robin stepped forward and offered his arm to Sophie. "Many happy returns, Miss Tresilian."

The warmth in his eyes made up for the formality of his words. "Thank you, Mr. Pendarvis," Sophie replied, just as circumspectly, though goodness knows, her face probably showed everything she felt at this moment: excitement, anticipation, and a happiness so intense she could have sung with it. She settled for tightening her grip on Robin's arm as he led their party, now suitably paired up, in to dinner.

❧

The original dining room of Pendarvis Hall still existed, Robin explained to his guests as they made their way through the passages, but he'd had one of the reception rooms on the ground floor converted into a much larger salon where the hotel guests would have their meals. And it was to this room that he led them now.

A footman in black and white livery opened the doors for them with a flourish and Sophie caught her breath for the second time that night. For the Grand Salon was easily twice the size of any dining room she had ever seen in any great house in Cornwall. And as elegantly furnished and decorated as if the Queen herself was expected to dine here.

Overhead, a fully lighted chandelier cast a bright glow over the entire room, illuminating tables draped in spotless white linen. The largest of these—a round table that could easily seat them all—stood in the middle of the salon. Every place was laid with gleaming silver flatware and Crown Derby china. And Waterford crystal goblets, in which a variety of wines would be served. A silver epergne occupied the center of the table, holding flowers: a glory of June roses in brilliant hues, vibrant reds, glowing yellows, and lush pinks.

Glancing at her companions' faces, Sophie saw that they were every bit as impressed as she was. "Mr. Pendarvis, this is—just splendid," she said fervently.

"Your staff has outdone themselves tonight, old fellow," Harry remarked.

"If not tonight, then when else?" Robin returned, still with that ease and assurance she loved to see in him. "Come, let's be seated."

The shape of the table rendered the whole order of precedence largely unnecessary. As they took their places, Sophie was irresistibly reminded of King Arthur and hoped that this Round Table would prove to be as harmonious. Much to her delight, Robin sat to one side of her, Harry on the other. Aurelia and James took up places to the other side of Robin.

"This is simply amazing," Aurelia declared, gazing about the dining room. "James has told me how this place has been coming alive. But I guess there's no substitute for actually *seeing* it."

Robin smiled at her. "I couldn't have imagined how well things would turn out myself when I first drew up the plans for the hotel. And I believe I have you as well as James to thank for his coming aboard with this scheme?"

"You certainly do," James affirmed, with a fond look at his wife. "Aurelia was nothing if not persuasive about my becoming a part of this. And based on the end result, I am exceedingly glad to have yielded to my uxoriousness."

Aurelia blushed, but laughed along with the rest of them. "Well, I knew you would be in favor of anything that benefited Cornwall," she told her husband. "You've said yourself that there must be some new industry here, if it is to continue to thrive. And I've heard there are many village girls who are pleased to have found positions here at the hotel."

"That's good to know," Robin replied. "I've retained my own staff at the Hall, but wherever possible I've hired local men and women for additional positions. From domestics to wait staff," he added, nodding toward a pair of liveried men now approaching the table with what appeared to be the first course.

Silence reigned for several minutes as the waiters set baskets of fresh baked rolls on the table, filled their glasses with a pale sherry, ladled out portions of steaming oyster soup from a silver tureen for each of them, and then withdrew with the same quiet efficiency with which they had entered.

Sophie sipped from the spoon, aware that Robin was watching her closely. The first taste of the soup fulfilled every expectation. "Oh, this is lovely! And richer than what we usually have at home."

He relaxed, just enough for her to sense the faint anxiety lingering under his surface calm. "Chef Renard adds a dollop of cream, and sherry to make it so."

"Well, you can present my compliments when next you see him," Sophie declared.

The others murmured their approval, spooning up their soup with enthusiasm. The fish course that followed was just as delicious: a whole poached salmon served upon a bed of tender asparagus, prawns baked in tiny pastry shells, and boiled lobsters with drawn butter. But where could one possibly find fresher fish than in Cornwall, with the sea at one's doorstep, Sophie mused as she finished the last of her salmon.

"I think even the most particular appetite in London would be satisfied with this dinner," James remarked, laying down his fish fork.

"I adore the lobster," Aurelia said, extracting another

morsel from a scarlet claw. "I don't think any of the hotels in Newport could produce anything better."

Robin laughed, the sound warming the very depths of Sophie's heart. "Well, it's not perhaps on the same level as the Savoy, but I think it'll do nicely. And there's more to come," he added, nodding toward the returning waiters.

More was a roast duck in a delicate orange sauce, and fricassee of chicken with truffles, succeeded by spring lamb with mint sauce and new potatoes.

"My favorites," Sophie said with a sigh of pleasure as the laden plate was set before her.

"So I've been told." Robin smiled at her. "Many happy returns, Miss Tresilian."

The same words he'd said to her before, but the tone was different: intimate and warm, a caress of velvet against her ear. Sophie suppressed a shiver, her skin deliciously atingle beneath the silk of her gown, and stole a glance at Robin beneath her lashes. Her pulse quickened when she saw that his eyes held some of that hazed, slumberous look she'd remembered from their first kiss in the garden. She dropped her own gaze hastily, half wishing it could be just the two of them dining alone together, rather than with her entire family looking on and—in the case of her mother, at least— speculating on how matters stood between them.

Robin tapped his fork against his wine glass, making the crystal chime, and his guests looked up at once from their plates. "If I may interrupt you for a moment," he began, "I should like to propose a toast. To Miss Sophie Tresilian, on the occasion of her nineteenth birthday!"

"To Sophie!" they echoed, and drank to her health while Sophie blushed, laughed, and then could not seem to stop smiling—grinning even—for all her attempts to appear serene and ladylike.

They all drank to the hotel after that, and the hard work of the partners and staff. And the dessert course was brought in, just as delectable as the courses that had preceded it: hothouse fruits, lemon and raspberry ices, exquisitely tinted petit fours, and most striking of all, a spun sugar and meringue confection in the shape of the Pendarvis Hotel itself. They drank another round of toasts, this time with an excellent French champagne that Harry, who prided himself on his cellar, insisted on knowing more about so he could purchase a case himself.

Sophie sipped at her own glass, savoring the fizz upon her tongue. A delectable meal, a beautifully furnished room full of the people dearest to her, a party in her honor held by the man she loved, on Midsummer Eve, no less—what could be more magical than that?

❧

She found out soon after the last dishes had been cleared away and Robin led them from the Grand Salon to the ballroom.

Much to Sophie's pleasure, the walls were the same delicate green, and the curtains still made of oyster satin, though a bit richer and heavier than the ones she remembered. Unshrouded from its holland cover, the crystal chandelier blazed forth in full magnificence, the light of its shining prisms reflected in the polished floor. More roses here too, snowy white alternating with soft damask pink, arranged in graceful celadon vases. And up in the gallery sat the musicians—a string quartet and a pair of flautists, Robin informed his guests. At his signal, they immediately struck up a lilting Strauss waltz.

"Not quite enough people for a quadrille," Robin explained. "But then, that's one advantage of an informal dance such as this. There can be as many waltzes as one likes."

"And everyone knows that one can never have too many waltzes," James remarked, exchanging a knowing smile with Aurelia. Watching them, Sophie wondered if, someday, she and Robin would share that sort of wordless intimacy. "May I have this dance, loveday?"

Her smile was answer enough, and soon they had all paired up, with the exception of John and Peter, the two spare gentlemen of the party, though Peter claimed not to mind. At sixteen, he still regarded dancing with any female as a penance rather than a pleasure.

Harry claimed Sophie as his partner for the first waltz—an older brother's prerogative, he said—and she danced with John, James, and Arthur before Robin stepped in, sweeping her into a waltz with that breathtaking new assurance of his.

"You've improved," Sophie observed with delight, as he led them into a graceful turn.

"Thank you. I did get some practice in while you were away."

"Oh?" Sophie raised her brows. "Might I inquire who your partner was?"

"No need—she's here tonight." He nodded toward Aurelia, circling the floor in James's arms. "Lady Trevenan did the honors, at least until the last part of her confinement."

Sophie couldn't restrain a smile. James and Aurelia always waltzed as though they were one person, not two. "I shall have to thank her as well. You're a credit to her teaching—I haven't enjoyed a waltz this much in, oh, ages!"

"With the cream of London Society vying for your dances? I find that difficult to believe, my dear."

"Oh, but surely you know that enjoying a dance has nothing to do with Society," she said lightly. "And everything to do with… finding the right partner."

He stilled for a moment, his eyes gone as dark as midnight as he gazed at her. "I would say the right partner can make all the difference in the world."

Sophie smiled up at him. "Then we're in perfect accord, aren't we? Although," she added, "since you *have* mentioned London, I've got some news to share."

His expression lightened. "Good news, I trust?"

She nodded. "I had a letter from my voice teacher

yesterday. He wants me to go on a singing tour with several other pupils."

"A tour? When would it start?"

"In autumn. September or October, lasting until December, and we'd be performing mostly in England, though we might travel up to Scotland as well. Getting our feet wet as professional musicians," she explained. "The biggest draws will be singers who are already established, but we'd support them—and a few of us will perform solos as well. And we—the ladies—would be duly chaperoned at all times, so that needn't be a problem."

Robin's eyes warmed. "That's wonderful news, my dear. Shall you go?"

"Perhaps," Sophie temporized. "I haven't written back yet. I felt I had to discuss this with my family first. And you."

His mouth firmed. "You should go, Sophie."

"Robin—"

"I mean it, my dear. You've worked too hard and have far too much talent to give up a chance like this."

"But everything's so unsettled right now!" Sophie protested. "Your hotel, and that *other* situation—"

"Will still exist whether you are in Cornwall or on tour," Robin broke in. "I have hopes of things being resolved before too long, but even under the best circumstances, it will still take time to… disentangle myself." He took a breath. "This could turn ugly—divorce often does—and I don't want you in the middle of it."

It was on the tip of Sophie's tongue to argue that she was already in the middle of it, but she stifled her protest when she saw the bleakness in his eyes. "Very well," she conceded. "I'll talk this over with my family, and if they have no objection, I'll go on the tour."

"Good." He relaxed then, the warmth creeping back into his eyes. "You'll take the rest of England by storm, I have no doubt. And Cornwall will still be here when you return—as will I."

Relief escaped in a gurgle of laughter at the familiar words. "You sound like *me*!"

"Do I, then?" He guided her into a swirling turn. "Your optimism must be rubbing off on me at long last."

"Better late than never," Sophie teased.

"Indeed. So let us maintain our optimism, and trust that all will turn out for the best. Are you enjoying your birthday celebration?"

"You know I am." She smiled up at him with all her heart. "It's been a wonderful night, Robin. Thank you—I feel just like a princess in a fairy tale."

"You look like one." Robin's gaze swept over her gown—a confection of rose-pink silk trimmed with ivory lace—and then up to the budding roses woven in her hair. "I'm partial to you in green, but you're lovely in this color too. Like a rose coming into bloom." He drew her closer to him as they danced, his voice low and caressing. "The fairest rose in the garden."

It seemed impossible to be happier than at this moment— this sure of him, and of herself, and the future before them. Wonderful, Sophie thought, her senses pleasantly blurred with love and champagne. This night could not be more wonderful...

Greatly daring, she let her head rest for a moment upon his shoulder, then pulled back in surprise when something hard pressed against her cheek.

"What's this—in your pocket?"

He smiled. "Something that might become you even more than that pretty locket you're wearing now."

"My locket?" Sophie's hand went to her necklace. While only a trinket, it had belonged to her mother and grandmother before her, and she was quite fond of it.

Robin stepped back, reached into his breast pocket... and an unfamiliar voice assailed them all, rising above the lilting music from the gallery.

"*Mesdames, m'sieurs...* can someone 'elp me?"

A woman's voice, clear, imperious—and not at all English. Robin's head snapped toward the sound, and the color drained from his face. Her own heart pounding, Sophie followed the direction of his gaze and felt her blood turn to ice.

A fair-haired woman—dainty, almost fairylike in her proportions—stood on the threshold... with a child of perhaps three clinging to her skirts and another, little more than an infant, slumbering in her arms. Straightening to her full height, diminutive as it was, she addressed the room at large.

"*Pardonnez-moi*, I am looking for a Monsieur Robin Pendarvis. I am Madame Pendarvis."

Ten

The ghost of folly haunting my sweet dreams…

—John Keats, "Lamia"

MADAME PENDARVIS.

Forewarned should have meant forearmed, but Sophie felt as dazed and stunned as if she were hearing of Robin's marriage and Robin's wife for the very first time. And all around her were people who were indeed hearing this for the first time, now staring transfixed at the woman before them. Even the musicians had stopped playing; Sophie wouldn't have been surprised to find them peering over the balustrade to get a closer look at the scene unfolding below.

Concentrate. With an effort, she forced herself to remain composed as she studied the self-styled Madame Pendarvis more closely.

Contrary to Sophie's secret perception of her, Robin's runaway wife did not wear the tawdry finery of a fallen woman, but a plain traveling dress of demure blue-grey twill. The only claim to frivolity was a slightly bedraggled ostrich feather on the crown of her otherwise undistinguished-looking hat. But even such drab apparel could not dim her ethereal beauty. The baby in her arms was swaddled in a heavy blanket, over which a tuft of fair hair was just visible.

The baby... Sophie darted a glance at Robin, whose face was still pale and set. How painful this must be for *him*, having to deal with not just his wife's reappearance but the all too evident fruit of her infidelity.

Madame, by contrast, appeared to feel neither shame nor discomfiture. Her gaze swept the ballroom and lighted at last upon her estranged husband. "Ah, Robin, there you are!"

"Nathalie." Robin's lips barely seemed to move; it was as if a stone had spoken. "What are you doing here?"

Silvery blue eyes, almost opalescent in hue, widened with an assumption of childlike innocence. "You 'ave been trying to find me, 'ave you not?"

"I tried to stop her, sir!" Praed, breathless and shaken out of his usual composure, burst into the ballroom. "I told you, *madam*," he emphasized the last word with chill formality, "that Mr. Pendarvis and his guests were not to be disturbed. I told her to wait in the reception room while I sent a footman to inform you of this, sir," he explained to Robin, who held up a hand, his gaze still intent on his wife. The butler subsided but continued to eye "madam" with suspicion and distrust.

"Nathalie, the children," Robin began hoarsely. "Whose—?"

"*Mon Dieu*," she broke in on a breathy little laugh. "Do you not recognize your own daughter? Sara, *ma petite*, this is your *bon papa*."

Sophie stifled a gasp. For the little girl clinging to the woman's skirts now lifted her head... and the eyes that gazed mistrustfully at the room of strangers were the exact same color and shape as Robin's. And her hair, cut in a short straight cap, would almost certainly be the same shade of dark brown in the sunlight.

"Papa." The word was scarcely more than a breath, but it seemed to echo through the now silent ballroom. And the look in Robin's eyes as he stared at his daughter—shock, followed by a dawning recognition… and a hunger that Sophie had never seen, not even when he looked at *her*, she realized with a flash of pain.

"And this is Cyril," Nathalie continued, folding back a corner of the blanket. The child in her arms stirred languidly. His skin was porcelain pale, his half-open eyes the same misty blue-grey as his mother's. His hair was perhaps a shade darker, but in all else he was her very image. Hard to guess his age—six months, perhaps, or very little older.

This couldn't be happening. This *couldn't* be happening. The ballroom swam and flickered before Sophie's eyes. She clenched her fists, feeling the points of her nails dig into her palms through her silk evening gloves, and forced herself to remain upright. Never in her life had she swooned like some milk-and-water miss, and she wasn't about to start now.

Robin's face was still pale under its summer tan, but his posture was erect and unbending, his voice completely level when he spoke. "Praed, will you escort—Mrs. Pendarvis to my study? And ask Mrs. Dowling if she would be so good as to take the children upstairs to my wing? The bedroom at the end of the passage will do, and a hot drink should be brought for them as well."

Praed recollected himself. "Very good, sir." He turned to—to Mrs. Pendarvis, his face once more unreadable. "Madam?" His voice was as cool and colorless as Robin's own.

For a moment, Nathalie eyed the butler, clearly taking his measure, then she gave a little shrug—so French, that gesture—and exited the ballroom with the children, Praed following her purposefully.

Robin looked at his guests—the friends and neighbors whose trust and friendship he'd striven to earn this past year—all staring back at him. His face was as closed and shuttered as Sophie had ever seen it, as if he hadn't been laughing and dancing with her mere minutes ago. "Pray excuse me. I have some important business to attend to." He paused, then resumed with that same excruciating courtesy. "Perhaps it might be best if you were to take Miss Tresilian home now."

❧

She sat in the chair by the fire, hatless now, her platinum ringlets loose about her shoulders, her feet and legs curled up beneath her like a cat's. Her silver-blue eyes were kitten-wide and innocent.

Deceptively innocent, as Robin had cause to know. He schooled his own features into impassivity as he walked toward her, feeling as if he were approaching a coiled adder.

"Well, *mon cher*, I 'ave come home to you." Despite her ever-present French accent, she spoke impeccable English, the native tongue of her long-dead father. She tilted an exquisite cheek toward him, as though expecting a kiss. Robin made no attempt to bestow such a salute upon her.

He raised a skeptical brow instead. "Cornwall was never home to you."

Her eyes widened. "But Robin, where else would home be but beside my 'usband?"

He'd used to love the way she spoke his name, with that tiny lisp that made it sound almost like "Wobin." Now it grated on him. And so did those too-wide eyes, that butter-wouldn't-melt expression. A naughty little girl trying to cozen her parents into forgiveness. At nineteen, those mannerisms had been charming; at twenty-four, they were much less so. Almost grotesque, given their history. How pitiful to grow older, without ever growing up.

So different from Sophie, always candid and honest in all her dealings. But the thought of Sophie felt like a knife in his heart, so he pushed it away. "Your husband in name only," he reminded her. "We have not lived as a married couple in nearly four years."

"So long? I 'ave forgot how fast the time does fly."

"No doubt," Robin said dryly. "But for those of us with less—convenient memories, the time had passed more slowly. Though *I* have attempted to put that time to good use."

She regarded him more narrowly, with less kittenish innocence and greater shrewdness. An assessing look that took in his immaculate evening clothes, of a cut and a quality he could not have afforded in Rouen. "I can see that," she acknowledged at last. "You look prosperous, Robin. But I am glad you 'ave not become fat."

He said wearily, "What do you want, Nathalie?"

"Why, *chèri*, I only want what is my proper due. The rights and station of a wife."

He heard himself laugh, short, sharp, and humorless. "You tired of those within a year of our marriage. Why do you claim them now?"

She made a little moue. "May not a woman change her mind, Robin? Especially when—circumstances change as well."

The shoe dropped with predictable force. "You mean now that I am a successful hotelier, instead of a penniless architect, you find me a far more appealing prospect."

A little to his surprise, she actually blushed. "You make it sound so… mercenary, *chèri*."

He crossed his arms. "I believe in calling a spade a spade."

She tossed her head, her ringlets dancing about her shoulders. "You say 'mercenary'—a horrid word. I say 'practical.' There is no woman on earth who would not prefer a man of means to a mere dreamer." Her gaze roved around his study, decorated in subtle coffee and cream tones, taking in the padded leather armchairs, the glass-fronted bookcases, and the mahogany writing desk, glossy with polish. "*Alors*, I am so glad that you 'ave chosen a more—lucrative career. We did not live so, in France."

"We did not live in squalor either," Robin reminded her. "I saw to that. You might have as well, instead of sulking over what we could not afford then."

Her lower lip, soft and full as a child's, quivered piteously. "I was young, and perhaps foolish! I 'ave learned better since, I swear!"

"So have I. And what I have learned is not to take a word you say at face value." Leaning against his desk, he regarded her with cool appraisal. "I suppose you thought *Raoul*—a better prospect? And after him, *Philippe*? And God only knows how many others after him."

Her eyes narrowed. "That wretched little man you sent to find me knows too, I am sure."

"And the rest of the world may soon know as well, since I intend to bring a divorce suit against you," Robin informed her bluntly.

Nathalie gasped, one hand fluttering to her throat in a dramatic gesture worthy of Drury Lane. "Divorce! But you cannot!"

"On the contrary, it would be all too easy to divorce you on the grounds of infidelity."

"You would not! You would brand yourself a cuckold." She made a gesture of horns upon her head. "You would be a laughingstock among the English!"

"Perhaps. But I would also be free, and that matters a good deal more."

"Free!" She almost spat the word at him. "Free to marry that little *ingénue*? That simpering English miss you were dancing with?"

"You will not speak of her." Robin scarcely raised his voice, but the tone was enough to silence Nathalie, at least for a moment.

Then she rallied, her eyes filling with tears. So had she twisted him round her little finger before, in the early days of their marriage. Now he watched the performance, unmoved. "But what am I to do then?"

"That is your own concern," Robin replied evenly. "But I daresay we can come to some sort of arrangement that will benefit us both. I do not believe you are any more desirous of living with me as my wife than you were four years ago."

"That is not true! I would be all that you required of me!"

"Including faithful? Loyal? A companion and partner, not a spoiled child who must forever be indulged?" He shook his head. "I do not believe you have that in you, Nathalie."

Silvery tears tracked down her cheeks. "You are so cruel, Robin."

"I did not say those things to wound you." How tired he was. "I am done with being angry with you, Nathalie. You are—as you are. But we were ill-suited then, and we are worse-suited now. Let's make a civilized end to our marriage and move on with our lives apart."

"Apart? But I 'ave children to think of!" she protested. "*Your* children."

"My child," he corrected her. "Singular. The girl may be mine, but you know as well as I that the boy cannot be."

She grew still. "And so you would throw him out in the street, and his mother with him?"

Her eyes challenged him to reply in the affirmative. Robin strove not to rise to the bait, knowing that if Nathalie suspected he cared for or felt any interest in either child, she would exploit that mercilessly.

"I will see that both children are provided for," he said at last. "And you as well. In exchange for the divorce, I am prepared to offer fair terms and a generous settlement." His solicitor would probably have an apoplexy when he heard the amount Robin had in mind, but it seemed a small price to pay for his freedom—and the children's security.

Because *that* mattered just as much. There had been nothing in Norris's reports about either child, Robin recalled; Nathalie had somehow concealed their existence all too well, even from him—*especially* from him. He had never once suspected that their brief, ill-starred marriage had borne fruit, but he'd seen the proof tonight: that tiny scrap with her dark hair and startling blue eyes, so huge in her tiny, almost elfin face… his daughter. Again he felt that fierce surge of protectiveness that had gripped him in the ballroom when he'd heard her call him "Papa."

Nathalie must have been with child when she fled with her lover. The age would be about right—he supposed it was possible that his estranged wife might be lying about her daughter's paternity, but there was such a look of his own mother about the little girl's eyes and mouth. Not to mention her name—what had prompted Nathalie to call her after the mother-in-law she had never met?

More importantly, what sort of life could Sara and her brother have known, dragged hither and yon at Nathalie's whim? Had there been nurses to look after them while their mother was—otherwise occupied? Or had Nathalie convinced her various lovers to provide care for the children, as a condition of their liaison? Well, whichever it was, that was about to end, Robin thought. Both children were little more than infants; they needed and deserved a more settled existence than their flighty mother had given them.

"Generous!" Nathalie echoed with a tinkling laugh that set Robin's teeth on edge. Once that laugh had sounded like fairy bells to his besotted ears, but there was a harsher note to it now, a discordancy that reflected the years and experiences between. "So I am to forfeit my reputation, my rightful place as Madame Pendarvis, and slink away like a thief in the night for a pittance that will barely keep body and soul alive?"

She was speaking in French now, the better to express her outrage and indignation. Robin replied in the same language, "You willingly forfeited your reputation and your position as my wife years ago when you first left. As to the settlement, it should suffice to keep you if you exercise some prudence and restraint." Neither of which Nathalie could be said to possess even on a good day, he reflected wearily. "And I will be providing whatever *both* children require. The boy may not be mine by blood, but he should not be made to suffer for your conduct."

Nathalie sprang up from her chair, eyes wide with what appeared to be genuine dismay. "So, you mean to take them from me? My children?"

Robin cursed inwardly. For all her flightiness, Nathalie could be quick enough when she sensed her own interests might be at stake. Stupid of him to forget that, even temporarily. "I have said nothing of the kind." He paused, choosing his next words with care, doing his best to sound reasonable. "You are their mother, and so I would not deny your claim to them. But they need more… stability in their lives. Surely you must see that yourself, or you would not have come here tonight." And if concern for her children's welfare had motivated Nathalie's appearance here in any way, he could—almost—forgive her for the shambles she had made of this evening.

Sophie's stricken face flashed into his mind with agonizing clarity. He suppressed the memory as best he could and continued, "I am in a better position to provide certain necessities for them: a home, a nursemaid, and schooling, in due course. Whatever happens between us, my primary concern is *their* security and well-being. I would hope that you feel the same, and that we could arrive at terms agreeable to us both." He grimaced inwardly, hoping the words sounded less stiff to Nathalie than they did to him.

No such luck to judge by the mulish set of her pretty mouth. "And if I do not like your terms, *chèri*? If I was to leave with *my* children, rather than comply with your so-generous offer, what would you do?" She took a step toward him, all pretense of innocence gone now, her eyes sharp with mingled challenge and calculation. "Will you risk losing both children, *husband*, simply to get rid of *me*?"

The threat chilled him to the bone, but he stared unflinchingly into her eyes until she flushed and looked down. "As

I recall, madam," he bit off each word with icy precision, "English law favors fathers when it comes to matters of custody. You would do well to remember that before you try to disappear with Sara and Cyril." He pushed away from the desk, strode over to tug the bell rope in the corner of the study. "A chamber has been prepared for you in the west wing. One of the maids will escort you there. We will speak again in the morning."

❧

The room was mostly dark, but for the light of a single lamp and a fire burning in the grate. Summer nights could be cool in Cornwall, with the wind coming off the sea.

A housemaid sat by the fire, poking the flames into greater life, but she rose when Robin entered and bobbed a quick curtsy. The children were in bed, she informed him in a low voice, and the boy had gone right to sleep. But the girl—Miss Sara—was still awake and inclined to be a little tearful. Missing her mum, the maid opined, then blushed at her own forwardness.

Unoffended, Robin thanked the girl—her name was Rachel, he remembered—and motioned her to resume her seat, then went over to sit in the chair beside the bed. Two small forms lay beneath the covers; the larger one stirred at his approach, and he found himself gazing into a pale face dominated by huge blue eyes, fringed in thick dark lashes. Those lashes were damp at the moment, and the child's rosebud mouth quivered with bewilderment and genuine misery. She looked utterly lost in that bed: tiny, helpless, and fragile.

Robin's heart constricted at the sight. He had to swallow several times before speech was even possible.

"Good evening, Sara," he managed at last, keeping his voice low and gentle. "I am your papa. Can you not sleep?"

She shook her head and breathed out a tremulous little sigh, her gaze now fixed on him.

Robin glanced about a little wildly and saw a small china pot and cup—both painted with roses—sitting on the bedside table: the hot drink he'd recommended. Relieved, he picked up the pot and poured a stream of gently steaming liquid (it smelled like some sort of milk posset) into the cup. "This may help, sweeting," he said, holding out the cup for her to drink from. "Will you try some? It is not too hot now, I think."

She stared at it uncertainly, then took a cautious sip, followed by another. After three sips, she pulled back, no longer tearful but still clearly anxious. Robin replaced the cup on the night table for the moment. "There, my dear. Let me know if you want any more."

Sara moistened her lips. "*Où est Maman?*" Her voice was barely a thread of sound.

Where is Mama? French—he should have anticipated that; he switched to that language at once. "*Maman* is resting, *ma petite*, in a chamber down the passage. You will see her in the morning, but for now, you must sleep, yes?"

She regarded him with those great eyes, then looked over at the cup on the table.

Robin smiled. "More milk first?"

At her nod, he picked up the cup again and held it as she drank more of the posset. Some splashed onto the coverlet, but Robin took out his handkerchief and quickly mopped up the spill. His fingers brushed against something hard when he slipped the damp, crumpled linen back into his breast pocket, and he froze in horrified recognition. Sophie's pearls—the necklace he had meant to give her tonight, in token and pledge…

"Papa." It was more of a sigh than a spoken word, but it recalled him to the present at once, to the little girl sitting up in bed, her eyes solemn and intent on his.

Robin mustered a reassuring smile. "Yes, *petite*, Papa is here. Are you ready to go to sleep now?"

After a moment, she nodded again, then yawned, surprising

them both. Robin coaxed her to lie back against the pillows, then drew the blankets up to her chin and stroked her hair, soft as down beneath his fingers. A ghost of a smile curved her lips, and within minutes, her eyes drifted shut and her breathing slowed, becoming soft and even.

Robin sat quietly for a while, until he was sure she was deep in slumber, then rose and made his way to the other side of the bed, looking down upon the second child.

If Sara looked lost in that bed, Cyril all but disappeared in it. Indeed, he looked scarcely larger than a child's doll. Difficult to pin down his age, but judging from his size, Robin would have guessed no older than five or six months. And Nathalie's very image, with her fair complexion and thistledown hair. He wondered, suddenly, about Cyril's father. Norris had believed Nathalie's latest lover to be an Englishman. Had Nathalie left him, the way she had Robin, years before? Or had the man abandoned both mother and child, leaving her with no recourse but to come here and appeal to a husband who wanted only to be free of her?

He felt a reluctant stirring of pity for her, but far more for Cyril. The cuckoo in the nest—the child who could most definitely *not* be his. Like his sister, the only true innocent in this wretched situation—and the one most likely to suffer, unless things were handled exactly right.

Cyril sighed and stirred restlessly in his sleep. Robin reached down to touch one half-open fist—about the size of a walnut—and astonishingly felt the child's fingers curl about one of his own. Robin swallowed painfully; there was a squeezing sensation in his chest now, as if those fingers had closed about his heart as well.

Sitting down on the bed, his finger still clasped in Cyril's fist, he forced himself to think rationally, even coldly, about the divorce and what it would mean—for all of them.

He could not be sure how much Nathalie knew of English divorce laws, but in recent years, *he* had become something of an expert in them. A husband could divorce his wife on the grounds of infidelity—but not without providing conclusive evidence of her misconduct. Proof of an illicit assignation or ongoing liaison, the identity of her lover, who would be named as co-respondent… a child obviously born out of wedlock.

Raoul or Philippe—to this day, he did not know with which one she had fled back in Rouen. Nor if either was still in France or could be easily located. The same could be said of Nathalie's other lovers. He could hire Norris to track down some of those men and try to uncover evidence of an affair, but there was no guarantee of success and little chance that any could be made to testify, if found—especially if their own lives and reputations were at stake.

The surest, swiftest path to what Robin wanted—the divorce, his freedom, *Sophie*—lay directly over two lives. Two young and innocent lives: the daughter of whose existence he had been unaware, and the boy he could not possibly have fathered. Children who clung to *Maman*—not knowing or caring that she was flighty and unreliable—because she was their one constant in an uncertain world.

Will you risk losing both children, husband, *simply to get rid of* me?

Dear God, what was he going to do? What *could* he do?

～

"Oh, my dearest child." Lady Tresilian folded her youngest daughter close.

Sophie leaned into her mother's embrace, breathing in the familiar scent of lemon verbena that had comforted her since she was a little girl. Strangely, despite having the perfect opportunity to do so, she did not weep. Her eyes felt hot and burning, but whatever tears she might have shed after the evening's debacle seemed to have congealed into a frozen weight inside of her.

Her family had been distressed enough *for* her. On their

return to Roswarne, Harry had stormed about the parlor, his face like thunder, raging over what he called Robin's duplicity and refusing to hear a word in his defense. It had been a relief to Sophie when Lady Tresilian had all but ordered her eldest son to leave the room until he had calmed down. John had prudently held his tongue and somehow influenced Peter to do the same, whisking the younger boy upstairs with him as soon as Harry's tirade began. Arthur and Cecily had merely embraced Sophie with silent sympathy before retiring to their own chamber, leaving mother and daughter alone in Sophie's bedroom.

"I cannot believe Mr. Pendarvis would deceive us like this," Lady Tresilian murmured, distressed. "And you, most of all…"

"But he didn't!" Sophie protested, pulling back from her mother's encircling arms. "I *knew*, Mama. I've known for months that he had a wife. But he told me he was going to divorce her." *So he could marry* me… She bit back the words just in time, but even unspoken they hung heavily in the air.

Lady Tresilian's face grew stern. "Did he importune you, dearest? Cajole you into a secret engagement?"

"He didn't need to cajole me into anything!" Sophie insisted. "*I* was the one who said I'd wait for him."

"Sophie—"

"And I meant it, Mama! I love him—I still do!"

"But a divorced man—"

"He married her when he was only a boy!" Sophie broke in. "And she left him for another man a few years later. Why *shouldn't* he be free as well?" Her voice was climbing, taking on an alarming shrillness. She struggled for composure, determined not to sound like a hysterical female, then resumed in what she hoped was a more reasonable tone. "I know you and Harry would like to believe I was led astray, Mama, but nothing could be further from the truth! Robin tried to break with me before I left for London—and I wouldn't let him."

"Oh, my love." Lady Tresilian stroked Sophie's hair.

"I told him I would wait, as long as it took, for him to be free of her," Sophie went on. Someone just had to understand. "He had inquiry agents looking for her, so he could initiate divorce proceedings. On the grounds of adultery," she added, flushing at having to reveal so intimate a detail to her mother. "He did not know about the child. Children."

"Clearly not, to judge from his reaction tonight. No man is that good an actor."

Sophie just managed to suppress a smile. Right or wrong, she couldn't help but feel slightly heartened by Lady Tresilian's dry tone. "Robin never intended to deceive anyone, Mama. He just didn't want that part of his past made public yet. Or to have people like that horrid Sir Lucas prying into his business. Surely you can understand *that*."

Lady Tresilian sighed, but Sophie thought she saw her mother's eyes and mouth softening with a reluctant sympathy. "Well, I can certainly understand wanting privacy in his particular situation. But I still think he should have been honest with us—with his *friends*—about his circumstances, especially once he started courting you."

"He *was* going to tell you," Sophie insisted. "He just wanted his wife found first, before he made any sort of offer to you or Harry. He meant honorably by me, Mama. He always has."

"I am relieved to hear that. And to be frank, I have never doubted that Mr. Pendarvis's intentions toward you were honorable, or I would never have permitted you to spend so much time in his company. But, my dear"—she regarded her daughter gravely—"have you considered how this latest development, with the children, may change things for both of you?"

"Of course it's going to change things," Sophie said, a little too quickly. "How could it not? But I know we can find a way to resolve this, in time." She ignored the treacherous small voice in her head that was wondering just *how* this could be resolved, and forced another smile. "I love Robin, and I know that he loves me. I have complete faith in him, Mama."

"Well, my love, I hope that faith will prove justified—for all our sakes." Lady Tresilian sighed again, reached out to smooth Sophie's disheveled hair. "I will talk to Harry and try to explain all this to him. And you should sleep now, dearest, if you can manage it."

"I am rather tired," Sophie admitted. Exhausted, really—but she could not afford to show fatigue, not while fighting for her future with Robin.

"That's hardly surprising." Lady Tresilian kissed her on the forehead and rose from the chaise they'd been sharing. "Let us hope the morning brings... rather better tidings."

✳

Morning brought Robin, soon after breakfast. Fortunately, Harry had left by then to oversee some business at the mine. Lady Tresilian had done her best to pour oil on the troubled waters, but he was still very angry with Robin, muttering direfully under his breath about fisticuffs and horsewhips. Difficult though it had been, Sophie had managed to hold her tongue, sensing that any defense of her love would only make things worse at this point.

She sat in the parlor with her mother, vainly trying to read a book even as her ears strained for a familiar voice, a familiar step in the passage. He would come. She knew he would. And once he did, they could work everything out between them.

Her heart nearly leapt out of her chest when she heard the front door open at last. Seconds later, Parsons appeared in the doorway.

"Mr. Pendarvis is here, my lady. He wishes to speak to Miss Sophie."

Lady Tresilian hesitated only a moment. "Very good, Parsons. Show him in."

Sophie clenched her hands in her lap as Robin entered the room. He wore riding dress, and his face was pale and haggard, as though he had not slept any better than Sophie had.

"Lady Tresilian, Miss Tresilian." His tone was almost painfully formal; Sophie's heart ached to see him retreat into punctiliousness, as if he were among strangers instead of friends.

"Mr. Pendarvis," Lady Tresilian returned with equal reserve. "I trust you are well?"

He nodded. "Quite well, thank you. And I hope you are the same?"

The stilted pleasantries continued for some minutes longer, with no reference to the events of the previous night. Just when Sophie thought she could bear it no longer, that she was seconds away from tipping over a table in her agitation, Robin turned to his hostess. "Lady Tresilian, may I have a private word with Miss Sophie?"

It seemed an eternity before Lady Tresilian replied. Then, "Very well, Mr. Pendarvis," she conceded. "I understand that you and my daughter have important matters to discuss." She rose from the sofa. "I will be in the morning room should you need me, Sophie."

Once the door had closed behind her mother, Sophie sprang up from the sofa and held out her hands to him, the words escaping in a fervent rush. "Robin—I am so glad that you've come!"

He moistened his lips, his eyes searching her face, but he did not take her hands—yet. "I had to see you. How are you, truly?"

"I'm well enough," Sophie lied, without a qualm. "A bit... surprised by everything, that's all. But *you* must be in absolute shock," she added, reaching out to touch his sleeve. "How are you holding up?"

Robin exhaled. "I'm managing. But it's a lot to deal with,

all the same." He paused, then said almost abruptly, "They're still at the hotel. Nathalie—and the children."

Sophie nodded. Of course they would be. He would never throw them out in the street. She waited for him to continue.

He looked at her, raw misery in his eyes. "I didn't know, Sophie. I swear I never guessed Nathalie might be with child when she left!"

"Of course you didn't know." She tried to keep her voice low and soothing.

"A lie of omission." His voice was as bleak as his expression. "Or perhaps, to be fair, Nathalie wasn't aware of her pregnancy either. But in all likelihood, she spoke the truth last night. The girl—Sara—is mine. Almost the image of my mother at that age. I've seen family portraits."

Sophie swallowed. "She has your eyes. Your coloring too. But the boy…"

"Cyril couldn't possibly be mine. But his father—whoever he is—doesn't appear to be involved. Dear God, Sophie, he's only a baby!"

"I know. And frail too, by the look of him." Half against her will, she felt a tug of pity for that tiny, swaddled atom in Nathalie's arms.

He nodded, raking a hand through his disheveled hair as he took a few agitated strides about the room. "Frail—and not quite well, even now. As near as I can tell, Nathalie's dragged them across Europe, and all over England. Norris had so much trouble finding her, because she kept changing her name and location."

He glanced back at Sophie, and she saw that the misery had given way to determination. "I have to claim them— *both* of them—as my own. They'll have some security, some stability that way. Cyril may stand a better chance of survival here, with me: a warm bed, regular meals, a doctor's attentions. Nathalie's given precious little thought to all that."

Not surprising. Nathalie Pendarvis—as she now called

herself—wasn't the sort to concern herself much with others' needs. Sophie nodded, lacing her fingers together and trying to ignore the chill spreading outward from the pit of her stomach. "Of course you must claim them. They're—they're the true innocents in all this." Somehow she dredged up a smile, though it felt stiff and unfamiliar on her face, like some ill-fitting garment. "You'll do your best for them, I know. You always do. Only… how will this affect your divorce from Nathalie?"

He stared at her as though she'd spoken in tongues, the color draining from his already pale face. "Sophie, there can't be a divorce. Not now. Perhaps—not ever."

❧

Not ever. A death knell in two words.

Sophie stood stock-still in the parlor as Robin struggled on with his explanation—the difficulty of locating Nathalie's lovers or concrete proof of her adultery, the impossibility of repudiating the children, the cruelty of branding them as bastards—but only one thing seemed to penetrate the fog surrounding her.

That the future they'd both longed for, the life that had appeared just within their grasp, was slipping away from them, receding faster than a wave at low tide.

Robin fell silent, his words stumbling to a halt. In the last five minutes, he looked to have aged ten years, the weight of the world—of fatherhood—bowing his shoulders. The shadows beneath his eyes were dark as bruises.

"You called the children 'the true innocents in this,'" he said at last, his voice leaden with regret. "But *you* are just as innocent. And you deserve better, far better, than a man who can no longer keep his promises. Forgive me." He spoke in a defeated whisper now. "If you can. And—forget me."

He turned to go, shoulders still slumped—and all the happiness in Sophie's world was going with him. That realization was enough to jar her from paralysis, though it took several tries to force words past the constriction in her throat. "Robin, wait!"

He turned back, his eyes as dark and hopeless as an eternal midnight.

Sophie swallowed and made herself continue. "I know—that your first duty must be to the children. You wouldn't be… the man you are if you didn't put them first. But I want you to know that—that my feelings are unaltered."

His mouth curved ever so faintly, forming an almost-smile of mingled grief and tenderness. "As are mine, my dearest girl."

"Well, then…" She cleared her throat. "If that is so, for both of us, then… why can we not still be happy? Even if it's not—*exactly* the way we had planned?"

He stilled, his gaze sharpening. "Sophie, what are you saying?"

She took a breath, bracing herself for the leap over the next hurdle. "I'm saying… I can still be yours, Robin. I *want* to be yours—whether we are married or not!"

"My God." Comprehension flashed across his face. "You're offering to be my mistress."

Spoken aloud, the words sounded unbearably stark. Sophie felt her cheeks burning, but there could be no turning back. She nodded, holding his gaze with her own. "It would be worth *everything* to me, simply to be together!"

For a split second she saw it in his eyes, everything *she* felt: the hunger, the longing… and the temptation. Then his face closed with that shuttered look she knew all too well, and he took another step back, shaking his head. "Sophie… no. This *cannot* happen. You would be sacrificing your whole future—your reputation, your career, everything you've worked for, even your family. I can't let you risk that or give it up."

"I don't care!" She caught his hands, cold as ice in her own. "Love always finds a way—and we *love* each other, Robin! Don't try to deny that!"

"I couldn't, not ever. And it's because I love you that I

have to let you go. To have the life you were meant to have, without me." He freed his hands from hers, his face ashen but resolute. "I wanted to *give* you the world, not force you to make an impossible choice. I couldn't bear to see you shunned—outcast—because of me."

"Robin—" Just one word, just his name, struggling past the tears rising in her throat.

He shook his head again, moving inexorably away from her. "I am not worth so great a sacrifice. And in time, you will see that I am right."

"Please, don't—"

"Good-bye, my dear."

And then he was gone, the parlor door closing behind him, his footsteps receding in the distance. Seconds later, she heard another door close with a terrible finality, marking Robin's departure from Roswarne—and her life.

Sophie stood where he had left her, the tears thick and hot on her cheeks, pain like a slow evisceration opening below her breastbone and spreading outward to her chest, her abdomen, to every part of her body. Gasping, she doubled over, arms crossed over her middle... and the gasps deepened into ugly, retching sobs that shook her from head to toe.

Sinking to the floor, she rocked back and forth, unable to silence those wracking sobs or stem the tears now pouring from her eyes, running into her open mouth, soaking the bodice of her morning dress. The world shrank around her, dwindling to pain and the hot, ceaseless flow of tears down a face already raw with them.

Lost in grief, she never heard the door open or the footsteps that hurried toward her. But when soft arms enfolded her and gentle fingers stroked her hair, she turned her face into that familiar bosom and sobbed afresh, the words finally shaking themselves loose.

"I wish I could die, Mama! Oh, God, I wish I could just *die*..."

Eleven

A heavy heart, Belovéd, have I borne
From year to year until I saw thy face...

—Elizabeth Barrett Browning,
Sonnets from the Portuguese

London, July 1896

SHE *HADN'T* DIED.

Even now, Sophie felt some surprise at that. Barely a day after that last, wrenching break, she was on her way back to London, accompanied by her mother. She remembered nothing of the journey; mercifully, the pain had given way to numbness and emotional exhaustion by then. According to Lady Tresilian, she'd spent the whole duration gazing out the window of their railway compartment, speaking only when spoken to, and eating only when coaxed and then no more than a sparrow would.

Sophie had no reason to doubt her mother's account. It had been days before the protective numbness had worn off, by which time she and Lady Tresilian were ensconced in the Sheridans' townhouse. Amy had welcomed them with open arms and, perhaps alerted by her sister, asked no questions about what had happened in Cornwall, but provided only boundless sympathy and comfort.

Gradually, as from a lengthy illness, Sophie had recovered. Or at least progressed to the point of being able to eat, sleep, and take some interest in the world around her. She'd stayed on with the Sheridans through the summer, even after her mother returned to Cornwall. In August, rehearsals for the tour had begun, and by early September, she was on the road with the other pupils, embarking upon the life of a professional singer.

But the memory of those agonizing first days in London was as vivid—and painful—as if no time at all had passed. And it was that memory haunting her now as she stared Robin down, awaiting his reply to her question.

He said at last, "Nathalie is—as she always is. She doesn't change."

The flat neutrality of his tone was a condemnation in itself. And it told her all she needed to know about his continuing marriage to a woman he no longer loved. Strangely enough, she felt no sense of triumph or even bitterness, just a weary pity for everyone concerned.

"I see." She tugged at a loose thread on her riding glove. "And I'm sorry, Robin."

His eyes had gone the color of a winter sea. "Don't be. I chose my lot four years ago, with no illusions regarding how things were likely to turn out. And it hasn't *all* been terrible," he added abruptly, answering her unspoken question. "I've had my work, and"—his eyes and voice softened fractionally—"the children."

Of course—the children. Had she really been so arrogant as to believe her happiness mattered more than their needs? And she did not doubt that Robin was a good father or that he made no distinction between his daughter and Nathalie's son. "They must be getting so big now. Children always grow so fast. Are they well?"

To her shock, a spasm of pain crossed Robin's face. "Sara is well. But Cyril, my son... died in January. The doctor said—he'd had a heart ailment since birth, and he was lucky to live even this long."

"Robin, I'm so sorry!" And she was. The memory of that child, pale and fragile in his mother's arms, rose in her mind, as sharp as the first and only time she'd ever seen him. She'd been too stunned that night, too shaken by the knowledge of what the children's existence might mean for her and Robin, to feel any particular sympathy for him. But now it flooded her from head to toe. Cyril couldn't have been more than four or five years old.

And Robin had loved him. She could tell that by the starkness of his eyes, the compressed line of his mouth. His grief was very real—and all too recent.

"He did not suffer, at the last. And we were all there for him. Even his mother." He stared out over the Serpentine, his hands lax upon the reins. "After a time, I found that his death—changed certain things for me. I discovered I was no longer content to leave things as they were, as they had been." He took a breath and met Sophie's gaze squarely. "I mean to renew my divorce suit against Nathalie."

"Divorce?" Sophie echoed. Questions crowded on her tongue, so many she couldn't begin to ask. Why now, when he had been so adamant before? What could possibly have happened to change his mind? Other than that poor little boy's death...

He nodded, his mouth still firmly set. "No one in the county questions that Sara is mine, and now—with Cyril gone—well, there's no sense in continuing with our farce of a marriage. We haven't lived as husband and wife since her return."

Sophie's heart gave a painful little skip at this disclosure, even as she sternly reminded it this was neither the time nor the place for such indulgences, not in the wake of Robin's loss and now this decision, over which he had agonized four years ago. Once again, she wondered what could have driven him to this point, and once again, he seemed to anticipate her question.

"She took another lover, Sophie." His tone had gone flat again. "Oh, it wasn't a shock—she's had several others since she came back. The only condition I laid on her when I agreed not to pursue the divorce four years ago was that she be discreet. As of the last fortnight, she violated even that."

Sophie regarded him closely, seeing no trace of jealousy, nor any sign of the anguish that a betrayed husband might feel under the circumstances, but his face was set, his mouth grim. A line had been crossed, then—some final condition had been breached, and this was the result. "But won't it be—difficult to obtain a divorce after you've lived together for several years?"

Robin shook his head. "Given the circumstances, it should actually be easier." He gave Sophie a wintry smile. "I caught them together—*in flagrante delicto*. You can't get much more blatant than that. And I shall have no compunctions about naming her latest lover as co-respondent in the divorce. Hell—I might even enjoy it!"

Sophie winced inwardly, not knowing what to say. This was a side to him she had never seen before—hard and cynical. It grieved her to think of his becoming so over the last four years. But then, she acknowledged ruefully, she herself was no longer the romantic, starry-eyed girl who'd trusted love to overcome all difficulties.

Robin sighed, some of the hardness leaving his face. He looked more like the man she remembered now, and she began to relax. "Nathalie is still Sara's mother, so I will not deny her access or forbid them to see each other. There's no need to make this uglier than it has to be."

"Will you petition for custody of your daughter?"

He nodded. "I firmly believe Sara is better off with me."

His expression softened in the way it had before when he mentioned the children. "We've grown very close these last four years. And Nathalie favored Cyril in any case, especially once Sara grew out of babyhood. She's had less and less time for our daughter, of late. I'd hoped it might prove otherwise, after we lost Cyril, but... things are what they are." He fidgeted with his reins, frowning to himself. "According to a more recent law, despite her infidelity, Nathalie could try to secure custody until Sara is sixteen, but she'd have to prove herself the more fit parent."

Sophie privately wondered how anyone could consider Nathalie Pendarvis a more fit parent than Robin, then told herself not to judge a woman she did not know. It wasn't as if she'd had the opportunity to witness Nathalie's capabilities as a mother, after all—or even wanted such an opportunity. It had been hard enough to imagine Robin and his wife raising their children together without actually having to see it.

Robin sighed again, patting his horse's neck almost absently. "Well, I'll cross that bridge when I come to it. Perhaps there's a chance Nathalie and I can settle the question of custody like the civilized adults we're supposed to be." He glanced at Sophie, his expression shifting again, still somber but with a hint of... diffidence? "And that is—essentially what I came to tell you, my dear. But... as it happens, there is something I should like to ask you as well. If I may."

Sophie swallowed dryly, her heart hammering against her ribs in slow, heavy strokes, every inch of her skin sensitized and tingling. "Robin..."

"I understand that I have no right to expect anything at all from you," he continued, and Sophie could not begin to guess how hard this was for him. "Not after—all this time. But... I love you." His eyes, dark as midnight, were intent on hers. "I have never stopped loving you. No other woman has taken your place in my heart, nor ever will. And so I must ask... now that I am to be a free man, is there any hope at all for *us*?"

Hope—the sweetest poison of all. Sophie closed her eyes, remembering the taste all too well. She'd lived on it for more than a year once she'd realized she loved him, and in the end, she'd been left with only the bitter dregs.

"Robin." It came out more strongly this time. She opened her eyes and gazed into that once dearly loved face. "So much has happened in the last four years."

"I know. Time hasn't stood still for either of us." He paused, then continued with almost painful precision, "And if, in that time, you have come to care for someone else, just tell me—and I swear I shall trouble you no more."

"Someone else? Who could I possibly—?"

"That young man you sang with last night—Mr. Cherwell. You seemed to be on the best of terms. I couldn't help but wonder…"

"Good heavens, no!" Sophie exclaimed. "David is a dear friend, nothing more." Despite the gravity of the situation, she felt a faint smile tug at her lips. "In fact, he once wished to play matchmaker between me and his brother. Fortunately for us all, Llewelyn had other ideas—and, as it turns out, another lady in his sights."

It was warming and more than a little gratifying to see the relief that swept over his face. "Then, you are—unattached?"

"At present, yes. *But*," she emphasized, looking him square in the eye, "I won't pretend that there haven't been other men in my life, Robin. Men whom I cared for, who were more to me than… simply friends."

A shadow crossed his face at her confession, but after a moment, he nodded. "Fair enough. And if you had honored one such with your hand and heart, I would have tried not to begrudge him his good fortune. And to wish you happy."

"I know you would have." It was what he had urged her to do, time and again: find another, worthier man. Her own folly that she could conceive of no one worthier than he—or had it proved, in the end, a greater wisdom?

He moistened his lips, as nervous as she, and no wonder. "But if you are yet heart-whole, and you are not indifferent to me—"

She gave a tremulous little laugh. "I couldn't be indifferent to you if I tried, Robin! And heaven knows I *have* tried!"

He smiled then, his eyes suddenly, suspiciously moist. "Darling Sophie. I have loved you since you were seventeen. That hasn't changed, whatever else has."

That hadn't changed for her either, even though the admission lodged like a bone caught in her throat. So much love, so much hope—all dashed in one midsummer night.

"Love…" she husked, then swallowed and tried again. "Love can't solve everything, Robin. We learned that four years ago."

"Perhaps not, but it's a start, isn't it?" He reached out, brushed the fingers of her nearest hand with his own. "And in the end, perhaps that's all we have. I know you have a brilliant future before you. That you are adored by half of Europe. That there are men far richer, handsomer, and grander than myself, without my encumbrances, all eager to court you. I have no right to ask this of you, but will you— will you wait for me?"

All the things she'd dreamed of hearing. The things she imagined on those lonely nights on tour, when she'd lain awake, remembering. And hoping in vain for some miracle that would allow them to be together at last.

How was it that, at this longed-for moment, she should feel as much fear as exultation? Who would have thought that finally being offered your heart's desire would be so terrifying?

Sophie swallowed. "I need time. Time to think about all of this."

"You'll have it. All the time you need, I promise." His mouth quirked in a wry smile. "That may be the one thing I *can* safely promise."

Twelve

When I am from him, I am dead till I be with him.

—Sir Thomas Browne, *Religio Medici*

THERE SEEMED LITTLE TO SAY AFTER THAT, AND THEY both lapsed into silence, riding sedately back the way they had come. Some part of Sophie longed to say something, *anything*, to shatter the constraint between them, but another part of her—the part that had known disappointment and learned discretion—kept her tongue in check.

Not until they had reached Hyde Park Corner did she muster up the nerve to speak. "How long will you be staying in London?"

"A few more days as yet. At least until my solicitor has finished preparing the divorce papers." He paused, then continued, almost abruptly, "Sara is staying with James and Aurelia at present. Their son, Jared, is her friend, and," a faint smile warmed his eyes, "she is also fascinated with their new baby girl. In any case, I didn't want her exposed to the unpleasantness between Nathalie and myself."

"Of course not. That was very considerate of you. And exactly how a father *should* think, in these circumstances."

"My motives weren't entirely selfless," he confessed wryly.

"I was safeguarding my own interests as well. James and Aurelia know that I intend to seek a divorce. With Sara staying at Pentreath, it would be just about impossible for Nathalie to run off with her, as she's threatened to do in the past."

His face had gone grim again—no surprise if he'd had to live with that constant threat hanging over his head for four years. Sophie felt a fierce spark of anger at the thought: however unhappy a marriage, parents should never use their children as weapons against each other.

She said in her most reassuring tone, "Well, as Earl of Trevenan, James wields quite a lot of influence in the county. If anyone can keep Sara safe in your absence, it would be he."

Robin sighed. "I tell myself the same thing. But I cannot deny that I think of her every day, and miss her sorely."

"At least you know she's in good hands, and that you'll be seeing her again soon."

The sound of laughter and approaching horses' hooves reached them, and they quickly drew their own mounts aside to make way for a small riding party—ladies and gentlemen both—heading for the Row. Fortunately, the newcomers seemed far too intent on each other to spare Robin and Sophie more than a passing glance.

"I must be going," Sophie said once the riding party was out of earshot. "I have an engagement this afternoon, and I should put in at least an hour's worth of technique beforehand."

He nodded acknowledgment. "I'm staying at Brown's Hotel at present. If you should come to a decision—about us—within the next few days, you can write to me there."

"Thank you." Sophie summoned a parting smile as she urged her horse forward. "I will try not to keep you waiting too long for an answer."

His own smile was bittersweet. "After the last four years, I assure you my patience is infinite. Take as much time as you need."

Lost in thought, Sophie rode back toward the livery stable. Divorcing Nathalie—so he meant to do it at last. The question was, did she have the stamina to see it through with him, after everything they'd endured?

Four years ago, she wouldn't have had to ask. But she'd been as confident then as she was apprehensive now. Afraid to hope, and haunted as well by how it had ended before. The pain might have faded, but she remembered all too clearly how much it had hurt. And how utterly helpless and bereft she'd felt in the face of Robin's decision to walk away from everything they might have shared. Even understanding his reasons hadn't diminished the agony.

Never again. She'd vowed that repeatedly to herself. No other man would ever have the power to devastate her like that.

And no other man had. She thought of the men whom she had described as "more than friends." Her lovers, spaced out over four years: the young violinist on her first tour who'd been as lonely and in need of comfort as she; the dashing French composer who'd written a charming bagatelle of a song just for her; Sebastian Brand, a promising baritone who'd stepped into the role of Almaviva during those nights she'd played Susanna. Not so many—three in all.

But however much pleasure they had all derived from their brief dalliances, it had been music that bound them—a strong connection, though not the only one lovers could share. As well she knew. For none of her lovers, however talented and accomplished, had come close to supplanting Robin in her heart.

There were times when she had almost hated him for that.

On her return to Curzon Street, she discovered that her drawing room was filled to overflowing with flowers, sent by admirers who'd attended the concert. Lavish arrangements of full-blown roses and calla lilies jostled for position with exotic orchids in varying hues and brilliant blue hydrangeas.

"Where should these go, ma'am?" the footman inquired, holding up a basket of the latter.

Sophie considered the offering. "Oh, I think upstairs in my sitting room, perhaps." The blue would go well with the color scheme there. "And that arrangement," she indicated the roses and calla lilies, "can stay in the drawing room. It's far too grand for any other place!"

"Very good, ma'am."

More flowers awaited her in her chamber—along with something else. Curious and apprehensive at once, Sophie opened the velvet box Letty handed her, and stifled a gasp at the diamonds sparkling up at her: a delicate bracelet made up of three strands of glittering gems.

"Oh, miss!" Letty breathed, her eyes round as saucers.

"Put this on my writing desk, Letty," Sophie said firmly, closing the box with a brisk snap. "I'll write a note of refusal to," she consulted the accompanying card, "Lord Ingram later."

Still wide-eyed, the maid accepted the box and carried it away, while Sophie unpinned her hat with hands that shook only slightly. This wasn't the first time something like this had happened, nor would it be the last if she continued in her chosen profession. No doubt Letty thought her touched in the head to refuse such a gift from a titled admirer. But magnificent as the diamonds were, Sophie knew they came with a price—a price she was not willing to pay.

She'd received her first offer of that nature several years ago, when her star had just begun to rise, and in retrospect, she'd been almost too astonished to take offense. What had *that* to do with singing, after all? Surely there were others more desirable and adept at such things than a provincial Cornish girl, green as grass and just beginning to spread her wings? Much to her relief, an older singer on the tour had seen her agitation and guided her through a polite refusal of the gentleman's terms. Sophie had adhered to that position ever since, declining subsequent offers with as much tact and delicacy as possible. She might no longer be the innocent she'd been at seventeen, but there were some lines she would not cross. She'd offered, out of love, to be Robin's mistress. Becoming anyone else's, for material gain, was unthinkable.

Calm, Sophie told herself. Whatever happened, she must maintain her composure and not succumb to vapors or dithering. She'd bathe, practice her technique—the work would steady her, as it always did—and then head over to the Sheridans'; her engagement there had to be her first priority. Putting thoughts of Robin and their tryst aside as best she could, she asked Letty to prepare her a bath.

❧

"Darling Sophie!" Amy, exquisite in apricot silk, kissed her guest lightly on the cheek. "So glad you've come. Welcome to Sheridan House. Are you quite recovered from last night?"

"Perfectly," Sophie assured her, returning the kiss. "Although rather relieved to have the luxury of a day off."

"You've earned it, after that wonderful performance." Taking Sophie's hand, Amy led her to a sofa brocaded in soft greens and blues. "So, what do you think of the new house?"

"What I've seen of it is quite lovely. And you have a bit of private garden too."

"That was one of its main attractions," Amy told her. "Along with not being sandwiched between two other houses. And Thomas is *very* pleased with his new studio. It's on this floor, facing east, so he gets the morning light, which he prefers. He's been there for hours working, but he'll be down to luncheon shortly. It's to be just the three of us," she added. "Mrs. Herbert has had to substitute at a garden party today for an accompanist who was suddenly taken ill. But she says if you'll write out the list of your songs for her, she'll come with the music tomorrow afternoon and you can go over the programme together before the soiree."

"That should work out reasonably well," Sophie conceded.

Fortunately, she and Mrs. Herbert had worked together before and had developed a fairly good understanding of each other as performers. "Is there anything you particularly wish me to sing tomorrow evening?"

"Well, I always love it when you perform anything by Mozart," Amy began, then broke off at the sound of approaching voices and footsteps in the passage. Much to Sophie's astonishment, she sprang up from the sofa and closed the drawing room doors, holding a finger significantly to her lips. Baffled but obedient, Sophie remained silent as the voices came nearer.

"Straighten up, Marianne!" a rich, dark contralto admonished severely. "Really, Thomas! I can't think why you are letting her slouch like that in her portrait. She'll have to spend at least an hour at the backboard today to counteract the damage."

"Miss Daventry feels most at ease in a reclining position, Charlotte. Additionally, she and I both prefer that she appear natural rather than overly stiff." Sheridan's cool, refined tones betrayed no sign of the irritation he must certainly be feeling. "It is, after all, her portrait."

"A portrait that will be hanging in her uncle's house and mine. On public display."

"Well, then, if Guy wishes to view my sketches and approve Miss Daventry's pose before I set paint to canvas, he is welcome to do so."

"Guy happens to be fully occupied with his Parliamentary duties at present. There is to be an important bill presented in the House." Sophie could picture the unseen Charlotte drawing herself up haughtily. "However, I shall tender him your invitation, and he may find occasion to call upon you as soon as he finds himself less busy. And speaking of callers, is this not Amelia's At Home day? Perhaps I should stop in for a few minutes and give her my regards."

Amy's eyes widened with almost comical dismay.

"I believe my wife is presently conferring with the singer who is to perform here tomorrow night. She would prefer not to be disturbed at this time. But I will convey your greetings to her when she is available, Charlotte. Now, Miss Daventry," Sheridan's tone grew warmer, "shall we say the same time, two days hence, for your next sitting?"

A lighter, much softer feminine voice murmured an inaudible reply, which must have been an affirmative, because Sheridan responded briskly, "Very well, Miss Daventry— until then. Ladies, allow me to see you to your carriage."

As footsteps receded down the passage, Amy breathed out an undignified "whew!" and returned to the sofa.

"Dear life, who *is* that Tartar?" Sophie inquired, *sotto voce*.

"Lady Charlotte Daventry. Thomas has been commissioned to paint her niece and ward, Miss Marianne Daventry. And while Marianne is complaisant enough, Lady Charlotte tends to be… domineering." Amy pulled a slight face. "Worse, she's a distant cousin of Thomas's on his mother's side, and her husband, who's an MP, is a favored protégé of his father, so he's obliged to tolerate her presence—and occasional interference—while he works."

Sophie grimaced in sympathy. "He must find that very trying indeed!"

"He tends to swear the air blue after she and Marianne are gone," Amy confessed with a giggle. "Not in front of me, of course, but I've eavesdropped a time or two. He's also trying to come up with some acceptable way to get her out of the studio so he can persuade Marianne to relax and appear less like a frightened rabbit during her sittings. Which isn't easy— she's just seventeen and thoroughly cowed by her aunt."

"*I'd* be thoroughly cowed with such an aunt!" Sophie said fervently.

Amy rolled her eyes. "So would I! She *means* well, I suppose. And perhaps she can't help being the way she is, and telling everyone what to do and how to do it. Her father is the Marquess of Dowbridge, who's rather overpowering himself, according to Thomas. I find Lady Charlotte easiest to tolerate in small doses—like medicine."

Sophie smiled at the comparison. "She does have a lovely speaking voice, though. I do notice that sort of thing in my profession," she explained at Amy's incredulous look.

"I suppose she does," her friend conceded reluctantly. "And considerable presence too. Thomas says that she used to play breeches parts when they put on amateur theatricals as children—the big parts, like Hamlet and Romeo. I can almost picture her doing them."

"Perhaps she's a frustrated actress at heart," Sophie suggested lightly. "I should think it would be far more interesting to play Hamlet than a political wife."

"Oh, no doubt. It's a pity women cannot stand for Parliament," Amy mused. "Guy Daventry is very charming, but Lady Charlotte has twice the push and all the connections. I wonder if she ever tires of being the woman behind the man. I know *I* would."

"Which is why I insist on your standing *beside* me instead," Sheridan remarked from the doorway. "Lovely to see you again, Sophie," he added, with a nod and a smile in her direction.

"Likewise," she replied, smiling back.

Sheridan turned back to his wife. "I have seen the Daventrys off in their carriage, my dear, so you may now leave the drawing room with impunity."

Amy flew to his side and kissed him soundly. "You are the very best of husbands!"

He returned the salute, cocking an ironic eyebrow. "Better love hath no man than to shield his wife from his most annoying relations?"

Amy pulled a face. "She calls me Amelia."

"*I* call you Amelia," he reminded her.

"Yes, but in an entirely different tone, which I don't mind at all. When your cousin does it, I feel like a schoolgirl being scolded by my governess. In any event," she added, "I am grateful to be spared Lady Charlotte's company until tomorrow night's soiree. Talking of which, Sophie, shall we discuss your programme further, over luncheon?"

"That sounds like an excellent idea," Sophie replied, accepting Thomas's proffered arm.

◦───◦

Luncheon was delicious, a selection of exquisitely prepared hot and cold dishes that made Sophie understand why her hostess was so envied and her chef so assiduously courted. A creamy tomato bisque was followed by poached salmon with chilled asparagus, chicken in béchamel sauce, and a salad of tender greens. Sophie, who'd eaten little at breakfast, found herself famished and did full justice to the meal, though she took care not to overindulge.

The conversation was as good as the food. Although Amy was strictly an amateur performer, she had a deep appreciation of music and a good instinct regarding what was most likely to please her guests. By the time the dessert course of peach galette and lemon ice had been brought, Sophie had selected most of the songs that would be on her programme, not only the classical compositions for which she was best known, but some lighter, popular works that would be familiar to the audience—including a smattering of Gilbert and Sullivan.

Afterward, the Sheridans led her to the music room, an airy salon furnished in white and ice blue that would look and feel cool on even the muggiest summer night. On a low dais stood an Érard grand piano. Amy seated herself at the instrument—she could play a bit, though not as well as her sister Aurelia—and provided an accompaniment to the simple folk song Sophie performed to test the sound capabilities of the room. Sheridan sat in the front row of chairs where the audience would be seated the following evening and offered a few suggestions of his own.

It was close to four o'clock when they returned to the drawing room. While they were all enjoying a restorative cup of tea, Isabella Beatrice Sheridan, aged nine months, was brought down by her nurse to be properly introduced and admired. Much to Sophie's amusement and delight, both parents immediately set their tea aside to dote upon their daughter. Like her mother, she was fair, with pale gold down crowning her head, but her eyes were the same brilliant green as her father's. Best of all, she appeared to have been blessed with a sunny disposition, gurgling and cooing at all and sundry while waving a tiny fist in either greeting or emphasis.

Amy kissed the top of Bella's head as she dandled the baby on her lap. "I was afraid Thomas would be disappointed at first, because I did not have a boy, but he absolutely dotes on Bella. He's got a sketchbook full of drawings of her alone."

"It pains me to contradict you, my love, but it's actually *two* sketchbooks." Sheridan leaned over the back of the sofa to stroke Bella's downy hair. "Or it will be soon enough, once I add more drawings of her in the bath."

Amy giggled. "Take care she doesn't drench the pages the way she did last time!"

"I underestimated the range and magnitude of her splashing ability," Sheridan explained with a crooked smile. "Not to mention her enthusiasm for making as large a mess as possible."

Sophie laughed. "Perhaps she has a natural affinity for water? You should bring her to Cornwall sometime."

The Sheridans exchanged a glance. "As a matter-of-fact, we're planning to do just that later this summer," Amy replied. "Relia's very eager to have us visit, and I want Bella to spend time with her cousins. Alexandra is just a few months younger than she, and I'm determined for them to be great friends. Jared too."

"And nothing stands in the way of Amelia's determination," Sheridan remarked fondly.

"Which should come as no surprise to you after five years," she retorted.

"No surprise, but a constant source of entertainment. We'll be heading off to Cornwall in August, as soon as the Season ends," he added to Sophie.

"I thought everyone in Society raced off to shoot grouse on the Glorious Twelfth."

"Not everyone," Amy corrected. "We've had our share of invitations, but Thomas would rather paint grouse than shoot them. And I've never felt much enthusiasm for tramping about the moors in the damp, either. The seaside strikes me as a much pleasanter place to be, and the company far more congenial."

"So you're a convert to Cornwall at last?" Sophie teased, masking a brief pang of what might have been envy. During the last four years, she'd made only flying visits to the county she'd formerly called home. Her family had never questioned the brevity of those visits, but she knew they all wished she would stay longer, especially her mother.

"In moderate doses," Amy admitted, smiling. "I'm still a city girl at heart, but everyone benefits from a change now and then. The sea air will doubtless do us all some good."

"Mr. Sheridan, Lady Thornley has arrived," the butler announced from the doorway.

"Thank you, Marsdon. A new commission," Sheridan explained to his companions. "I'll be in my studio for the next hour, at least."

"I'll have dinner put back until seven, then," Amy told him.

"Excellent." Sheridan kissed his wife and daughter, touched Sophie's shoulder, and strode from the room, with the abstracted air Sophie had often observed in artists and musicians.

Amy watched after him fondly for a moment, then turned back as Bella's questing fingers seized upon her mother's cameo pendant, which she promptly tried to convey to her mouth.

"No, no, my love." Amy pried her necklace loose from the child's fist. "You wouldn't like the taste at all."

Bella squawked a protest, clearly holding a different opinion.

"Shall I take her for you?" Sophie asked. "Just until you tuck that away." She nodded toward the pendant. "I'd love to hold her in any case."

"Then of course you may." Amy yielded up her daughter with a smile.

It had been several years since Sophie's nieces and nephew had been small enough to hold like this, but some things the body did not forget. Bella squirmed for a moment in Sophie's unfamiliar arms, but calmed down almost at once and lay smiling up at her newest admirer. Sophie cradled the baby close, marveling at the warm, light weight in her arms. Not for the first time, she felt a wistful ache about her heart. Sometimes, especially on tour, when she was lonely and weary from travel, she would find herself imagining another life: a home, a husband, children. And then, almost instantly, she would shut the door on that fantasy—because the husband of her imaginings too often wore Robin's face…

As he did now, so she pushed the idea away determinedly, almost angrily, and summoned a smile for Bella's mother. "Amy, she's an absolute darling."

"*We* think so." The necklace now safely out of reach, Amy leaned over her daughter. "Thomas, especially. Sometimes he takes her into the studio with him and tries to show her how to hold a brush properly, though she usually tries to gnaw on them instead. Your daddy spoils you rotten, doesn't he, precious?" she crooned as Bella gurgled agreement. "Do you know, Sophie, I wasn't sure I was ready to become a mother? But now that she's here"—her smile grew tremulous—"well, I can't imagine our lives without her. And Thomas feels just the same way. Mama once told me there's nothing like sharing a child to bring two people closer. I think I'm even more in love with him now than I was five years ago—" She broke off, her eyes widening in dismay. "Sophie, are you all right? You've gone white as a sheet!"

The memory conjured by Amy's words had taken Sophie unawares, as sharp and painful as a dagger thrust between her ribs: Nathalie standing on the ballroom threshold, Cyril in her arms, Sara clinging to her skirts. And Robin's face with its mixture of shock, disbelief, and—when he looked at Sara—longing.

Those children… he'd wanted them. He'd chosen them and Nathalie over *her* and the life they might have had together. Or so the nineteen-year-old girl inside of her tearfully insisted.

Shut up. You know it wasn't as simple as that. And you know that if he could have divorced her without risking the children's welfare, he would *have. Blame the law, not Robin. And not Sara and Cyril.* She used their names deliberately, making them real, not abstractions.

"It's nothing," she managed at last. "I'm fine."

"Well, you certainly don't *look* fine!" Amy retorted, reclaiming Bella. "You look like you're about to cry—or possibly be sick! And don't tell me you've got stage fright about tomorrow or some such nonsense like that. You're usually as cool as a cucumber when it comes to my soirees. So you might as well come out with it. You know I'll give you absolutely no peace until you do!"

Sophie choked out a laugh that sounded and felt more like a sob. And the confession spilled out of her, a gush of blood from an open wound. "Robin Pendarvis is in London. And I've spoken to him."

Amy grew very still, registering all the implications of that news. "I think, my dear, you had best tell me everything," she said.

⚜

"You must think me such a fool," Sophie said shakily, dabbing at her eyes.

They sat on the sofa together, another half-empty teapot

before them, several damp handkerchiefs crumpled around them. The nursemaid had long since borne Bella back to the nursery for her afternoon nap.

Amy, her own eyes wet with sympathy, shook her head. "Never a fool, dearest. Just young—and very much in love. Because you do still love Mr. Pendarvis... don't you?"

Sophie tucked her handkerchief away, avoiding her friend's gaze—and her question. "I'm not nineteen anymore. I no longer expect love to solve everything."

"Of course not. But in my experience, love can simplify as well as complicate matters."

"How can love simplify anything?"

Amy smiled. "Well, either you still care for Mr. Pendarvis enough to wait for him to divorce his wife, or your feelings have changed to the point where you no longer desire a life with him. If you know the answer to either question, then you also know what course to take."

Sophie stared down at her hands, lying clenched in her lap. Like Aurelia, Amy had become family—and Thomas as well. Four years ago, they had provided a safe haven when her world had fallen apart. Only her mother had borne closer witness to her heartache then.

"Whatever your choice, I am always on your side," Amy continued. "I want whatever makes you happy, my dear. That includes keeping Mr. Pendarvis at bay should you choose not to see him again and he fails to respect that."

"He wouldn't do that!" The protest was automatic. "Robin's never been one to intrude where he's not wanted." Sophie mustered a wan smile. "He's punctilious to a fault that way."

Amy smiled back. "I remember you saying something like that about him when you were here for your Season. About his insisting that you find a worthier man."

Sophie gave a watery laugh. "And, of course, *I* insisted there was no worthier man. At least, not for me!"

"And do you feel the same way now?" Amy asked.

"I don't know—perhaps. I do know that I've never stopped caring for him. I'm just not sure that's enough. I've learned to be... *content*, Amy. Even happy, at times." She paused, swallowing painfully. "I remember how much it hurt, four years ago. To love someone that much, and have it end the way it did. I don't know if I have the courage to do it again."

"Understood." Amy squeezed her hand. "Is there anything I can do to help?"

Sophie took a breath before she spoke. What came out surprised them both.

"I realize this is short notice, but... would you consider adding one more person to the guest list for tomorrow night?"

❧

The dolls stood on the shelf, immaculately dressed and erect as a line of soldiers on parade. Robin stared up into innumerable pairs of glass eyes in various shades of blue, brown, grey, and, in one case, a brilliant green that reminded him painfully of Sophie.

"Which one did you fancy, sir?" the shopgirl asked brightly.

Robin started, then indicated a very pretty doll with soft golden-brown hair and slate blue eyes, wearing a dress and pinafore reminiscent of *Alice's Adventures in Wonderland*, currently Sara's favorite book. "That one."

"An excellent choice, sir," she approved, taking it down for him.

The doll boasted a jointed body and eyes that opened and shut. She also came with several changes of clothes, and in a fit of extravagance, Robin selected them as well, along with a toy steamer trunk to contain them. Sara did have other dolls, but this one would be the most fashionable by far.

His purchases accruing on the counter behind him, he made one last circuit of the shop. Spying a toy sailboat on a nearby shelf, he automatically began to reach for it, when the memory of Cyril caught him by the throat.

"Let's be sailors, Papa—let's run away to sea! I'll be better there."

Even after six months, even after knowing how peaceful the boy's end had been after his long illness, the grief was sharp enough to steal his breath. He closed his eyes until the pain subsided, and then took down the sailboat anyway. Sara had shared her brother's fondness for boats and the sea. They could sail it in his memory, perhaps on the lily pond on the hotel grounds. Or the bathtub, should the craft prove less than seaworthy.

Lastly, from a curio cabinet toward the back of the shop, he chose a music box shaped like a harpsichord, which played a lilting minuet when one lifted the lid. According to Miss Polgreen, Sara's former governess, the girl loved music even more than her dolls. He paid for his items, then arranged to have them sent to Miss Sara Pendarvis, care of Lord and Lady Trevenan at Pentreath. His daughter loved receiving things by post. Just a few days ago, he'd sent her some books from Hatchards, including *Through the Looking-Glass*, which she hadn't yet read, and a book of Andrew Lang's fairy tales. According to a telegram from James and Aurelia, they had already arrived and Sara was enjoying them immensely. Aurelia had taken to reading a fairy tale to the children every night before bedtime, rationing them out like sweets.

Robin left the shop with his resources slightly depleted but his spirits more elevated. Imagining Sara's pleasure when she opened her parcels was almost enough to dispel the cloud over his head. His meeting with his solicitor had left him in a somber mood… and there had been that matter of seeing Sophie again.

Sophie. Robin's footsteps faltered momentarily. Impossible not to think of her, and their strained meeting this morning. Even knowing their complicated history, even recognizing how much time had passed and how tortuous the road ahead

was likely to be for them, he'd still found himself wanting...
more than he probably had any right to expect.

Well, what had he *thought* would happen? That she would
cry, "Yes, of course I'll wait for you!" and fall into his arms
straightaway? *Conceit, my boy, pure conceit*, Robin told himself
sternly. Sophie could have anyone she wanted, just as she
had in Cornwall. Only it was still more likely now, because
of what she had become. It was sheer happenstance that she
was presently unattached. Otherwise, he doubted he'd have
had the nerve even to speak of a reunion. That, and the sheer
panic that had gripped him at the thought of losing her again,
just when he was reclaiming his life and freedom at last.

He remembered that shining young girl who'd enchanted
him at their first meeting, not least because she seemed the
embodiment of everything he desired and had denied himself
since his ill-starred marriage. Coming to know her better,
as a person rather than an ideal, had deepened rather than
diminished the attraction for him. A goddess was meant to
be worshipped, but a woman like Sophie was meant to be
loved. And so he'd loved her, reluctantly, almost unwillingly
at first, and with heedless, whole-hearted abandon—as she
had loved him.

Correction. As the younger Sophie had loved him.

Because the woman he'd met today—still lovely, compassionate, and generous—was so much warier and more
guarded than the girl he remembered. And a large part of that
was *his* doing. He'd promised her a future together, a future
for which she'd been willing to wait, to stand by him through
gossip and scandal, and then reneged on it. That he'd been
convinced it was the right and only thing to do didn't negate
that he'd let her down. She might still care for him—he
hoped to God she still cared for him—but the absolute trust
she'd had in him was gone.

Robin sighed sharply and rubbed his aching temples. The
right and only thing to do... More and more he'd come to

question the wisdom of his decision. It couldn't have been wrong, ever, to protect the innocents, but when the price was remaining in a loveless marriage, with a spouse for whom you felt indifference at best and contempt at worst...

Perhaps there was no right thing to do in this situation. Perhaps there was only the *least wrong thing*. And he'd chosen that course four years ago. He'd no business whining about it now just because it had proven more difficult to live with than he'd anticipated. For Nathalie too, he suspected. Because he hadn't given her what *she* wanted, either. Not in Rouen, or in Cornwall.

Unbidden, the memory rose to the forefront of his mind, in all its stomach-turning detail.

It had happened a few months after his break with Sophie—in autumn, when even Cornwall's mild climate held a slight chill in the air. When days were shorter, nights longer, and everything seemed to be drawing to a close. While he was reeling from the news that the girl he'd loved and renounced had embarked upon her tour, leaving him behind. As he'd wanted and *intended*, but the loss still dragged at his soul. He'd sat up long into the night, drinking brandy by the fire, and, despite his efforts, brooding over the way things might have been, if only. *If only.*

Finally, disgusted with his maudlin mood, he'd gone to bed, where he'd dreamed, not unexpectedly, of Sophie: the taste of her kiss, the delicate heart of her face, the scent of violets wafting from her satiny skin.

Even in sleep, he'd felt the mattress dipping beneath him and registered the added warmth and weight of someone climbing into bed beside him. Sara, perhaps? Once or twice, his daughter had slipped out of the nursery to seek comfort she could not find from her nurse or her mother. But some instinct had prompted him to pull away rather than draw close, even as he'd struggled back toward consciousness, fighting to raise his heavy eyelids.

It had been the scent that finally roused him: not essence of violet but something muskier, more exotic. Opening his eyes at last, he'd seen the female silhouette beside him in the darkness. As his eyes had grown accustomed to the dark, he'd seen that the hair cascading over the pillow was moonlight-pale, not dark chestnut. And Nathalie had smiled at him in blatant invitation, drawn back the sheet to show him her naked body. Confident to the point of insolence in her charms—after all, they'd caught him once before, hadn't they?

He'd got up at once, without a word, pulling on his robe, and walked into his dressing room, where he'd shut the door and lain down upon the couch there. He'd made no reference to what had happened the following morning at breakfast, and Nathalie, slightly to his surprise, had not mentioned the incident either. But then, it did not exactly reflect well on her that she'd attempted this in the first place. Toward the end of the meal, however, she had lifted her gaze briefly from her plate, and the anger and affront in her eyes had startled him.

Had she really thought him so enamored of her, so easily manipulated, that one glimpse of her unclad form would have brought him into her toils once again? He could not believe that she truly desired him as a lover—she'd tired of that soon enough in Rouen—so it was most likely mastery and power over him that she craved. Either way, he had no intention of cooperating.

From that night on, he locked his chamber door on retiring. While he trusted the restraints of his own body, he was less confident of Nathalie's scruples. At that point he'd not have put it past her to spike his food and drink with Spanish fly, or some other such substance. He'd taught the children a special knock, though, in case they should want Papa at night.

Not long after, Nathalie had apparently taken her next

lover, though she had respected their original agreement and conducted the liaison with discretion, away from the Pendarvis Hotel and the eyes of the children. For his part, Robin had poured his energies into work and fatherhood… and occasionally indulged in brief interludes of his own.

One could always find some way to assuage one's appetites, if necessary. So, a few times when he'd come up to London on business, he'd availed himself of a courtesan. But those excursions into bought pleasure only left him feeling emptier and lonelier than ever.

He'd known love, real love, and without it, the physical act was meaningless. Better to devote himself to other things—his work, the children… Strangely enough, he'd found it less difficult than expected to lead a celibate life. Better abstinence than this grotesque travesty of love. It had been almost two years since his last assignation, but he'd felt no desire to change that. Not even now, with his marriage finally, indisputably *done*.

Standing in the empty passage, hearing the sound of Nathalie's laughter, tinkling and bright, but always now with that hard, almost mechanical note to it. A chamber door opening, and the sight of her lying there, pale hair outspread upon the pillow, the diamond necklace gleaming about her throat. And the man starting up beside her, every bit as naked.

And a feeling, deep inside, of a last link sundering. An obligation ending.

He supposed he should have felt outraged, humiliated. The wronged husband, cuckolded again, this time under his own roof. Instead, he had felt mainly relief and emptiness.

It was over. It had been over for a long time. And now even the pretense was over as well. The divorce would be just a formality. Granted, there was Sara to consider, and he did not delude himself that her parents' divorce would be easy for her. But he would do his best to shield her from the worst of it. And selfish though Nathalie was, he did not believe she would do anything to deliberately harm or distress their daughter.

The past was the past. Time he stopped living in it, trying to make amends for the foolish youth he'd been and that foolish youth's foolish choices. The present was what mattered, and the future, even if—he steeled himself—Sophie ultimately chose not to be a part of his.

Squaring his shoulders, Robin paused to take stock of his present surroundings, which had gone unnoticed for a good twenty minutes. And a short, sharp laugh broke from his throat when he saw the print shop window almost directly in front of him.

Flanked by photographs of the reigning professional beauties, Sophie, in costume as Cherubino, smiled winsomely out at the world.

Fate had a perverse sense of humor, Robin reflected. But after only a brief hesitation, he entered the shop and bought the picture, along with a silver filigree frame. The clerk tried to persuade him to purchase a second photograph—of Rosamund Langley, a striking young widow who was the current beauty of the Season—but Robin politely declined.

Leaving the shop, he turned his steps in the direction of Brown's Hotel, studying Sophie's photograph as he walked. The face he loved and had pictured so often in his mind. She looked radiant here, her dark hair pulled back into a queue, her eyes bright, her dimples bracketing a mischievous, even slightly roguish smile. Perfectly in character, for Cherubino was an enchanting young rogue, forever falling into love and into scrapes with equal abandon. Sophie had received glowing reviews in the part from the London papers, all of which Robin had clipped and kept. And she regularly performed "Voi che sapete," Cherubino's best-known aria, as part of her programme.

Robin tried not to think too much about the very real possibility that newspaper clippings and this photograph might be all that he would ever have of her now. A great singer belongs to the world, after all. With a sigh, he tucked the photograph away into his breast pocket and turned onto Albemarle Street.

Late afternoon, and Brown's Hotel was doing a brisk business serving tea. Robin considered the tearoom for a moment as he'd not eaten for some hours, but decided to go up to his room and order sandwiches instead.

He paused at the concierge desk to ask, though not with any real hope, if any messages had come for him. Much to his surprise, the attendant on duty handed him a single envelope, sealed with deep red sealing wax. Delivered by hand that very afternoon, he informed his guest.

Robin's heart bounded in his chest at the news—until he looked more closely at the writing on the envelope. Not Sophie's. After their year of correspondence, he'd come to know her handwriting intimately. Unless that too had changed, along with everything else. For a moment, he wondered if he'd received someone else's message by mistake, but the name and direction were indisputably his own. Walking away from the desk, he located a convenient wing chair in the lobby and sat down to open the envelope.

Breaking the seal, he extracted a gilt-edged invitation… requesting his presence at a soiree at eight o'clock the following evening, to be held at the Park Lane residence of Mr. and Mrs. Thomas Sheridan. Musical entertainment would be provided.

Robin's mouth went dry, and his heart began to beat in slow, painful strokes. But it wasn't the invitation itself that provoked that response, but the short note that accompanied it—penned, almost certainly, by his hostess.

For reasons of her own, Sophie wishes you to attend. I hope you will not disappoint her.

Warning as well as cautious acceptance in that brief communication.

Robin closed his stinging eyes and silently thanked whatever gods existed for the mercy of a second chance.

Thirteen

Who chooseth me must give and hazard all he hath.

—William Shakespeare, *The Merchant of Venice*

WILL HE OR WON'T HE?

Sophie stared into the glass, and her reflection—perfectly tinted, not a hair out of place—stared serenely back. But it was another face she saw: a lean, angular face dominated by intense blue eyes, a face she'd tried for four long years to forget...

Is there any hope at all for us?

She closed her eyes, hearing that question echo over and over in her mind. And no nearer to an answer than she had been when he first asked her.

He'd promised her all the time she needed. But how much did she need, truly, to make up her mind on this? Did she already know, deep down, the answer she wanted to give? Might it be something else that was holding her back?

At her request, Amy had sent the invitation to Brown's Hotel. Short notice... but all the same, Sophie did not yet know how Robin had responded. Amy had dozens of other things to attend to regarding her soiree for Sophie to want to trouble her about one particular guest. Her friend had already done more than her share over the last four years. Besides, even if Robin had sent an acceptance, he might still change his mind at the last minute and not attend. Convince himself that it was in her best interest for him to stay away.

It wouldn't be the first time he'd thought that way. But it might be the last time she was prepared to accept it. Because if he was serious about their having a future together, he had to commit to it fully. She would accept nothing less.

This evening, then, would tell the tale.

She did not like that she was thinking of tonight as a test. In general, she had little use for women who continually demanded proof of devotion. But after the lonely years they'd both endured, the hopes that had been raised so high, then dashed so cruelly, the broken promises...

She needed to know, for once and for all, if he was prepared to fight for them. As he had not fought four years ago.

Come to me. Take a chance on being seen with me. At least some of my life will be lived in the public eye. Are you willing to join me there, and let the world know you mean to be a part of it?

A small test—nothing as dangerous as tossing one's glove into a pit of rampaging lions and expecting him to retrieve it, as a lady had done in a poem she'd read as a schoolgirl. But a test, all the same. *He loves me, he loves me not...*

"Miss, are you ready for your gown yet?" Letty inquired.

Sophie came to herself with a start. "Yes, yes, of course."

She glanced at the clock, grimaced. The Sheridans' carriage would be here soon—and a fine spectacle she'd make, sitting here in her dressing gown and mooning over the past.

Rising, she crossed to the open wardrobe to inspect the contents. She'd narrowed her choice of which gown down to two: an ice-blue satin draped with an overskirt of silver lace, and a pale gold silk—the color of candlelight—sewn with sparkling crystal beads on bodice, sleeves, and skirt. Both had the extravagant balloon sleeves that were still all the rage after three years, probably because they made the wearer's waist look tiny by comparison. In Sophie's opinion, these sleeves had reached absurd extremes of fullness this Season, to say nothing of how tiring it could be to carry the weight of so much fabric on one's upper arms. While in Paris this spring, she'd been relieved to hear that sleeves would be much less voluminous next season.

She'd almost decided on the pale-gold gown, was just reaching for it, when she heard the faintest whisper in her memory: *"I'm partial to you in green."*

Then more faintly still—*You look like a Nereid in that dress. My idea of one, anyway.*

Try as she might, she could not push those whispers away. Almost of their own volition, her fingers sought and located the delicate confection of sea-green silk gauze over oyster-white satin that hung in the wardrobe as well.

"I'll wear this tonight," she found herself saying.

Not that it was any less fine. Far from it—there were seed pearls and silver bugles on the bodice that would shine just as brightly as the crystals on the gold gown. She'd purchased it just before leaving on her European tour and hadn't found the right opportunity to wear it yet.

Letty made an approving sound as she lifted out the gown for her mistress. "You do look a proper treat in green, miss. I've always thought so."

Feeling as mindless as a life-sized doll, Sophie let herself be dressed for the soiree. The green gown, with its matching slippers, then her jewels for the night: teardrop pearl earrings, then her pearl necklace, a single creamy strand. She restrained a shiver as their cool weight settled about the base of her throat with the intimacy of a lover's touch.

Come, and I will lead the way / Where the pearly treasures be.

When had she last sung that song? Surely she must have performed it since that long-ago afternoon at Pendarvis Hall, she was sure of it… but no other occasion sprang to mind.

The past was all around her now, a living, breathing entity. And only time would tell whether she'd been wise or foolish to resurrect it, whether she should have let the ashes lie rather than stir the fire.

Letty's voice broke into her thoughts. "Your shawl, miss?"

Sophie hurriedly recollected herself. "Of course. Thank you, Letty." Obediently, she let the maid drape the folds of white silk about her shoulders and hand her a beaded reticule. "I don't know quite when I'll be back. Mrs. Sheridan's soirees have been known to continue past midnight, so pray just go to bed. Waiting up for me twice this week is above and beyond the call," she added with a smile.

"Very well, miss," Letty conceded. "I suppose I could do with an early night."

"Couldn't we all?" Sophie observed lightly. "But that's London during the Season for you." She looped the cord of the reticule about her wrist, tilted her head as the sound of carriage wheels reached her from the street below. "Until tomorrow morning, then."

Tomorrow morning, she thought as she descended the stairs. By which time she would know whether she and Robin shared a future… or merely a past.

❧

On arriving at the Sheridans' house, she was shown into the music room, where Amy, Thomas, and Joanna Herbert, the accompanist with whom Sophie had worked on other occasions, were already assembled. Earlier, she and Mrs. Herbert had gone over tonight's programme, though Sophie had sung only briefly, intending to save her voice for the actual performance. Amy, resplendent in a gown of coral and silver silk, greeted her with an affectionate embrace. "Darling Sophie, you look simply wonderful tonight! Is that a new gown? From Paris?"

"I bought it in London before my tour," Sophie confessed. "But the modiste was French."

Thomas nodded sagely. "I thought as much. You can

always tell French fashion from the line and the cut alone. And Amelia is right—you do look wonderful this evening."

Sophie smiled. "Thank you. I hope my performance gives equal pleasure."

"Based on what we heard this afternoon, it could hardly do otherwise," he replied.

"Indeed, and I expect to be the envy of every other hostess in London for having engaged you for the night." Amy linked her arm through Sophie's. "I know you never eat much before a performance, but would you care for something to drink? We have lemonade, or my special iced tea, if you prefer. I had it brewed with mint this very morning."

"Iced tea would be lovely, thank you," Sophie replied. She'd developed a fondness for iced tea ever since Amy had first served it to her years ago, asserting that Americans found the drink very refreshing during the hot summer months.

Amy hurried to the sideboard and poured out a glass at once, while Thomas secured Mrs. Herbert a glass of lemonade. "Our guests should be arriving within the next ten minutes. And from the looks of it, we'll have a full house this evening. Though not *too* full," she added, bringing the tall, icy glass over to Sophie. "It's always better to have more chairs than guests at a musicale, although I'm sure many would be willing to stand for the privilege of hearing you."

Sophie inhaled the fragrance of the tea and sipped at the amber liquid, relishing the crisp bite of the mint. "I'm flattered that you think so."

"I know so." Amy paused, then resumed almost too casually, "And—one in particular, I might add."

Sophie froze, her hand tightening about her glass. Swallowing, she looked at her friend, who gave the tiniest nod of confirmation.

So Robin *would* be attending tonight—or at least he'd sent an acceptance. But until she actually *saw* him, here in Amy's music room…

Sophie's mouth dried, and she took another, more deliberate swallow of tea. Nerves, she thought—but nerves that had nothing to do with tonight's engagement. All the same, it was time to put them away. Whatever happened or did not happen between her and Robin, she had a performance to give, and she particularly wished to do her best for the Sheridans, who had been such constant friends to her.

Amy had turned away and resumed talking—chattering almost—in a light diversionary way that Sophie could only appreciate. "And the Kelmswoods are up from Kent, so they'll be attending too. Can you believe what a staid, contented married man he's become these last few years?" Amy shook her head over her erstwhile suitor, but her expression was indulgent.

"Not so unbelievable," her husband demurred. "Sometimes, all it takes is—meeting the right woman."

Their eyes met in a glance so intimate Sophie had to look away. She remembered all too plainly how that felt—the moment when no one else in the world existed but the one you loved. Those golden months in the summer of 1892 had been full of such moments. Robin had stopped trying to deny what he felt for her, had even begun to imagine their future, and she… she had never been happier. Music had bubbled up from her like a hidden spring, a fitting accompaniment to the joy she felt at loving and being loved in return. She'd been so certain, then, so sure that nothing could mar their happiness—and then fate had proven her wrong.

Could she face such a possibility again? Did she even want to? A divorce could take years, especially if Nathalie found ways to contest the suit. And there was Robin's daughter to consider too, a child who might resent having to share her father and who would not unnaturally regard Sophie as an interloper and a usurper.

But in the end, it all came down to one question: Did she still want Robin?

If you know the answer, then you know which course to take,
Amy had said.

Tonight was meant to help her discover the answer—and
until that occurred, she would obsess no further about this. She
drank more tea and surveyed the room instead. "You've done
wonders with this salon, Amy. Everything looks beautiful."

She spoke no less than the truth. While handsome enough
by day, the music room blossomed into an oasis by night.
Amy had tastefully distributed a few floral arrangements
throughout the room: tall spires of delphiniums mingled
with clusters of gardenias, their rich blue and white a perfect
foil for the color scheme. Half of the French windows stood
open, letting in just enough of the balmy evening air, though
the rows of chairs had been carefully arranged so that no one
would find himself sitting in a draught.

Nor had Amy stinted on refreshments: pitchers of
lemonade and iced tea stood on the sideboard, along with
trays of tiny pastel-iced cakes and bite-sized savories, especially for the benefit of guests who might have foregone
dinner. Heartier refreshments and wine would be served after
the entertainment. Best of all, the whole salon was bathed
in the even glow of a large electric chandelier, cooler than
gaslight or candle flames. The last must be entirely Amy's
doing; Americans set such store by modern conveniences, but
in this case, Sophie could only approve.

Amy beamed. "Thank you. I know I should be used to this
after almost four years as a hostess, but you can't think how
much it means to me when a friend approves my efforts."

"Well, this friend certainly approves," Sophie assured her,
handing back her now-empty glass. She glanced toward Mrs.
Herbert who was finishing her lemonade. "Now, is there
time for Joanna and me to look over our music before your
guests arrive?"

"Yes, I really do think we should," the accompanist chimed
in. "One cannot be too prepared, after all."

"Of course. There's a little antechamber just off the music room too." Amy indicated a small side door just beyond the grand piano. "Shall I let you know when we're ready for you?"

"Excellent," Sophie said with a brisk nod, then beckoned to Mrs. Herbert to follow her.

❧

The knock on the door came perhaps twenty minutes later. No words were necessary.

Smoothing her skirts, Sophie followed Mrs. Herbert out into the music room. The low hum of murmured conversations ceased as Amy's guests caught sight of them, but Sophie refrained from looking back. Instead, she mounted the performers' dais and positioned herself beside the piano as the accompanist took her seat behind the instrument. Only then did she turn her head to face the audience.

Amy hadn't exaggerated before; every chair in the salon appeared to be occupied, at least from Sophie's vantage point. As always, the faces blurred into a sea of featureless blobs for her in the first moments. Only the music and the training existed.

She took a bracing breath as Amy introduced them to a scattering of applause, then discreetly withdrew. Mrs. Herbert, who had nerves of steel, played the introduction to her first song. Almost at once, Sophie sensed the pleased expectancy in the room at hearing something familiar. Many of Amy's guests would have seen her in *The Marriage of Figaro* last year, and while she wasn't wearing breeches tonight, she knew Cherubino inside and out—certainly enough to give a sense of the character, even in full evening dress. Assuming an expression that was half-mischievous, half-wistful, she raised her head and launched effortlessly into the opening phrase of "Voi che sapete," letting the music carry her away.

The audience clapped more warmly at the close, and with

the opening song behind her, Sophie found it possible now to smile and look more directly at them all. Glancing down from the dais, she saw Amy beaming at her from the front row, with Thomas beside her looking equally pleased. And just beyond them…

Her breath caught in her throat when she saw him: the tall, dark man with his air of restless energy, now gazing at her as if she were his hope of heaven.

He'd come tonight. Just as he'd said he would.

❧

From his chair, Robin stared up into her eyes, those brilliant green eyes that always made him think of a sunlit summer sea. And for just a moment, as their gazes met, he thought he saw the young Sophie looking out of those eyes. All else faded into insignificance as the connection they'd shared since their first meeting vibrated between them like a plucked string, an echo that reached all the way down to his soul. One word, one gesture from her, would bring him to her side, to her feet, wherever she wanted him… anything to bridge the distance between them.

Then, just as quickly, the moment passed. Sophie turned her head and the girl was gone, leaving the composed, soignée singer back in command. Which was as it should be, Robin told himself, even as he struggled against an ache of loss. The last thing he wanted to do was to fluster her or mar her performance in any way. Sophia Tresilian was nothing if not professional.

All the same, watching her now, he couldn't help the bittersweet pang that shot through him. Sitting this close to the stage, much closer than he'd been at the Albert Hall, he'd experienced a clearer understanding and appreciation of the skills she'd honed and polished to such dazzling effect. So poised, so confident, enrapturing the audience with every note and phrase… Despite his resolve, the old doubts assailed him once more. The spark between him and Sophie might still burn after all these years, but having tasted fame and success, would she truly be happy as the wife of a country hotelier? Might he have lost her, after all, to the very life he'd encouraged her to pursue?

If he had… well, he would just have to face it, Robin thought as he turned his attention back to the stage, where the accompanist was now eyeing Sophie with a touch of concern. She relaxed at Sophie's quick smile of reassurance, turned the page of her sheet music, and played the introduction to the next song.

More Mozart, Robin observed, as Sophie began a melting rendition of "Deh, vieni, non tardar," Susanna's aria from the last act of *The Marriage of Figaro*. According to critics, Sophie was fast becoming a consummate interpreter of the composer's works. Robin was especially impressed by the genuine pathos that crept into the song. Sophie's Susanna began by teasing her beloved—the eavesdropping Figaro who wrongly suspected her of infidelity—but ended her song with real tenderness, laced with an aching regret for the masquerade that necessitated his thinking the worst of her, even briefly. Robin had to remind himself that everything was happily resolved in the end, even for the couples estranged at the start of the opera.

He could only hope that matters between Sophie and himself turned out even half as well.

From Mozart, Sophie moved on to songs by Handel, Haydn, and Purcell, all of which had English lyrics—the better to engage the audience, Robin suspected. The strategy proved successful, and when Sophie followed Purcell's "Music, for a while" with a lighthearted selection of Gilbert and Sullivan tunes, the wave of delight that rippled through the salon was almost palpable. Her interpretation of those was sprightly and beguiling, but the atmosphere grew electric when the accompanist played the opening of Sullivan's famous solo composition, "The Lost Chord." Her expression instantly shifting from gay to grave, Sophie began to sing, pitching her clear soprano almost to an alto's range:

> *"Seated one day at the organ,*
> *I was weary and ill at ease,*
> *And my fingers wandered idly*
> *Over the noisy keys.*
>
> *I know not what I was playing,*
> *Or what I was dreaming then;*
> *But I struck one chord of music,*
> *Like the sound of a great Amen!"*

She sang it without irony or bombast, inviting the audience to share the momentous discovery with her, and mourn along with her the inability to find that angelic chord again. Robin had heard many moving renditions of the song, including one by Mrs. Ronalds, Sullivan's particular companion, but Sophie's sent a shiver down his spine. Perhaps only someone who was a born musician could do full justice to that song, he thought. Someone who understood the unexpected discoveries that went into making music: the joys, the frustrations, and the occasional blind luck that yielded the greatest rewards. Rewards that might prove fleeting, but were no less glorious for that.

The applause that greeted "The Lost Chord" was the loudest of the evening. Robin clapped until his hands tingled within his gloves, his chest tight with mingled pride and pain. This was what Sophie could give the world, what she was *meant* to give to it... How in God's name could he possibly compete with that?

He forced back the pain until there was only the pride, and made himself look up again at the stage, determined to savor Sophie's triumph.

She was gazing directly down at him, her eyes glowing, her lips softly parted in the way he remembered, the way he'd pictured time and again.

Robin swallowed, almost resenting the hope that her smile revived in him, but unable to resist it nonetheless. What more did he have, after all?

So he smiled back, trying to convey all the love and admiration he felt for her. The faith he'd always had in her talents, the pleasure he took in her success. Trying *not* to convey the fear that shadowed his heart—that he had lost her long ago, to this brilliant, glittering world she had made her own.

'Twere all one / That I should love a bright particular star / And think to wed it…

She is so above me.

✧

Buoyed by the applause that greeted "The Lost Chord"—the last song on the programme—Sophie took the opportunity to catch her breath… and let herself dwell, for the first time since they'd locked eyes, on Robin's presence here tonight.

He had come. With no guarantee of what answer she might give him tonight, he was here. The knowledge had sent a flood of warmth through her, melting away some of the doubts and anxieties that had plagued her before. A part of her had wanted to shriek with exultation and spin in circles like a giddy schoolgirl, but fortunately for her professional reputation, she'd managed to refrain from doing any such thing.

But it was a start, the cool rational voice in her head had conceded. *A step in the right direction.* Her mind and heart could agree upon that much at least. And then she'd put them both away—the rapture and the reason—for there was a performance to be given.

Now, she bowed, acknowledging the audience's enthusiasm, and let her gaze drift almost casually down to a certain seat in the front row.

He was still sitting there, applauding like the rest, and in his eyes she saw everything she had ever dreamed of seeing: pride, tenderness, passion... and hope. The same hope that had sustained her five years ago, when she'd foolishly believed that love could conquer all. Seeing it reflected in his eyes now sent a shaft of pain through her heart.

Pain—and something more.

This was the man who had believed in her from the start, who had always striven to put her first, even when she hadn't agreed with the ways he'd done so. The man who had encouraged her to pursue this dream, even at his own expense.

Why had he never understood that *he* was her dream too, that he mattered to her every bit as much as the music?

And with that acknowledgment, something shifted inside of her—and the rest of the world shifted along with it. Looking down at him, she felt again what she had not felt in four years: a sweet certainty that banished all the lingering doubts and fears.

Robin was her dream, her reality... and her love. Still. Forever.

Time she let him know that.

The applause was still ringing in her ears, interspersed now with calls of "Encore!" Recollecting herself, Sophie smiled again at the audience and turned to Mrs. Herbert. They had arranged for this eventuality—but the title Sophie now whispered to the accompanist was neither of the songs she had chosen earlier. Mrs. Herbert's brows rose in surprise, but she recovered at once and began to play.

Another song the audience would recognize, though Sophie doubted whether many of them remembered it had come from an opera more than half a century old. But whatever its origin, this song embodied the message she wished to convey more clearly than any other.

Drawing herself up to her full height, she began to sing, her voice carrying to every corner of the salon but colored with an intimacy that suggested the song was meant for one person alone:

> *"I dreamt that I dwelt in marble halls,*
> *With vassals and serfs at my side,*
> *And of all who assembled within those walls,*
> *That I was the hope and the pride.*
> *I had riches too great to count,*
> *Could boast of a high ancestral name;*
> *But I also dreamt, which pleased me most,*
> *That you lov'd me still the same*
> *That you lov'd me, you lov'd me still the same,*
> *That you lov'd me, you lov'd me still the same.*
>
> *I dreamt that suitors sought my hand;*
> *That knights upon bended knee,*
> *And with vows no maiden heart could withstand*
> *They pledg'd their faith to me;*
> *And I dreamt that one of that noble host*
> *Came forth my hand to claim.*
> *But I also dreamt, which charmed me most,*
> *That you lov'd me still the same*
> *That you lov'd me, you lov'd me still the same,*
> *That you lov'd me, you lov'd me still the same."*

She let her voice build to a crescendo on the last chorus, transforming the song into a triumphant paean to love that withstood any test, any change in circumstances.

Much to Sophie's relief, the audience responded with as much pleasure as they'd shown before—one could never predict how encores might be received. As the applause swelled around her, she bowed her head, taking a moment to compose herself. The salon seemed almost unbearably warm, and her pulse raced as though she'd just run a mile—uphill and in bad weather.

At the same time, she felt as though she had shed an enormous burden. She'd sung her heart; all she could do now was hope that he'd heard her.

Raising her head, she risked another glance down at the front row—and found Robin, clapping almost mechanically as he stared up at her.

He looked... stunned. There was no other word for it. She could see the hope still in his eyes, but it was tempered with uncertainty—as though he were on the brink of understanding what she had sung, of grasping her deeper meaning, but feared to be wrong at the same time.

Her heart went out to him in a rush, and she sent him the faintest of smiles, along with a silent message.

Soon, my love.

❧

Such a resolve proved easier to make than to carry out, however, as a number of Amy's guests wished to meet Sophie at the conclusion of her programme. Introductions passed in a blur, as she smiled, answered questions, and accepted compliments as graciously as she could, even with every fiber of her being yearning toward Robin, wanting only to find and speak to him.

Casting a quick glance about the room, she located him in a far corner. Their gazes met for a split second, but it was enough. Anticipation shivered through her, like the wind through a grove of aspens. *Not long now...*

Amy, who was performing the introductions, caught her eye just then, and Sophie sent her a look of entreaty. With a hostess's unerring instincts, Amy caught on at once.

"I think we'd best let Miss Tresilian catch her breath now, Regina," she said briskly to Sophie's current well-wisher, a fashionable middle-aged matron. "Or to take some refreshment. Singing must be thirsty work, after all."

"Of course," her guest agreed, sounding immediately

contrite. "You must be parched, my dear," she added to Sophie. "I know *I* would be, after a performance like that! Thank you for giving us all such a delightful evening."

Sophie smiled. "You're very welcome, Mrs. Dalton. Singing always gives me great pleasure. But Mrs. Sheridan is right—I would be most glad of refreshment now."

"Then, by all means, come and have some," Amy invited. "A cold supper will be set out momentarily. And I've included the dressed crab you like so much, Regina," she added, deftly steering Mrs. Dalton away and slipping Sophie a quick wink in the process.

Alone at last, Sophie exhaled thankfully. *Bless Amy for understanding.*

She turned to go in search of Robin—only to find someone else was standing directly in her path. Two someones, she amended: a tall, thin woman, perhaps in her late thirties, and a slight, fair-haired girl who might be seventeen.

"Miss Tresilian," the woman began in a deep, rich contralto that sounded vaguely familiar. "I had hoped to have a word with you."

Sophie bit back an unladylike oath and managed a smile instead, mindful of the courtesy she owed to Amy's guests. "Of course, ma'am. And whom have I the honor of addressing?"

"I am Lady Charlotte Daventry." She spoke with as much majesty as if she were Queen Victoria herself. "And this is my niece, Marianne Daventry," she added, her tone a little more perfunctory this time. "My husband, Guy, is the member for Shenstone."

The names, along with Lady Charlotte's arresting voice, jarred Sophie's memory. So this was the overbearing connection who plagued Sheridan's sittings and whom Amy could tolerate only in small doses. Studying the woman more closely, Sophie could understand why she might have such an effect. Lady Charlotte's features were too strong for beauty, and her figure spare and angular, but she had a presence any diva might have envied and she carried herself with the dignity of an empress. No wonder poor Miss Daventry was so intimidated! "I am pleased to make your acquaintance, Lady Charlotte," she said politely. "And yours, Miss Daventry."

Miss Daventry murmured an inaudible response as Lady Charlotte inclined her head. "Likewise, Miss Tresilian, and my compliments on your performance tonight," the older woman replied. "My personal taste runs rather more to… weightier material—I am very partial to Mr. Wagner's operas—but overall, I thought your songs were quite charming."

The faint condescension in her tone rankled a bit, but people had a right to their own preferences, Sophie reminded herself. "Thank you."

"Indeed, I was hoping I might engage you to sing at a soiree of my own," Lady Charlotte continued. "In early August, before Parliament adjourns."

"I'm afraid I am not accepting any engagements after this one," Sophie replied, trying to sound apologetic. "I shall be leaving London within a few days, for a month's holiday at least."

She had the distinct impression that Lady Charlotte was not accustomed to being refused. The woman's brows drew together in a mixture of surprise and annoyance.

"If it is a question of remuneration, Miss Tresilian, you may be assured that your commission will be most generous."

"I assure you, Lady Charlotte, it is nothing of the sort," Sophie said with a placatory smile. "I have not been to visit my family in more than a year. It is high time that I saw them again, especially as one of my brothers is soon to wed."

"I see." Lady Charlotte still sounded none too pleased by Sophie's refusal. "Well, should you reconsider, here is my card." She extracted it from her reticule and held it out. "My direction is in Belgrave Square."

Sophie accepted the card with murmured thanks, which seemed more prudent than flatly stating that she had no intention of reconsidering. Granted, this wasn't the first time she'd been offered an engagement while fulfilling another, but Lady Charlotte's autocratic manner rubbed her the wrong way. Perhaps, as Amy had suggested, the woman couldn't help being overbearing, but that didn't make the idea of working for her any more appealing.

"Ah, Charlotte." Sheridan spoke up from behind Sophie, much to her relief. "Pardon me for interrupting you and Miss Tresilian, but Eamon Fitzgerald is attempting to press Guy on the subject of Irish Home Rule, and I suspect he would appreciate your help in extricating himself."

Lady Charlotte clicked her tongue in annoyance. "That, again! I'd have thought the last defeat would have put paid to that issue. Pray, excuse me—Miss Tresilian, Thomas." She nodded to them both, then hurried off in a rustle of plum taffeta, Marianne trailing behind her.

"Thank you," Sophie said fervently, once the Daventry women were out of earshot.

Sheridan smiled. "You're welcome. I could not help noticing how cornered you looked."

"I declined an invitation to sing at a soiree of hers. She did not wish to take no for an answer," Sophie explained.

"Very few people are able to say no to Charlotte," Sheridan observed dryly. "Or to Guy, for that matter, but the reasons are quite different."

Curious, Sophie followed the direction of his gaze and saw a tall, athletically built man standing in the midst of a small crowd. Mr. Daventry, she realized when she caught sight of Lady Charlotte navigating purposefully toward him. The contrast between the two was striking, and not just in the physical sense. While Lady Charlotte was intense and rather haughty, her husband was relaxed and convivial, as well as attractive in a typically English way: blond and blue-eyed, with an engaging, almost boyish smile. Good teeth, Sophie observed, white and even—perhaps it was no surprise that he smiled so often. Regular features too, and a cleft in his strong, square chin. Most women would agree that he was a handsome man, and yet for all his clean-cut good looks, he held not a particle of the attraction Robin held for her and always would.

Robin. Recalled to her purpose, she looked for him at once, and to her surprise and delight, saw him approaching, accompanied by Amy in full hostess mode.

"Sophie, my dear, this gentleman has requested an introduction," she said brightly, for the benefit of whoever might be listening—or watching.

Of course—the forms must be observed, especially in London, where no one except the Sheridans knew of their prior acquaintance. Sophie assumed the polite expression of one encountering a complete stranger while Amy performed the necessary honors.

Robin bowed over her hand, clasping her gloved fingers lightly in his own. "Enchanted to meet you, Miss Tresilian."

"The pleasure is mine, Mr. Pendarvis." Sophie tried not to sound as breathless as she felt. "I am—happy to see you in attendance tonight."

His eyes, as deeply blue as an evening sky, met hers. "I gave my word that I would be here. And I mean to keep my promises."

The unspoken message in his words took her breath away. Lost for words herself, she let her hand linger in his and feasted her eyes on the face she'd loved since she was seventeen.

Amy looked from one to the other with an air of satisfaction. "Well, then, it looks as if my work here is done," she observed. "Thomas, my love, I am famished. Shall we take some supper now?"

"Assuredly." Sheridan offered his arm to his wife. "You might want to consider doing likewise," he advised Robin and Sophie over his shoulder. "Music may be the food of love, but I've found that lobster salad and champagne seldom come amiss."

Robin smiled at his host. "Duly noted, Mr. Sheridan."

"We'll be along shortly," Sophie added, knowing that discretion was still required of both of them. "I'm sorry," she said in a low voice as she turned back to Robin. "I wanted to find you sooner, but there were all these other guests, and then—"

"Lady Charlotte Daventry," he supplied. "So I saw—no further explanation is needed."

"You know her?"

Robin shrugged a shoulder. "Only by sight. She and her husband stayed at the hotel for a few days at Easter. They're a difficult pair to overlook, especially Mr. Daventry. According to Praed, he had the housemaids all in a flutter—they thought him 'ever so handsome.'"

"To each her own," Sophie said absently, still studying the face she much preferred.

"And they found *her* a touch high-handed, so they were relieved she kept mainly to herself during their stay. Sophie," his tone shifted abruptly, "what you sang. That last song. Did you—did you mean… what I hoped you meant?"

Sophie swallowed. But the time for prevarication was over. "Every word."

Robin's breath caught, his eyes blazing a brilliant electric blue. The air between them was electric too, crackling with suppressed longing and desire. He leaned toward her across the short distance that separated them, and Sophie felt herself swaying toward him as well.

Only to pull back as her stomach chose just that moment to complain about how hollow it was. She blushed and saw the heat in Robin's eyes bank down to an amused warmth.

Ruefully, Sophie pressed a hand to her midriff. "My dear life—how embarrassing!"

Robin smiled, an easy, unguarded smile that recalled the

earliest days of their friendship. "I'd call it normal myself—
reassuringly so. And perhaps it's just as well," he continued,
with a meaningful tilt of his head. "We're still in the public
eye, after all."

Sophie glanced around at once and saw with a touch of
dismay that several people were eyeing her and Robin with
open curiosity. Time to don the masks again.

Prompted by a similar instinct, Robin held out his arm.
"Come, Miss Tresilian. Let us go and try the lobster salad
our host recommended. Besides, it will be like old times," he
added in a lower voice, "feeding you after a performance."

Smiling, Sophie took his arm and they proceeded sedately
toward the refreshment table.

⁕

They arranged their movements over the next hour like the
steps of an elaborate dance. He stayed by her as they supped
on lobster salad and champagne, along with other delicacies,
then tactfully withdrew as more guests approached to speak
to her and praise her performance.

Sophie, for her part, acted the consummate professional:
gracious but humble, and showing no sign of wanting to be
other than where she was—although Robin knew she longed
as much as he for the moment when they could be alone
together. Finally, he saw her approach Amy and murmur
something that brought a knowing smile to the other woman's
face. Amy had whispered a reply that made Sophie blush, and
then had turned to catch Robin's eye and give him a meaningful nod. The next part of their plan had been set in motion.

Separate, discreet exits: they'd worked out the details over
supper. Robin went first—as one guest among many, his
departure would scarcely be noticed. Whereas a fair number
of eyes would be on Sophie when she left. People would
be more likely to remember who followed her than who
preceded her.

Now he waited in the Sheridans' brougham, shifting restlessly on the well-padded seats. Time passed—perhaps ten minutes, which felt like ten years—and then the door was opening and a footman was handing Sophie into the carriage. She settled next to him on the seat, in a whisper of silk, a drift of scent. He could feel her warmth, hear the quickened rhythm of her breathing, as the brougham pulled away from the curb.

"Where are we going?" he asked.

"Back to my house… eventually."

He raised his brows at the deceptively demure note in her voice. "Eventually?"

"Curzon Street, by way of Hyde Park." He glimpsed a flash of her dimples in the shadowed interior. "Amy suggested… taking the long way round."

So that, in all likelihood, was what their hostess had whispered to Sophie before. Robin exhaled. "I'm grateful that she appears to be on our side. Your side, at any rate."

"So am I. But I thought she and Thomas received you cordially enough?"

"They did." Although Sheridan had been more guarded than his wife, more openly protective of Sophie, which Robin could appreciate. "They love you like a sister."

"I love them too." He heard the smile in her voice.

They lapsed into silence as the carriage neared Marble Arch, its massive bulk ghost-pale in the moonlight, then turned left onto Bayswater Road to begin its circuit of Hyde Park.

The whole scenario felt increasingly unreal to Robin. But here was Sophie beside him, riding with him in a carriage… his dream of a second chance suddenly a reality. Thank God for that—and for her. He hadn't dared to hope, not until the encore.

But I also dreamt, which pleased me most, / That you lov'd me still the same …

Even now, he could scarcely believe this was real. Mouth dry, heart pounding, he reached for her hand—and felt her fingers curl around his with surprising strength.

"I'm here." The words were breathed rather than spoken.

"Yes," he husked, and drew her tenderly, even reverently, into his arms.

Sophie made a soft, needful sound low in her throat, and pressed against him. He breathed in her scent—not violets tonight, but something sultrier and more sophisticated. But she was Sophie still, and improbably and wonderfully *his* Sophie.

Their lips met, restraint and reserve going up like tinder as passion flared between them, all the more intense for four years of privation. They clung together, the only sound in the carriage their ragged breathing as they kissed and kissed again.

Oh, my love. My love.

He did not realize he'd spoken—groaned—the words aloud, until he heard her whispered response. "Yours, Robin. Always yours."

"It's more than I deserve," he told her thickly.

"Very likely." He heard the smile in her voice, the wry humor only time and maturity could have given her. "But true just the same. I'm done with trying to deny what I feel."

"So am I."

"Well, it's about time." She softened the tart rejoinder with a kiss, then settled back in his arms. "We've waited long enough for each other, I think."

"That we have," he agreed, resting his cheek against her hair.

She took a breath. "So—how are we to manage this?"

And there it was, that clear-eyed practicality that he'd missed every bit as much as her warmth and sweetness. As deeply as he'd hungered for her kisses, she was right to turn her thoughts—and his—in this direction.

"Quietly and discreetly?" he suggested.

"Quietly and discreetly, I'll grant. As long as you don't mean 'chastely' as well."

"Sophie—"

She placed a finger over his lips. "I want to be with you, Robin. I always have. We have already waited years, and we may have to wait still longer until your divorce is granted. Why can we not take—just a little time for ourselves alone?"

Just a little time. A brief interlude with the woman he meant to spend the rest of his life with. A fleeting taste of sweetness after four lonely, barren years. He would have to be made of iron to resist that—or her. *Not this time.*

He swallowed. "Where, then?"

She hesitated. "Curzon Street? No one is waiting up for me—I sent my maid to bed."

"No." Robin put all the firmness of which he was capable into that one word. "Not under your own roof, my love. I'd be doing you no favors by embroiling you in a scandal—twice."

He exaggerated, but not by much. In the wake of Nathalie's appearance in Cornwall, gossip and unkind speculation had circulated about him and Sophie, especially after her hasty departure for London. But in the end, most of the scrutiny had focused on Robin himself and what he meant to do about his errant wife and the children he'd never known existed.

Still, he had no wish to bring anything like that into Sophie's life again, or risk harming her reputation and career. As desperately as they wanted each other, they could not afford to let passion make them reckless or stupid. This would have to be carefully thought out.

"Robin, I haven't lived like a vestal virgin these past four years," she reminded him.

"Perhaps not, but I'll wager you've been careful. You have too much sense not to be."

"Yes," she acknowledged after a moment. "There seemed no point in inviting trouble. All right, then—not my house. And," she added on a sigh, "not your hotel room, either. But surely there must be some obscure corner of London for us to hide in."

"Perhaps. But your picture must be in all the print shops in town," he pointed out. "I bought one just yesterday. Wherever we go, you might still be recognized."

She tensed in his arms, struck by a new thought. "Which would do *you* no favors, either. Especially if you hope to gain custody of Sara."

He hadn't considered that, and the implications chilled him to the bone. While Nathalie had betrayed their marriage first, he still had to show that he was the more responsible parent. They weighed their options in bleak silence, each arriving at the same unsatisfactory conclusion.

"Damn." Sophie's voice sounded small and chastened. "I'm so sorry, Robin. I wasn't thinking." Her hand crept into his again.

He gave it a comforting squeeze. "Not your fault—I wasn't thinking either. Who'd have imagined that you'd become so famous that even London isn't big enough for you?"

She stilled. "Perhaps... it's not a city we should be thinking of at all."

"Sophie—"

"No, listen!" She turned in his arms, and he could see the urgency on her face even in the faint glow of the carriage lamps. "I have an idea, Robin. There may be a way for us, after all."

Fourteen

When her loose gown from her shoulders did fall
And she me caught in her arms long and small
Therewithal sweetly did me kiss,
And softly said, "Dear heart, how like you this?"

—Sir Thomas Wyatt, "They Flee From Me"

AT ANY HOUR OF THE DAY, PADDINGTON STATION swarmed with activity as hordes of travelers descended from the trains or rushed to board them. Shrouded in steam, the engines squatted in position like mechanical dragons, their doors gaping open to receive or disgorge passengers. Now and then a whistle blew, mournful and imperative at once.

Valise in hand, a copy of *The Times* tucked under one arm, Robin strode along the platform toward the first-class carriages, glancing through the windows of various compartments. At last he spied one that looked almost empty, except for a veiled woman in a plain dark dress sitting by the window, her nose buried in a book.

Without hesitation, he opened the door and stepped up into the compartment.

"Madam, if I may?" he inquired with perfect formality, as he closed the door behind him.

The woman glanced up from her book, bestowed upon him a look of cool appraisal—just discernible through her veil—and inclined her head, before returning her attention to whatever she had been reading.

Curious, Robin glanced at the spine of her book: *The Huntsman Winds His Horn* by Lewis Wells, a popular author of detective stories. Well, at least it wasn't Marie Corelli or someone equally dire. Amused all the same, he stowed his valise in the overhead rack, took the seat opposite her, shook out his newspaper ostentatiously, and began to read as well. A lady and a gentleman, sitting in silent, solitary decorum: two strangers who could not be less interested in one another. A few minutes later, the train's whistle wailed and they pulled out of the station.

Much to Robin's relief, no other passengers entered their compartment. After the conductor had collected their tickets and departed, he moved almost casually to sit beside his fellow passenger. He felt her entire body relax as he seated himself, and caught the glimmer of laughter in her sea-green eyes beneath that absurd veil.

He found himself grinning like a schoolboy, caught up in the lunacy of this entire escapade. "Minx! A Spanish duenna couldn't have improved upon that look!"

Sophie stifled a giggle. "Was I that convincing? I did feel I had to be, just in case we acquired an audience."

"You effectively *thicked my blood with cold*," he assured her. "Fortunately, we're still alone, so you can dispense with the basilisk stare for now."

"With pleasure. But I must confess," she added in a low voice, tucking back her veil, "I feel as if I'm performing in a French farce."

"The only thing missing is a bed," he murmured, and saw her flush deliciously.

She lowered her gaze, deceptively demure. "That will come into play soon enough."

The thought was enough to send a hot rush of arousal through him, but, mindful of their surroundings, he contented himself with taking her hand. Their fingers twined together, as intimate as a kiss.

"So, where are we going, exactly?" he asked as they leaned back against the seat, shoulders brushing. "Oxfordshire?"

"Yes, not far from the Cotswolds," she informed him. "Lord and Lady Warrender have a cottage to let on their estate. As Thomas is such an old friend of theirs, he vouched for me, and they were more than willing to let me stay here for a short holiday, after I finished my engagements in town. I've heard it's a charming place—Thomas stayed there himself while he was painting a portrait—and bound to be very private, since the Season's still in full swing."

"It sounds just about ideal. How long were you planning to stay?"

"Oh, I had thought about a week, although Lady Warrender assured me I could stay a fortnight, if I wished." Sophie paused, studying him with searching green eyes. "But I know you'll want to return to London—and Cornwall—sooner than that."

"Yes," he admitted on a sigh, touching his lips to her brow. "Far sooner, I'm afraid."

She grew still against him. "How long do we have?"

"My solicitor told me the papers should be ready on Tuesday." Mr. Halifax had offered to mail them to Nathalie, but Robin had refused. His ill-starred marriage had been undertaken face to face; it should end the same way, no matter how enraged Nathalie became once he told her he'd filed for divorce.

Still… Tuesday was a mere four days from now. Sophie's lovely face paled as she absorbed that unwelcome but inescapable fact, and Robin could almost *see* her dredging up a smile from somewhere.

"Well, then, we'll leave at first light on Tuesday morning,

so you can have the papers in hand by noon," she said with a creditable attempt at briskness. "And as to the rest, we'll just have to make the most of our time away."

"Agreed." Robin put an arm about her shoulders, drawing her close. His regrets ran as deep as hers. After so many years apart, so much longing and loneliness, this interlude seemed like a crust thrown to a starving man.

But a crust was better than nothing at all, he reminded himself. Who knew how long it would be before they could be together lawfully, especially if Nathalie resisted the divorce? At least they could have this interlude, snatch a few days of happiness, before he returned to Cornwall and began the lengthy process of ending his marriage once and for all.

Four days… but he was determined to make the most of them—as was Sophie, he knew.

The train wound along, and they sat together, fingers still entwined, and watched through the window as London slipped away.

∝

Less than two hours later, they stood with their valises on the platform at Witney, having changed trains at Oxford. The mid-afternoon sun shone down on them beneficently from a cloudless sky.

A beautiful day, Sophie thought. The thought struck her that she'd have found it beautiful even in the pouring rain, simply because she was here with Robin. Besotted… just as she'd been as seventeen, though she hoped she'd acquired more sense and perhaps even some wisdom in the ensuing six years.

"What now, my love?" Robin spoke the words lightly, almost carelessly, but they sent a pleasurable shiver through her just the same.

"Well, we should go into town first and wire Amy to let her know we arrived safely. *And* when we'll be coming back to London," she added. "Someone should know where we are, just in case. And we can trust her and Thomas to keep our confidence."

"We owe both of them a great deal," Robin agreed, offering her his arm.

They did indeed, Sophie reflected somberly as they left the station. Amy had been delighted to hear of Sophie and Robin's reconciliation, and Thomas, while more reserved than his wife, had expressed similar wishes for their happiness and offered practical assistance in arranging their brief holiday. At Thomas's invitation, Robin had checked out of Brown's Hotel and moved his trunks to Sheridan House; he'd also arranged to have any correspondence forwarded there too.

They found a post office easily enough and sent the telegram. Afterward, they hired a hackney carriage and were soon on their way to Wyldean Hall, located perhaps five miles south of the town.

"The staff knows to expect me today," Sophie explained to Robin as they bowled along the country roads. "I sent a wire this morning, so they'll have got the cottage ready for guests: food, fresh linens, candles, anything we might need." She smiled. "Lady Warrender told me there's even a piano in the parlor—a small one."

"The parlor or the piano?"

Sophie giggled. "I think she meant the piano, but I suppose the parlor might be on the small side too. Never mind, I think we'll have all the room we need. Downstairs—and upstairs."

He touched her cheek. "It was upstairs I was thinking of."

Upstairs, where the bedchambers were most likely to be.

Sophie leaned into Robin's caress. Useless to deny she was thinking of that too. Of the moment both had thought would never come. Sitting beside him in the carriage, she was all the more conscious of his proximity—the warmth of his body, the coiled energy in his lean frame, and the familiar scent of bay rum that set every nerve ending atingle. Desire curled through her: she burned to kiss him, to touch him as they'd touched last night in the Sheridans' carriage—but they'd had the advantage of darkness then. Daylight provided no such protection, she thought with an inward sigh. They must be discreet a while longer.

Still, to be here, with him, was more than she had ever dared to dream for the last four years. The rest would come soon enough.

So she sat quietly with her hand in his and gazed out the window at the scenery: the yellow stone houses, many half-timbered in Tudor fashion; bushy hawthorn trees studded with dark fruit; and the graceful willows lining the banks of the Windrush, its waters glowing amber in the sun. There was something curiously soothing about watching a river flow, she mused, much more restful than watching the sea. And her eyelids felt as heavy as stone shutters; she'd risen early this morning to prepare for the journey, and after last night's performance and everything that followed, the effort had been little short of Herculean. Perhaps if she closed her eyes for just a moment…

The next thing she knew, Robin was gently shaking her awake. "We're here, my love."

❧

Sophie fell in love with the cottage at first sight. Built of honey-colored Cotswold stone— like the main house—it gleamed among the beech trees like a perfectly set jewel. In autumn, when the leaves had turned to copper and flame, the sight must be truly dazzling, she thought.

While Robin took down the valises and settled with the hackney driver, she went up the walk and unlocked the door with the key the housekeeper had given her. Entering, she breathed in the scents of beeswax and lemon thyme, and took a long look around.

Two large rooms—a kitchen and parlor—appeared to

dominate the ground floor. The former came equipped with a modern cookstove and an impressive array of pots and pans; the latter was comfortably but tastefully furnished, with William Morris chairs, a well-padded sofa, and the promised piano standing in a corner. Everything was as clean and tidy as a new pin, the stone floor swept, the surfaces of tables, chairs, shelves, *and* piano all gleaming with polish.

"This *is* something like," Robin remarked with approval as he stepped over the threshold, closing the door behind him.

Sophie turned in a slow circle, feeling happiness bubble up as from an underground spring. "It's perfect!"

"Why don't we wait until we see the rest of the place before making such a declaration?" Robin suggested, but he was smiling.

"I know it's small. You could probably fit it into a corner of Pendarvis Hall—"

"I stayed in far less commodious places following the regiment. This will more than do," he assured her. "Shall we go up and see the first floor?"

Upstairs, they found two good-sized bedchambers, one papered in pale blue stripes, the other in rose sprigs; a bathroom with a full-length tub; and even a water closet containing a flush commode with an embossed bowl. The sight of the last left them temporarily speechless.

"Well, it's not primitive, at any rate!" Sophie remarked at last, stifling a giggle. "We shan't be living like Robinson Crusoe while we're here."

Robin smiled, the rare, unguarded smile that always turned her bones to water. "He had only Friday for company. I have you—that makes me better off than he already." He drew her into his arms and kissed her, a light, soft caress that hinted at much more to come. "Are you hungry? We had no luncheon."

"Famished," she admitted, still nestled within the circle of his arm. "But, oh, Robin—I would dearly love a bath first!"

"Then by all means have one," he proposed. "In the meantime, I'll go down to the kitchen and see about putting something together for us both."

"I don't want to leave all the work to you," she protested, but he shook his head.

"It's not that hard to brew a pot of tea and open some tins. Besides, I find that fixing a meal relaxes me—and we'll have to heat some water anyway for your bath."

This was a domestic side of him she hadn't seen before, but one she found instantly appealing. And he did look less tense—the set of his shoulders was looser, and his expression more open. Not as tightly wound as he'd been in London.

"Very well," Sophie conceded, capitulating without any real resistance. "And perhaps we can have a morsel or two while we wait for the water to boil."

⌘

The bath was lovely, the water just the right temperature, and there was Pears soap with which to wash—an additional luxury. Feeling much refreshed, Sophie climbed out, swathed herself in a thick, soft towel, and padded into the rose-papered bedchamber, seeking her valise and a change of clothing.

A charming room, she mused idly, as she located the valise and began to sort through what she had packed. Lady Warrender, or whoever had decorated this chamber, had exquisite taste. The floral theme was prevalent throughout, from the sprigged wallpaper to the patterned curtains to the bowl of potpourri on the dresser, breathing out a faint odor of roses. The furnishings were also well chosen: an elegant dressing table, a pair of wing chairs upholstered in moss green, and a bed with a carved oaken stead, just big enough for two.

Her mind stuttered to a stop. The bed... the one she and Robin would share tonight, as lovers, for the very first time. Anticipation quickened her pulse and sent a rush of heat flooding through her body—to be with him at last, the way she'd dreamed of for so long.

And yet... there was apprehension mixed in with the eagerness too. These last four years had changed them both, especially her: she was no longer the untouched innocent whom he had first known. He had accepted or seemed to accept her history, but in the end, would he be disappointed—that he was not her first and only lover?

Sophie pulled herself up sharply. She was being ridiculous—and she needed to stop borrowing trouble. In all their dealings, Robin had never said anything to her that he didn't mean. So if he said her past relations with other men made no difference to him, she should take him at his word.

She took a few deep breaths to steady herself, then looked down into her valise again. And broke into a smile when she saw a fold of pale rose peeking out from under a shirtwaist, recognizing the nightgown she'd bought in Paris, the exact shade of the Maiden's Blush roses that grew in the garden at Roswarne. The color, however, was the only maidenly thing about it, Sophie thought as she lifted it out. Both the nightgown and its matching robe were made of sheer silk gossamer, shot through with gilt threads.

Her smile grew as she held the nightgown up to the light, which turned it almost translucent. Yes, a garment like this was meant to reveal even more than it concealed—and once it was donned, very little would be left to the imagination, especially if she chose not to wear her combination underneath.

Humming softly, Sophie took out the robe as well and began to unwrap the towel from her body. Perhaps there were some advantages, after all, in *not* being an untouched innocent.

❧

Freshly arrayed in the nightgown and robe, her unbound hair tumbling down her back, she went down to the kitchen to find Robin brewing the tea, his back to her.

"Ah, there you are, my dear," he said, without turning around. "Did you enjoy your bath? I had a bit of a wash myself, and put on a clean shirt. No objection to a cold collation, I trust?"

"None at all. It sounds delightful," Sophie replied. "Thank you for making dinner."

"You're very welcome." He turned then, and she had the satisfaction of seeing his eyes widen as he took in what she was wearing. For a moment he just stared, heat kindling in his eyes, then the heat mounted to his face as he *realized* that he was staring. "My God. Sophie."

She laughed delightedly, did a little turn so that the gossamer skirts floated and shimmered around her. "Do you like it?"

"*Like* it? Ask me if I have a pulse," he retorted, smiling. "And I'm heartily glad that I'm the only one to see you in it. I *am* the only one, aren't I?" he added, with just a touch of unease.

Sophie smiled back, loving him. "You are. I bought this in Paris, and I've worn it only for myself so far."

And now, for you was the unspoken message, which Robin deciphered without any difficulty. "Then I count myself even more privileged," he said lightly. "Now, come and have some dinner, before I start thinking of ways to get you out of that very fetching nightdress."

"*I* wouldn't mind," she said, deliberately provocative. He looked good enough to eat himself, his shirt collar open to expose the column of his throat and a patch of lightly tanned skin, his sleeves rolled back over muscled forearms, his dark hair damp with comb marks but still appealingly mussed.

"First things first. You did say you were famished before," he pointed out, pulling out a chair for her at the wide kitchen table. "And you wouldn't want my culinary efforts to go to waste now, would you?"

"Well, when you put it like that..." She seated herself

in the chair and let him serve her from the spread he'd put together while she bathed.

He'd done a very creditable job with what he'd found: cold ham and potted chicken, fresh bread and butter, a wedge of cheese, almonds and a bunch of fat purple grapes, and a tin of sweet biscuits. A rather light meal, but after their travels and in this heat, neither desired anything heavier. There had been eggs in the larder, Sophie had noticed earlier, and a flitch of bacon. They could have a more substantial breakfast if they fancied one. There was something deliciously domestic about this interlude, and they found themselves content merely to savor it.

All around them was silence. One could not imagine such silence unless one had lived in a great city like London, where silence was so rare. Only in the hours before dawn was London quiet, and not for long even then.

"More ham?" Robin asked, as he filled Sophie's teacup again. "Or bread? I can slice more of both, if you'd like."

She shook her head. "No, thank you. I've had quite a sufficiency. But I will take a chocolate biscuit—I still enjoy ending my meals with a sweet," she confessed, smiling.

He passed her the biscuit tin. "A pity there's no cake to mark the occasion."

"Occasion?"

"Belated occasion. Your birthday was at Midsummer—*a fortnight and odd days* ago."

"Oh." She felt herself flushing. "I hadn't thought—I mean, I don't… oh, dear."

His eyes were intent on her face. "What's wrong, my love?"

She shook her head, impatient with herself. "You'll think it's silly."

"Never," he assured her, covering her hand with his own.

"Well…" Sophie hesitated a moment longer, then said with a wry smile, "It occurred to me, a while ago, that I hadn't had much luck with birthdays in recent years. Not just because of *that* night," she hastened to add, when she saw the shadow cross his face. "But the year before, you and James and Harry were facing those awful slanders, and then there was the year I caught the influenza while on tour and couldn't speak, much less sing. I suppose it's made me a touch superstitious. So now—when Midsummer Eve comes round, I tend to celebrate my birthday *very* quietly. A good dinner and some small indulgence, like a new frock or a night at the theater."

"Understood." Robin squeezed her hand. "All the same, I should like to mark the occasion. Perhaps between us, we can exorcise the ghost of Disappointing Birthdays Past?"

She managed to smile. "That sounds like something straight out of Dickens. What did you have in mind?"

"Wait here." He got up and strode from the kitchen. When he returned, he was carrying a black velvet box that he held out to her, almost diffidently. "I bought these for your nineteenth birthday but never had the chance to give them to you. I hope you can bring yourself to accept them now." He swallowed before continuing, "And the heart that goes along with them."

Sophie's breath caught on a sob when she opened the box and saw the double strand of pearls, gleaming against the black silk like a string of tiny full moons. "Robin…"

"I'm sure that you've seen or been offered far grander—" he began.

"These come from *you*," she broke in, blinking back tears. "That makes them the grandest of all. Oh, my dear heart, you don't need to buy my affections, you never have—"

"I know." He brushed away her tears with a gentle, if slightly unsteady, hand. "And I'm not fool enough to think you *can* be bought. But I purchased these with you in mind, and it's time they were given to their rightful owner. If I may?"

She handed him the box, and he lifted the pearls from their silken nest, fastening them about her throat.

"Many happy returns, my love." His lips brushed her nape as he fastened the clasp, then knelt down by her chair to study his handiwork. "I used to imagine how they'd look against your skin. And I can tell you the sight does not disappoint."

Sophie fingered them, cool, silken spheres of graduated size. While she could not see the effect without a mirror, she'd always loved the way pearls felt to the touch. "So beautiful. Like moonlight on a string. And you kept them all these years?"

"In the safe at my bank. I never meant for anyone but you to wear these. My Nereid."

Pearly treasures. "I'll cherish them always," she told him with a tremulous smile.

"My mother once said that pearls go with everything. I'd like to add that they look magnificent with… almost nothing too." His gaze, now an intense smoky blue, lingered once again on her diaphanous nightgown.

Sophie felt her lips quirk, an imp of mischief taking hold of her. Leaning forward in her chair, she twined her arms about his neck and drew his head down until their lips were nearly touching. "Would you like to see how they look— with nothing at all?"

His kiss, soul-searing and intense, was all the answer she needed.

❧

If only this could have been their wedding night, in truth. The night they'd both dreamed of, before that Midsummer Eve when everything had been shattered. A night that would have enshrined him forever as her first, last, and only love.

But then, he already held that distinction, Sophie realized, no matter who else had shared her bed in their years apart. She was no longer a virgin. But her heart beat as rapidly, her breath came as quick and fast, as if she were still that untried girl anticipating their nuptial night.

In the rose-sprigged room, they stole kisses as they undressed, buttons flying apart, shoes and slippers being kicked aside, discarded garments dropping at their feet.

"Sophie." Naked save for his drawers, Robin set his hands upon her shoulders, gazed down into her eyes. "My dearest love."

Her nightgown slipped to the floor. His drawers followed seconds later.

Sophie looked down, flushing when she saw the proud jut of his erection. Knowing *she* was responsible for that sent a fierce triumph surging through her, and she reached forward to touch it, touch him...

He nudged her hand aside, not in repudiation, but because he was holding something in his own hand. "Sophie, this is—"

"I know what it is," she broke in, recognizing it at once. "Several years ago, on tour, an older soprano took me and some of the other young singers aside and explained about rubber sheaths and Dutch caps."

"Dutch caps?" Robin echoed, astonished.

"They're a bit like sheaths, only for women." Sophie's cheeks grew warm, but she met his gaze squarely. "As it happens, we're doubly prepared tonight."

He shook his head, befuddled. "I cannot believe we're having this conversation. We couldn't have four years ago."

"Yes, we could. Only it would have taken longer, and involved much more blushing."

A laugh broke from him at that, and the lingering tension shivered apart until there was only desire. Once the condom was in place, Robin drew her into his arms.

"Sophie." He studied her for a moment—naked save for his gift, gleaming about her throat—before deftly undoing the clasp and dropping the necklace onto the dressing table behind them. "Believe me, love, you need no adornment. Especially tonight."

His hands slid down from her shoulders to cradle her

breasts, then traced a sinuous path over her ribs and belly like an explorer charting the course of a river, or an undiscovered country. *License* his *roving hands and let them go…*

Sophie's skin sang beneath his fingers. She'd known other caresses, by lovers far more experienced, but no other man's touch inflamed her as his did. No other man had ever sounded the deepest chord within her, rousing a host of emotions she could not begin to name.

A moan of pure pleasure escaped her as his fingers found and parted her seam, began to stroke back and forth over moist folds, lightly at first, then with a deepening pressure that sent shocks of pleasure reverberating through her. Gasping now, she surged forward, her mouth fastening on his, her hands gripping his shoulders convulsively. From their first kiss at the Hall, he'd awakened the woman inside of her. And that woman now responded, matching him touch for touch, kiss for kiss.

Through a haze of pleasure, she registered that his fingers were gone and his hands were clasping her hips, tilting them forward… and then he entered her with a thrust that rocked them both from head to foot and drove a hoarse cry from her throat.

Robin's eyes flew open, shock and self-reproach blazing across his face in an instant. "Oh, God—*Sophie*…"

She gulped in a breath, shifted her weight… and let the laughter bubble up, exhilarated and exultant as she relished the feeling of him, hot and hard inside her. Where he was meant to be. Some advantages to no longer being an innocent. "Don't stop, Robin!"

His expression changed from guilty to wondering. "Sophie—"

"Don't stop," she repeated, stroking his face. "And don't apologize." She angled her hips, rocked against him provocatively, and heard his breath roughen and catch. "Just—carry on."

He sagged with relief, but not—fortunately—where it

mattered most. Instead, he began to move, slowly and gently at first, then with increasing speed and force. In and out, in and out, plunging deeper with each thrust… Sophie held onto him as her knees trembled beneath her, and fiery pinwheels spun behind her closed eyes. And the sensations between her legs built and built, bearing her aloft like a cresting wave or a choir in full voice…

Then she was falling, tumbling off the edge of the world into Robin's arms, his cry mingling with hers as their shared climax tore through them. And in that moment, Sophie thought she heard the Lost Chord, transcendent and divine, echoing within the very depths of her being…

When they came to themselves, they were lying entwined upon the carpet, her head pillowed on his chest as it rose and fell with his still-ragged breaths. His heart pounded like a drum—just like hers.

Minutes or years passed before Robin spoke, his voice not quite steady. "My love… are you all right?"

Sophie put all the conviction she felt into her reply. "Much better than that."

He relaxed. "I've pictured this so often over the years. Dreamed of it."

She kissed his shoulder, tasting the salt on his damp skin. "So have I."

"I used to imagine making love to you—gently. Tenderly. The way a husband *should* make love to his new bride." He huffed a rueful laugh. "I never pictured anything so—immoderate!"

"Disappointed?" Sophie asked, stroking his face.

He shook his head. "Astonished, amazed, but—very far from disappointed. You?"

"Not disappointed at all," she said staunchly. "Besides, given how long we've waited and how much we've had to overcome," *still have to overcome*, her mind supplied, "perhaps it's not too surprising that our first time as lovers was like *this*."

Robin gave a slow nod, conceding her point. "Perhaps not. All the same, I intend for things to be a bit different next time."

Sophie stretched luxuriously, savoring the sensation of his lean, hard-muscled frame against her own. "In what way?"

His eyes glinted. "Well, for starters, I insist on our making it over to the bed first!"

Amidst her laughter, he swept her up from the floor and carried her over to that article of furniture, which, on close inspection, proved to be more than satisfactory for their purposes...

Fifteen

Now let us sport us while we may;
And now, like amorous birds of prey,
Rather at once our time devour,
Than languish in his slow-chapped power.

—Andrew Marvell, "To His Coy Mistress"

MORNING BROKE SOFT AND DOVE-GREY IN OXFORDSHIRE. Sophie woke first, and lay listening to the soft trills of birdsong outside the cottage. Nature's music—one of the loveliest ways to wake up, she thought with a smile of drowsy contentment.

And waking up with a lover made it even sweeter. Raising herself on one elbow, Sophie studied the man still fast asleep beside her: the strong, angular features, the sweep of his lashes, the way his dark hair fell over his brow. There were lines about Robin's eyes and mouth that hadn't been there four years ago, lines attesting to the strain he'd lived with as an unwilling husband. Tolerating his wife's many lovers, compensating for her neglect of their children, and at the same time, doing his best to run the hotel and make it provide for them all.

Last night had been both consummation and release for them, an unquenchable fire burning away years of hopeless longing, loneliness, and stoic endurance. Her loins still throbbed pleasurably when she remembered their first joining, so fierce, so hungry, so *immoderate*, to use Robin's word. Later, at moonrise, he'd made love to her again, slowly this time, with all the tenderness, care, and... moderation of which he was capable. And Sophie had reveled in that second coupling, not just for its sweetness, but for what it revealed about him: that he was still, at heart, the gentle, considerate, chivalrous man with whom she'd fallen in love. Their years apart hadn't changed him beyond recognition. Nor had Nathalie.

Nathalie... Sophie fretted her lip, suddenly uneasy. She did not want to think about Robin's wife, not now and not *here*, the place where their love was to have free rein at last. But sooner or later, the subject would have to be dealt with. Nathalie Pendarvis was not an abstraction, but a person... if not a particularly admirable one.

For so many years, Sophie had thought of the woman— when she could bear to think of her at all—as the wicked witch in a fairy tale. Someone who had calculatedly, maliciously destroyed her happiness and Robin's by appearing, with children in tow, to stake her claim anew. Perhaps she'd been less than fair. Nathalie might be malicious and calculating, but surely she was human too. Maybe it was desperation as well as greed that had driven her to Cornwall. Desperation not just for herself but for those two young children.

And now, four years later, Nathalie Pendarvis was a wife whose husband did not want her, who wished only to be free of her. And a bereaved mother, who had lost a son and who might have to forfeit custody of her daughter, if she and her estranged husband could not come to terms. Perhaps Sophie erred in giving Nathalie the benefit of the doubt, but it was possible that she was unhappy too, and lashing out in the only way she knew how—by making others as miserable as she. If she could be brought to see there was another way, even for her...

Robin was right; there was no point in making this situation uglier than it had to be. Sophie did not have to like
her rival, but she could perhaps try to understand her. And
do her part to improve things by whatever means possible.
They would have to tread carefully, but there must be a
solution with which all of them could live. She would not
believe otherwise.

The young Sophie, so sure in the sanctity of her love,
rearing her head? Perhaps, but she might be a little wiser
now—and more patient. Barely a week ago, she'd never
thought this was possible. She'd resigned herself, four years
ago, to a life without Robin—and now the promise of it was
within her reach again. What lay ahead would not be easy,
but then, if she had wanted easy, she wouldn't have fallen in
love with this man in the first place.

She looked down at him again, love a warm weight inside
of her: tender, passionate, and fiercely protective at once.
Hers to cherish—and cherish him she would, till death did
them part.

He stirred in his sleep, a faint frown etching itself between
his brows. Even as she watched, the frown deepened and his
head moved restlessly from side to side on the pillow.

Dreaming, she realized—and perhaps, to judge from his
reaction, not particularly pleasant dreams. She reached out a
hand, laid it against his cheek. "Wake up, dear heart."

His breath hitched, and his hand seized hers in a grip so
strong she cried out in surprise and pain. Robin's eyes flew
open, and he stared wildly at her before recognition came
rushing back into his gaze.

"Oh, God!" He released her hand, instantly contrite. "I'm
sorry, love! I don't know what I was—"

"You were dreaming," Sophie told him soothingly.

He closed his eyes for a moment, swallowed hard. "Yes."

"And—not a good dream?" she ventured.

Robin exhaled shakily, tried to smile. "On the contrary,

it began as a *very* good dream, about us. It just... took an unexpected turn."

"Do you want to talk about it?" she asked, still studying him.

"I'd—rather not, if you don't mind. Thank you for waking me." He caught sight of her surreptitiously rubbing her hand, and his eyes darkened with remorse. "Sophie—"

"It's nothing," she assured him, showing her hand. "See? Not so much as a bruise."

He captured the hand, bestowed a gentle kiss on it. "No thanks to me."

"Hush! No one's to blame for what happens during a nightmare." Sophie stroked his hair. "But I'm sorry you had such a rude awakening."

"It's over now—no need to dwell on it," he said, with a firmness that reminded her a little too much of the old Robin, protective to a fault and secretive as an oyster. "Besides, I would much rather talk about last night than this morning."

She smiled, even as she recognized the diversionary tactic. "Last night was wonderful."

His expression eased. "For me as well. Everything I ever dreamed it would be." He reached out to gather her in, and she snuggled against him, her head resting on his shoulder.

Robin let a lock of her hair spill over his fingers. "Your hair smells like violets. The way I remember it."

She had combed a few drops of the scent through her damp hair after bathing. "I couldn't bear to wear that scent for years," she confessed. "Because of what it made *me* remember. But now... it seems only fitting to wear it again, and for you."

"Thank you." He touched his lips to her brow. "I've always thought of violets as a—hopeful flower. A promise that spring is coming and the world will be made over. They took on a whole new meaning when I fell in love with you. No doubt it was sentimental folly on my part, but... every spring, I would find or buy some violets and keep them in my chamber, to remind me of you. And the time we had together." He took a breath. "And perhaps, deep down, I was hoping that someday, somehow, you and I would have—a second spring."

Sophie swallowed, her eyes stinging. He'd never spoken so openly or at such length of their past and his own secret hopes. "We'll have it," she promised. "Another spring and every other season, for the rest of our lives."

His arms tightened around her. "What could be better than a love for all seasons?"

"A love for all seasons, followed by breakfast?" she suggested after a moment.

Robin raised amused brows. "You're hungry again?"

"Remember how we spent the night. You know I'm *always* ravenous after a performance. To say nothing of the encores!" she added mischievously.

He laughed then, and gave her a quick kiss. "Point taken. And now that you mention it, I should be glad of breakfast myself. It must be a good twelve hours since we last ate."

"Well, then, let's get dressed, and I'll start breakfast," she said briskly. "It seems only fair, since you made dinner for us last night."

"Dressed, washed, and in my case, shaved." Robin rubbed a hand over his stubbled chin. "I'll see you downstairs, then." He kissed her again and sat up, tossing the bedclothes aside.

Sophie watched from the bed as he moved about the room retrieving his garments. The morning light, stronger now and faintly tinged with gold, played along his lean, hard-muscled frame, illuminating angles and contours like the hand of a master painter. She feasted her eyes without shame: Robin, her lover now, in every sense of the word.

Despite her present happiness, the look on his face and the shadows in his eyes when he'd awakened still niggled at her. Whatever lay at the root of that dream he so adamantly refused to discuss was clearly not some vague phantasm but something real and disturbing… that disturbed him still.

She did not want to pry. Courtesy dictated that she respect Robin's wish for privacy and not force the issue. But secrets had torn them apart before.

"Robin," she said, after he had pulled on his drawers and donned his shirt again.

He glanced up from buttoning his shirt. "Yes, love?"

She hesitated, then began, "You know you don't need to protect me anymore, don't you? Not as you did when I was seventeen."

His brows rose. "I know you have grown into a formidable young woman. But you must understand that it's second nature for a man to want to protect the woman he loves."

"Yes, but it's also second nature for a woman to want to support the man she loves," Sophie countered. "To be his partner in good *and* bad times. After all these years, you should know that I'm not a fair-weather friend. Nor will I be a fair-weather wife."

Their gazes locked, and his fell first. "I do know that," he said, not looking at her.

"I am glad to hear it." Sophie let her voice soften. "So, dear heart, if you should wish to discuss what was troubling you earlier, I am here. Ready to listen—and to help, if I can."

He looked up, his expression unreadable but a trace of warmth in his eyes. "Thank you. I will—bear that in mind."

Sophie smiled at him. "That is all I ask."

～

Robin stared at his lathered reflection in the glass as he shaved.

Why couldn't he tell her?

This was the woman with whom he wished to spend his life. Intelligent, perceptive… He'd known since the earliest days of their acquaintance that Sophie would not stand for being shut out. That was why he had ultimately trusted her with the truth of his life.

Trust had never been the issue. Was it that he feared to hurt her again, when he had hurt her so deeply before? That must be part of it, surely. She knew some of his life with Nathalie, but he'd tried to spare her the more sordid details.

For whose sake—hers… or his?

You know you don't need to protect me anymore. Not as you did when I was seventeen.

He grimaced, acknowledging the truth of her words. The innocent girl he'd once wished to shield from every harsh wind had grown into a strong, sophisticated woman who could hold her own on stage, in Society… and in bed. Thinking of how she'd matched him passion for passion last night was enough to arouse him all over again.

And remembering what he'd dreamed was enough to drive all physical desire away, as effectively as a freezing shower bath.

Who are you really protecting with your silence—Sophie or yourself?

The answer gave him no satisfaction. Mouth tight, he scraped the last of the shaving soap from his cheek and wiped his face clean with a damp cloth.

Time to stop being a bloody coward, Pendarvis.

He heard Sophie singing from the kitchen—a merry Gilbert and Sullivan air from *The Mikado*—when he came downstairs, and the sound lifted his spirits at once. Standing in the doorway, he watched her, fresh and pretty in a green skirt and lace-trimmed shirtwaist, as she put the kettle on to boil, then began to carve slices from yesterday's loaf for toasting.

She broke off in mid-chorus when she saw him and smiled brilliantly. "Good morning, dear heart! How many eggs would you like? It always seems a waste to dirty a fork on just one."

Robin returned her smile. "Two, then. Is there anything I can do to help?"

Sophie shook her head. "I have everything under control. Just make yourself comfortable over there." She waved the bread knife in the direction of the table.

He sat down, still watching her. "You were right, you know."

"Hmm?" she returned absently, reaching for the toasting fork.

"My dream did disturb me. And I am—ready to talk, if you are still willing to listen."

Her gaze went to him at once, and she gave a tiny nod. *Go on.*

"I said I started out dreaming about us," Robin began. "Which was true. We were lying in bed, and you were wearing your pearls," he added, smiling a little despite knowing what followed. "Except that as I looked at you, you disappeared... and Nathalie was there instead. Laughing at me. Taunting. Saying I'd never be free of her."

Sophie's green eyes brimmed with sympathy. "Oh, Robin."

"That's not the worst of it. Looking at her, I felt such *rage*. All I wanted was to wipe that smile off her face. She was wearing a necklace—this gaudy diamond pendant. I grabbed the chain and started to twist—" He broke off, swallowing convulsively.

Sophie dropped the toasting fork and went to him at once, putting her arms around him. "It was a dream, my love," she soothed. "Just a dream."

He leaned into her embrace. "I know. I know. And you woke me before I could... But it's not something I can easily forget!"

She stroked his hair, not saying anything, just letting him speak.

The words spilled out of him, all the pent-up strain and longing of the last four years. "I said Nathalie and I weren't living as husband and wife. That is entirely true. But one night, not long after you'd left Cornwall, she climbed into my bed while I was sleeping. Her scent awakened me, and thank God it did, because otherwise…" Robin shook his head, suppressed a shudder. "I got up and went to my dressing room. And barred my chamber door ever after."

Her arms tightened around him. "She meant to seduce you."

He nodded weary acknowledgment. "I can't think why, though."

Sophie pulled back a little, her expression quizzical. "Can't you? It seems to me that Nathalie had everything to gain if she'd succeeded. Security, respectability, power—and you."

He rubbed a hand over his face. "But she didn't love me, nor I her."

"I wonder."

Robin glanced up sharply at her soft, almost musing tone. She raised her brows. "Why does the idea surprise you so much? I saw her face that night when she came back and found us dancing together. You say that she didn't love you, and perhaps she never had. I may not have understood everything back then, but I can tell you this much: Nathalie did not like seeing me with you, not one bit."

"Her vanity was injured, nothing more." He shrugged a defensive shoulder. "She probably hoped I'd turn into a sot or blow my brains out when she left me."

"Instead, you thrived," Sophie pointed out. "Eventually, anyway. You returned to England, became a successful architect, inherited the Hall, and turned it into a profitable business. You are so much more than the boy she married and abandoned, the struggling young apprentice. You're a man of means now—and a handsome one." She paused, stroking his hair, then continued levelly, "She may not have loved you, but I think, on some level, that she *wanted* you. And you didn't want her. *That* would have made you irresistible."

Robin shifted in his chair. What Sophie said made a certain degree of sense, even though he felt uncomfortable as hell admitting it.

"Nathalie may have hoped that, in time, your marriage would become a complete one again," Sophie continued, still sounding eerily composed, even detached. "Getting into bed with you may have been her most blatant attempt at winning you over. But I am sure she tried other means as well. Subtler ones."

A harsh bark of laughter escaped him. "Subtle and Nathalie were poles apart!"

He remembered her swathed in frivolous bits of silk and lace, trying on him all the coquettish little tricks that had worked so many years ago—the pout, the fluttering lashes, the near-lisp he'd once found charming. And her barely concealed rage when they availed her nothing, culminating in the night when she'd got into bed with him.

More memories bubbled up, like corruption from a poisoned wound: Nathalie taking over the music room he'd decorated with Sophie in mind, and playing would-be seductive French *chansons* on the piano in his hearing. (He'd refrained from locking her out only because Sara loved the music room too and had asked to have piano lessons.) Nathalie flirting with his neighbors and guests, always with one eye on him to gauge his reaction And he remembered the book of clippings he'd made, following Sophie's career, and how he'd found it torn and damaged on the floor of his private study. No need to ask whose work *that* had been, and from that point on, he'd kept that notebook and any other news regarding Sophie under lock and key.

"Come back, dear heart."

He surfaced, shuddering, aware that his face was damp with perspiration.

Sophie's gaze was compassionate. "Where did you go?" she asked, smoothing his hair.

Back to hell. He managed a wan smile. "Trust me, love, you don't want to know."

Sophie worried her lower lip, clearly tempted to argue

the point, but much to Robin's relief, the kettle whistled behind them.

"Drat!" Sophie muttered, and went to rescue it. "Shall I make the tea, then?"

Without waiting for a reply, she spooned tea into the pot, then poured in the boiling water; her brow was still creased in a frown that had nothing to do with her current task.

Bracing his forearms on his knees, Robin took several composing breaths. There had been times, these last four years, when he'd felt as though he were living in an armed camp. But he was free now, and *never* going back to how things had been. Nor was he going to waste any more time dwelling on it, not when he was here, at long last, with the woman he truly loved.

"Here." Sophie placed a steaming cup of tea before him. "Drink this; you'll feel better."

Robin took a careful sip, appreciating both the hot drink and the familiar ritual. "Forgive me. I never wanted to burden you with this."

She squeezed his shoulder. "Burdens shared are burdens halved. But I am sorry to see you in such distress."

Robin blew out a breath. "You'll think it's strange, no doubt, but I was more disturbed when Nathalie climbed into my bed than when I found her entertaining her latest lover in her own. Not that I enjoyed that," he added, "but I didn't feel... manipulated to the same degree."

Sophie said slowly, "You don't think she... arranged for you to find her so? In hopes that you would be outraged or inflamed with jealousy?"

"Perhaps she did—I don't know. But if she was expecting some big dramatic scene, she was doomed to disappointment." He felt his mouth crook. "In retrospect, I think I felt mainly distaste, and some surprise that she showed such poor judgment in her choice of bedfellow."

Sophie fretted her lip. "Did Nathalie—seduce a guest at the hotel?"

Robin smiled without humor. "Oh, nothing so common-place as that, my dear. She set her sights much higher—or lower, depending on how one looks at it. Nathalie's current lover is Sir Lucas Nankivell."

❦

For a moment Sophie just stared at him, convinced her ears were playing tricks on her. Then, "Sir Lucas?" she echoed faintly.

"None other," Robin replied. "He's held a grudge against me since the day we met. And I won't deny it became mutual quite soon after that."

She reached behind her for a chair, sank down on it without looking. "Because of me?"

"Oh, in part." Robin caressed her cheek. "I won't deny it, love. Nankivell's wanted you from the first. Not that I blame him, but that certainly lent an edge to our dealings. It would have only got worse after we uncovered his slanders that summer."

Sophie pulled a face. "Oh, I doubt he was heartbroken over losing me—not that he ever had me to begin with! Any halfway pretty girl with a large dowry would have done for him, and yes, I figured that out a long time ago. Without my fortune, he'd never have approached Harry for my hand. Besides, didn't he marry an heiress just a year or two ago?"

"Yes, an industrialist's daughter from Birmingham," Robin confirmed. "But no one with eyes to see would mistake it for a love match. Not on his side, at any rate. His title, her fortune—that seems to be the way of things these days."

"If she does love him... poor girl," Sophie said feelingly. "Especially now that he's unfaithful." She spared a moment to be thankful she'd never felt an attraction to Sir Lucas.

"Our mutual grudge notwithstanding, Nankivell and I generally try to avoid each other, so I can't begin to guess how Lady Nankivell feels about her husband. But according to recent rumor, she's left him—for now." Robin's mouth quirked. "I don't know whether Nankivell's affair with Nathalie predates this separation, and I don't much care. It's possible Lady Nankivell left when she found out about it. If so, I hope she still has some control over her fortune. I'd hate to think how much of *his* wife's money Nankivell spent on that diamond necklace for mine."

Sophie stared at him, aghast. "The necklace? The one in your dream?"

His eyes were winter-cold, his mouth crooked in a mirthless half smile. "She was wearing it when I caught them together. The necklace—and nothing else."

"Oh." The single appalled syllable was all Sophie could manage at that. She wished fervently for a cup of tea herself—or a glass of something considerably stronger.

"Nankivell's idea. From what little I heard before interrupting them, he enjoys seeing his mistresses wearing his gifts during—intimacy. It satisfies his sense of proprietorship." Robin's mouth twisted wryly. "Adding my wife to their number was particularly gratifying for him."

Sophie shuddered. "Hateful man."

Robin shrugged. "He's not worth hating—not really. As far as I'm concerned, he's welcome to Nathalie's favors, and I don't doubt she was a willing participant. Possibly even the instigator. The irony is that in seeking to serve me another ill turn, he actually handed me the key to my cage. Doubtless it would gall him if he knew."

"And Nathalie herself? Do you think she loves him?"

"I doubt it. More likely it was sport for her—taking another lover, right under my nose *and* under my roof this time." Robin's voice hardened. "Well, she can have all the lovers she wants now, and I'll even grant her an annuity toward a separate household, but I'm done with this sham of a marriage. I won't live like this any longer!"

He broke off then, struggling to contain his anger—anger

that was all the more intense for being held on such a tight rein these last four years, Sophie realized. She covered his hand with her own, and after a moment, he turned his hand palm up and twined their fingers together.

"I want an end to this," he said more calmly. "An end to bitterness and resentment, mine *and* hers. This arrangement benefits no one anymore, not even Sara." His eyes, clear unclouded blue, met Sophie's. "And I want a fresh start with the woman I love."

"You have it." She drew their linked hands up to her lips and kissed his fingers. "And you have me. The rest will come in time, Robin. We'll simply wait it out, together."

"Together," he agreed, his mouth softening into a genuine smile this time. "That's becoming one of my favorite words."

"Mine too." She smiled back. "Now, let me get breakfast ready, and then we can take on the world. Or go for a walk in the woods, if you prefer."

He released her hand. "The woods, I think. The world can wait a few more days."

"So it can," Sophie agreed, sobered afresh by the reminder of how short this respite was.

So, make the most of it. Pushing back her chair, she asked brightly, "Bacon or fried ham with the eggs?"

❧

Four days, one for each year they'd spent apart. That was how Sophie came to think of it afterward. Four days in which they lived only for love and each other. Rising when they chose, fixing themselves a leisurely breakfast in the cottage kitchen. Walks in the woods, or down to Wyldean itself, a charming village made up of yellow stone buildings, like the manor and the cottage. And talking about everything under the sun, from weighty subjects like politics and the state of the world to the more intimate and personal matters that concerned only themselves.

The staff at Wyldean Hall seemed to have a sixth sense about when to visit the cottage. Or perhaps they were merely respecting the tenant's expressed wish for privacy. In any case, Sophie and Robin would return from their rambles to find that the rooms had been cleaned, the beds freshly made up, and more food delivered in their absence, but no sign of any person in sight. It was like living in a fairy tale, Sophie told Robin, in which one was waited on by elves or invisible servants.

"And their invisibility must be respected," she added lightly, "or the enchantment ends, and everything will vanish in a clap of thunder."

"*This* enchantment will last, I promise you," Robin said, and kissed her until fairy tales were the furthest thing from her mind.

Sometimes Robin played the upright piano in the parlor. He'd acquired a measure of competence that surprised her. "Music was a way of keeping in touch with you," he explained. "And Sara is learning to play now, herself."

And Sophie would sing—not opera, but the less demanding, though still beautiful, songs she'd learned as a girl. Some of them he knew as well, and they would sing together, her soprano mixing with his passable baritone.

There were books in the parlor. Not many, to be sure, but a pleasant enough collection of novels, poetry, and even a few volumes of history. Occasionally they read aloud to each other, although Robin teased her for her choice of reading material on the train. "I never imagined you'd acquire a taste for sensation novels!"

"Detective novels," she corrected him. "Much more respectable, and some of them are quite ingenious too. In any case, I needed something to entertain myself with during my travels. David introduced me to Lewis Wells's work when we last toured together. Apparently he's well-acquainted with the author." She fingered the binding of her book. "Conan

Doyle's Sherlock Holmes is more brilliant, but Mr. Wells's detective is more human, which I rather like. Mind you, my *first* preference is for a good romance—with a happy ending, of course."

Robin's eyes warmed. "I'll see what I can do about that," he said, drawing her closer to him on the sofa.

One afternoon, surprised by a rainstorm while out walking, they hurried back to the cottage and built up a fire to drive away the chill, curling up together on the hearth rug to watch the cheerful blaze.

Warm and secure in Robin's encircling arms, Sophie said, "Tell me about your children."

He pulled back a little, looked searchingly at her. "Do you truly want to know?"

Sophie smiled her reassurance. "Why wouldn't I? Sara is your daughter, and in the eyes of the world, Cyril was your son. More important, he was the son of your heart, and I can tell that you grieved—and still grieve—for him."

"Thank you." Robin's expression eased, though she could see the sorrow in his eyes.

After a while, he said, "The doctor told me we were always living on borrowed time with Cyril. But he had so much love to give, perhaps because he sensed he'd so little time to give it. I won't say he was an angel—he had bad days, when he was peevish and hard to please, and I know he'd have given much to be strong and active, like James and Aurelia's son."

A wistful smile tugged at his mouth. "But they managed to be friends just the same. Whenever Jared came to visit, he brought toys and books to share. Cyril was as bright as a button, and he loved to be read to. Sara would sit beside him with her books and try to share her lessons with him."

"So they were close."

"Very much so—just as a brother and sister should be. And they enjoyed many of the same things, like the sea."

Robin's eyes had gone dreamy, even distant. "Sometimes I would wrap Cyril in blankets, put him and Sara in the carriage, and drive down to the beach. Sara would look for shells, and Cyril would just sit and watch the water, the waves coming in and out. And the boats—he always dreamed of going to sea. Last summer I managed to take him and Sara aboard James's new yacht a time or two, just for a gentle sail round the harbor."

"They must have loved that."

"They did. And no *mal de mer*, either," Robin said, with a hint of pride in his voice. "Cyril turned out to be a natural sailor. Sara was a little queasy at first, but she was fine once she got her sea legs."

Where had Nathalie been in this? Sophie wondered. Had she accompanied Robin and the children on their outings? For that matter, how involved had she been in her children's lives from day to day? The questions crowded on her tongue, but she swallowed them back, not wanting to upset Robin; Nathalie was already a sore subject for him.

He was still speaking, his thoughts, like his gaze, a million miles away. "By autumn, he'd grown too frail for such outings, so I bought some watercolors of the ocean and hung them in the nursery, where he could see them from his bed. Sara brought him shells—scallops and whelks. And James and Aurelia gave him a conch for his fourth birthday, so he could hear the sea.

"On his last night… he fell asleep listening to it."

Robin's voice caught. Sophie turned and wrapped her arms around him, drawing his head down to her shoulder. He shuddered once, then stilled, but she could tell from the rhythm of his breathing that he was fighting back tears.

Four years ago, she'd resented Nathalie bitterly, and she'd resented the idea of those children, links between Robin and his estranged wife that could not be severed. And yet, at the last, she had managed not to resent those children themselves.

Hearing now of Robin's love for them, she could only be glad that they'd had the father they deserved.

He raised his head at last, thrust a hand across his eyes. "Forgive me, I still—"

"Don't apologize," Sophie broke in vehemently. "Don't ever apologize for loving that little boy! I think you made all the difference in his life, and I'm glad, truly glad, that you had each other."

Robin leaned his forehead against hers. "I am glad it was peaceful for him at the end. That he didn't suffer. And when I think of him now, I like to imagine him as the man he might have become, if fate were kinder. Strong, hearty, sailing the seven seas…" He exhaled slowly. "Sara was devastated, even though we tried to warn her about Cyril's condition. How can you truly explain death to a seven-year-old?"

"*A simple child, / That lightly draws its breath, / And feels its life in every limb, / What should it know of death?*" Sophie quoted, stroking his cheek. "She must miss him terribly."

"She does. I think she's the one who mothered him, more than Nathalie ever did. She hasn't been sleeping well since he was lost. She's a grave little thing, my Sara, and she's had to grow up far too fast. I did not want her exposed to the friction between Nathalie and myself, not after everything else she has endured." Robin looked up, more composed now. "I'm hoping that her stay at Pentreath will help her heal. James and Aurelia have an excellent nursemaid who was willing to look after Sara along with the other two. And Sara enjoys playing with Jared, and Aurelia lets her help with baby Alexandra sometimes."

"I am so glad you've become such good friends with James and Aurelia."

"So am I. Harry and I still consider ourselves friends, but things were strained between us for a while after you left Cornwall."

"I know." Sophie's mother had written of the ongoing

tension between Harry and Robin. Judging from more recent letters, Sophie had inferred that they were on better terms nowadays, but perhaps more guarded with each other than they'd formerly been. "Well, I hope you can patch them up now. Especially since you're going to be making an honest woman of me at last."

Robin huffed a small laugh. "Harry would probably say it was the other way round—you'd be making an honest man of me. Emphasis on the word 'honest.'"

"Hush, that's in the past now," Sophie reproved. "And no one can deny that you've conducted yourself openly *and* honestly since Nathalie returned."

"Thank you. It hasn't been easy, but I have tried to balance honesty with discretion—there's no benefit to airing our dirty linen before the county." His face grew somber. He rubbed the back of his neck. "I've asked James and Aurelia not to tell Sara about the divorce. Such news is best coming from a father. And I don't wholly abandon hope that Nathalie and I can come to some sort of—arrangement."

Given what she'd heard, Sophie had her doubts, but she kept them to herself.

Robin sighed. "I don't hate her, Sophie. Not even now. Although there were times in the last four years... but she's Sara's mother, and she grieved for Cyril, in her way. It was a sorrow we shared, at least for a little while. I even thought we could..." He broke off, shaking his head.

"Go on," Sophie prompted.

He ran a hand through his hair. "Well, I wondered if we could—not reconcile, exactly, that was never in the cards—but find a way to be *kinder* to each other. I'd thought perhaps we might travel up to Yorkshire as a family, have Sara meet my mother's kin. They'd love her—and they'd have been courteous to Nathalie, if only for my sake. However... other things came to light before I could even make the suggestion."

The affair with Nankivell, Sophie translated without difficulty.

Robin's mouth twisted in a wry half smile. "So, that was that—the end of the last illusion. Or simply the end, if you prefer." He sighed again. "I've heard it said that the opposite of love isn't hate but indifference. And that is mostly what I've felt for Nathalie these last four years. Hardly an incentive to remain in a marriage, even one such as ours. We both deserve better."

Sophie wondered if Nathalie would have preferred Robin's hate to his indifference, but that was perhaps too dark an insight to share. "Well, if you do not hate her, then I can manage not to hate her too," she replied instead. "Life is too short for that."

Robin's arms tightened around her. "No looking back?"

"No looking back," Sophie agreed, nestling her head on his shoulder.

∽

Four… three… two… one. The days flew past like birds on the wing. Robin wished he could catch them all in their flight, to live them over again.

And now it was their last night in this refuge. Tomorrow loomed large for them both: the return to London lay ahead… and so did their inevitable parting. Even knowing the latter was temporary did not ease the ache in their hearts.

But at my back I always hear, / Time's wingéd chariot hurrying near…

Slim and pliant as a willow, she rose over him in the bed. "Let *me* make love to *you*, dear heart." Her smile was as enchanting as Circe's and as old as Eve's. "You'll enjoy it, I promise."

Intrigued, Robin acquiesced, then watched, marveling, as she straddled him, one knee on either side of his hips. In the lamplight, she seemed lit from within, her ivory skin luminous as the pearls he'd given her, her dark hair showing glints of chestnut and copper as it rippled over her bare shoulders. No erotic fantasy in which he'd ever indulged could match the reality of *her*.

Now she curled her hand about his rearing shaft, stroking up and down its length. Even through the condom, he felt the heat of her palm, and his loins ached with need. It took all his restraint not to seize her by the waist and tumble her onto the mattress beneath him. Instead, he reached up to stroke the undersides of her breasts, brush the rose-brown nipples until they hardened into stiff little peaks.

Sophie closed her eyes, gave a pleased little hum low in her throat. "Patience, my love," she murmured, then angling her hips, she lowered herself onto him by exquisitely slow degrees. Inch by inch, until all his length was tightly sheathed in moist feminine heat.

Robin sucked in air as arousal pulsed through him. "My God, Sophie…"

But she was nowhere near finished with him. Instead, she began to move, raising and lowering herself repeatedly, building up a delicious friction that spread outward from their joined bodies like ripples in a pond. Stifling a groan of impatience, Robin grasped her hips and urged her onward, faster and faster, until they reached the peak, the world flashing white around them.

She climaxed first, head flung back, gasping, triggering his release seconds later. They cried out together—and then she was falling, toppling like a felled tree, but he was there to catch her and enfold her close.

Shuddering, he wrapped his arms around her, burying his damp face in her hair. Her body still rippled and shook in the grip of her orgasm. Fascinated, he pulled back to watch her face, glowing and transfigured in its ecstasy. Full of surprises, his Sophie. Much as he'd adored the girl, he found himself continually challenged and delighted by the woman. A lifetime might not be enough to uncover all her mysteries, but he meant to have the time of his life exploring them.

Afterward, they lay entwined and talked of this and that, as lovers will. Inevitably, the subject of tomorrow's journey arose. They'd already been down to the village to hire a carriage that would take them to the railway station. If all went as it should, they would arrive in London by late morning. Robin could collect the papers from his solicitor and catch an afternoon train to Cornwall—a far longer journey, but he would reach home by nightfall.

"You could stay here at the cottage, you know, instead of going to London," Robin suggested. "You do have it until the end of the week, at least."

Sophie shook her head. "I don't want us to part a moment before we must. And it will be too lonely without you." She smiled tremulously. "All the memories we've made here! The cottage will surely be haunted by them."

"Ah, if these walls could talk." Robin played with a curling lock of her hair. "So, where shall you go instead?"

"Well, I shan't stay long in London, not after telling everyone who wished to engage me that I was going on holiday. Perhaps," she ventured, "I might go and visit Cecily in Veryan? That way I would still be in Cornwall, but far enough away not to cause problems while you and Nathalie are discussing the divorce."

His heart leapt at the thought of her being in the same county, even if propriety dictated that they keep apart for now. "I would be very glad to have you even that close. But only if you are willing to make the move."

"I'm resolved to do my part in keeping the situation as civilized as possible."

"I appreciate that, but keeping things civilized will be largely my responsibility, and I cannot guarantee success," he warned. "Nathalie may well pitch the tea service at my head."

"Have you thought of asking your solicitor to come

down to Cornwall?" Sophie asked. "I've heard there's nothing like the presence of lawyers for ensuring a professional atmosphere."

"You have a point, love. I'll take it under advisement. Now," he added, running a caressing hand down her side, "as this is our last night here, I refuse to spend another moment thinking about lawyers, divorces, or anything except you, me, and our time together."

She dimpled at him, once more the carefree girl he remembered. "*Carpe diem*?"

"*Carpe noctem*," he corrected, and kissed her.

Later, as she slept beside him, he thought of one other thing he'd meant to give her.

Something that, like the pearls, he had kept in his vault in London and meant only for her. But the time was not quite right for that, he sensed. And he did not want to foredoom the moment by acting too precipitately. Better to wait until he was truly free to offer that last gift. When he could call her affianced wife not just in the eyes of God, but in the eyes of the world.

❧

They left at first light, just as they had planned. From Witney to Oxford, Oxford to London—the train connections were made quickly and easily.

Sophie dozed with her head on Robin's shoulder, lulled by the rhythmic clacking of the train's wheels, bearing them closer to their final destination. He shook her gently awake as the engine pulled into Paddington.

"This isn't the first time I've fallen asleep on you," she observed, sitting up and stifling a yawn. "After this past week, you must be getting weary of it."

Robin smiled. "Perhaps after forty years I will. But for now, I find it infinitely comforting, because it means you're *here*, with me."

They collected their valises and stepped out onto the fog-shrouded platform, hoping to locate a hackney.

"Sophie. Pendarvis."

Sophie almost jumped out of her skin at the disembodied voice emerging from the fog. Peering through the mist, she saw a tall figure striding toward them. With a shock, she recognized Thomas Sheridan, but his face was drawn and grimmer than she'd ever seen it.

Dread gripped Sophie's heart. If anything had happened to Amy or little Bella...

"Sheridan?" Robin sounded puzzled. "What are you doing here? Is something amiss?"

"I'm afraid so," Sheridan replied. "A telegram's come, not two hours ago, from Cornwall." He hesitated a moment, then grasped Robin's arm. "There's no easy way to tell you, Pendarvis. Your wife has been murdered."

Sixteen

Cover her face. Mine eyes dazzle. She died young.

—John Webster, *The Duchess of Malfi*

ONCE AGAIN SOPHIE EMBARKED UPON A RAILWAY journey she could remember nothing about afterward. Well, nearly nothing… she remembered Robin, pale as a ghost beside her, his mouth set like stone, and his eyes as far away as his thoughts clearly were.

The news of his wife's death had stunned them both. No question of an accident, illness, or even a suicide, in this case. According to the telegram and the subsequent telephone conversation Thomas had had with James, someone had choked the life out of Nathalie Pendarvis the previous night. Her hysterical lady's maid had discovered the body in the morning, lying crumpled beside her dressing table. Most of Nathalie's jewels were missing, suggesting that she had surprised a thief at his work.

Robin's face had grown greyer with every detail he'd absorbed, but speech had seemed beyond him just then. Sheridan had instantly borne him and Sophie off to Sheridan House, where Amy had plied them with food and strong black coffee, insisting they break their fast before undertaking the necessary arrangements. Two hours later, their trunks packed and the Pendarvis Hotel informed of Robin's imminent return, he and Sophie were aboard the Sheridans' private railway coach, bound for Cornwall.

Sophie longed to say something comforting, but all that came to mind were soulless platitudes. Her rival, Robin's wife, the mother of his child, was suddenly and horribly dead. What could she possibly say that wouldn't sound banal, insincere, or worst of all, ghoulish?

In the end she settled for saying nothing, but remained close beside him throughout the four-hour journey. At least he had accepted her presence. Once his initial shock had worn off, he had tried to persuade her to remain in London, shielded from the ugliness that awaited him in Cornwall, but she'd flatly refused to let him make this terrible passage alone. This wasn't the way they'd expected or wanted it to happen, but they were a couple now, for better or for worse.

It was late afternoon when they arrived in Newquay, and a carriage was already waiting for them at the station. They got on in silence, and were soon driving through the gates of the Pendarvis Hotel. Glancing out the window, Sophie saw a man standing on the front steps and recognized him, with a shock, as her eldest brother.

The moment the carriage door opened, Harry was there, his face strained and anxious.

"Thank God you're here, Rob." The words tumbled out of him. "I'm so sorry—"

Robin held up a hand and climbed down from the carriage. "Where is she?"

"Upstairs—in her chamber." Harry swallowed, as distraught as Sophie had ever seen him. "I wasn't sure what to do. Whether to have her remains taken to the mortuary—or leave her where she was until you came. Because you are still her husband, in spite of—" He broke off, his whole face changing as he caught sight of his sister alighting in Robin's wake. "Good God, Sophie, what are *you* doing here?"

"I was present when Robin received the news," Sophie replied evenly. "So I traveled down with him. I felt he should not make such a journey alone."

She could almost see the questions forming on Harry's tongue, but after a moment's visible struggle, he capitulated. "No, of course not. I'm—glad you had one of us there to support you," he added to Robin, stepping back so the coachman could unload the trunks.

Robin glanced at Sophie, his bleak gaze warming fractionally. "Miss Tresilian was a great comfort to me" was all he said, before turning back to his partner. "You did the right thing, Harry—I wouldn't have wanted Nathalie moved, not until I had the chance to see her. I assume the police are here?"

"Two constables, a sergeant, and an Inspector Taunton, sent over from Newquay," Harry confirmed. "They're waiting inside. With the coroner."

"Do our guests know of this?" Robin asked. His professional facade was firmly in place, Sophie saw: the hotelier whose first concern was the safety and comfort of his guests.

Harry nodded. "No way of avoiding it, I'm afraid. A few wanted to depart the moment they heard, but cooler heads prevailed. Besides, Taunton's confined all the guests to the premises until things are more—resolved." He passed a weary hand over his face. "Praed and I have been trying to keep them calm and contained. Mrs. Dowling has been doing the same with the staff. *They're* all at sixes and sevens, especially that wretched maid—" He broke off, jerked his head toward the steps, where a sandy-haired man in a plain overcoat was now standing, flanked by his subordinates.

"Mr. Pendarvis?" the sandy-haired man inquired.

Robin nodded. "I am he."

"Inspector Taunton," the other man identified himself. "I am sorry for your loss."

"Thank you," Robin returned levelly, his expression giving nothing away.

"I regret the necessity of this," Taunton continued, "but would you be so good as to accompany me—upstairs?"

Robin did not hesitate. "Of course," he said, and followed the inspector into the hotel.

Sophie watched him go, her heart aching for him. However well he hid it, she knew this loss was a blow for him. And he would have to break this terrible news to his daughter too…

Beside her, Harry cleared his throat. "Sophie, what were you—"

"Not now, Harry. Robin's situation is what matters. Everything else can wait," she added, not ungently, as she turned to look at him—the beloved older brother who'd been almost a father to her after their own father's untimely death. As a child, she'd eagerly sought his approval and good opinion. She would always love and respect him. But she was of age now, a grown woman who made her own choices and was not obliged to answer for them, even to her family.

Something of that realization flickered across Harry's face as he studied her, taking in her subdued but fashionable traveling dress, her modish hat, and, perhaps most persuasive of all, the added inch or two of height she'd attained in the last four years. "Very well," he conceded with a sigh that told her how much strain he was under at present. "But we *will* speak of this, later."

"Of course." Sophie paused, then held out her hands. "It's good to see you, Harry. I've missed you and everyone else dreadfully."

He gave her a lopsided smile and took her hands, squeezing them gently. "I've missed you too, Snip. Welcome home."

No one who has been strangled is ever beautiful.

Robin stared down at the body, laid out carefully upon the bed. For a mercy, someone had closed Nathalie's eyes and mouth so her tongue did not protrude, but her face was still congested and livid, and the reddened abrasion around the tender skin of her throat—where a garrote of some sort had been wound and then pulled fatally tight—betrayed just how determined her killer had been. When Robin's mother had died so many years ago, she'd looked for a time as if she were merely sleeping. Nathalie looked dead.

The worst thing was that he could still recognize the woman he'd married in this pallid corpse. The silver-gilt ringlets, the triangular shape of her face, the dainty figure—all were horribly familiar. So were the pretty hands, now piously crossed upon her breast—he remembered how they'd used to flutter, like little white birds, when she was excited. Strange to see them so still now. She wore no rings, not even a wedding band, and the ink stains on her right middle and index fingers stood out dark as bruises against her porcelain fair skin. She'd kept a diary—*un journal*—when she was a young girl. He wondered suddenly if she still did… had… What could it matter now? Whatever essence or spirit that had made Nathalie who and what she was had gone forever.

He was faintly surprised that he did not feel sick. Perhaps that would come later, when the reality of what he was seeing had finally sunk in. The younger of the two constables looked slightly green about the mouth, though his colleagues appeared to be made of sterner stuff.

"Sir?" the older constable prompted.

Robin suppressed a shiver, feeling cold and somehow insubstantial—almost as if he were dead himself, and it was his spirit standing there, identifying Nathalie's remains. Forcing that gruesome thought away, he straightened up. "Yes, that is—was—my wife. Nathalie Pendarvis."

His voice sounded very far away in his own ears. At a

nod from Taunton, the coroner drew the sheet up over Nathalie's face.

Robin exhaled slowly and turned away from the bed, trying to focus on something—anything—else. In their four years of uneasy coexistence, he had entered Nathalie's chamber no more than a handful of times, usually on some matter pertaining to the children. Now his gaze swept restlessly over the room: the pale blue wallpaper, the even paler blue window curtains, the gilt chair lying overturned before the white-draped dressing table… a stark reminder of how and where she'd met her death. His mind shied away from that as from an open grave, and he registered with relief the sound of a throat being cleared, a reminder that he was *not* alone.

"Mr. Pendarvis." Taunton exchanged a glance with his sergeant. "Will you come down to the police station and give us your statement? There are some questions we wish to ask you."

Robin took a breath and said evenly, "I will answer whatever questions you have, but not today. I have been traveling for the last four hours. I have a hotel to run, guests to reassure and, most important of all," he held Taunton's gaze, "a daughter who doesn't yet know that her mother is dead. My place is with *her* now."

"Understood." Taunton inclined his head. "Tomorrow morning will be soon enough. Meanwhile, have we your permission to remove…" He gestured toward the bed and its shrouded occupant.

Robin nodded. "You do."

Steeling himself, he turned and watched without flinching as the woman who'd once borne his name and honor, only to shame them both, departed from Pendarvis Hall forever.

⁓

"Robin." Sophie touched his hand, felt a flash of alarm at how cold it was. "Dear heart, you must eat something," she cajoled.

They were sitting alone, in his private parlor, a plate of sandwiches and a pot of tea before them. Robin had just got back from consulting with Praed and Mr. Pascoe, the concierge, on how to handle this crisis at the hotel. Meanwhile, Harry was continuing to soothe and reassure the most anxious guests that this tragedy was an isolated incident, not a harbinger of future mayhem. Moreover, it had occurred not in the hotel itself but in the private residential part of the Hall, where the security was far lighter. And the police had been on the scene all day, searching for evidence to identify Mrs. Pendarvis's killer.

Sobered by the reminder of the victim's identity, the guests were quick to express their sympathy for their host and willing to cooperate with Taunton's request—for now, at least. Sophie had remained discreetly in the background, letting her lover and her brother handle their business and clientele as they saw fit. From what she heard and saw, however, she gathered that the hotel staff respected "the master" and Sir Harry highly, and were doing their best to help them through this "dreadful business." What any of them felt toward Nathalie she could not begin to guess, although she had not witnessed any great outpouring of grief thus far, more a sense of general disquiet and distress than any personal loss.

To Sophie's surprise and gratification, some of the staff recognized and remembered her—perhaps even with affection. So when she asked for tea and sandwiches to be sent up to the master's parlor for his return, her request had been speedily granted.

Robin had appeared soon after, composed but still ashen. Sophie did not think he'd had normal color in his face since he'd first got the news. Sustenance was called for—hours had passed since the breakfast Amy had pressed upon them, and he'd eaten little enough of that. So she poured out a cup of tea, added sugar liberally, and set it before him, then piled a plate with three sandwiches—not bite-sized cucumber and cress dainties, but hearty constructions of ham and roast beef on thick new bread—and handed that over as well.

Still dazed, he stared down at the plate. "I don't know if I can—"

"You *must* eat," Sophie broke in sternly. "You'll need your strength if you're to be of any use to your daughter."

Robin roused at that and took the topmost sandwich, slanting her a guilty glance. "I'm a rank coward, my love," he confessed. "I told Taunton that my place was with my daughter, and yet, here I am, no closer to Pentreath than I was half an hour ago."

Sophie touched his arm. "No one can blame you for not rushing to tell her *this*. Or for taking the time to—find the right words. If they even exist," she qualified with a wry smile. "But in my experience, bad news can usually wait. Take a little time now, for yourself."

He nodded, took a listless bite of his sandwich, and then another as hunger suddenly revived. Devouring the rest of it, he reached for a second and was halfway through that when Harry walked in, looking almost as weary as Robin. Unlike Robin, he required no urging to take some refreshment, falling upon the sandwiches like a man who hadn't seen food for a week.

"Things appear to have settled down, for now," he reported around a mouthful of ham and cheese. "Of course it helps that the police appear to have left for now, and that none of the guests appear to be under suspicion."

Robin took a sip of tea, blinked as though registering its sweetness for the first time, but swallowed anyway. "Praed tells me their movements are accounted for last night?"

"Surprisingly, yes. They were all abed when it happened, and the staff as well. Not that I *want* anyone here to have done this," Harry added hastily. "But if not them, then…" His voice trailed off and he shook his head.

"Then who?" Robin finished for him, his mouth twisting in a parody of a smile.

Sophie suppressed a shiver and drank some tea herself. *Who, indeed?* If no one—guest or staff—on the premises had killed Nathalie, then it *must* be an intruder. Perhaps a thief, as had been previously suggested—and the missing jewels seemed to bear out that theory. But why only Nathalie's? Surely there were women staying at the hotel who owned more costly jewels and valuables. Unless the thief had known Robin's wing of the Hall was essentially unguarded...

"—Dowling's got a bit more sense out of Enid, the lady's maid." Harry's voice broke into her thoughts. "I don't know how much stock to put in what she says, she was still half-hysterical at the time, but... she claims she heard a sound coming from her mistress's chamber last night and got up to investigate."

Sophie tensed in her chair, her attention now fully engaged. Beside her, Robin's gaze sharpened. "She did?"

"She says," Harry resumed slowly, "that she opened the connecting door, just a crack—and saw a tall, thin man standing behind Nathalie's chair, throttling her."

Robin's breath hissed between his teeth. "Christ! Why didn't she—"

"She fainted," Harry said succinctly. "And she was unsteady on her pins as it was. Nathalie had dismissed her early because she had a toothache—Enid, I mean—and she dosed herself with some tonic that had laudanum in it. I'm surprised she could see straight at all, much less through a barely open door in the dark. When she came to, it was morning, and she thought she'd been dreaming or hallucinating, but—" He broke off, grimacing.

"Has she told the police any of this?" Sophie asked.

Harry nodded. "Once she was halfway coherent, Mrs. Dowling had her talk to the sergeant about what she saw—or thought she saw. Pity she only saw the fellow from the back, but it's a start, I suppose."

"Not much of one, though," Sophie observed with a sigh. "Cornwall and the rest of the world are full of tall, thin men."

Robin's mouth crooked. "*I* see one whenever I look in the glass."

"You're not a suspect," Sophie said sharply.

"Not yet, perhaps." He set his now-empty plate aside. "But Inspector Taunton wishes me to come down to the police station tomorrow morning and give a statement."

"Well, you should have all the proof you need to show you were elsewhere at the time," she said bracingly. "And the word of others to back you up, including the Sheridans and myself."

Much to her disquiet, his face had taken on that too-familiar shuttered look. "Thank you, my dear. But I hope they won't require too much evidence to establish my whereabouts when—when Nathalie was killed." He stood up abruptly. "I must go to Pentreath now, while there's still some daylight left."

"For God's sake, take the carriage, Rob!" Harry ordered. "After today, the last thing you should be doing is making the trip on horseback. And if Sara needs you to stay, then do it. *I* can stop over at the hotel tonight—once I take Sophie home, that is."

Sophie nodded at Robin's questioning glance. "I'll be all right with Harry. Go and see your daughter, dear heart."

He could not kiss her, not with Harry present. But the warmth in his eyes, the faint smile he gave her, was all the caress she needed for now.

"Thank you. Both of you," he added, including Harry in his gaze. "At times like these, it's good to know how fortunate I am in my friends."

James and Aurelia were sitting on the sofa together when their butler, Pelham, showed Robin into the family parlor at Pentreath. Aurelia rose to embrace him.

"James has just told me everything. I'm so sorry, Robin. What can we do?"

Fortunate in his friends, indeed. "You've done so much for me already," Robin said, returning her embrace. "And for Sara. She hasn't heard anything, has she?"

Aurelia exchanged a glance with James. "Not that we know of. After Harry gave us the news, I made a point of keeping the children at Pentreath today. We didn't go into the village or any place where Sara might hear accidentally."

Robin nodded tautly. "Thank you for having her—and for shielding her from this until I came. But I need to see her now."

"I'll go up to the nursery and bring her down at once." Aurelia touched his shoulder in passing as she headed for the door. "You're staying here tonight," she added, in a tone that brooked no argument. "I'll have a bedchamber made ready for you."

Robin knew better than to resist. "Thank you."

Once they were alone, James crossed to the sideboard and poured Robin a stiff whiskey. "Here. You look like you could use this."

Robin tried to smile. "What, no cider?"

"A crisis like this requires something a good deal stronger." James handed him the glass. "An ugly business, murder. How are you holding up?"

Robin took a gulp of whiskey, almost welcoming the burn. "As you see. Shaken but still standing. I have to be, for Sara's sake."

"That doesn't mean you have to deny your own feelings," James pointed out. "I know you and Nathalie have been living essentially separate lives, but she was your wife, after all."

"And Sara and Cyril's mother. I don't forget that." Robin took another drink. "I wanted to divorce her, James. But I never wished her dead, least of all murdered."

James laid a hand on his shoulder. "I know you didn't. Are the police giving you any trouble? They were still questioning people when I left the hotel two hours ago."

Robin shook his head. "Not so far. But I'm to come down to the station tomorrow, for further questioning."

"I should think you had an ironclad alibi, being in London all this time," James observed.

Not all this time, Robin thought, remembering those four blissful days in Oxfordshire. But it was true he'd been far from Cornwall when Nathalie was killed. "Sophie thinks so too."

"Sophie?" James's gaze sharpened. "She's in Cornwall?"

Robin chose his next words carefully. "I—saw her after a concert in London, and we spent some time together. She was with me when I received the news about Nathalie." Was it really only this morning? "And she thought I shouldn't make the journey alone."

James regarded him narrowly. "Am I to infer that you and Sophie are…?"

"It wasn't planned, James," Robin said quickly. "We weren't together by design. Before Nathalie—did what she did, I'd no plans to go to London. I'd half forgotten about Sophie's concert when I arrived. My sole thought was how to be free of my marriage at last. But once I knew… I had to see her. I had to know if there was any kind of future for us."

James's expression softened into compassion. "I know how much the two of you cared for each other. And how hard it was to separate, when Nathalie came back."

"I never dreamed she'd give me another chance," Robin confessed. "When I saw her again, I half expected her to tell me it was finished between us. That she'd found someone else, or that she preferred to concentrate on her career. But I couldn't let it be, James. I had to know, one way or the other."

"Hope is a very different thing from expectation," James observed. "But from the sound of it, you forgot the family legacy."

"Not for long. *Swans and Tresilians mate for life*," Robin quoted. "And God bless them for it." He sighed. "I just wish I could protect her from this. When I first heard the news, I tried to persuade her to stay in London. She wouldn't have it."

"Of course not. If I know her, she's trying to work out how to protect *you*."

Robin raked a hand through his hair. "She shouldn't have to. This is my disaster. If I'd handled things differently four years ago—"

"You did what you thought best at the time. And I know it couldn't have been easy to choose between Sophie and your children. Perhaps you made the wrong decision, perhaps not, but you have another chance to get it right. Not everyone is so fortunate. And don't underestimate Sophie," he added. "She's always been much stronger than she appears. So is my Aurelia, and I couldn't have got through what happened five years ago without her support."

For a moment, their thoughts sped back to that fateful summer, when they'd both faced ugly slanders implicating them in the violent death of James's cousin and predecessor.

"If Sophie wants to stand by you, let her," James told him. "You ignore women at your peril, especially when they're as determined as *ours* are."

Ours. So James had accepted that he and Sophie were together. Robin feared the rest of her family would be less receptive when they heard. He might no longer be a married man, but being a possible suspect in his wife's murder was hardly an improvement in his circumstances.

"As you may remember, I've been in your shoes," James

continued, as though reading his mind. "And Aurelia's faith in me then meant the world. *All* of my in-laws were supportive, and I thanked God for them before the end." He paused. "Harry and Aunt Isobel will be on your side, Robin. Whatever reservations they may have about you and Sophie resuming your relationship, they would never believe you capable of murdering Nathalie."

The door opened then, and Aurelia came in, leading Robin's daughter by the hand.

The girl's face brightened when she saw him. "Papa!"

Robin knelt at once, and Sara flew into his arms. "I missed you so much, Papa!"

"I missed you too, sweetheart." He stroked her hair, the same dark brown as his own, but with a natural wave that was entirely hers. "Have you been a good child?"

"Sara's always good as gold," Aurelia told him.

"It's been ever so nice here." Sara smiled up at her father. "We go down to the beach almost every day, and I picked up some beautiful new shells. And Jared and I found a sand crab, but we let him go. And I started reading *Through the Looking-Glass*—could you teach me how to play chess someday?"

Robin sighed inwardly, wishing he didn't have to shatter his daughter's newfound contentment. This was the most animated he'd seen her since Cyril's death. "Of course, sweetheart, though I must admit, I'm not very good at it." He stroked her hair again, as much to comfort himself as her. "I'm—very glad you've been enjoying your stay here. But… there's something I need to tell you now."

By this time, James and Aurelia had withdrawn discreetly, leaving father and daughter alone together. They wouldn't have gone far, Robin knew—they'd be lurking just out of earshot, ready to help in any way they could.

"What, Papa?" His daughter's gaze was infinitely trusting.

"Sara, sweetheart." Robin swallowed, hating what he had to do. "I'm afraid I have some very bad news." He tightened his arms around her. "It appears that there was a robbery at the hotel, while I was in London, and your mother was killed."

She paled, her eyes going wide and frightened. "*Maman* is—dead? Like Cyril?"

Her slight body was trembling like a sapling in a gale. "I'm afraid so."

Sara's breath caught, tears welling in her eyes, but her gaze was fixed on his. "Was it—was it quick?"

Oh, God. For a moment Robin saw Nathalie's congested face, the livid marks on her throat. "I don't know, my darling. Let us hope it was, and that *Maman* didn't suffer." Although he knew that she must have, fighting for breath, struggling against her attacker. But he would not burden Sara with the image.

Tears spilled down Sara's cheeks but she brushed them away, almost absently. "Do you think she's in heaven now, with Cyril?"

Robin forced the words past the tightness in his throat. "I am sure of it, my dear. If heaven is what it is meant to be, then your mother and brother must be together. And you and I are here, together, and we must be strong and comfort each other."

She nodded, then buried her head in his shoulder and wept as she clung to him. Not in the same passion of grief with which she'd received news of Cyril's death, but in confusion and bewilderment that were no less real.

"I'm here, darling. Papa is here." He heard his voice crack, felt the hot press of tears in his own eyes. Not so much for Nathalie, whom he'd lost long ago, but for the pain their child, the last link between them, was suffering now.

After a time, her sobs eased, and he gave her his handkerchief. Obediently, she wiped her eyes, blew her nose, and asked in a quavering little voice, "Am I to—to come home now, Papa?"

"Not just yet, sweetheart," he told her. "I want you with

me, of course, but the police are going over the hotel to see if they can find anything that might help them catch whoever killed *Maman*. So I would like you to stay here with Lord and Lady Trevenan until it's quite safe for you to return to Pendarvis Hall."

She nodded. "Will you stay here too?"

"I'll be here tonight, certainly," he promised. "And perhaps a few nights beyond that, if the Trevenans are willing to have me. But in any case, I shall visit you every day and make sure to kiss you good night—even in the middle of the afternoon."

She gave a small watery giggle, then looked a little shocked at herself for having done so. Robin dropped a kiss upon her head for reassurance. "There's my brave girl."

Her answering smile was still a faint, trembly thing, but genuine enough for all that. Hugging her close, Robin vowed silently that he would do all he could to find Nathalie's killer and see him brought to justice. Their daughter deserved nothing less.

Seventeen

In all the woes that curse our race
There is a lady in the case.

—W. S. Gilbert, *Fallen Fairies*

THE POLICE STATION AT ST. PERRAN WAS SMALL—no more than two or three rooms, Robin estimated, including the holding cell—and sparsely furnished: chairs, desks, and not much else.

Taunton appeared uncomfortable here, as though accustomed to a greater space to work in, which was probably the case, as Newquay was a far larger town.

The inspector looked younger this morning than he had the previous afternoon: Robin's age or perhaps even a few years younger. His sandy hair was untouched by grey, his face youthful and unlined, and his slate-blue eyes round and deceptively guileless. Deceptive because Robin suspected the mind behind those eyes was fairly keen—or Taunton wouldn't have reached his present position so young.

Sergeant Jenkins—dark, greying, and stocky—had a good ten years or so on the inspector but showed no resentment at taking orders from a man a decade his junior. He sat stolidly at his desk, taking down Robin's statement and letting Taunton ask the questions.

"So, Mr. Pendarvis, you left for London two weeks ago—is that correct?"

"Close enough." Robin kept his voice steady. Had it really only been a fortnight since he'd found Nathalie in bed with Nankivell? It seemed so much longer... another lifetime.

Nathalie's lifetime. The thought chilled him to the marrow. Just two weeks ago she'd been alive: laughing as she writhed under another man, diamonds winking at her throat, meeting his eyes defiantly from across the room. And now she lay, white and silent, in the mortuary, that tinkling laughter forever stilled, bruises instead of diamonds encircling her neck.

Forcing that morbid image aside, he made himself concentrate on the task at hand. "I left Cornwall twelve days ago. And did not return until yesterday morning, when I received the news of my wife's death."

Taunton leaned against the desk, his gaze on Robin. "And for what purpose did you travel to London, Mr. Pendarvis?"

"On personal business," Robin replied, careful to show no hesitation even as his thoughts stuttered slightly over the answer. "I often go up to London to consult with my banker or solicitor. On this occasion, I met with both."

"Over a period of twelve days?" Taunton raised his brows. "It must have been an important matter to require so long a stay. Weren't you concerned about your business?"

"The matter concerned my daughter's future, so yes, it was indeed important," Robin said evenly. "As for the hotel, I had every confidence that my partners, Sir Harry Tresilian and Lord Trevenan, would handle things capably—more than capably—in my absence."

Taunton's eyes narrowed and he inquired, almost too casually, "And how did Mrs. Pendarvis react to the prospect of your absence?"

With great glee, most likely, Robin thought. But surely there was no need to mention Nathalie's indiscretions or the divorce papers he had never collected from his solicitor. Aloud he said, "I don't believe it affected her one way or the other, Inspector."

"Indeed?" Taunton's brows rose again. "Your wife did not object to your being so long away from home?"

"Not to my knowledge. You will doubtless discover this, if you have not already done so, but Nathalie and I led mostly separate lives—and have for some years," Robin informed him. "Our children, Sara and Cyril, were our main point of communication."

"Ah, yes—you mentioned your daughter? Who, I under-stand, is presently staying with Lord and Lady Trevenan at their estate, Pentreath," Taunton added. "Any reason she was not left at the hotel with her mother?"

Steady, Robin reminded himself. *Steady and calm*. "Sara has been much distressed by her brother's death in January. And Nathalie was perhaps too preoccupied with her own concerns to pay her sufficient attention. I had thought staying with friends would be good for Sara, especially as they've children of their own to be companions for her."

"My condolences on your loss." The response was automatic, but Robin thought he detected some genuine sympathy in the inspector's tone.

"Thank you," he acknowledged. "Under the present circum-stances, I cannot regret my decision where Sara is concerned."

"Of course not," Taunton agreed. He paused, then abruptly changed tack, much to Robin's relief. "So, where did you stay while you were in London?"

"At Brown's Hotel at first, then I accepted an invitation to stay with friends, Mr. and Mrs. Thomas Sheridan, at 21 Park Lane." And that was the truth, in the general sense of the word; the Sheridans would confirm his statement, if asked. Unless there was no way to avoid it, Robin saw no need to

mention the few days he and Sophie had stolen for themselves in the Cotswolds. Four short days of bliss, balanced
against four long years of hell. He clung to the thought of
their future—the one bright spot in this nightmare.

But he was determined to keep her out of this entirely.
Bad enough that he'd allowed her to come down to Cornwall
and get involved in this mess. At least he could spare her the
indignity of being questioned by the police.

The rest of the interrogation—for so it was, however
Taunton chose to phrase it—proceeded smoothly enough.
Robin answered all their questions, taking time to phrase
his replies carefully. He stifled a sigh of relief when they
were through with him, and Jenkins laid the pages aside. It
had been more difficult than he'd anticipated to omit any
mention of Sophie and their reunion, but he prided himself
on pulling it off.

Or did, until a constable—the younger one Robin remembered from the previous day— appeared in the doorway.
"Inspector Taunton," he began uncertainly, "there's a lady
here. She says she wishes to give her statement—about what's
happened up at the hotel?"

Taunton blinked, momentarily nonplussed. "Very well,
Constable. Show her in."

Robin sat stock-still, dread stealing over him. *Oh, God—
she wouldn't…*

"Good morning, Inspector Taunton." Sophie spoke up
from directly behind him.

Her voice, as always, was silvery clear. And Robin had
never been less pleased to hear it than at this moment.
Clenching his teeth, not trusting his voice, he risked a glance
at his love.

She wore the dark green riding habit he remembered
from London, cut with a severe simplicity that flattered her
slender figure and made her look taller and slightly older.
A high black riding hat crowned her head, the veil folded

back to expose her heart-shaped face: the fresh skin, brilliant green eyes, and warm lips, curved in a faint but sweetly obliging smile.

More striking even than her sophisticated clothes was her air of self-possession. The presence she exuded onstage was on full display now, shining like an electric chandelier: here was Somebody to be reckoned with, her demeanor announced. The young constable was staring at her, not quite openmouthed but close enough, and even the stolid sergeant looked impressed.

As did Taunton himself. His eyes widened, then he rallied, "Good morning, Miss—"

"Tresilian," she supplied, extending her hand. "Sophie Tresilian. You've already met my brother—Sir Harry Tresilian?"

"Ah, yes." Taunton took Sophie's hand. "How do you do, Miss Tresilian? Pray, be seated." He gestured to a vacant chair just a few feet from Robin's. "I understand you are here to give a statement?"

Sophie sat down with perfect composure, close enough for Robin to catch the faint perfume of violets wafting from her skin. "Indeed I am, Inspector. I'd heard that you wished to question Mr. Pendarvis, and I wondered if you would find it useful to speak to me as well."

"Inspector, do you believe Miss Tresilian's statement to be strictly necessary?" Robin asked, pointedly ignoring her.

Taunton glanced at him with an expression as bland as milk. "I appreciate any information that might help clarify the events of yesterday, Mr. Pendarvis. And I commend Miss Tresilian's willingness to cooperate with this investigation."

Damn. Stymied, Robin sat back in his chair as the inspector and the sergeant turned their attention to Sophie.

"Name, Miss?" Jenkins inquired, pen now poised over a fresh sheet of paper.

"Sophia Catherine Tresilian," she supplied.

Robin did his best to sit stoically as Sophie replied to

their most basic questions, giving her age (twenty-three) and current place of residence (Roswarne House). But he felt his pulse quicken and his stomach knot when Taunton inquired with studied nonchalance, "Now, Miss Tresilian, how exactly did you come to be involved in this matter?"

"Purely by chance. I happened to be present when Mr. Pendarvis received the news of his wife's death, and we traveled down to Cornwall together."

The way Taunton's gaze sharpened at this detail had Robin tensing in his chair. "Indeed? And how was it that you 'happened to be present' then?"

Sophie did not turn a hair. "I am a professional singer, based in London, Inspector. Last week, I gave a concert at the Royal Albert Hall, which Mr. Pendarvis attended. He came backstage afterward to offer his congratulations. Two nights later, I performed at a soiree given by Mr. and Mrs. Thomas Sheridan at their Park Lane residence, and Mr. Pendarvis was among the invited guests. We have been continually in each other's company since then."

"Continually?" Taunton echoed, looking nonplussed. "Then you and Mr. Pendarvis are on terms of intimacy?"

Robin just managed not to flinch at Taunton's choice of words. *Intimacy... dear God.*

"I consider Mr. Pendarvis a close friend of the family, as well as a business associate of my brother and cousin," Sophie said smoothly. "And I was delighted to see a familiar face, as I have not been back to Cornwall in over a year." She gave Taunton her most winsome smile. "There was a great deal of catching up to do."

In other circumstances, Robin might have been amused to observe that Taunton was no more immune to that smile than he was. All the same, he could tell that the inspector was preparing to probe further. "So you accompanied Mr. Pendarvis to Cornwall out of *friendship*?" he asked, his tone suggesting a wealth of hidden meanings.

Sophie raised her brows. "Naturally." She sounded surprised that he would even ask. "I shouldn't like to think of anyone making the journey alone, in such circumstances—least of all, a good friend. Besides, I had no further engagements or commitments keeping me in town."

Taunton regarded her searchingly. "How well-acquainted were you with the deceased?"

"With Mrs. Pendarvis?" Robin felt his pulse jump, but Sophie gazed steadily back at the inspector. "I didn't know her at all well. We met on only one occasion, four years ago, and did not speak."

The inspector's brow creased slightly. "You did not know the wife of a man you consider a *close family friend*?"

"Mrs. Pendarvis took up residence in Cornwall while I was finishing my training in London," Sophie replied with perfect truth. "As I have been continually touring for the last four years and seldom came home to visit, our paths did not cross. But it was a shock to hear that she had died so suddenly—and by such violent means." She paused, then looked Taunton square in the eye. "I hope that you catch whoever is responsible."

And that too was no less than the truth, Robin thought. Even Taunton seemed convinced of that much, because he changed tack, much as he had done with Robin. At any rate, he asked Sophie only a few more questions, none of which ventured into potentially dangerous territory, though Robin could not help wondering if Taunton suspected the true state of things between Sophie and himself. The thought was like an itch between his shoulder blades, making him edgy and uncomfortable. He had never been more relieved than when Taunton thanked them both for their cooperation and told them they were free to go, although he might have further questions for them at a later time.

Robin broodingly watched Sophie's slim, straight back as she preceded him out of the police station. The innocent girl he'd thought to shelter, the formidable woman she'd become—once again, she'd surprised him, steering her way through the interrogation with the assurance and expertise of an old salt navigating through stormy seas: presenting an honest account of their meeting in London, while avoiding the Scylla and Charybdis of their past romance and recent reunion. Moreover, she'd firmly established that they were both far from Cornwall at the time of Nathalie's murder. Almost certainly that had been her motive for coming to the police station in the first place.

He did not know whether he wanted to kiss her breathless—or shake her thoroughly.

❧

"I'd hoped to keep you out of this, entirely."

Robin's voice was as stiff as his backbone. Sophie could sense the irritation rolling off him in waves as she had from the moment they'd left the police station. Fortunately, he'd held his tongue until they were safely out of the village and riding back along the main road, toward Roswarne and the hotel.

"Well, I am *in* it now, so there's no point in stewing about it," Sophie said bracingly.

He cast her a darkling glance. "On the contrary, I would say that possible damage to your reputation is well worth 'stewing about,' as you put it."

"My reputation? Because I mentioned we spent some time together in London? What nonsense!" Seeing his mouth tighten, she added defiantly, "I daresay there'd be whispers about me in any case, considering my profession, and I'm used to that sort of thing. So let them whisper—we have more important things with which to concern ourselves than gossip!"

"Don't underestimate the damage gossip can do," Robin warned. "You might want to consider being more circumspect in future. And marching into the police station to defend a man being questioned in his wife's murder isn't exactly circumspect. I'll warrant Taunton and his lot are already speculating as to why a young lady of good family would put herself out like that for 'a close family friend.'"

I came to confirm your alibi, you ingrate! Sophie bit back the angry words and glared at him instead. "I don't care if they—or the whole county, for that matter—think I have more lovers than the Whore of Babylon, as long as you're cleared of suspicion in Nathalie's death! And I told you before, I mean to be your partner in all things, not some helpless infant who has to be protected all the time, so stop trying to wrap me in cotton wool!"

Robin's eyes blazed back at her, burning blue, then just as quickly, the anger faded and he dropped his gaze with a sigh. "I *was* doing that, wasn't I? Forgive me—old habits die hard." He stared down at his horse's neck. "I just—wanted to build something entirely new with you. Unconnected to the past, and untainted by it."

"Well, that's a lovely thought, but not exactly practical," Sophie remarked. "Because what's between us already has roots in the past, just as much as your marriage to Nathalie." She urged Tregony closer to him on the road and added more gently, "Let's not quarrel, dear heart. We *are* on the same side."

"So we are," Robin conceded, after a moment. He rubbed his brow under the brim of his riding hat. "Forgive me, Sophie. I'm like a bear with a sore head this morning."

"Naturally you are, after yesterday," she said, instantly remorseful. "And you look exhausted. Did you sleep at all last night?"

"Oh, now and then. But Sara needed me, so I spent a fair portion of the night sitting up with her."

"She must be devastated, to lose her brother and mother this close together."

"She's mostly confused and sad right now. And frightened—because of *how* her mother died. I've told her

I want her to stay at Pentreath until I'm sure it's safe for her to come home."

"A wise decision," Sophie approved. "And you're staying there too?"

"For the next few nights, at least. But I must go to the hotel now, make sure things are under control. The guests will have concerns, as will the staff, and it wouldn't be fair leaving Harry to cope with all this alone. There's certain to be an inquest," he added abruptly. "And anyone who might have seen or heard *anything* that night will be expected to testify." He rubbed his forehead again, pinched the bridge of his nose. "God in heaven, how I hate this!"

Sophie reached across the short distance between them to touch his arm. "We'll get through this, dear heart. I promise we will."

A corner of his mouth lifted, ever so slightly. "Together?"

"Together," she agreed, smiling back.

❧

They parted, reluctantly but of necessity, at the crossroads marked by the hawthorn tree. Loath as Sophie was to let Robin go—especially after they'd so narrowly averted a quarrel—she had no wish to make things more difficult for him. He had a business to run, a wife to bury, and a child to comfort, all of which had to come first. She wouldn't dream of adding to his burdens by thrusting herself to the forefront of his life and making demands he was in no position to fulfill. *Their* time would come, someday.

Sighing, she turned Tregony homeward. It was lovely to be back in Cornwall, she reflected as she rode. And lovelier still to be reunited with her family, who'd greeted her like the prodigal daughter, all but killing a fatted calf in her honor. But then, her mother had hoped for years that she would make an extended visit. How tall Peter, now in his first year at university, had grown! And how much more confident

John appeared, newly established in his profession and soon to be a married man!

Absorbed in these pleasant musings, she rode up the drive to Roswarne, only to pull up short when she saw a woman in a dark blue habit dismounting gracefully from a white—or rather, grey—horse just before the front steps. The visitor's hair glinted dark gold beneath the brim of her hat, and Sophie's spirits lifted at once.

"Aurelia! What are you doing here?"

Lady Trevenan looked up with a smile. "I came to see *you*, of course. James told me you were back."

"Yes, I arrived yesterday afternoon," Sophie replied, alighting from her own horse and hastening to embrace her friend and cousin by marriage. "It's delightful to see you again! Won't you come in for some refreshment?"

"Nothing would please me more," Aurelia assured her, returning the embrace.

Linking arms and talking animatedly, they entered the house together.

❧

As always, Sophie was struck by how similar and yet how different Aurelia was from her twin, Amy: both tall, slim, and golden-haired, with brilliant blue eyes. Aurelia bore a faint scar on her cheek from a riding accident some years before, and there was a slight hitch to her step at times of fatigue. But a more significant difference was the expression in her eyes—more pensive and reflective—and her smile, which held a wistful sweetness every bit as captivating as Amy's ebullience. Both were loyal to the bone, however, and Sophie knew just how fortunate she was to have their friendship. While Amy had provided her with a safe haven when her world had fallen apart, Aurelia had been her confidant and advocate during those halcyon days when she'd first discovered her love for Robin.

"So, how are the children?" she asked, pouring out tea for them both. "Jared must be all of four years old now."

"Four, and the very image of James," Aurelia reported with pride. "Dark hair, dark eyes, and the same—well, intensity, for lack of a better word."

"And the new one, Alexandra—does she favor you or James?" Sophie inquired.

"She has dark hair, but my eyes, and James swears she has my smile too. She's got him wrapped round her little finger already. And how is my niece? I gather you saw her in town."

"Oh, Bella is thriving. She's fair like Amy, but she's got Thomas's green eyes. And the sunniest nature too. Amy hopes to bring her down to Cornwall later this summer."

"So she's informed me. I count it a victory that she wishes to spend her summer holiday here, city girl that she is!" Aurelia declared, smiling. "By the way, she wrote that your concert at the Albert Hall was a great success. I'm sorry we never got up to London to see it, but there was so much to do here."

"You saw me in *Figaro* last year. And, under present circumstances," Sophie hesitated before continuing, "perhaps it's just as well that you and James were *here*."

Comprehension flickered in Aurelia's eyes. "You may be right. I don't like to think what might have happened to Sara if we *hadn't* been here." She paused in her turn, then ventured, "I gather from what James has told me that you and Robin are—reconciled?"

Sophie nodded. "When he was in London, we… talked. The bond we shared is still there. He told me he'd decided to proceed with the divorce, because he'd learned Nathalie was unfaithful again. He asked me if I would wait for him." A smile tugged at her mouth. "I did not take long to decide."

"Oh, I'm so glad!" Aurelia squeezed her hand. "I know how much you loved each other, and how it broke your heart to leave him, even though you had no choice back then! But now you have a second chance."

"I know. I just wish it hadn't come at such a price," Sophie confessed. "It's terrible that this should have happened. I know Robin did not want to remain married to Nathalie, but he never wished anything like this on her. He never wanted her dead."

"Of course he didn't," Aurelia said swiftly

Sophie wished her own conscience were as clear. But was wishing your rival gone really the same as wishing her brutally, senselessly murdered? On further reflection, she thought not. If Nathalie had succumbed to an illness, like Cyril, or died in some sort of accident, it would have been a tragedy still—but a clean tragedy. The sort of misfortune that could befall anyone.

But this... strangled in her own chamber by some unseen intruder and left to lie there undiscovered until morning? She suppressed a shiver at the thought.

"And *you* needn't feel guilty either," Aurelia added, as though reading Sophie's mind. "You would have had to be a saint not to resent Nathalie for taking everything you wanted. But I know you'd never have wished such a fate even on her."

Sophie took a deep breath. "No, I wouldn't. I just hope—Robin isn't regretting his choice." And there it was, the unspoken fear that had gripped her from the moment they'd heard the news but which she hadn't been able to utter, until now.

"Good heavens, why ever would he? You *know* he loves you."

"We were—together, when his wife was murdered." Sophie bit her lip. "I can't help worrying that it might be an ill omen, somehow."

Aurelia laid a hand on hers. "You *mustn't* allow yourself to think that way. What happened to Nathalie was tragic. But

Robin could have been anywhere in England at the time. And at least he needn't fear being blamed for it, because he *was* with you."

Sophie didn't know which surprised her more: that Aurelia showed no shock on hearing that Sophie and Robin had been together or that she'd instantly grasped the advantages of such an alibi. She choked down a lunatic giggle: Americans were nothing if not practical!

Regaining her composure, she managed to say, "I thought it might help if I could vouch for his whereabouts over the last week or so." She recounted her visit to the police station that morning. "They did seem inclined to believe me. At least, they found nothing to contradict what Robin had already told them. So—they had no choice but to let him go, for now."

"Naturally, you had to clear his name," Aurelia agreed. "The only thing to do with ugly rumors is nip them in the bud before they grow into even uglier scandals. And goodness knows what's happened is ugly enough!"

"And there's certain to be more ugliness, when the inquest is held," Sophie said, sighing.

Aurelia pulled a face. "Robin's going to have his hands full keeping Nathalie's little—indiscretions a secret."

"Her affair with Sir Lucas, you mean?"

"Among others. I don't like to speak ill of the dead, but Nathalie had an eye to several women's husbands." A hint of frost crept into Aurelia's voice. "Including mine."

Sophie dropped her teaspoon with a clatter. "Nathalie went after *James*?"

"On more than one occasion. We wished to remain friends with Robin, and that meant being civil to his wife. No easy task, especially after she set her sights on James. Oh, she didn't slip into his bedchamber at night or disrobe in front of him, but she'd flirt with him at dinner parties and contrive to catch him alone. Or stand too close to him when they were in the same room. James didn't want to make anything of it, at first, but she finally overplayed her hand—by suggesting that he might enjoy the novelty of making love to an *unblemished* lady."

"Oh, Aurelia…"

"Not to worry. James set her to rights in no uncertain terms." There was no mistaking the satisfaction in Aurelia's voice. "I was privileged to overhear him, in fact. It was—wonderful."

"I'm so glad," Sophie said fervently. "Not that James would ever betray you—"

"Oh, *I* know that." Aurelia dismissed the incident with the assurance of a wife wholly confident of her husband's fidelity. "The strange thing was, I don't think it was James's looks or fortune or even his title that made Nathalie act as she did. I think she was doing it to cause trouble for *Robin*. To drive a wedge between him and James."

Sophie remembered what Robin had told her in Oxfordshire. "Sadly, I find that all too easy to believe. It would have been about power for her, not love. Not even lust."

Aurelia nodded. "That's it exactly. Robin doesn't know," she added. "James never told him—he thought Robin had enough on his plate without having to deal with this. Fortunately, Nathalie never tried again, and James and I took care to avoid her whenever possible, unless Robin or the children were present." Her voice warmed and softened. "Now *they* were darlings, Sara and Cyril. Has Robin told you about them?"

At Sophie's nod, she continued, "Robin would bring Sara to Pentreath to play with Jared. She adored Cyril, but it did her good to have a healthy playmate now and then. James and I like to think that Sara had a chance to be a little girl during her visits to us."

"And Cyril?"

"We'd visit him at the hotel. And it wasn't easy for him, being unwell so often, but he tried to be patient, and he really was good as gold most of the time. And Robin was—well, he was just what a father should be, to both of them."

Sophie blinked her stinging eyes. "I could tell he loved them very much."

"Oh, no question of that," Aurelia asserted. "There was talk, of course, about poor Cyril, and who his father might have been—especially since most of the county knew Robin couldn't possibly have sired him. But Robin would not have any of that in his hearing. He accepted Cyril as his own from the first day, and never swayed from that."

"It wouldn't have been fair to blame a child for his mother's failings."

"And Cyril adored him too. I think, in spite of everything, Robin, Sara, and Cyril managed to form a fairly happy unit." Aurelia paused, her expression clouding. "I'm worried about Sara. Robin left her with us when he went up to London. He said he thought it would be good for her to spend time in a happy place. But she still misses Cyril terribly, and now—"

"Now her mother is dead as well," Sophie finished, then winced at the starkness of it.

"Yes," Aurelia said on a sigh. "Granted, Nathalie wasn't the most attentive of mothers—even to Cyril, whom she favored. Robin was the one who played with them, took them for outings, and sat at their bedsides. But all the same, it's a huge loss for a child of seven, especially so soon after losing her brother. Nanny Odgers has been wonderful with her, and Sara knows she has only to ask if she needs something. Jared doesn't quite understand what's happened, but he's being very solicitous of her, lending her all his toys and books to cheer her up. They've become good friends, in spite of the age difference."

"Robin mentioned that. I'm glad his daughter has a playmate in your son." Sophie fiddled with her teaspoon. "Aurelia, do you think *I* could meet Sara sometime? Just as a friend," she added hurriedly. "Just so she can start getting…

used to me. And I wouldn't tell her about Robin and me, not yet," she rushed on. "That's *his* responsibility, in any case. But I know how important she is to him, and I don't want her to feel that she's going to be cut out, or that I'm going to be this evil stepmother who'll steal away her father's love, or make her wear rags and sleep among the ashes, or—"

"Sophie," Aurelia broke in gently, her eyes brimming with amused affection. "Darling, no one who knows you could possibly think you'd do any such thing!"

Sophie exhaled shakily. "I've never had to face the prospect of bringing up someone else's child. It terrifies me," she admitted.

"It would terrify anyone." Aurelia squeezed her hand. "But Sara herself isn't the least bit terrifying. She's serious and sweet, and very grown-up for her age. Granted, a meeting between you *should* be handled carefully—and discreetly." She tapped a forefinger against her chin as she thought. "Perhaps you could come to tea at Pentreath some afternoon. *After* the funeral, I think—Sara needs more time to come to terms with losing her mother. I'm not sure it's completely sunk in for her yet."

"Of course," Sophie said quickly. "Whenever you *and* Robin feel she's ready. The last thing I want to do is force myself upon her."

"Don't worry, my dear. Personally, I think you and Sara will get along famously, once you get to know each other."

"You sound so certain of that."

"I am." Aurelia smiled at her. "Mainly because I happen to know that Sara is *passionately* fond of music."

Eighteen

…machinations, hollowness, treachery, and all ruinous disorders, follow us disquietly to our graves.

—William Shakespeare, *King Lear*

"EARTH TO EARTH, ASHES TO ASHES, DUST TO DUST."

The words of the burial service rang in Sophie's ears as she stood with her family about the new grave in the churchyard. So deep a hole, to house so small a casket, scarcely larger than a child's. But then, Nathalie had been tiny—*mignonne*, as Robin had once said.

Thankful for the veil that covered her face, she stole a glance at him, standing remote, black-clad, and impassive on the other side of the grave. One gloved hand grasped the brim of his hat, while the other rested on the shoulder of his daughter.

Sophie's gaze went to the child: seven years old—soon to be eight, according to Aurelia—and much taller than she'd been when Sophie had last seen her clinging to Nathalie's skirts in the ballroom. Sara was so like her father, the same dark brown hair, the same intense blue eyes. Her complexion—emphasized by her mourning frock—was fairer, and the shape of her face softer and more feminine, but beyond that, Sophie saw little of the girl's mother in her.

Not that that made a difference, she reminded herself hastily. Even if Sara had been Nathalie's spitting image, she was a part of Robin, and that made her important to Sophie too. And *any* child who'd lost her mother and her brother just months apart needed sympathy, attention, and care. She was getting all of that from her father and from the Trevenans, but Sophie hoped she might have the chance to offer those things to the girl as well. She too knew what it was like to lose a parent at a young age, though her father hadn't died under such terrible circumstances as Nathalie.

Her thoughts turned to the inquest, held mere days ago. While she had not been summoned as a witness, both Harry and James who'd arrived on the scene soon after Nathalie's body was discovered had been called to testify, as had Robin. It hadn't taken long for the coroner's jury to return a verdict of murder, at the hands of persons unknown, and the search for those persons unknown was continuing under Inspector Taunton. Though barely thirty and new to the county, he was apparently as "keen as mustard" to find the murderer. According to Harry, at least; Robin had said almost nothing about him. Robin was saying next to nothing about *anything* these days, and certainly not to Sophie.

She tried to be patient, which wasn't easy, especially when she saw so little of him. And it was all too easy to remember what had happened the last time a crisis had arisen in his life. Logically, she knew that the obstacles that had kept them apart four years ago were gone. Emotionally… was a different matter altogether.

Fortunately, she had Aurelia to confide in, and her cousin-in-law was, as always, a sympathetic and discreet listener. Sophie's family seemed reluctant to initiate any sort of discussion about the nature of her current relationship with Robin, although she sometimes caught her mother eyeing her speculatively. But even Harry appeared to have backed off for now. Sophie didn't know whether to be glad or sorry about that.

"Amen."

Jolted back to the present, Sophie quickly murmured "Amen" along with the other mourners to mark the end of the service. She just managed not to flinch as the first handful of dirt struck the coffin—always so final, that sound. How often Robin must have heard it himself, and at so many burials: his brother, his parents, his son, and now his wife. A few more clods of earth followed, then Sara took a tentative step forward and threw a tiny nosegay of white flowers into the grave as well, before retreating into the protective circle of her father's arm.

As the vicar withdrew, the crowd began to disperse, many of the mourners now approaching Robin and Sara to offer further condolences. Sophie suspected that most of those in attendance had come because of Robin. Indeed, she'd heard that some of his relations on his mother's side had traveled from Yorkshire for the funeral. She was glad that however they might have felt about his ill-starred marriage, they were here to support him today.

James and Aurelia were speaking to Robin now, their voices almost inaudible at this distance. But Sophie noticed the way James laid his hand upon Robin's shoulder and the warm sympathy in Aurelia's gaze as she stooped down to Sara's height. Setting her hand in Aurelia's, the girl looked up at her father, who gave her a quick kiss and embrace. One more exchange with Robin, and the Trevenans left the churchyard with Sara, heading toward their waiting carriage.

More people came, spoke to him, departed, and then the crowd thinned out, and Sophie, along with the other Tresilians, came face to face with the widower.

She hung back discreetly, letting Harry take the lead when it came to offering formal condolences on behalf of the family.

"Mama, I would like a private word with Robin," she told Lady Tresilian in a low voice.

Her mother hesitated only a moment, appearing to grasp that Sophie was not asking for permission. "Very well, my dear. We will be waiting for you in the carriage."

Sophie watched with gratitude as Lady Tresilian guided her sons before her, even Harry who might otherwise have balked. Despite his restraint, her eldest brother was still a little uneasy about how matters stood between her and Robin.

Now, she studied the man she loved, noting his pallor and the shadows beneath his eyes. He looked thinner too—no doubt he was missing meals, along with sleep. Most worrying of all was the sense that he carried some other burden, some new sorrow, beyond those he'd already shouldered—and which, she thought with an inward sigh, he was not yet willing to share with her. "My dear, I am so sorry," she said. "Is there anything I can do?"

Because there was so much she could *not* do at this moment, such as kiss or embrace him, though she longed to do both. But the world was still watching them, even here, among the quiet gravestones. There might even be some mourners—other than Sophie's own family—who remembered the budding romance between them four years ago.

Best not to give the gossips any morsel to chew on, Sophie conceded with an inner sigh. But she could offer Robin her hand, and take some comfort from the way his closed around it, warm and firm even through the black gloves they both wore. And from the way his eyes and the set of his mouth softened when he looked at her. Life was still present, in spite of everything.

"Thank you, Miss Tresilian," he replied formally, then added in an undertone, "Just stay as you are—that is all I ask."

Another squeeze of hands, imparting all they wanted to say but could not—here. And for a moment, they allowed their hands to remain linked, while Sophie envisioned her own strength and energy flowing into him, sustaining him for the difficult days ahead.

Robin released his grip first and took a step back. "I am glad that you came," he said, again in that formal tone. "You and your family. Shall I be seeing you back at the hotel?"

Sophie smiled, hearing the faint entreaty in those words. They were getting better at listening to each other, she thought—at discerning the faint signals and subtle cues that every couple in love develops. "Yes, we're heading there now. Do you need a ride back yourself?"

He shook his head. "My own carriage is waiting. But I thought I'd take a few more minutes here—Cyril is buried in this churchyard too."

"By all means," she said at once. "Take all the time you need. I know Harry can see to things in your absence."

His smile, though faint and weary, was real enough. "I will come presently."

Sophie murmured a last good-bye and turned away, setting her feet on the winding path that led out of the churchyard. She could not help but glance back, however, to where Robin still stood beside his wife's grave.

And then, frowning, she looked again, focusing not on Robin but on a headstone just a few feet away from him—and the man standing behind it, watching. He looked up and for a moment Sophie was staring directly into his face, then he lowered his head, pulled down the brim of his hat, and moved off, losing himself among the sea of stones and crosses.

Sophie gazed after him in shock, wondering if her eyes were deceiving her.

Had Sir Lucas Nankivell truly had the effrontery to attend Nathalie's funeral?

"Sophie!" Her mother's voice reached her from the carriage lane. "We must be going!"

Sophie shook her head and hurried on.

The summer sun lay across Robin's back like a heavy hand. Sighing, he loosened his collar, undid the first few buttons of his shirt, and closed his eyes, breathing in the scents of grass and newly turned earth. If it weren't for the almost preternatural silence, he could forget he was standing in a graveyard, having just seen his wife's coffin lowered into the ground.

The funeral itself had passed in a blur for him. There had been flowers, he knew: tuberoses and lilies, their scent heavy, almost oppressive in the air. And he recalled snatches of the vicar's eulogy, which seemed to have been written for a very different woman than the one he'd married. And the coffin, barely larger than Cyril's, that housed her elfin frame.

Barely six months ago he'd buried the child he'd come to love as a son; today he had buried the boy's mother. His estranged wife, whom he'd loved when he was a callow stripling, grieved and raged over when she'd betrayed and abandoned him, and for whom he'd felt mainly indifference these last four years.

Had any part of what they'd shared been real? Before boredom and resentment had set in for her, disenchantment and impatience for him? But something good had come from this ill-starred match: Sara. He thought of her now, heading back to Pentreath in James and Aurelia's care. Best for her to be there rather than at the hotel, where Taunton's ongoing investigation still had everyone on edge.

And to think he'd worried about the upheaval connected with a divorce suit! That would have been *nothing* compared to this, the doubt and uncertainty surrounding Nathalie's murder.

Robin opened his eyes and stared bleakly down at the grave. He did not think there were many here who had mourned Nathalie's passing. She'd remained an outsider until the day she'd died, as bored by provincial Cornwall as she'd been by provincial France.

But had anyone here actually hated her enough to kill her?

He rubbed his forehead, recalling willy-nilly the details of the inquest—and all the questions that had remained unaddressed. But then, an inquiry was only meant to establish the cause of death. The exact circumstances surrounding the death would only be explored during a trial… if there was one. If a killer was even found.

So far, the evidence seemed to support the theory that her murder had been merely the unfortunate consequence of a robbery, most likely committed by an intruder who'd broken into the separate wing of the hotel, made off with Nathalie's jewels, and was now long gone from the area. Who could be anywhere in England—or Europe at this moment.

But if it had been robbery, if Nathalie had surprised a vicious thief at his work, why hadn't she screamed the place down? Or had she been the one surprised, moving about the chamber, preparing for bed, unaware of an intruder's presence until it was far too late?

And the method of the killing—wouldn't a blow to the head have been swifter? Or a knife, under the ribs or across the throat, quick and soundless?

But there was something oddly personal about a strangling. As if the murderer had derived an obscene satisfaction from watching his victim struggle for breath. He remembered the livid mark about Nathalie's throat, how tightly the garrote must have been wound.

What if she'd opened the door to the killer? What if she'd known him?

And what if the killer had known or at least suspected… something about her? The very same thing that Robin now knew, courtesy of the coroner's postmortem. Something that might be allowed to remain concealed during an inquest, but which must surely emerge in the event of an arrest and a trial. Something he'd been unable to share, even with Sophie.

Nathalie had taken one last secret to her grave.

At the time of her death she'd been three months pregnant.

Nineteen

Women are naturally secretive, and they like to do their own secreting.

—Arthur Conan Doyle, "A Scandal in Bohemia"

"I CANNOT DECIDE—SHOULD IT BE PICKLED SALMON OR poached?" Lady Tresilian mused, studying the menu before her. "What do you think, Sophie?"

"Poached is more elegant, I think," Sophie replied. "And don't forget the lobster puffs John likes so much."

"Oh, Cook is already making those. Should we have dressed crab too?"

"Why not? Amy served dressed crab at her last soiree—it was very popular with her guests. And this is Cornwall, Mama," Sophie reminded her, smiling. "Where else can one find the freshest fish and shellfish in England?"

"Very true," Lady Tresilian agreed, adding it to the menu.

From sorrow to celebration in barely a day, Sophie mused. Just yesterday she'd stood beside a grave, watching the coffin of her murdered rival being lowered into the earth. This morning she was sitting in the parlor at Roswarne, helping her mother choose the refreshments for the engagement party they'd be hosting for John and Grace three evenings from now. She longed to see Robin; worry for him fretted her like a sore tooth, but she could think of no reasonable pretext to ride over to Pendarvis Hall. And he must have his hands full in any case, keeping his guests appeased in this situation.

"Miss Tregarth is here, my lady," Parsons observed from the doorway.

Lady Tresilian rose from her desk. "Thank you, Parsons. Show her in at once."

"Good morning, Lady Tresilian!" Grace Tregarth, tall, fair, and pretty, entered with outstretched hands and a smile as bright as her sunny hair. "And Sophie too! I am so glad to find you both at home."

"I shall always be at home to you, Grace dear," Lady Tresilian fondly assured her future daughter-in-law as they sat down upon the sofa. "Now, what brings you over here so early?"

"Well, in truth, I had a favor to ask. Both of you," Grace added, including Sophie in her smile. "I know you've sent out the invitations weeks ago, but would you be willing to add someone else to the guest list? A particular friend of mine?"

"That can be arranged quite easily," Lady Tresilian told her. "Now, which friend is this?"

Grace hesitated, then ventured, "Constance Nankivell. She returned to St. Perran three days ago."

Constance Nankivell? Sir Lucas's *wife*? Sophie barely kept her mouth from dropping open. Glancing at her mother, she saw that her expression had grown slightly rigid. "I see."

"I know you're none too fond of Sir Lucas," Grace rushed on apologetically. "And I can hardly blame you for that! But Constance and I have become good friends, and I shouldn't like her to feel unwelcome. I imagine it was difficult enough for her to come back here in the first place. Especially since Sir Lucas wasn't exactly an ideal husband," she added significantly.

So the baronet's peccadilloes were at least partly known.

Sophie wondered how many in the county knew he had been Nathalie's lover, and winced to think of Robin's humiliation.

"Well, I suppose… we could make an exception in this case," Lady Tresilian conceded at last. "It isn't fair to punish Constance for Sir Lucas's dreadful behavior, then or now. And the party *is* in your honor, my dear, and John's. Have you consulted him on this, by the way?"

Grace nodded. "John says he's willing to tolerate Sir Lucas's presence on this occasion, for my sake. He likes Constance too, and has always felt rather sorry for her."

"Very well," Lady Tresilian acknowledged. "I shall see that an invitation is sent to the Nankivells. *And* I'll talk to Harry to let him know how matters stand."

"Thank you." Grace laid a hand over the older woman's. "I appreciate that, immensely. And now, on to a less—fraught matter," she added with her winsome smile. "Sophie, would you be willing to sing at our party? It would mean so much to us both."

"Grace, dear, it is your evening—yours and John's," Sophie began.

"And I can't think of a better way to celebrate that than with music. We met at one of your family's concerts, after all," Grace reminded her. "Having you sing would be like… commemorating our first meeting. And you needn't fear we'll ask you to sing the whole score of *Figaro*," she said with a gurgle of laughter. "Just a few of our favorite songs will suffice."

Sophie smiled back. "Well, if you're sure about it. What would you like me to sing?"

"I'll talk to John and we'll give you a list tomorrow, if that's soon enough?"

"That will be fine. And Cecily would probably be willing to play the accompaniment," Sophie added. "Just as she did back then."

"That would be delightful!" Grace clasped her hands.

"I am so happy to be gaining you both as sisters. You can't imagine how lonely it is, being an only child!"

"We're delighted to have you joining our family too," Lady Tresilian told her, smiling. "Now, would you mind looking over the menu with me? I'd appreciate further suggestions."

"Of course." Grace bent her head to study the bill of fare.

"And Sophie"—Lady Tresilian turned to her daughter—"I was wondering if we might invite Robin Pendarvis to dinner this evening. I couldn't help but notice how tired and thin he looked yesterday at the funeral," she went on, as Sophie stared at her. "This has been such a difficult time for him, and I think it would do him good to spend an evening among friends."

Sophie felt a rush of gratitude, recognizing that this was her mother's way of giving her blessing to Robin and Sophie's relationship. "I think that's a fine idea, Mama. May I ride over to the hotel and give him the invitation in person?"

"You may. Indeed, I had rather suspected you would want to," Lady Tresilian observed, a touch dryly. "Only—try to be back before dinner yourself, my love."

Sophie blushed, kissed her mother decorously, and went to change into her riding habit.

❦

At the hotel, Praed welcomed Sophie warmly, but an air of abstraction hung about him. The master was in his office, being questioned by "that inspector," he informed her, his tone halfway between censure and apprehension.

Sophie inferred without difficulty that Taunton was by no means popular with the staff. "I see. Has Mr. Pendarvis left specific orders *not* to be disturbed?"

"On the contrary, Miss Tresilian, he has done nothing of the kind."

They regarded each other with perfect understanding,

then, "Thank you, Praed," Sophie said brightly, and set off at once toward the west wing.

She remembered from the floor plan that Robin's office was on the ground floor. But even without that, she'd have located it quickly, by the voices that carried into the passage. Voices that sounded anything but friendly, she noted with alarm, and quickened her pace until she was standing just outside the door.

"—a matter pertaining to your late wife?" Taunton was saying, his tone sharp and inquisitorial. "Were you in fact seeking to bring a suit of divorce against her?"

Sophie held her breath as Robin replied, his own voice level, calm, and cold as the grave. "I came to London to seek a divorce, yes. You can confirm as much with my solicitor."

"And yet you chose to omit that detail when making your statement?"

"There seemed little point in mentioning it, as the news of Nathalie's murder reached me before I could collect the papers from Mr. Halifax," Robin retorted. "The dissolution of my marriage was a private matter. Under the circumstances, I preferred that it remain so."

"I see. Well, the timing certainly worked to your advantage."

"I beg your pardon?" The chill in Robin's voice had deepened.

"Your wife's death occurred *before* the divorce could take place, sparing you no small amount of expense and embarrassment. The tragedy could not have occurred at a more opportune moment... than if you had arranged it yourself."

Sophie stifled a gasp at the blatant innuendo. Peering around the slightly open door, she saw the two men standing face to face, their postures equally stiff and unyielding.

Robin did not pretend to misunderstand. "Inspector, let us deal plainly with one another. If I were already going through the proper legal channels of divorcing my wife, I would scarcely imperil my future or that of my daughter by murdering her mother."

"You still might have found it easier and less expensive to have her killed, rather than waiting for a divorce that might not be granted!" Taunton pointed out, almost triumphantly.

From her vantage point, Sophie saw Robin's hands fist; she could only guess at the anger and offense surging through him. *Keep calm, dear heart*, she willed. *This is what the inspector* wants.

Much to her relief, he unclenched his hands after a moment, then said evenly, "I had good cause to believe the divorce *would* be granted, as I possessed incontrovertible proof of Nathalie's infidelity. However, as the mother of my child, she was entitled to some degree of maintenance, and I intended to confer an annuity upon her. But no amount of expense or embarrassment would have deterred me from pursuing the divorce." He took a breath. "And now, if I might inquire as to the source of your information regarding my plans?"

"I am not at liberty to divulge—"

"Was it Sir Lucas Nankivell?"

Positioned as she was, Sophie did not have the best view of Taunton's expression, but the faint shift in his stance betrayed him.

"You may wish to question *him* more closely," Robin continued coolly. "He may have a number of interesting things to impart—as my wife's last lover and the possible father of the child she was carrying."

Sophie's eyes widened, and she heard Taunton catch his breath, then swallow audibly. As well he might… Nathalie with child? By Sir Lucas? When had Robin discovered *this*?

He was still speaking, and she hurriedly recollected her thoughts to listen. "Moreover, Inspector, as one new to St. Perran, you are likely unaware that five years ago, Sir Lucas attempted to slander me, Lord Trevenan, and Sir Harry, by accusing us of conspiracy to murder Trevenan's predecessor.

His slanders were exposed, and he was persuaded to confess his wrongdoing and make reparation."

Sophie would have wagered her violin on Taunton not knowing that, and what she could glimpse of his profile looked sufficiently nonplussed to confirm as much. "I am not sure what bearing the events of five years ago have on this present investigation—"

"A great deal, I should think," Sophie surprised herself by saying. Then, as both men turned toward her, sporting identical startled expressions, she stepped out from behind the door and walked boldly into the room.

"Pardon me, gentlemen," she said with her brightest smile. "I could not help but overhear. Inspector, I can personally vouch for what Mr. Pendarvis has told you about Sir Lucas. Indeed, I was present when his lies," she chose the word deliberately, "were revealed. He bears a grudge against my family and Mr. Pendarvis to this day. As a result, we seldom meet socially."

Taunton regarded her with narrowed eyes. "Why would Sir Lucas invent such a slander in the first place, Miss Tresilian?"

Sophie matched him stare for stare. "For several reasons, no doubt, but my brother's rejection of him as my suitor was among them. I possess a comfortable fortune, Inspector, which Sir Lucas coveted, just as he coveted some railway shares held by Mr. Pendarvis," she added, with a nod toward Robin. "I'm sure we're *all* aware that unscrupulous men will say and do just about anything to get what they want. Even something as petty as revenge."

She knew she was laying it on a trifle thick, but to judge from his expression, Taunton appeared to be listening—or at any rate not dismissing what she said out of hand. By contrast, Robin's face had gone completely unreadable.

"Indeed," Taunton said, after a moment. "Thank you for your cooperation, Miss Tresilian. Mr. Pendarvis." He sounded almost conciliatory. "I will be sure to take what you have both told me into account. Good day."

"Good day," Sophie said quickly. Robin merely inclined his head as Taunton withdrew.

"That didn't go *too* badly," she ventured once they were alone.

Robin raised a sardonic brow. "No?"

"At least he knows better now than to swallow everything Sir Lucas tells him about you."

"True enough," he conceded, then sighed, looking unutterably weary. "Not that I'm not pleased to see you, my love, but why have you come?"

"To invite you to dine with us tonight, at Roswarne. Mama's idea," she added, smiling.

His eyes warmed. "I accept with pleasure. Now, how long were you hiding behind that door?"

Sophie considered dissembling, then discarded the idea. "Long enough to hear you say Nathalie was pregnant by Sir Lucas when she died."

"She was pregnant, yes. But it's not yet certain Nankivell was the father," he corrected.

She fretted her lip. "Then who else could it have been?"

"Any man who shared her bed in the last three months." His lips twisted. "Not that I kept a tally. And I'd swear there was no one during Cyril's last illness, or right after his death."

"So that would mean… April or thereabouts?"

He nodded, tight-lipped. "I don't know if she and Nankivell were involved then. I suppose it's possible. To be frank, I didn't care to know."

"He was at the funeral yesterday. Not among the mourners," she added, as Robin glanced at her sharply. "But I saw him, afterward, standing behind a gravestone, watching you. I couldn't believe he had the gall to come!"

"Neither can I." Robin shook his head. "I thought for certain he'd be lying low, especially now that Lady Nankivell's returned to Cornwall."

"That's what I heard from Grace." Sophie grimaced.

"Under the circumstances, Lady Nankivell would've been wiser to stay away. And now Sir Lucas is trying to make trouble for you again. I wonder how he found out about the divorce."

"From Nathalie, I suspect. She may have guessed my intent when I left for London." Robin rubbed a hand over his face. "Well, however Nankivell found out, he knows casting suspicion on me would divert suspicion from *him*. A preemptive attack, I suppose, since I hadn't so much as mentioned his name to the police before today."

"Well, now you've pointed the finger right back at him," Sophie said with satisfaction. "Tit for tat!"

"Perhaps." Robin paused, then said abruptly, "You know, Taunton might not be the only one who thinks I arranged to have Nathalie killed."

"He's wrong," Sophie said at once. "And so is everyone else who thinks that. No one who knows you *could* think that."

His smile was faint but genuine. "Thank you for your faith in me."

She took his hand, held it to her cheek. "I've always had faith in you, Robin."

He lowered his head until his brow rested against hers. "I have to do something, Sophie. I can't just sit idly by and leave all this to Taunton, especially not after this morning. If Nankivell continues to spread his poison…"

Sophie did not need to be told how damaging this could be. If Robin's innocence wasn't established beyond all doubt, he could face professional ruin. Who would frequent a hotel run by a suspected murderer? Harry had mentioned they were lucky the hotel was only half-full at present, and that they'd managed to keep the news of Nathalie's murder fairly quiet. But the Season would end soon, and a flood of summer guests would descend on Cornwall. If Nathalie's killer hadn't been found by then, the backlash against Robin and the Pendarvis Hotel could be disastrous. And then there was the far greater personal cost, uppermost in both their minds.

Robin exhaled slowly, his breath warm against her cheek. "Sara had another nightmare last night—crying out for her mother and Cyril. She's afraid to come home, and I'm almost as afraid to bring her. I *can't* bring her, not until I'm sure she'll be safe."

Sophie stroked his hair, saying nothing, just letting him unburden himself.

"I have to do my part in solving Nathalie's murder," he went on. "For her own sake, because whatever she was, she didn't deserve such a fate. And because someday I'll have to look into our daughter's eyes and tell her I did everything I could to catch her mother's killer."

She kissed him, touching her lips lightly to his. "Then tell me what you mean to do, dear heart. And I will help you in any way I can."

༄

"So, what are we looking for?" Sophie asked.

They stood on the threshold of Nathalie's chamber, all icy blues and whites. All evidence of violent crime had been cleared away: the bed was freshly made, the furniture right side up. The occupant might have simply gone away on a trip, rather than been buried the day before.

"Anything the police might have missed," Robin said with an apologetic grimace. "Not much to go on, I'm afraid, and Taunton's men were fairly thorough when they searched this room before. But a fresh pair of eyes couldn't hurt."

Sophie walked gingerly over to the dressing table, where Nathalie's body had been discovered. "If this were a Conan Doyle or even a Lewis Wells story, we'd find some brilliant clue that everyone else had overlooked. A distinctive button behind the vanity, perhaps, or a missing glove, or a monogrammed handkerchief. Pity reality is seldom as cooperative as fiction."

He gave her a rueful smile. "And I'm no Sherlock Holmes, my love, but perhaps chance will favor us in spite of that. I'd rather make the effort than not."

"Of course," Sophie agreed. She turned back to the dressing table, noticing for the first time a photograph in a pretty silver frame. The children, unsurprisingly—Sophie recognized Sara straightaway, and the fair-haired boy of perhaps three, all dimpled cheeks and chin, must be Cyril. That cherubic smile… she paused, her memory teased, but she couldn't quite lay her finger on why that smile seemed familiar.

"We had that taken last year," Robin said over her shoulder. "We—weren't sure how much longer we might have with Cyril. James recommended the photographer he employs for family portraits. It's a good likeness of them both—I keep the same photograph in my office."

"They're adorable," Sophie told him, with complete sincerity. "Cyril favored Nathalie?"

He nodded. "It's probably just as well that he resembled her so closely."

"Have you ever wondered about…?"

"Wondered, yes—but never for long. What would be the point? Cyril was *my* son."

"He was indeed." Sophie turned away from the vanity. "Where shall we begin?"

"If you take the wardrobe, I'll search the dresser."

They set to work without further ado. Sophie tried not to feel like an intruder as she opened the wardrobe. Nathalie Pendarvis was buried and—one hoped—at peace, not hovering like some malevolent ghost as they sorted through her gowns and unmentionables.

Very fine gowns, as it turned out, and unmentionables trimmed with lace. Easy to tell that Nathalie had spent much of her pin money on clothes. Evening gowns, lavishly trimmed and beaded, with an almost shocking amount of décolletage. Airy negligees and robes that made the one

Sophie had worn in Oxfordshire look as demure as a nun's habit. And because Nathalie had been French, after all, numerous pairs of perfectly matched gloves—several of them perfumed—and slippers.

Robin was going through the contents of the dresser, his face stonily impassive. Sophie wondered, with an unpleasant twinge, if Nathalie had worn any of these garments to entice him, then mentally kicked herself for being obtuse. Of *course* she had.

In the end, however, they had to admit defeat: their search yielded nothing of note.

"Well, we knew it was a slim chance at best," Robin said as he closed the last drawer.

Sophie shut the wardrobe door. "Yes, but I couldn't help hoping for better." She glanced about the chamber. "Is there no other place we might search? How did Nathalie pass the time? Besides entertaining her latest lover," she added as Robin cocked an ironic eyebrow at her.

"I asked Enid how Nathalie spent her last few days," he replied, after a moment. "Apparently, she'd go riding in the mornings, then drive into St. Perran, or more often Truro, to shop, usually after luncheon. The afternoon before she… died, she ordered some new dresses from a ladies' establishment in Truro. I received the bill a few days ago," he added dryly.

"What else? Would she dine here or somewhere else?"

"She took her meals here, mostly in her chamber or her sitting room."

"Nathalie had her own sitting room?"

"Not hers, precisely. It's not connected to her chamber. But I did have a sitting room furnished for… a lady's particular use." He did not look at Sophie when he spoke, and she realized with a bittersweet pang that he'd planned that room with *her* in mind.

"Have the police searched there as well?" she asked, in a brisk tone that forbade regrets.

"Yes, though they found nothing unusual—just some dressmakers' bills and a meal menu intended for the next day."

"What about correspondence?" Sophie asked. "Might she have written to someone—Sir Lucas, perhaps? They must have had some way of setting up their assignations."

"Nothing was found, but…" Robin's brows drew together in thought. "She had ink stains on her fingers, so she must have been writing at some point that day."

"Why don't we search the sitting room too? We've nothing to lose, after all."

Robin acceded readily enough, and they left Nathalie's chamber, closing the door behind them with unspoken relief.

The sitting room, located two doors along the passage, was furnished and decorated very differently, and Sophie again felt a wistful pang. Yes, she would very much have liked a room like this: the wallpaper was a light, clear celadon, and curtains of willow-patterned Morris chintz decked the windows. The furniture was graceful and well-proportioned without appearing spindly or insubstantial: armchairs, sofas, tables…

Sophie paused, eyes widening. "That secretary in the alcove—Nathalie used it?"

Robin glanced at her, no doubt surprised by such an obvious question. "I believe so." A faint, reminiscent smile softened his mouth. "Cyril hid under it once. He was too frail for most games, but he could play hide-and-go-seek. Nathalie found him and chased him out, though—it was one of the few times I remember her scolding him."

Only half listening, Sophie crossed over to the desk, running her hand along the smooth mahogany top as she studied the arrangement of drawers: two large ones below, a set of smaller ones in the cabinet-like upper portion. "A bit too early to be Hepplewhite or Sheraton," she mused, excitement sparking within her. "Chippendale? Or something very like."

"I hadn't realized you were such an enthusiast about writing desks," Robin remarked.

"It's not that, or not entirely." Sophie looked up, took a breath to steady herself as her mind speculated furiously. "Chippendale, and other furniture makers of the time—they designed things—desks, sideboards, chests-of-drawers—that had hidden compartments."

"Hidden…" Robin echoed blankly. "But the police didn't find any—"

"You'd have to know *where* to look; they aren't necessarily where you'd expect to find them. They're *meant* to be a secret, to everyone except the owner and the craftsman."

Robin shook his head in obvious chagrin. "I can't believe I never thought of that…"

"No reason you should," Sophie said consolingly. "Your expertise lies in buildings, not antique furniture. And I'll wager Taunton and his men never thought of it either. It's not that I'm such an expert myself, but I have a desk in my London home that's very similar to this. Made a bit later, though," she added. "Sheraton's work—it doesn't have those ball-and-claw feet."

Robin eyed the desk. "How many secret compartments could that thing hold?"

"I don't know. They tend to vary in size—some can be almost as large as a drawer, while others are just pigeonholes." Sophie took a breath, mentally rolling up her sleeves. "Anyway, *my* desk has sixteen compartments—shall we get started?"

❧

An hour and nine compartments later, they stared down at their findings: a few stamps, a handful of stray coins, a small notebook in which columns of numbers had been entered, and a tarnished silver ring, too large for a woman's hand. From one of Nathalie's lovers? Sophie wondered; it seemed the most likely assumption.

The stamps and coins held no mystery, being neither rare

nor valuable, so she picked up the ring instead. "It looks like some sort of signet, but it's so old—and worn. You can barely make out the crest." She held the ring out to Robin. "A boar's head?"

"I don't think so. No tusks. But those do look like horns—a ram, perhaps. Or a bull."

"And there's a collar too." Sophie peered at the ring again. "Do you know of any families in England that have a bull's head as part of their coat of arms?"

Robin shook his head. "I know next to nothing about heraldry. And coats of arms weren't particularly important to *my* branch of the family. And don't forget that could be a French signet just as easily. We don't know how long Nathalie's had that ring in her possession."

"It could be her father's, I suppose," Sophie acknowledged reluctantly. "You mentioned that he was an Englishman. What was his name?"

Robin's mouth quirked. "Edward White—very prosaic, I'm afraid. Nathalie and her mother called themselves 'Leblanc,' instead."

For which Sophie couldn't blame them: "Leblanc" did sound more impressive than its English equivalent. "Then the ring's *not* likely to be his. May I take it, for now? Our library might have a few books on heraldry. And James almost certainly has some at Pentreath."

"Very well," Robin said, almost absently, as he started leafing through the notebook.

"Anything useful?"

"Not sure—maybe a little. This seems to be a record of Nathalie's private expenses—money coming in and going out. Unsurprisingly, the latter exceeds the former," he added dryly.

He turned over a few more pages in silence, then paused, his brows lancing together.

"What is it?" Sophie asked at once.

"A loose page, tucked into the notebook." Robin pulled it out and unfolded it, his frown deepening. "It looks like part of a letter," he reported, after a moment. "In French."

Sophie's own French was passable, but Robin was the one who'd lived in France for four years. Concealing her impatience, she waited until he had finished reading.

When he looked up from the page, his face was pale and as grim as she'd ever seen it.

"A *billet-doux*?" she ventured.

"Not exactly." He folded the page again, his expression now carefully impassive. "Unless I'm very much mistaken, Nathalie was writing to the father of her baby. Asking for money—and threatening exposure."

Twenty

Music for a while,
Shall all your cares beguile,
Wondering how your pains are eased…

—Henry Purcell, *Tiresias*

From Aurelia, Lady Trevenan, to Sophie Tresilian

…While still adjusting to her loss, Sara seems to be in better spirits today and perhaps in the mood to be diverted. I think, my dear, the time might be just about right for that matter we discussed last week. Shall we say, four o'clock tomorrow afternoon?

❧

Sophie had spent less time choosing what to wear for a concert held before half of London than for tea at Pentreath with Robin's daughter. To dress too frivolously—lacy gown and lavishly trimmed hat—would be insensitive. Sara was in mourning, after all—indeed, she'd probably been wearing black frocks since January, after Cyril's death. Yet neither did she wish to appear gloomy and forbidding. The child had surely had her fill of sorrow this year. This visit was meant to cheer her.

Finally, she chose one of her more subdued costumes: a dove-grey suit with black piping, over a silk shirtwaist in a muted rose. Her hat, plain black straw trimmed with a band of ribbon and a small spray of pink and white flowers, was equally simple. And she borrowed the carriage, as befitted the slightly more formal circumstances of her visit.

Aurelia, wearing a lavender afternoon dress, greeted her warmly on her arrival at Pentreath. "Lovely to see you again. My, you do look smart!"

"Not too stiff, I hope?" Sophie couldn't quite keep the anxious note from her voice.

"Not at all." Aurelia paused, then added with her surprising perception, "Just be yourself, my dear, and Sara won't be able to help liking you, any more than *I* could when we first met."

Sophie managed a smile. "Thank you. I do hope you're right."

"I'm sure I will be about this." Aurelia gestured invitingly toward the sofa. "Sara's upstairs getting ready, by the way, and tea will be brought shortly."

They sat down together. The drawing room at Pentreath was always such a pleasant place, Sophie thought as she looked around: gracious and intimate at once. There'd been some changes since her last visit: family photographs on the mantel, an antique globe in one corner of the room, and a tan-and-white King Charles spaniel dozing in a basket by the unlit fireplace.

"How is Sara doing, truly?" Sophie asked. "She looked so fragile at the funeral the other day. I can't imagine how horrible it is to lose your brother and your mother so close together."

"The days aren't so bad. We've managed to keep her occupied with other pursuits. But at night—" Aurelia shook her head. "We go in to her, of course. I don't believe in letting children cry alone in the dark. And it helps that Robin is still spending his nights here, but I think it will be best when she can finally go home with him."

"I know. Robin misses her dearly, but until the investigation into Nathalie's death is complete, he believes Sara is safest and happiest with you, at Pentreath."

"How *is* the investigation going?" Aurelia asked. "Neither James nor I have heard much."

"It's—coming along," Sophie said cautiously, unsure how much to reveal even to her close friend and cousin-in-law. Robin was still seething over Sir Lucas's latest attempt to cause trouble for him, and none too pleased with Inspector Taunton for accepting the baronet's insinuations so readily. "Robin's determined to be part of it, though."

"That doesn't surprise me. He's not the sort to sit idly by while his life and reputation are at stake—no more than James is. And sometimes you just *have* to look into matters yourself, especially when you're the one who best knows the people involved."

Sophie gave a reluctant nod, remembering how diligently James and Aurelia had searched for the source of the slanders against him, Harry, and Robin five years ago. "All the same, I hope he doesn't end up antagonizing the police. That won't help *anyone*."

She'd had the devil of a time persuading Robin to show what they'd found in Nathalie's desk to Taunton, after their earlier clash. But while the inspector might have been too credulous about Sir Lucas Nankivell's so-called evidence, he still struck Sophie as an honest man who genuinely wanted to find the murderer. Better to have him as an ally than an adversary. So Robin had agreed to take Nathalie's notebook and the letter down to the police station today.

That letter… they'd speculated continually about it, wondering why it was written in French and why it hadn't been sent. Robin had pointed out logically enough that the father of Nathalie's unborn baby was not necessarily French himself—merely capable of reading the language, as many

English gentlemen probably were, having been taught French in the schoolroom. Sir Lucas therefore could not be ruled out as the father.

Only had he—or whomever the intended recipient was— even received the news of Nathalie's pregnancy? While that letter had gone unsent, another might have been mailed in its stead. Or perhaps Nathalie had found another means to convey her threats and demands.

And possibly sealed her own fate, Sophie thought with a shiver. And remembering Robin's face after he'd read the letter, she knew the same idea had occurred to him.

"Sophie, are you all right? You looked a million miles away."

Sophie roused and mustered a quick smile. "Sorry—I was just… wondering. Aurelia, might I borrow some books from your library—on heraldry?" She'd already exhausted the scant resources in Roswarne's library in a fruitless search for the ring's possible coat-of-arms.

"Of course you may, but—heraldry? I didn't know you had an interest in it."

"Not a great interest," Sophie admitted. "It's just that— well, Robin and I did find something yesterday. Mind you, it could turn out to be completely useless, but—"

She broke off as Aurelia held up a hand, then nodded significantly toward the doorway. "Sara, dear, are you ready to join us? Do come in."

With a shy smile, the girl stepped into the room. She looked less overwhelmed than she had at the funeral, Sophie thought: her face less pinched and with a little color in her cheeks. She still wore black, which made her look older than her almost-eight years, though her brown hair had been simply plaited and tied with a mauve ribbon.

"Sara, this is my good friend and cousin, Sophie Tresilian," Aurelia began. "You know her brother, Sir Harry Tresilian, is your father's partner in the hotel. Sophie is a professional singer, who's come back to Cornwall for a visit."

Sara made a little bob, then held out her hand. "How do you do, Miss Tresilian?"

Her voice was soft but clear. Sophie took the offered hand and shook it gravely; the girl's fingers were slight and delicate, and colder than they should be on a summer's day. "Very well, thank you. I'm pleased to meet you, Sara. Aurelia has told me so much about you."

Sara blinked, clearly surprised, but she did not look displeased. Just then, the spaniel, roused from his slumbers, uttered a happy bark and scampered toward them, his feathery tail waving like a banner.

Aurelia smiled. "Lovelace here has taken quite a shine to Sara."

The girl's cheeks pinked with pleasure, but she said conscientiously, "He belongs to Lady Trevenan, though, and maybe to Jared too."

The spaniel was presently gazing from Aurelia to Sara and back as though unsure of which goddess to worship first. Then he noticed Sophie and trotted over to make her acquaintance instead.

Sophie fondled the dog's silky ears. "What a pretty fellow you are—though quite a shameless flirt."

Sara smothered a tiny giggle. "Do you have a dog, Miss Tresilian?"

"Alas, no. I'm fond of dogs, but they're such social creatures, it wouldn't be fair to have one when I must be away so often. I do have a cat, though," Sophie added. "A beautiful Russian Blue." She'd left Tatiana with Amy when she departed for Cornwall. While she knew her staff wouldn't forget to feed the cat, Tatiana tended to become fractious when Sophie was gone for longer than a few days. Even the most independent pets needed some companionship.

"I like cats too," Sara replied. "I should like to have a kitten of my own someday. And maybe a puppy too, if they can get along."

"They can be trained to get along," Aurelia said, smiling. "We had cats *and* dogs at our home in New York when I was growing up. And horses at our country home."

Nothing like animals for breaking the ice, Sophie thought. They were still discussing the merits of various pets when the tea arrived.

Perhaps Aurelia had given particular instructions for the staff, because everything might have been designed to tempt a child's appetite. The sandwiches were cut in fanciful shapes, and the cakes, while plentiful, were dainty things, bright with pastel icing. The scones, however, were generous, and the bowls were heaped with clotted cream and strawberry jam.

Sara took tea with a liberal dash of milk in it, then accepted a scone. Much to Sophie's delight, she proceeded to apply butter, jam, and clotted cream in the true Cornish fashion.

Smiling, Sophie prepared a scone for herself in the exact same way.

Aurelia held out the plate of sandwiches to the child. "I asked Cook to make deviled ham sandwiches just for you, my dear. I know you're partial to them."

Sara took one, hesitated, then took another, murmuring a polite thank you. But both sandwiches were eaten, along with the laden scone and a Bakewell tart.

"May I give Lovelace a sandwich, Lady Trevenan?" she asked. The spaniel, seated at her feet, was gazing up at her with hopeful, melting eyes.

"Just one," Aurelia cautioned. "He's indulged enough as it is. And perhaps one of the egg sandwiches—the spices in the deviled ham might not agree with him."

Sarah set an egg-and-cress sandwich down before the dog, who devoured it with surprising daintiness.

"Are James and Jared anywhere about?" Sophie inquired, selecting a cake decorated with a crystallized violet. "I'd have expected them to descend on this bounty as well."

"Later, no doubt, but they're at the stables just now. James

316 PAMELA SHERWOOD

is teaching Jared to ride—or, rather, he's leading him around the paddock on a very old and placid pony," Aurelia qualified. "He might be ready for a pony of his own next year."

"So he's not afraid of horses?"

"Not in the least—no fear, no sense," Aurelia said with mingled pride and exasperation. "Typical Trelawney, according to James. Typical male, *I* say."

They all laughed, even Sara, though Sophie wasn't entirely sure how much the child understood. But there was something cozy and familiar about this whole scenario: women sharing a jest about the exasperating nature of men.

"So, Sara, Aurelia tells me you're fond of music?" she inquired, offering the girl the plate of sandwiches again.

Sara nodded, her eyes brightening, and took another ham sandwich. "It's my favorite subject. Along with French."

"Are you learning to play an instrument?"

"Miss Polgreen started me on piano before she left to get married last month," Sara replied. "She said I was making progress, but I was only playing scales then."

"Well, we all have to start there," Aurelia said consolingly.

Sara turned to Sophie. "Do you play an instrument, Miss Tresilian?"

"Yes, the violin. I started when I was just about your age. My brothers used to claim I made the most dreadful noises at first, just like a cat yowling." Sophie made a sound similar to Tatiana at her most vocal, and Sara giggled. "But I did improve with time—and practice."

"Sophie's a very good violin player, but an even better singer," Aurelia told Sara. "My dear, would you give us a song or two?" she appealed. "I still regret being unable to see you at the Albert Hall."

"Well, if Sara would like it," Sophie began.

The girl nodded vigorously. "Oh, yes, please!"

"And you're willing to provide the accompaniment—"

"Of course," Aurelia agreed, smiling.

"Then I'd be happy to," Sophie finished, setting her plate aside and rising to her feet.

❧

The voice, silver-clear and limpid as spring water, stopped Robin in his tracks.

Transfixed, he stood and listened as it wove a familiar spell around him, soothing away the ravages of a trying day like the stroke of a gentle hand.

No need to inquire the source. Handing his hat and coat to Pelham, he followed the sound down the passage to the drawing room. He found himself smiling as he recognized the words: "The Mermaid's Song," as sung by a Nereid.

Sophie had embarked on the second verse by the time Robin reached the drawing room. Loath to disturb the performance, he hovered in the doorway, watching her, slim and straight beside the piano. Aurelia was providing a deft accompaniment, the instrument trilling merrily beneath her fingers. And Sara sat listening raptly, her eyes dreamy, her lips curved in a smile of pure pleasure.

Robin's heart ached at the sight. It seemed a lifetime since he'd seen his daughter smile like that, with such unguarded happiness—since before Cyril's death, surely. He already loved Sophie to distraction, but he loved her just a bit more for giving Sara such a treat. He hoped that boded well for their eventual future as a family.

The song ended, and Robin joined his daughter in applauding the performers. Hearing the sound of two more hands clapping, Sara glanced toward the door and broke into a smile.

"Papa!" She sprang up from her chair and rushed to meet him.

"Hullo, sweeting." He stooped to embrace and kiss her, then turned to the ladies, smiling beside the piano. "Aurelia, Miss Sophie—that was charming. Pray, don't let me interrupt."

"That's quite all right; we were just finishing up." Sophie's dimpled smile flashed briefly. "The performer's motto: always leave the audience wanting more!"

"I can't persuade you to give an encore?" he asked.

She hesitated, then smiled more brilliantly. "Only if Sara's willing to join us." She turned to Robin's daughter. "Has your governess taught you to sing as well?"

Sara gave a shy nod. "Mostly folk songs."

"Have you a favorite?"

"I like 'English Country Garden.'"

"So do I." Sophie held out a hand to her. "Why don't we all sing it, just for your papa?"

Sara blushed but joined her willingly at the piano, as Aurelia played the introduction. While hesitant at first, Sara soon joined her sweet-toned treble to Sophie and Aurelia's sopranos, the three voices weaving a delightful harmony. Robin applauded more vigorously at the close.

"Brava!" he declared. "Excellently done!"

Smiling, Aurelia rose from the piano. "Such appreciation surely deserves a reward. I'll have more tea brought at once."

Sara perched on the arm of Robin's chair as he had his tea, talking more animatedly than she had since learning of Nathalie's death. Much to his relief, she seemed to have taken a genuine liking to Sophie, who—even better—appeared to reciprocate. "Can Miss Tresilian come to the Hall and see our music room, Papa? We have a piano *and* a harpsichord," she added proudly to Sophie, who was sitting opposite them on the sofa.

"Oh, can you play the harpsichord too?" Sophie asked with unfeigned interest.

"A little. It's not too different from a piano, except the sound's all… silvery—like a music box. Only," a shadow crossed her face, "*Maman* wouldn't let me play it last time. She said it was out of tune, and made me leave the music room."

"Is it? Then I'll have someone in to fix it, sweetheart," Robin promised.

Sara bit her lip. "I was mad at her," she confessed in a low voice. "And now…"

Robin put his arm around her. "I am sure *Maman* knows you aren't mad at her anymore," he said gently. "And that she has long since forgiven you."

Or she would have if she'd ever devoted as much attention to your feelings as to her appetites. But that was a bitter thought, and unworthy to share with his daughter. Sara looked slightly consoled by his words, which was all that mattered.

They were spared further awkwardness by the entrance of James and Jared, the latter boisterous from the excitement of his first riding lesson. Aurelia's spaniel, resting at her feet, leapt up and frisked over to the new arrivals. A noisy, cheerful family interlude ensued, in which everyone seemed to be talking at once. Not even attempting to compete, Robin leaned back in his chair, let the day's frustrations and annoyances fall away, and enjoyed it all.

Perhaps someday he too would experience this sort of happy chaos, when he, Sophie, and Sara had formed their own family. Cyril's place would always be vacant, but perhaps, God willing, other children would come along to make places of their own. He caught Sophie's eye and suspected from the softness of her smile that her thoughts were running along similar lines.

Eventually, Nanny Odgers appeared to reclaim her charges, ushering them upstairs for baths before supper. Sophie asked Aurelia if she might look through those books on heraldry she'd mentioned earlier, and Robin quickly offered his assistance in fetching and carrying. They withdrew to the library, leaving their hosts to enjoy some much-desired privacy.

"I was surprised to see you here today," Robin told Sophie as they stepped over the threshold. "Delighted, but surprised."

"Aurelia invited me to take tea with her this afternoon, and mentioned Sara would be present. So I couldn't pass it up. Your daughter's lovely," she added, smiling. "I look forward to getting to know her better."

Robin spared a moment to be grateful for Aurelia's handling of the situation. He'd wanted Sara and Sophie to meet as well, but he suspected he wouldn't have arranged their first encounter nearly as deftly. "She appears to have taken to you also. I was glad to see all of you having such a pleasant time together."

"From the look of it, I'd say we had a better afternoon than you," Sophie observed, eyeing him closely. "What's wrong, dear heart? Did things not go well with Inspector Taunton?"

"Things did not go *at all* with Taunton—he's been sent back to Newquay."

"What? When did this happen?"

"Early this morning, according to the constables," Robin replied. "He and Sergeant Jenkins have both left St. Perran, though no one could give me the particulars of their removal. So I rode over to Newquay in search of a fuller explanation."

"Did you speak to Taunton?"

"He wasn't available to be spoken to, but his superior was." Robin took a breath, trying to quell the anger that rose to the surface when he remembered their exchange. "I'll spare you all the infuriating details, but the police have decided not to proceed further with their investigation at this time."

Sophie stared at him. "But... how *can* they? Nathalie's killer—"

"Was most likely some chance intruder whose main interest was in Nathalie's jewels. They believe that he has long since left the area with his ill-gotten gains and will be difficult, if not impossible, to trace," Robin finished stonily.

"That wasn't the song they were singing yesterday when Taunton all but accused you of arranging to have Nathalie killed."

"No. And moments later, I put Taunton onto Nankivell's

scent. My guess is that he proceeded to interrogate Nankivell or went straight to his superior with the information. Whichever it was, the timing is—interesting, to say the least."

Sophie nodded her understanding. "Because, barely a day later, he's removed from the case and sent back to Newquay. Do you think Sir Lucas complained to his superior?"

"Nankivell or someone with even more influence in the county. My money's on George Boscawen, personally."

Her eyes widened. "Sir Lucas's *stepfather*?"

Robin gave a grim nod; the baronet's widowed mother had remarried not long after Nankivell succeeded to his title. "Major Henshawe retired as magistrate last year. Captain Boscawen took his place and is now cutting quite a figure in St. Perran. And I have no doubt that Mrs. Boscawen—the former Lady Nankivell—would exert whatever influence she has on her husband to prevent the police from looking into her son's part in all this. I could almost sympathize—if it weren't for the possibility that her son murdered the mother of my daughter."

"Do you *truly* believe Sir Lucas killed Nathalie?"

Robin barked a laugh. "He's slandered me. Cuckolded me. Served me any ill turn he can. Why should he balk at widowing me too?" Then, before Sophie's steady gaze, he admitted grudgingly, "I don't know, to be honest. Initially, I wouldn't have thought so. Not because he's incapable of murder, but because I can't envision him committing *this* one." He vividly recalled the livid weal about Nathalie's throat, a silent testament of the killer's rage. "There was… passion in the deed—and Nankivell is too cold, too calculating for that. I doubt he'd go to such an extreme unless he felt himself to be severely threatened. Even when he was slandering me, James, and Harry five years ago, he endeavored to keep his own hands clean."

"You don't think *he* could have hired someone to kill her?" Sophie asked.

"That's slightly more plausible, but still…" Robin shook his head. "I just don't know."

"What do you mean to do, now that the police have backed off?"

He met her gaze squarely. "Keep searching on my own. What else *can* I do?"

Sophie nodded, not questioning, not protesting, and his heart seemed to swell at how perfectly she understood him. He wouldn't have blamed her, or any woman, for asking him to accept that the investigation was closed and to let the matter drop. Instead, she turned briskly to the bookcases looming before them. "We should get started, then. That ring's the only other evidence we've got so far, and I'm nowhere near to identifying the coat of arms yet."

Relief poured through him in a sweet, sustaining flood. His partner, his true mate—at long last, he'd got it right. "Did you bring the ring with you?"

She shook her head apologetically. "I was worried about misplacing it, so I left it behind at Roswarne, among my things. But I made a wax impression of the crest," she added. "And it's definitely a bull's head, wearing some sort of collar. I couldn't find anything like it in our heraldry books, but we only have two in our library, so that wasn't surprising. Aurelia says they've got a much wider selection here—at least two shelves devoted to the subject!"

Robin felt his spirits lift, in spite of everything. "Then let's get started, my love. Against the left-hand wall, wasn't it?"

As one, they turned to the task before them.

Twenty-one

And graven in diamonds in letters plain
There is written, her fair neck round about…

—Sir Thomas Wyatt, "Whoso List to Hunt"

ENTERING THE BALLROOM AT ROSWARNE, SOPHIE caught her breath. Mama had done a beautiful job with the flowers: arrangements of white calla lilies and golden roses—Grace's favorites—stood in green jasperware vases, placed throughout the room. The sunny hues brightened the room even more than chandeliers.

"Lovely, isn't it?" Cecily remarked, coming up behind her. "I always wish *I* had Mama's eye for flowers."

Sophie murmured her assent. "Grace will be delighted, and John is pleased by whatever pleases her, so they should both be very happy."

They exchanged a smile. "Someday we'll be celebrating *your* engagement here," Cecily predicted. "Yours and Robin's."

Sophie felt herself flush but made no demur. "Perhaps."

"Almost certainly." Cecily slipped her arm around Sophie's waist. "It's high time you were happy, Lark. I know how hard these last four years have been—for both of you. Just know that we're all behind you on this."

Grateful beyond measure, Sophie returned her sister's embrace. "Even Harry?"

"Even Harry," Cecily confirmed. "I know he wasn't happy about the way Robin handled things before, but he's come round. And he's finally accepted that, as far as you're concerned, the choice was made long ago. As he should," she added a touch critically. "He's seen this often enough in our family. And I'll wager he'll be just the same when he meets *his* future wife."

Sophie couldn't help but smile. "I don't suppose he's any closer to finding her, is he?"

Cecily shook her head, smiling too. "No, but there are several ladies who aspire to the position. Mama is trying to make sure he cultivates their acquaintance, but so far he's eluded the net. *I* think it's time he settled down, rather than continue with his—present association."

She meant the widow with whom Harry had kept discreet company for the past two years. From what Sophie had heard, Mrs. Bettesworth enjoyed her freedom far too well ever to remarry, her late husband having been something of a martinet.

"Maybe he just hasn't met the next Lady Tresilian yet," she observed, then tactfully changed the subject. "Have you a moment to go over the programme, Cecy? Grace got her list of songs to me this morning. Nothing too complicated, but have we ever performed *this* one?"

Cecily glanced over the list Sophie handed her. "I'm not sure, but let's see if one of our songbooks has the words."

Arm in arm, they started for the music room.

"You look splendid, by the way," Cecily added, regarding Sophie with an approving eye.

"Not too splendid, I hope. This is Grace's evening, after all." Sophie glanced down at herself a trifle anxiously. Given the circumstances of her return, she'd left her grandest evening gowns in London, packing only a few of the more subdued ones. But she'd found a way to brighten this one—silk faille in a dusky shade between wine and rose—with a band of paler rose ribbon, so it didn't look *too* somber.

"No, not at all," Cecily assured her. "Just stylish and sophisticated. I can scarce recognize my little sister. Even that necklace looks right—and normally I don't care for jet at all."

Sophie touched the sparkling collar of Whitby jet at her throat; matching earrings dangled from her lobes. "It doesn't look like mourning jewelry?" She'd thought of donning Robin's pearls for the occasion, but the timing just hadn't felt—appropriate.

Cecily shook her head. "It's fine. The color of the dress helps. I could never wear anything so vivid myself."

"Well, I don't think *I'd* look as well as you in powder blue," Sophie told her. "And that lace is gorgeous—Valenciennes?"

Her sister nodded. "This gown is one of Arthur's favorites," she began, then stopped short on the threshold of the music room. "Oh, Essie—no!"

Three-year-old Esther Penhallow stood on the piano bench, dangling her doll over the inside of the instrument. Shaking her head, Cecily hurried to retrieve her youngest daughter.

"*Not* in the piano, my love," she said firmly, scooping the child up in her arms. "Mummy won't be able to play tonight if you put Dolly in there."

Sophie frowned, something tugging at the back of her mind. But before she could get a hold on whatever it was, the Penhallows' nursemaid arrived, pink-cheeked and panting. "I'm that sorry, missus!" she apologized. "I turned my back on Miss Essie for just one minute—"

"That's quite all right, Mary. I know just how active children are at this age." Cecily handed Esther over to the nursemaid. "But it's high time she was in bed."

"Yes, missus." Mary whisked her charge away.

Cecily turned back to Sophie. "Now, where were we?"

They found the song in a book of Scottish and Irish airs,

and rehearsed it twice before setting the book on the music stand with the other sheet music and returning to the ballroom.

Guests began to arrive around seven o'clock, and the Tregarths were among the first wave. Sturdy, practical Mr. Tregarth, his slender, elegant wife, and Grace herself a charming blend of the two, with her mother's looks and her father's common sense. Tonight she wore a gown the same shade as the golden roses in the ballroom and her bright grey eyes shone like stars. John's face lit up at the sight of his betrothed: it had been a long wait for them, while John had studied and finally established himself as a lawyer.

As long as for Robin and herself, Sophie thought with a slight pang. But John and Grace had had the privilege of a pledge and a promise, and they could acknowledge their love openly, without fear of censure. But self-pity was pointless and self-indulgent—all that mattered was that she and Robin could, at long last, have a life together. And someday, perhaps, they could enjoy a night like this, surrounded by family and friends wishing them well.

She had just exchanged pleasantries with the Prideaux family, when she caught sight of a familiar dark-haired figure, lingering by the doorway.

Robin. As always, her heart gave that little skip when she saw him.

Even fully and formally dressed, he drew her gaze like no other man in the room. Granted, that might have to do with her intimate knowledge of how he looked *undressed*. In her mind's eye, she could see his lean, hard-muscled torso as vividly as she had during those stolen days and nights in Oxfordshire. She could imagine his touch, the sensation of his cheek against her brow, his warm breath stirring her hair…

Shameless, Sophie told herself sternly. That even in the shadow of grief and mourning she could still desire him like this. Then his gaze, burning blue, locked with hers, and she knew from the rush of heat that swept through her body that he wanted her just as intensely.

It took a little time and some discretion, but eventually she managed to drift away from the guests in her immediate vicinity and toward the corner in which he was now standing.

He wore impeccable evening dress, along with a black armband. His face looked drawn and shadowed with fatigue, but he mustered a smile for her that held just a hint of the smolder she'd seen in his eyes before.

"Robin." She extended her hand, aware that they might be watched. "I am so glad you chose to come tonight." He'd been undecided as of yesterday, she knew, and hearing that the Nankivells were likely to attend hadn't made the prospect any more appealing for him.

He took her hand with equal formality, but the contact was still electric for them both. "Well, I accepted this invitation long before Nathalie's death, so I thought I'd put in a brief appearance, just to wish John and Grace well. I won't dance, of course, but I'd be happy enough to drink their health."

She squeezed his hand lightly before letting go. "They'll be pleased that you're here too."

Robin lowered his voice. "Sophie, I don't wish to cause any sort of difficulty for you by having come tonight."

"You won't," she insisted. "You're Harry's friend and business partner. No one will question your being here tonight." A man in mourning could rejoin society far sooner than a woman in the same situation. Unfair as that was, Sophie couldn't summon the necessary indignation tonight, when it meant seeing Robin. "And as for me, no one present would dare to criticize me here, in my family's home—it would be the height of rudeness. Besides, tonight is about John and Grace, so the attention will be on them and rightly so. Grace wishes me to sing a few songs. Nothing too elaborate, just some of her and John's favorites."

His eyes warmed, beacons in his tired face. "Another

reason I am glad to have come. You've always managed to transport me when you sing. For a time I forget all else, everything difficult or wretched, when I listen to you."

"What higher accolade can any singer hope for?" Sophie asked, smiling. "Now, please go and help yourself to some supper from the buffet. I can tell just by looking at you that you haven't been eating properly today."

"I suppose I haven't found the time for a full meal," he admitted. "We're getting ready for a flood of new guests at the hotel. And there's been Sara to think of."

"You're making certain that *she* eats, aren't you?" she countered. "It's only common sense that you do so too, and not just when your friends are watching you to make sure. Why are you smiling like that?"

"Something James told me. That you would start looking after *me*, rather than the other way around, and if I had any sense, I would let you."

"And do you intend to?" Sophie inquired, raising a brow at him.

Robin smiled as he began to move off. "I shall bow to my friend's superior wisdom, and do just as he suggests."

Sophie lost track of time for a while, helping to greet other guests who arrived with warm wishes for the betrothed couple. But she next glanced over toward the corner where the buffet stood and observed with satisfaction that Robin had acquired a plate of food, which he was consuming steadily, if absentmindedly.

Soon after that, the entertainment began, the guests filing into the music room and taking their seats. Cecily sat down at the piano, while Sophie positioned herself beside it. They exchanged a smile, remembering all the times they'd done this over the years, then Sophie turned to face the audience.

"Good evening, everyone," she said, pitching her voice effortlessly to fill the salon. "Thank you all for coming. My future sister-in-law," she smiled at Grace, sitting in the first row of chairs, her hand linked with John's, "has asked me to sing a few songs that are especially dear to her and my brother. I dedicate this performance to them, along with my warmest wishes for their happiness. To John and Grace!"

"To John and Grace," the audience echoed, and Sophie nodded at Cecily to play the introduction to the first song.

The performance went smoothly—even the song she and Cecily had just rehearsed—and the audience was in a mellow mood, willing to be pleased by Grace's selection of sweet, simple love songs. Sophie even persuaded them to sing along with her on the choruses, and soon the room echoed with their joined voices. Buoyed along by song and sentiment, Sophie let herself relax and enjoy the moment, as she seldom had leisure to do during her formal concerts.

Four songs in the programme—just the right number for an occasion like this. But Sophie's heart had turned over just a little when she'd recognized the last one on Grace's list: the song she had sung in Robin's pavilion five years ago, the true beginning of it all. Her gaze sought and found him now, sitting a few rows back from John and Grace, watching her with that heart-stopping intensity. She sent him a smile and embarked on the final song, her sense of their history—the bitter and the sweet—lending the words a deeper poignancy:

> *"Once in the dear dead days beyond recall*
> *When on the world the mists began to fall,*
> *Out of the dreams that rose in happy throng*
> *Low to our hearts Love sang an old sweet song.*
> *And in the dusk where fell the firelight gleam,*
> *Softly it wove itself into our dream.*
>
> *Just a song at twilight, when the lights are low,*
> *And the flickering shadows softly come and go,*
> *Tho' the heart be weary, sad the day and long,*

> *Still to us at twilight comes Love's old song,*
> *Comes Love's old sweet song."*

The audience joined Sophie on the chorus, but her voice rang out alone and triumphant in the last verse, affirming love's power to transcend pain, hardship, even the end of life itself:

> *"Even today we hear Love's song of yore,*
> *Deep in our hearts it dwells forevermore.*
> *Footsteps may falter, weary grow the way,*
> *Still we can hear it at the close of day.*
> *So till the end, when life's dim shadows fall,*
> *Love will be found the sweetest song of all."*

The applause was enthusiastic, but it was the glowing pleasure on Grace and John's faces that made Sophie's evening. Afterward, while graciously accepting her performer's due of praise, she made sure to direct the attention back to the betrothed couple as quickly as possible, then looked about for Robin.

As before, he'd found a quiet corner, and she made her way unhurriedly to his side.

"I hope you enjoyed the performance, Mr. Pendarvis." She kept her tone light and casual.

"Yes, very much." His tone was equally light, but the warmth in his eyes was like a caress. "I've developed a certain fondness for that last song."

"You do not find it hopelessly sentimental?"

"Sentimental, yes, but far from hopeless. I've come to understand, at long last, that love should never be without hope."

"At long last, indeed," Sophie observed, smiling to take the sting from the words.

"Not before time, you'll agree. Do you know, I could almost envy John and Grace, just a bit, for being at the beginning of it all?"

"We're at the beginning of it too," Sophie reminded him. "An interrupted beginning, to be sure, but no less sweet for that."

"Perhaps even sweeter," Robin agreed, mouth curving in a faint smile. "I should go and congratulate the happy couple. We haven't spoken much before—" He broke off, stiffening beside her, his gaze arrowing across the room over her shoulder.

"Robin, what's wrong?"

His voice was taut. "Look, over there."

She turned her head, following the direction of his gaze. "Sir Lucas and—his wife?"

They were standing by Grace and John, offering their good wishes no doubt. Sir Lucas looked uncomfortable, Sophie was pleased to note, but Constance Nankivell, a petite brunette with a round, softly pretty face, was smiling.

Robin's hand closed about her arm like a vise. "Lady Nankivell is wearing Nathalie's diamond necklace."

Sophie snapped her attention back to him. "What? Are you sure?"

He nodded, tight-lipped and flint-eyed. "Entirely. The circumstances in which I saw it are impossible to forget."

Sophie winced, remembering what he'd told her in Oxfordshire. "What do you want me to do, dear heart?" she asked, pitching her voice for his ears alone.

His mouth twisted in a parody of a smile. "Why, procure me an introduction, of course."

"Of course." Sophie kept her tone mild and pleasant as she slipped her own social mask back into place.

She stole a glance at Robin as they crossed the room, uneasily aware of something... dangerous behind his eyes, something more than anger—tightly contained for now, but lethal if allowed to escape. Even when she looked away, she could feel it radiating from him like heat from a furnace.

The Nankivells were just turning away from the engaged

couple as Sophie and Robin approached. Sophie glanced first at Sir Lucas, and saw a look of dismay cross his face before his gaze slid away from them both. Remembering the many times he'd tried to injure or humiliate Robin, the last just a few days ago, Sophie felt a stab of vindictive satisfaction at his discomfiture. Suppressing it as best she could, she turned to his wife.

Constance Nankivell looked younger than she had from a distance, nearer to Sophie's own age, and her round brown eyes, along with the pale pink gown she wore, added to the impression of youth and artlessness. Trying not to stare at the diamond pendant blazing splendidly, even garishly about her smooth throat, Sophie opened her mouth to begin the introduction, but Lady Nankivell spoke first.

"Miss Sophie Tresilian?" The brown eyes were guileless, even friendly. "I wanted to tell you how well you sang tonight."

Any opening was a start. Sophie smiled brilliantly. "Thank you, Lady Nankivell. I am glad you enjoyed my performance."

"Oh, call me Constance, please," Lady Nankivell entreated. "I still haven't got used to my title, even hearing it from friends—or those I should like to consider friends."

Sophie decided Lady Nankivell was much nicer than her husband deserved. "Constance, then," she agreed. "Grace tells me you have but recently returned to Cornwall?"

Constance colored slightly. "I've been visiting my parents in Birmingham for the last few weeks. But Cornwall is my home *now*."

Sophie did not miss the emphasis on that last word, and wondered whom it was Constance was trying to convince. "And a wonderful home it is," she agreed. "I've been away for several years myself, but I still consider Cornwall the home of my heart."

Beyond his wife's shoulder, Sir Lucas was shifting from foot to foot, clearly desiring nothing more than to remove himself and his wife from the vicinity. Fortunately, Constance showed no inclination to oblige him. "That's not surprising if your roots are here. I understand the Tresilians are one of the county's oldest families?"

"Oh, we are, along with many of our neighbors." Sophie sensed Robin coming to a point beside her, like an actor preparing to make his entrance. "Talking of which, may I present to you Mr. Robin Pendarvis, an old friend of the family?"

"Pendarvis?" Constance's eyes widened, then a slight flush mounted to her cheeks. "Oh, you are... pray accept my condolences on the loss of your wife. I was—not well-acquainted with her," she rushed on, her flush deepening. "But what a terrible thing to happen, all the same."

"Thank you, Lady Nankivell," Robin returned, bowing punctiliously over her hand. "It was terrible, indeed."

His grave, measured tone seemed to irritate Sir Lucas beyond bearing. "In light of your *terrible* bereavement, Pendarvis," he broke in, "I am surprised to see you in attendance tonight."

Sophie stiffened, thinking the same could be said of the baronet. Had he not lost a mistress, after all? To say nothing of the baby he might have fathered. She leveled a withering stare at him. "Mr. Pendarvis is here at *our* express invitation, Sir Lucas. We do not deny our friends the comforts of our home and our companionship in times of trouble."

Constance looked uncomfortable, but Robin did not even deign to acknowledge Sir Lucas's remark. All his attention, his single-minded focus, was on the baronet's wife. "What a magnificent necklace you're wearing tonight, Lady Nankivell. Might I ask how you came by it?"

Constance touched the pendant. "It was a gift from Sir Lucas, on my return." She paused, eyeing Robin uncertainly. "Why do you ask, Mr. Pendarvis?"

Robin swallowed, but his gaze and voice were perfectly steady. "Because the last time I saw that necklace, it was around the throat of my late wife, Nathalie."

Constance stared at him, the color draining from her face as the significance of his words sank in. "But Sir Lucas…" Her voice trailed off in confusion.

"Absurd!" the baronet interrupted again. His face was flushed—with anger or with nerves? Sophie suspected it was both. He stabbed a furious forefinger at Robin. "*You* are delusional, Pendarvis! I gave this to my wife and my wife alone!"

Now Robin looked at his nemesis, and Sophie caught her breath at the icy rage that had uncoiled in his eyes. Only his voice was colder. "I know what I saw, Nankivell. And when I saw it. As should *you*, for you were present at the time."

"Come, my dear." Sir Lucas took his wife's arm. "I will not stay here to be maligned."

"Oh, I think you will, Nankivell," a new voice remarked.

Harry had appeared behind Sir Lucas—and he was flanked by James, John, and Arthur. Silently, the four men formed a circle around the baronet, cutting him off from the rest of the room. Sir Lucas's eyes darted from one face to the other, but found no mercy in any.

Was he remembering how they'd taken him down five years ago? Not for the first time, Sophie wished that she'd seen it.

"I suggest we remove ourselves to the library," Harry continued. "As we did before."

Mouth tightening, Sir Lucas drew himself up haughtily. "I don't have to go anywhere with you, Tresilian. Let me pass, all of you!"

No one moved. Robin said coolly, "Shall we send for Inspector Taunton? I am sure that he, and perhaps even his superior, would be interested in knowing just where my late wife's stolen property has turned up."

Constance stifled a gasp, her hand straying to the pendant, then dropping away at once in revulsion. Sophie felt a pang of pity for her—the innocent dupe of an unscrupulous man.

Sir Lucas, who'd paled visibly at the mention of Taunton, now rounded on Robin. "How dare you distress my wife,

Pendarvis, with your talk of police and stolen property! I will not stay to be insulted further!" He bent over Constance in a display of solicitude as fulsome as it was false. "Come, my lady, let us depart at once."

"No." The word was faint but definite. To everyone's amazement, Constance swallowed and repeated more firmly, "No." Freeing her arm from her husband's clutches, she straightened to her full height and faced them all. "I am not going anywhere at present, Sir Lucas. I want to hear what Mr. Pendarvis has to say. All of it."

※

Sophie knew from bitter experience that there was no easy way to break a woman's heart—or shatter her illusions, at the very least.

To his credit, Robin made the effort to do so with a minimum of cruelty, speaking calmly and without heat of finding Nathalie and Sir Lucas together—his tone left no doubt as to his meaning—and seeing the necklace around Nathalie's throat. All the same, it was painful to watch the color, along with any remaining vestige of hope, drain from Constance's face as she listened.

Sir Lucas had lapsed into defiant silence, arms crossed, refusing to look at anyone in the library. No doubt he was recalling his previous defeat at the hands of Robin, Harry, and James—and seething that they'd brought him to this point again. John had gone back to the party with Grace, but quiet, watchful Arthur remained, pen and paper close at hand should some record of this meeting become necessary. Sophie herself had flatly refused to be dismissed.

"So, how did that necklace come to be back in your possession, Nankivell?" Harry inquired conversationally. "Did you pinch it when Nathalie wasn't looking, or did she throw it at you in a fit of pique? I can't see her parting with it otherwise."

The baronet glanced at him with dislike, his mouth compressing mutinously.

"Answer him, Sir Lucas," Constance spoke at last, her voice pitched high and taut with strain. "I want to know how I came to be wearing your dead mistress's jewels!" She reached up, fumbling with the necklace's catch, and all but flung it from her when it came undone. It fell almost soundlessly to the carpet, where it glittered like a diamond snake.

Sir Lucas lurched forward in his chair as though he meant to scoop it up, only to desist at a barrage of condemnatory stares. He slumped back, sullen and defeated.

"Nathalie and I parted company a few days before her death." He gave a short, forced laugh. "To tell the truth, I can't think what I ever saw in her. And as our association was at an end, I demanded the return of the necklace."

"And she gave it to you, just like that?" James sounded skeptical.

Sir Lucas shrugged. "There was a bit of a scene—she was a Frenchwoman, after all. But in the end, I convinced her to part with it."

"So you took the necklace when you broke with my wife." Robin's tone was neutral, his face expressionless, but for some reason, Sophie felt her scalp prickle when he spoke.

Nankivell contrived to look down his nose. "That's what I just said, Pendarvis."

"You lie."

In an instant, Robin had surged from his chair and seized Sir Lucas by the throat. Constance made a sound that was half gasp, half shriek, as the other men leapt to their feet.

"You lie," Robin repeated through clenched teeth now, as he drove the struggling baronet backward, slamming him hard against the nearest wall. "Nathalie's maid, Enid, saw the necklace among her things when she undressed her for the night. It was in her jewel box—and you know that because you were *there*! You killed her, didn't you? You murdered my wife!" His hand tightened about Sir Lucas's throat, and the man began to choke and gag, his face turning an alarming shade of puce. "She was *pregnant*, you bastard—and you killed them both!"

Sophie heard a faint whimper from Constance, then someone—probably Harry—swore. But her own attention was fixed on her lover, and the murderous rage darkening his eyes. "Robin, no!" she said sharply. "Let me summon the constable!"

Harry and James had already converged on the pair, trying to wrest them apart.

"Let him go, Rob!" Harry caught his friend by the shoulder. "He's not worth soiling your hands on."

James had pinioned Sir Lucas's arms, but the baronet, doubled over and crowing for breath, made no attempt to resist.

"I didn't kill her!" he rasped out, hanging limp in James's grasp. "As God is my witness, she was dead when I got there!"

❧

"I took the necklace," Sir Lucas repeated, some minutes later, his voice still hoarse but clearer. "But I swear she was already dead when I entered her chamber—just after midnight."

He sat slumped in his chair again, pale, disheveled, all his arrogance gone. Robin's attack and the threat of arrest had taken the remaining fight out of him. Now he swallowed painfully. "It was—*horrible.* Her face…"

He paused, looking about the room with the air of one expecting… sympathy? understanding? Encountering only stony stares, he dropped his gaze to the carpet.

"We *had* broken with each other, before."

"Her decision or yours?" Sophie surprised herself by asking, but she was even more surprised when Sir Lucas responded.

"Hers, damn her. She said she was weary of me." Insult

flickered briefly in his eyes. "Not as weary as I was of her, I told her, and I demanded the necklace back. She laughed in my face." His hands clenched in his lap. "Mercenary bitch. But I still had the key she gave me. I knew where she kept her jewels, and that she slept like the—like the dead, after…"

After sex, Sophie finished silently. Sir Lucas had probably hoped to enjoy Nathalie's favors one last time. She stole a glance at Robin and saw by his sardonic expression that he'd arrived at a similar conclusion.

"Anyway, she was dead," Sir Lucas resumed, his voice and expression harder this time. "I could not tell how long. I didn't want to touch her. And there was her jewel box, just sitting on the vanity. I took what I'd come for… and a few other things as well."

No comment greeted this disclosure, but the accusing silence said it all. *Adulterer. Coward. Thief.* Sophie did not know whether she was more appalled by the baronet's theft or his self-serving decision not to raise the alarm when he discovered Nathalie's body hours before her maid.

"Well, why shouldn't I have taken it?" Sir Lucas demanded, looking up defiantly. "The necklace was mine, bought and paid for—it wasn't going to do Nathalie any good."

"*Mine* bought and paid for, you mean," Constance reminded him. "You used my family's money, my dowry, to buy gifts for that—that French slut!" She flushed at having to utter such a vulgar word, but she did not retract it.

"And I realized not a moment too soon that you were worth twenty of her!" Sir Lucas broke in hurriedly.

Constance stared at him, then turned away, the soft planes of her face hardening into something flinty and unyielding.

"Nathalie was already bleeding me dry. I can't think what I saw in her," he said again.

A way to get revenge on Robin, Sophie thought. Too bad for Nankivell that the petty satisfaction had been outweighed by the demands of a cold, calculating mistress.

"And the child?" Robin asked in a level voice. He had himself under control again, but Sophie sensed that the veneer was very thin.

Sir Lucas rubbed his throat and looked away. "There truly *was* a child?"

"She was three months along," Robin confirmed, after a moment.

"It wouldn't have been mine," Sir Lucas said, perhaps too quickly. "Our—arrangement began only in May. And we always took preventive measures. Besides," he added, with what might have been relief, "I noticed she was putting on weight the last time we were together. She was undoubtedly *enceinte* by then."

Constance closed her eyes as though gripped by a spasm of pain. Sophie wished she could say something comforting to her, but feared to make bad worse. And for all her seeming softness, Lady Nankivell appeared to have her share of pride.

Robin's brows drew together. "So you were not her only lover."

Sir Lucas's lips thinned. "No. And as to whom else Nathalie was entertaining in her bed," he added with a lingering spurt of malice, "why don't you start by looking for the blond man I saw her trysting with at Easter?"

"A blond *Englishman*?" Sophie asked at once, seeing the temper spark in Robin's eyes.

"I assume so," Sir Lucas said, shrugging. "They appeared to be speaking English when I saw them. Not that I heard much. I was too far away."

Robin had got hold of himself again. "Where did you see them?"

"The churchyard. I was there seeing to my father's headstone. I assume Nathalie was there because of the boy." To Sophie's relief, there was no sneer or disparagement in Sir Lucas's voice when he mentioned Cyril; she doubted anyone could have restrained Robin in that case. "Deuced odd place to meet a lover, I thought," he went on. "But I saw them leave the churchyard together, arm in arm. Just like old chums."

Twenty-two

It is a wise father that knows his own child.

—William Shakespeare, *The Merchant of Venice*

"WELL, ROB, SHALL WE CALL THE CONSTABLE?" HARRY inquired, eyeing Sir Lucas with distaste. "You could have him up before the magistrates for petty theft, at least."

The baronet went a sickly shade of grey. And Robin, to Sophie's watchful eye, looked very little better—more shaken by this latest revelation than he cared to admit.

"Gentlemen."

To everyone's surprise, it was Constance who spoke, rising shakily from her chair. She was still pale, but her eyes were dry and her spine poker-straight as she gathered the remains of her dignity around her. Recognizing the pose all too well, Sophie ached with pity for her. "I don't deny that my husband has behaved disgracefully"—Sir Lucas shifted uncomfortably in his seat at those words—"but please, I ask you—I *beg* you—not to contact the police! Please don't make his shame public as well!"

Harry and James exchanged an uneasy glance, but it was to Robin that Constance directed her appeal and her gaze. "Mr. Pendarvis, Sir Lucas claims not to have killed your wife or…

got her with child. I understand why you would doubt his word, but there appears to be no evidence contradicting that claim. As for the misdeed of which he *is* guilty—if your wife's jewels were returned to you, would that end the matter?"

Robin looked at her for a long moment, his face unreadable, but Sophie thought she saw a slight softening in his eyes. "It would, Lady Nankivell," he said at last.

Constance stooped to pick up the fallen necklace from the carpet. "Here." She dropped it into Robin's hand. "I will see that the rest of your wife's belongings are returned to you tomorrow. And if any are missing, I will ensure that you are fairly recompensed for their value."

The necklace glittered passively in Robin's palm. "Thank you, Lady Nankivell."

Sir Lucas cleared his throat. "My lady—"

Constance rounded on him, a look of scathing contempt on her mild face. "Not one word more, *husband*!" The word dripped with scorn. "You have already shown yourself to be a liar, a coward, and a thief! Pray don't make things worse by being an ass as well!"

The baronet's mouth dropped open, but no sound emerged. Sophie suspected no one had spoken like that to him in years, if ever, least of all a woman.

Constance turned back to the others. "Now, gentlemen, if you will excuse us, it has been… rather a trying evening, and I should like to go home now."

"I'll have the carriage brought round at once," Harry replied, and after a quick exchange of glances with Robin, who merely nodded, he escorted the Nankivells from the library.

Sophie watched them depart, Constance in the lead, her head held high, and Sir Lucas following with an almost hangdog air. Would he be a good and faithful husband now? She doubted it, but perhaps he might be more discreet. Whatever the Nankivells' marriage had been like before, Constance's expression seemed to presage some changes in the wind, and Sophie suspected few of them would be to the baronet's liking. She permitted herself a private little smile. Sometimes fate had a way of serving up one's just deserts, after all.

James and Arthur were the next to leave, the former clapping Robin briefly on the shoulder as he passed. A corner of Robin's mouth lifted in acknowledgment, but he continued to stare down at the diamond pendant winking in his hand.

Sophie crossed to the sideboard where the decanters stood, poured out a measure of whiskey, and brought it to him. "Here, dear heart. You look like you could use this."

Robin took the glass with a murmur of thanks, tossed off the contents, and drew a long, not entirely steady breath. "What a night."

Sophie put her hand on his arm. "Don't let that vile man upset you."

He looked up, his eyes bleak. "I have to wonder if it's ever going to end. Or if Nankivell will go on looking for new ways to stab me in the back."

"I think his stabbing days may be over—you frightened him tonight. You frightened *me* a little too," she confessed.

"Oh, God." He closed his eyes. "I'm sorry. That's the last thing I ever wanted to do. I saw the necklace, and then he *lied*, and I just—"

"Shhh." She put her arms around him. "No one here blames you for losing control, under the circumstances. *I* certainly don't."

He opened his eyes, regarded her somberly. "Do you think he was telling the truth? About not being the father?"

"Perhaps. Granted, he could have been lying to save his skin," she added, "but he did seem genuinely surprised about the pregnancy."

Robin gave a slow nod. "Nathalie didn't tell him. Either because she hadn't the chance to—or because it didn't concern him."

"That makes it more likely that he wasn't the intended recipient of that letter."

So who was? The question hovered unspoken between them.

"A blond man," Sophie said, thinking aloud. "Most likely an Englishman."

"Who was here at Easter, and trysted with her in the churchyard," Robin supplied.

"A gentleman, sufficiently well-educated to read a letter written in French."

"A man of means, almost certainly. Nathalie wouldn't have pursued someone who wasn't successful." His mouth crooked wryly. "No more struggling architects or obscure artists."

"A man of means," Sophie agreed. "With something to lose, if their affair came to light."

Their eyes met, and the same thought flashed through both their minds.

"A married man," they said, almost in unison.

❧

The clock chimed ten, and Sophie woke with a start, her head jerking up from where it had been resting on her folded arms. Yawning, she rubbed her eyes and gazed blearily around her chamber, wincing a little at the sun now gilding the walls.

She stifled a groan, reached for the cup at her elbow, and took a swallow of now-tepid tea. Her brain felt as if it were wrapped in cotton wool this morning. But of the five books on heraldry she'd borrowed from Pentreath, there were still three more to get through—more crests and coats of arms to study, even if by now she was no longer sure just what she was looking for.

All the same, she had to keep searching. She couldn't bear to admit defeat and let Robin down, not after last night. He'd departed soon after that confrontation in the library, slipping through the throng of guests all blissfully unaware of the drama. As calm as he'd appeared on the surface, Sophie had known he was in turmoil, reeling from the latest of Nathalie's secrets. The sooner all those unwelcome revelations were rooted out and brought to light, the sooner he could begin to heal and truly put the past behind him.

She bent determinedly over the book again. While they'd found the answers to some of the questions surrounding Nathalie's unfinished letter, the ring remained an unsolved part of the riddle. Sophie picked it up now, studying it critically: the silver tarnished, the crest scratched and worn... such an unprepossessing piece, nothing like that gaudy diamond pendant or the other glittering baubles Nathalie had hoarded against a rainy day. But she'd kept it, carefully hidden away in one of her desk's secret compartments. That had to mean something: a token from a past lover, or—which seemed more likely—from her present one, that blond Englishman with whom she'd supposedly trysted at Easter. The monied, *married* blond Englishman, who'd got Nathalie with child and perhaps found her a liability he could no longer afford...

Sophie shivered at the thought and forced herself to focus on the page before her. Bull's heads—she must have encountered several dozen families whose crest included that emblem, but even when comparing them with the seal she'd made, she hadn't yet found an exact match. Nonetheless, she had drawn up a list of the most likely candidates.

She rubbed her eyes again and turned another page. This book was twice as thick as the last volume she'd read, but it included detailed sections on families throughout England, and even areas of Scotland.

"Turnbull," she murmured, scribbling the name down.

She turned a few more pages—and froze.

The name had caught her attention first. Swallowing dryly, she read over the information again, to make sure of what she'd seen. Then, almost tentatively, she picked up the wax seal and laid it alongside the one in the illustration.

She stared at the results a moment longer, then marked the page with a stray scrap of paper before snatching up book, ring, and seal, and rushing from the room.

⚜

The jewels made a glittering heap on Robin's desk: sapphire earrings, an amethyst brooch, strands of amber and pearl, a filigree comb… he could hardly bear to look at them.

Lady Nankivell's note informed him that this was all she'd found in her husband's possession, but if he knew of any other missing valuables, please write and let her know.

Robin exhaled, bracing his forehead against his interlaced hands. Again he saw Nathalie, supine against the pillows, her pale ringlets forming an aureole about her head, naked except for the necklace—brilliant, garish, and insolent—blazing about her throat. And Nankivell starting up beside her, his face turning a dull mottled red as Robin's gaze raked over him…

"No." His voice sounded unnaturally loud in the quiet office. "No more." Bitter as that memory was, he was through with it. Through letting it haunt him further. Let it die and be buried with Nathalie.

Resolved, he looked again at the jewels on his desk. He neither knew nor cared to know how Nathalie had acquired them. But what to do with them now? Frowning, he glanced away, his gaze alighting upon the photograph of his children. Sara—perhaps he should keep the jewels for her. She should have at least some of her mother's things.

Except the diamond pendant… There were too many evil memories attached to that, and he could buy Sara something much more suitable when she was of an age for diamonds. Maybe he'd sell the pendant for a good price and donate the proceeds to a worthy cause. Something to benefit Cornwall—a fund for miners' widows and orphans, perhaps. That would annoy the hell out of Nankivell, if he heard, but Constance might actually approve.

Slightly cheered by the thought, Robin replaced the jewels in the casket they'd come in and placed it, along with Lady Nankivell's note, in a desk drawer for the time being. He was just turning the key in the lock when he heard running footsteps in the passage. A moment later, Sophie erupted into the room, brandishing a heavy book.

"Robin!" She was flushed and breathless, her green eyes ablaze. "Thank heaven you're here—you *must* see this!"

Robin started from his chair. "Good Lord, Sophie, what—"

"You *must* see this!" she repeated, thrusting the book before him.

She all but vibrated with urgency. Taking the book, he opened it to the marked page, ran his eyes over the illustration and its accompanying description.

> *Family crest: a bull's head, ducally gorged, proper. Coat of arms: a bend, argent, on a field, sable, between two gold cotises, engrailed.*
>
> *Daventry.*

Recognition struck him like a blow in the stomach.

Guy *Daventry*—tall, blond, and smiling. Daventry, who had been a guest at the hotel in April and had the housemaids sighing over how handsome he was. Daventry, the charismatic MP with an aristocratic wife and a brilliant political future before him.

"He was here." Robin barely recognized his own voice. "At Easter."

"I remember." Sophie's voice, along with the touch of her hand, was impossibly gentle.

He swallowed, willing himself not to be sick, and looked into compassionate green eyes. "It fits—all of it." With stunning, merciless clarity.

"I know."

A knock at the office door startled them. "Come," Robin responded automatically.

The door opened to reveal Bert Vigus, the sturdy Cornish handyman who kept all the instruments at the Hall in tune. "Mr. Pendarvis, sir—just wanted to let you know the piano in the music room's all right and tight now."

"Ah." Robin collected his straying thoughts. "Thank you, Bert. And the harpsichord too?" Sara had particularly wanted that fixed, he remembered.

Bert's square, good-natured face went puzzled. "Aye, but as to that, sir—there was naught amiss with it in the first place."

Robin rubbed his forehead. "I don't understand. I'd heard it was out of tune?"

"Not out of tune, sir," Bert explained. "But it couldn't have been played, not with this great lot inside of it!" He held out a thick packet of—something, wrapped tightly in a yellowed linen kerchief and bound with twine. "Don't know what this is, but I found it hidden in the instrument. Thought you'd best know what to do with it, if anyone did."

❧

"What a strange hiding place," Sophie remarked in bemusement as Robin sliced through the bindings of the packet with his penknife. "I wonder why she chose it."

"We'll never know, but I would guess she moved this from wherever she was keeping it before. Possibly to keep it separate from everything else she was hiding." The bindings cut, he folded back the creased linen to expose the packet's contents.

Letters, written on good-quality stationery and addressed in a strong, slanting hand. Robin picked up the topmost one and scanned the direction. "His to her. There look to be about a dozen or so here," he added as he rifled through the stack.

A dozen letters—the implication seemed clear enough: this

hadn't been a fleeting dalliance, but a liaison of some duration. Sophie remembered Sir Lucas's description of how Nathalie and her lover had appeared in the churchyard, walking arm in arm "like old chums." She stole a glance at Robin, but his face gave nothing away. She bent over the packet again.

"Not just letters," she observed. "There's something else… newspaper clippings?" Carefully, she extracted a yellowed column for a closer inspection.

And caught her breath when she saw Guy Daventry smiling up at her from the page.

He'd the sort of features that photographed well, and the camera had captured him full-face: high brow, beneath an almost boyish thatch of fair hair, wide-set eyes and straight nose, genially smiling lips parted to show even teeth, and a firm square chin, marked with a cleft.

That cleft… She stared at it a moment longer, wondering if her eyes were deceiving her, as she had when she'd first discovered the Daventry coat of arms. Then she lunged across the desk to catch up the photograph of Robin's children.

"Sophie?" Robin roused from his brown study at her movement. "What's wrong, love?"

She laid the newspaper clipping flat on the desk, then placed the photograph beside it, her hands trembling slightly. "Tell me what you see, dear heart."

He looked down—and went white to the lips. "My God…"

The answers they'd sought, in a pair of photographs. A cleft in a man's chin, a dimple in a child's. A smile, less cherubic and more calculating thirty years later, but still recognizable.

"You see it, don't you?" Sophie said gently. "Guy Daventry didn't just father Nathalie's unborn child. He fathered Cyril too."

❧

If either had any remaining doubts after that, reading the letters silenced those forever.

Not a constant record of correspondence, by any means. The earliest was dated several weeks before Nathalie's arrival in Cornwall, inquiring after the health of baby Cyril—named, apparently, for Daventry's father—and promising to send money as soon as Nathalie was settled in her new residence. The letter also urged discretion, entreating her to keep future communications brief and infrequent, though assistance would be provided at certain intervals.

Sporadic as they were, the remaining letters followed a similar pattern: inquiries after the child's welfare and progress, insistence on Nathalie's discretion, and promises of remuneration. And yet, for all that, they weren't *cold* letters, Sophie mused. The tone was one of cautious affection, and Daventry's interest in Cyril appeared genuine. If he were fond of children, as he appeared to be, he must feel some regret over this son he could not publicly acknowledge

The last letter was dated February of this year—just a few weeks after Cyril's death, according to Robin—and the tone was markedly different:

> *…oh, my dear, words are inadequate to convey my sorrow for your loss. Our loss. My heart aches to think of what might have been—and of our boy's last hours. You must let me know if you need anything, anything at all. I cannot get away just now, but I promise to be there in the spring. And we may mourn together then…*

Sophie looked up from the letter into Robin's bleak face. And yet—not wholly so; she thought she saw a faint trace of pity about his eyes and mouth. Unlike Daventry, he could mourn Cyril openly. And he was the man the boy had called Father. Papa. The man who'd taken him for outings, nursed him through illnesses, and sat by his bedside as he slipped into that final sleep.

"It's fairly clear what happened next, isn't it?" Robin said at last. "Daventry came down at Easter, Nathalie took him to see Cyril's grave. And then, I suspect, one thing led to another."

"I'm surprised Nathalie would take such a risk again."

"Perhaps she felt she needed comfort. God knows *we* were little enough comfort to each other. And Daventry was grieving too." Robin looked up from the photograph. "They don't have any children, do they—Daventry and his wife?"

Sophie shook her head. "Just their ward—his niece, Marianne." She gazed down at the letter again. "She must have written him—to tell him she was with child by him again."

Robin's face darkened. "God, he must have been furious when she threatened him. He'd have known just where to find her—and how to silence her."

"But would he truly have done so?" Sophie asked, troubled. "He sounds genuinely grief-stricken about Cyril. Even if he were angry with Nathalie, how could he kill a baby—*his* baby?"

"A baby who wasn't yet born," he pointed out. "Some men find it easy to dismiss whatever they can't see or hold in their hands. And he'd have so much more to lose now if this got out. How long would he keep his seat in Parliament if it were known he had a mistress and had fathered not one but two illegitimate children upon her? And I knew Nathalie," he added. "She'd have milked this and him for everything she could get."

Just as she did with every man, and it had finally cost her her life, Sophie thought.

Aloud she asked, "What do you mean to do now?"

He took a breath. "Show these to the police. In light of this new evidence, they might be persuaded to reopen the investigation. At the very least, it would be easier to have their authority on my side. But even if they don't, I'll be arranging a trip to London in the next few days."

"I'm coming with you," Sophie said at once.

Robin nodded. "Naturally, you are."

She raised her brows. "Not even a token protest, Robin?"

He laid his hand over hers. "Nary a one. I've learned to my cost that I ignore you at my peril. Together, my love?"

She linked her fingers with his and smiled. "Together, dear heart."

Twenty-three

Other sins only speak; murder shrieks out.

—John Webster, *The Duchess of Malfi*

Three days later

A HEAVY SILENCE PERVADED THE LIBRARY AT SHERIDAN House, broken only by the faint dry sound of pages turning as Sheridan read over Daventry's letters.

Laying down the last one, he drew a long breath before looking up at Robin, seated on the other side of his desk. "Damning indeed. Though I can scarce believe it. Oh, not that Guy had a liaison with your wife," he added. "I find that entirely too believable. But that he would commit murder…"

Amy spoke up from the sofa where she and Sophie were sitting. "He had a lot to lose, Thomas. And Mr. Pendarvis said his wife was almost certainly trying to blackmail him. Who knows what any of us might be capable of when our backs are to the wall?"

"True enough," Sheridan conceded. "How do you intend to proceed with this, now that you're in London, Pendarvis?"

"Some of it's out of my hands," Robin said somberly. "The Cornish police reopened the investigation when Sophie and I showed them our new evidence." They could hardly have done otherwise, if they wished to preserve their own reputation, he reflected with grim amusement.

And robbery as a motive had been discredited with the return of Nathalie's jewels. "Traveling up to London was inevitable, after that. Inspector Taunton—he was handling the case in Cornwall—came with us. The plan is to show the evidence to the London police and request their assistance in this matter." In the spirit of cooperation, Robin had agreed to submit the letters to the police once an arrest was made. But until then he'd insisted on retaining possession, and the Cornish authorities, aware of how they'd bungled matters so far, had reluctantly accepted his condition.

Sheridan nodded. "Always best to have the support of the local authorities. Where are you and Sophie staying, by the way?"

Robin began, "We thought we'd take rooms at Brown's Hotel—"

"Oh, don't be absurd," Amy broke in. "You're both staying here, of course. Sophie, darling, you look exhausted," she added. "Let me take you up to your room right now."

Sophie roused with a heavy-eyed, guilty smile. "So sorry. It's just that we've spent so much time traveling today—"

"No need to apologize," Amy assured her. "I remember just how long it takes to travel from Cornwall to London. I'm always dead on my feet when I arrive."

"Go up and rest, my dear," Robin told her. "You'll feel the better for it later."

It was a sign of how fatigued Sophie was that she obeyed without question this time. The two women went out together, talking softly, their arms about each other's waists.

Alone, Robin turned back to Sheridan, who was now replacing the letters in the envelopes, a faint groove visible between his brows.

"Guy Daventry is my father's protégé," he said, without

looking up. "A rising star in the House of Commons. And his wife, Charlotte, is a blood relation, though a distant one."

Thanks to Sophie, Robin was already aware of those things; that was partly why they'd shown the letters to the Sheridans. "You must rue the day I ever set foot in your house."

Sheridan looked up with what appeared to be genuine surprise. "No—why would you think that?"

Robin took a breath. "Nathalie… wasn't exactly an admirable person. I'm aware that very few mourn her death, though they'd never be discourteous enough to say so. And people you know could be destroyed over this. At the very least, their lives will never be the same."

"*Your* life isn't the same," Sheridan countered. "Neither is your daughter's. I would say that whatever may happen with the Daventrys pales in comparison to what you and she have suffered." The artist's green eyes were unexpectedly compassionate. "And no matter what sort of woman your wife was—if Guy killed her and the child she carried, then he must answer for it. I only wish the damage to innocent parties could be… minimized, somehow."

"I wish the same."

"You mean to accompany the police when they question Guy?"

Robin nodded. "The evidence was found in my home, after all, *and* I can claim some prior acquaintance, since Daventry stayed at the hotel. Besides, if he's unwilling to talk to the police, perhaps he can be persuaded to speak to—the man who raised Cyril." The boy they'd both loved. Robin would concede that much to Daventry, if nothing else.

Sheridan studied him a moment longer, then held out his hand. After a moment of blank incomprehension, Robin took it.

"I wish to be present as well, when you call on Guy," the artist said in a tone that brooked no argument. "He's a connection of mine, through his marriage to Charlotte. And if Scotland Yard's finest can't get you past the front door, then I can."

❧

"I've put you in the Green Room," Amy told Sophie as they walked along the passage. "And Mr. Pendarvis in the Amber Suite, just across the hall."

"The Green Room? What could be more appropriate for me?" Sophie asked, smiling.

Amy laughed. "I confess, I had a similar thought. But really, it's one of our nicest guest chambers, with its own little parlor as well. Although," she added mischievously, "I cannot guarantee you complete solitude. You'll have a companion—of the feline persuasion."

"Oh, Tatty!" Sophie exclaimed, feeling ridiculously pleased by the news. "Is she well? And has she been behaving herself?"

"As to the first, yes, she's fine—living on the fat of the land," Amy assured her. "As to the second, she's behaving about as well as one can expect—from a cat. She's taken a fancy to Thomas, as most females do. I may have to acquire a Russian Blue of our own when she goes home with you. Or perhaps a Siamese—they're very striking, if one can get used to their voices."

"Amy, thank you," Sophie said, stopping to embrace her. "For the hospitality, for looking after Tatiana—and, well, everything. And I'm so sorry if we've brought trouble to your door by coming here."

Amy returned her embrace. "Nonsense! You've done nothing of the kind."

"Well, the Daventrys *are* connections of yours," Sophie pointed out. "That's why I thought you and Thomas should know what Robin and I discovered. I didn't think you should hear about it by accident."

"Better to know than not know," Amy said bracingly. "I shall be sorry if Guy does turn out to have murdered Mrs.

Pendarvis, but not so sorry as to want him to get away with it. And no matter what happens, my dear, you and Mr. Pendarvis have our support." She paused, her lips quirking in a wry half smile. "Remember that—unpleasantness in Cornwall, five years ago?"

"I've never forgotten," Sophie confessed.

"Nor have I, actually. Relia jumped right into it, for James's sake," Amy added, her smile turning fond and reminiscent. "*I* held back—I was afraid of getting too involved. And of making bad worse. But sometimes you *have* to get involved, don't you? Especially when it comes to people you care about." She kissed Sophie on the cheek. "Have a good rest, my dear. And if you should need anything else, just let me know."

The Green Room was every bit as nice as Amy had promised: light, cool, and pretty, with walls tinted a delicate jade and graceful furniture fashioned of some pale wood, ash or maple. Glancing around, Sophie spied Tatiana perched on the window seat, gazing down into the street below, and called softly to her.

Ears pricking, the cat looked around, then leapt down to greet her errant mistress with a plaintive mew. Sophie scooped up the cat and cuddled her close, taking comfort from the rich, throaty purr.

"So, am I forgiven?" she asked, sinking down on the bed with the cat still in her arms.

Tatiana purred even louder, and Sophie scratched her under the chin. Sara had mentioned wanting a kitten, she mused. Until that could be arranged, perhaps the girl would enjoy spoiling Tatiana? Not that the cat *required* further spoiling…

Despite her fatigue, her mind insisted on remaining active, sifting restlessly through all that had happened and still was to happen. Disconcertingly, in the midst of more serious reflections, her thoughts kept returning to the minor, though not insignificant, detail that Robin would be lodged just across the hall from her—in closer proximity than he'd been in weeks.

Yearning pulsed through her, sharp and sweet. It seemed an eternity since their brief idyll in Oxfordshire when they'd been all in all to each other, before tragedy had caught them up in its toils. And hard to banish the fear that they might never know such happiness again.

We will, Sophie told herself firmly. This was no time to lose faith in him, in them.

But just now Robin was preoccupied with thoughts of Nathalie, Cyril, and that baby who would never see the light of day. Little wonder if he'd no attention to spare for anything or anyone else. At least he was no longer shutting her out—that, in itself, was a victory. Indeed, it seemed tacitly understood by everyone that she meant to accompany him tomorrow—to Scotland Yard and the Daventrys'. They could hardly stop her from doing so, after all.

Sophie set Tatiana gently down on the carpet, then lay back against the pillows and closed her eyes. She'd need a clear head and all her wits about her to see this through with Robin, right to the bitter end.

The bitter past, more welcome is the sweet. She only hoped that would prove to be true.

❧

Early August now, and the close of Parliament was less than a fortnight away. On arriving in London yesterday, Sophie had noticed that the crowds seemed sparser. According to Amy, the exodus to grouse moors or seaside villas was imminent. Many families had already left town, though the Sheridans were among those staying until the very end of the Season.

As were the Daventrys.

Sophie glanced at her companions, standing with her before the MP's Belgrave Square townhouse. Robin, his face impassive, his bearing almost militarily erect; Inspector

Taunton trying not to look intimidated by the massive facade of the Daventrys' terraced townhouse; Inspector Seymore, of Scotland Yard, some ten years Taunton's senior, doing rather a better job of that, although it was entirely possible that he *wasn't* intimidated, after his years on the force; and finally, Thomas Sheridan, very quiet and grimmer than Sophie had ever seen him.

She'd been surprised at first by his insistence on joining them. But on further reflection, she couldn't help but be grateful that he had. His presence might make a huge difference as to how willing Daventry was to speak to them and how much he might say. The man was a politician, after all, and no doubt accustomed to talking his way out of trouble.

The door finally opened to reveal a stern-faced butler, who appeared none too pleased when the inspectors identified themselves and asked to speak to Mr. Daventry—the police in general weren't exactly welcome visitors at any home. But his face and demeanor changed the moment he recognized Thomas.

"Mr. Sheridan."

Thomas nodded. "Good afternoon, Grimsby. *Is* Mr. Daventry at home?"

Grimsby hesitated a moment before replying. "He's just returned from the House, sir."

"It is of vital importance that we speak to him," Thomas said, holding the butler's gaze with his own. "Would you be so good as to show us up?"

"Very good, sir," Grimsby conceded, and admitted them at last.

The interior of the townhouse was almost oppressively grand, Sophie found. Compared to Sheridan House, which wore its splendor lightly, even insouciantly, the Daventrys' home was stiffly formal. And, to her critical eye, overly decorated—the most elaborate furnishings seemed to have been positioned to call attention to themselves: the huge ormolu

mirror in the entrance hall, the marble-topped Baroque table
on the first floor landing, and the Louis Quatorze chair just
outside the drawing room, for example.

The drawing room showed a similar French influence,
heavy on gilding and marquetry. Sophie wondered which of
the Daventrys was the ardent Francophile. Lady Charlotte?
Decor tended to be the provenance of the lady of the house.
Perhaps Mr. Daventry was content to collect French mistresses,
she reflected as she seated herself gingerly on a brocaded chair.

The men remained standing, Robin taking up a position
behind Sophie's chair. He had agreed to let the inspectors and
Thomas take the lead when it came to questioning Daventry.
But Sophie could feel him vibrating like a plucked string. She
laid a hand over his, where it rested on the back of her chair,
and studied the other three men.

Thomas was leaning against the sideboard, his posture
nonchalant, his expression carefully neutral. All but his eyes,
which had darkened to a muddy green—always a sign of
disquiet, according to Amy. By contrast, Seymore looked
calm to the point of stolidity, while Taunton appeared to
be fidgeting slightly—he'd been eager to be put back on the
case, Sophie remembered. He'd also done his best to clear the
air earlier, informing Robin that he had never truly believed
him guilty of Nathalie's murder. Robin, for his part, had
accepted the olive branch. All that mattered now was finding
and apprehending the true killer.

They all looked toward the door at the sound of approaching
footsteps. Seconds later, Guy Daventry—tall, blond, and even
handsomer than in his photograph—strode into the room. His
gaze, blue and direct, went to Sheridan first.

"Thomas—what brings you here today, old man?" he
inquired, almost jovially.

"A matter of some urgency, Guy." Sheridan nodded
toward Seymore and Taunton. "These two inspectors will
explain further."

Daventry's fair brows rose quizzically as he regarded the two policemen. "Inspectors? This must be serious indeed. What can I do for you, gentlemen?"

No sign of nerves, so far, Sophie observed. He appeared to have no inkling of why the police were here.

"Inspector Seymore, Scotland Yard," the London detective introduced himself. "And this is Inspector Taunton, of the Newquay police," he added, gesturing toward the younger man. "Forgive the intrusion, Mr. Daventry, but we wish to ask you a few questions."

Daventry's brows climbed higher. "I have no idea what this is about, Inspector, but naturally, I'll—" He broke off abruptly, staring at Taunton with an arrested expression, then, "Newquay?" he repeated, a faint apprehension creeping into his tone. "From Cornwall?"

"That's right, sir," Taunton said evenly.

Daventry continued to eye him. "You're quite far from your usual patch, Inspector."

Taunton exchanged a glance with Seymore, who said, "Inspector Taunton requested Scotland Yard's assistance in regard to a crime committed in Cornwall."

Daventry gave an uneasy laugh. "So far away? I don't see how I can help you there."

"Did you not spend part of the Easter holidays in Cornwall?" Taunton asked. "During which you stayed at an establishment known as the Pendarvis Hotel?"

The MP flushed, slightly but noticeably—the curse of a fair complexion. "Yes, for a few days," he conceded. "But that was months ago. I've hardly set foot out of London since the Season began. I certainly haven't made any recent excursions to the West Country."

"Be that as it may, sir," Seymore resumed, "the police are in receipt of evidence suggesting that you might have some knowledge pertaining to this crime. The murder of one Nathalie Pendarvis."

The name dropped into the quiet room with all the force of a bomb. Daventry's face went the color of whey, and his eyes were suddenly all pupil, the blue swallowed up by black. He shook his head a little dazedly, lips parting as though he would speak, but no sound emerged.

"Guy." Thomas strode over to stand at his side, laying a firm hand on his shoulder. "Before you say anything, anything at all, there's someone else you should meet." He motioned to Robin to come forward. "This is Mr. Robin Pendarvis, owner of the Pendarvis Hotel—and husband of the deceased."

Robin stepped out from behind Sophie's chair and directed a level look at his wife's lover, who went even paler.

"Mr. Pendarvis." He swallowed audibly. "Pray accept my condolences on your loss."

"Thank you," Robin returned. "Allow me to extend mine—on the loss of your son."

"M-my son?" Daventry echoed feebly.

Still holding the other man's gaze, Robin drew the packet of letters from inside his coat, and held them out so that the handwriting on the envelopes was plainly visible.

Daventry's gaze dropped, along with the last vestiges of his pretense.

"I told Nathalie to burn those," he said dully.

❦

"We met six years ago on the Côte d'Azur." Daventry stared down at his hands, twisting a gold signet ring on his little finger. Sophie could not see the design, but she suspected that it bore the crest of a bull's head, ducally gorged.

The drawing room had fallen so silent one could hear the proverbial pin drop. Thomas had retreated to his former place by the sideboard, though Sophie could tell he was still listening intently, as were the two inspectors. And Robin, now standing before Daventry's chair—strangely, he was the only person of whom the MP even seemed aware.

"I was smitten, instantly," Daventry went on, still not looking at any of his hearers. "It was like a—madness, being in love with Nathalie. For a time I couldn't get enough of her. And she... she seemed to feel the same." A faint, bittersweet smile tugged at his mouth. "She begged my ring from me—just an old signet ring with my family crest. Nothing costly or valuable, but she swore she'd cherish it more than diamonds. And I could deny her nothing."

"We found the ring among her possessions too," Robin said colorlessly.

A spasm of pain crossed Daventry's face; after a moment, he gave a tight nod and resumed, "I set her up in her own establishment in town. We did our best to be discreet, careful... but then we learned there was to be a child." He looked up then, and Sophie could see the hunger in his eyes. "My wife and I hadn't been able to... I wanted..." He paused, drawing a ragged breath before continuing. "Nathalie made me promise I'd support her once the baby was born. How could I *not*?

"We had a son, Cyril—named for my father. He wasn't—wasn't very strong, but I made sure there was enough money for medicine and a nursemaid. Nathalie had a daughter too," Daventry added, with a tentative glance at Robin. "Yours, I suppose?"

Robin gave a curt nod. "I never knew about her."

Daventry's gaze fell. "Nathalie never spoke much of her marriage. I think, after Cyril, she hoped that I might... but it was quite impossible. I couldn't promise her more than what we had. And in the end"—he shifted in his chair, avoiding everyone else's eyes—"I had to break with her. Completely. I couldn't risk the scandal to my career—or my marriage. Charlotte... I'm not proud of how I deceived my wife. I owe her and her family so much."

He exhaled, looked up again. "Nathalie was distraught, angry—as she'd a right to be! She told me she meant to return to you, that *you* would do right by her and the children."

He scrubbed his hands over his face. "God forgive me, I was *relieved* to hear it! But I couldn't bear to lose all contact with Cyril. So I arranged to send money when I could, in exchange for news of him. But I swear, I never intended to see Nathalie again.

"When she wrote and told me Cyril had died…" Daventry's eyes glistened with moisture. "My son. My only child. I had to go and see where he was buried, at least." He met Robin's eyes. "Thank you—for accepting him and treating him so well."

Robin's face was still, austere. "I thought of him as my son too."

Daventry nodded, swallowing hard again. "What happened then, between Nathalie and myself—it wasn't planned. She was crying, she clung to me—and then…" He shrugged, helplessly. "I told her, afterward, it must never happen again. That it was grief that had drawn us together. That I wished her well, but we must never see one another again. And we haven't. I heard nothing from her, about her—until you came to my door today."

Robin's gaze sharpened. "Then you didn't know about the baby?"

Daventry's breath caught. "What baby?"

"According to the coroner, Nathalie was three months pregnant when she died."

"Oh, God." Daventry's pallor was now tinged with grey.

"We found the draft of a letter hidden among her papers," Robin continued. "Addressed to the father of her child, informing him of her pregnancy. I assumed she had written or was in the process of writing to you."

Daventry stared at him, then shook his head, slowly, as if it took all his strength. "I didn't know. I received no letter, no word at all…" Voice trailing off, he lowered his face into his hands, clearly struggling to absorb what he'd just been told.

An uneasy silence fell. Watching Daventry, Sophie found it hard to believe that he could feign such a reaction to this news, politician or no. The mingled shock and regret in his eyes had appeared genuine too. Because if he'd loved Cyril as much as he claimed… She felt her conviction about his guilt—not particularly deep-rooted in the first place—begin to waver, and wondered if Robin's did as well.

"Mr. Daventry." Seymore broke the silence at last. "Would you be so good as to tell us where you were on the night of this past July thirteenth?"

Daventry looked up, dazed and glassy-eyed. "The night of…" he echoed blankly, then his face sharpened into awareness as the implications of the question sank in. "Wait! Inspector, are you—are you suggesting that *I* killed Nathalie? The mother of my child?" His voice rose, incredulous and indignant. "How could you even think that?"

"The question, if you please, Mr. Daventry," Seymore repeated inexorably.

The MP gripped the arms of his chairs, his hands white-knuckled as he fought for composure. "I did *not* kill Nathalie! I told you, I've spent almost the entire Season in London. And that night, July the thirteenth you said"—he paused, doubtless attempting to reconstruct the events of that evening—"I dined at the home of one of my fellow members, Mr. George Mallinson at 11 Portland Place! We did not part company until half-past ten. There were five other gentlemen present who can vouch for my attendance!" he added, almost triumphantly.

An ironclad alibi—or seemingly so. Sophie stole a glance at Robin, but she could not tell what he was feeling at this moment: relief that Cyril's father had not killed Cyril's mother, or disappointment that their search for the murderer appeared to have hit another dead end.

"What is the meaning of this?"

A new voice—rich, imperious, and distinctly displeased— spoke up, drawing everyone's attention to the doorway where Lady Charlotte Daventry now stood.

"I should like to know why my drawing room appears to be full of strangers," Lady Charlotte remarked, entering with her usual regality, Marianne a pale shadow behind her. "Two of whom"—she eyed the inspectors with cool disfavor—"appear to be policemen. Or so Grimsby informs me." Her gaze swept the rest of the room, alighting not on her husband, Sophie observed with interest, but her cousin. "I trust a fuller explanation is forthcoming, Thomas?"

"The police will provide one, Charlotte," he replied. "I suggest you listen to them."

Lips pursed with displeasure, she turned back to the inspectors. "Well, gentlemen?"

Seymore introduced himself and Taunton at once. "Pardon the disturbance, Lady Charlotte," he began, "but Inspector Taunton and I are investigating a crime that was committed a few weeks past, in Cornwall."

"In Cornwall?" Lady Charlotte's brows arched. "How extraordinary. But how can that possibly concern us?"

"We had reason to believe Mr. Daventry has some knowledge pertaining to the crime," Seymore explained. "The murder of one Nathalie Pendarvis."

Lady Charlotte paused in the act of pulling off her gloves, a marble calm settling over her strong features. "Indeed?" She regarded her husband with a notable absence of warmth. "Is that so, Guy?"

Daventry swallowed, nodded. "Charlotte, I have—something to tell you."

She held up a hand. "If that—something involves one of your numerous indiscretions, you may spare your breath." Her voice held a chilly detachment. "I am well aware of your infidelity, and have been for years. That wretched creature in Cornwall was your mistress, wasn't she?"

Marianne uttered a faint squeak, while Daventry flinched as if his wife had struck him. "How—how could you know?" he husked.

Lady Charlotte lifted an aristocratic shoulder. "I would not be the first wife to employ a detective to investigate an adulterous husband. Or the first who chose to overlook that husband's sins in private life to preserve his public reputation." She stared down at him in wintry disdain. "I know that not only was Nathalie Pendarvis your mistress for more than a year, but she conceived an illegitimate child with you, whom you supported with *our* money until he recently died."

The woman was uncanny, Sophie thought with a shiver. Terrifying, actually. And to judge from the expressions of everyone else in the room, she wasn't alone in her opinion. Even Thomas, a master of ironic detachment, looked unnerved by Lady Charlotte's clinical recital, while Marianne appeared ready to faint—or weep at the very least.

Ashen-faced, Daventry moistened his lips. "What more do you know?" he asked finally.

"As much as I care to." Lady Charlotte turned back to the policemen. "Is Mr. Daventry officially a suspect in this woman's murder?"

"The police have taken an interest in Mr. Daventry for several reasons, Lady Charlotte," Taunton explained. "For one thing, he matches the general description of Mrs. Pendarvis's attacker, whom her maid identified as a tall, thin man—"

"England is full of tall, thin men," Lady Charlotte interrupted. "Have you come all the way to London on the strength of that detail alone? How singular!"

Taunton flushed at the slight mockery in her tone. "For another," he resumed, as if she hadn't spoken, "Mr. Pendarvis," he nodded toward Robin, "discovered correspondence of an intimate nature between his wife and Mr. Daventry, which he brought to our attention."

"I see." The mockery vanished as Lady Charlotte's gaze alighted upon Robin. "Mr. Pendarvis—my condolences on your loss." Her tone was a model of perfunctory politeness. "But as you have perhaps been made aware by now, Mr.

Daventry has spent almost the entire Season in London, attending to parliamentary matters, as his fellow members can likely attest. Regardless of his past association with your wife, he certainly could not have made an excursion to Cornwall without my knowledge. While I hope for your sake that the person responsible for Mrs. Pendarvis's murder is found, I suggest that you look elsewhere."

A dismissal, if Sophie had ever heard one—faultlessly courteous, but clearly meant to intimidate and discourage.

Robin, however, was not so easily dismissed. "I believe that is for the police to decide, Lady Charlotte," he returned, and Sophie had the sense of him planting his feet more firmly on the expensive Aubusson carpet.

Annoyance flickered across Lady Charlotte's face, but before she could give vent to it, Seymore said, "Mr. Daventry told us that he dined at the house of one George Mallinson on the evening of July the thirteenth. Were you present as well?"

"July the thirteenth?" She paused, then gave a dismissive shrug. "No, I was not."

"May I ask where you were instead?"

"In Berkshire, visiting my sister Henrietta. She was widowed at this time last year, and, not wishing to mark such a sad anniversary alone, requested my presence. I was away for no more than three days."

"And your sister can attest to your presence there?" Seymore inquired.

"Of course." Lady Charlotte sounded almost impatient.

If Sophie's glance had not strayed for just a moment, she might have missed Marianne's sudden start at those words, then the flush that mounted almost to her hairline—a flush that looked almost... guilty. But what had that shy creature to feel guilty about?

One always overlooked Marianne, Sophie realized. As she existed in the shadow of a charismatic uncle and a domineering aunt, that was hardly surprising. And yet surely she must have thoughts, opinions, and feelings of her own. Thomas had wanted to draw out the girl's true self in her portrait, only to be continually thwarted by Lady Charlotte's overbearing presence.

Could Marianne be the key? What might the girl know about her aunt or uncle that could prove helpful? Or knock a hole in the fortifications that Lady Charlotte was attempting to erect about herself and her husband? Clearly *something* was amiss here—and it jarred on Sophie like a wrong note in an aria. She glanced toward the two policemen, who had drawn aside and appeared to be conferring on something—the Daventrys' apparently unshakable alibis, perhaps.

"Miss—Tresilian, is it?"

Startled by the sound of her name, Sophie turned her head to find Lady Charlotte eyeing her with mingled curiosity and censure.

"I confess, I am surprised to see *you* here," the older woman remarked. "Indeed, I cannot conceive how this concerns you in the least."

Sophie looked straight at her and summoned her most ingenuous expression. "I am here to support Mr. Pendarvis, Lady Charlotte. He is a dear family friend, as well as my brother's business partner. And I happened to be present when he first received the tragic news of his wife's murder."

"How distressing for you," Lady Charlotte said coldly.

"Oh, far more distressing for him," Sophie insisted, ignoring the probing look she could sense Robin directing at her. "And for his young daughter too."

Out of the corner of her eye, she saw Marianne bite her lip, even as her gaze remained fixed on the floor. Compelled by some instinct she could not yet identify, Sophie went on, "Such a sad thing, to lose a parent so early. And in such— violent circumstances," she added with a shudder. "Especially since her younger brother died only a few months previously."

The other men were also staring at Sophie now, no

doubt wondering at her sudden effusiveness. Robin and
Thomas, at least, both knew she wasn't the sort to gush
like this. Sophie could only hope they guessed she might be
doing so for a reason.

"My heart just… breaks for little Sara." She let her voice
quaver; no hardship as the sentiment was wholly true, though
she would never have expressed it so blatantly, especially to
an unsympathetic stranger. "Seven years old is far too young
to lose your mother."

"Indeed." Lady Charlotte's voice and expression were as
cold as ever, but Marianne had glanced up sharply at that,
revealing a stricken face and suspiciously liquid eyes. Sophie
wondered fleetingly how old the girl had been when *she*
was orphaned.

"And she's so frightened too, because of the *terrible* way
poor Nathalie died," Sophie continued, noting how Marianne
had now pressed one hand to her mouth. "Mr. Pendarvis says
she wakes up screaming from bad dreams every night."

Lady Charlotte's eyes sparked, a flash of temper as sudden
as it was surprising. "I don't doubt this is all very affecting,
Miss Tresilian. But if Mrs. Pendarvis had devoted more attention to her child and less to other women's husbands, perhaps
this tragedy could have been avoided!"

And there it was: the first crack in that icy facade, and the
glimpse of hot fury beneath.

Sophie wasn't the only one shocked by the venom in her
words. She felt Robin stiffen beside her, heard Marianne utter
a soft, distressed cry, and saw Daventry, formerly dazed and
enervated, jerk upright in his chair like one galvanized.

"Charlotte!" he protested hoarsely.

Ignoring both her husband and her niece, Lady Charlotte
turned to Seymore. "Inspector, I believe we have answered
your most pertinent questions for the time being. It has been
established and can be verified that neither Mr. Daventry nor
myself were anywhere near Cornwall when Mrs. Pendarvis

was murdered. Now, if you have concluded your business here, would you—*all* of you," she added, with another sweeping glance over the room, "be so good as to see yourselves out? We have a dinner engagement this evening."

Sophie stifled a rush of disappointment. She'd felt so close to breaking through, certain that Marianne might be on the verge of saying *something*, but the girl had retreated into cowed silence. She could not look at Robin; he'd been so sure this visit would yield the answers they were seeking. And here was Lady Charlotte, masterfully preparing to sweep all else before her. Taunton was shifting from foot to foot, and even Seymore looked uneasy now, clearly racking his brain for a way to prolong his investigation in the face of such high-handedness.

"Lady Charlotte," he began doggedly.

She contrived to look down her nose at him, aided by her considerable height. "I hope I will not be obliged to report you for insolence, Inspector."

The colors were about to be struck, Sophie sensed with a sinking heart.

"No, wait!" a shaky female voice broke in.

And all heads turned toward Marianne, white as paper and trembling like an aspen, but determination etched on her every feature. Sophie was suddenly reminded of Constance Nankivell, unexpectedly strong beneath her soft, mild exterior, and prayed that Marianne might be finding some of that hidden strength in herself.

"I have—I have something to say," the girl began haltingly.

"What is it, Miss Daventry?" Seymore said gently.

Lady Charlotte made an impatient gesture. "Really, Marianne, what can you possibly—"

"My uncle has an alibi," Marianne interrupted, her voice still not entirely unsteady. "He was in London, when Mrs. Pendarvis was killed. But my aunt was not."

Lady Charlotte said, as though addressing a backwards

child, "You know very well I was in Berkshire, Marianne—visiting your Aunt Henrietta."

"That's what you *said*," Marianne countered, shooting her a nervous but defiant glance. "You even left *me* behind, which you've never done before. All these years, you've scarcely allowed me out of your sight or permitted me to take a breath without your approving it first!"

"I hardly see what this signifies," Lady Charlotte began, but Marianne rushed on.

"I couldn't believe you'd leave me to myself for *three whole days*! I was so grateful to Aunt Hen for inviting you, I didn't care that I hadn't been included. Except"—she paused, breathless and still trembling slightly—"the morning after you'd gone, a letter from her arrived—mailed two days before, from the *Lake District*."

The words fell into the silence like stones in a millpond, the ripples spreading far and wide. Marianne looked directly at her guardian for the first time since she'd begun to speak. "Aunt Hen *wasn't* in Berkshire. And neither were you."

For just a moment, Lady Charlotte stared at her niece, nonplussed. Then she rallied, "Rubbish, Marianne—you don't know what you're talking about! My sister can verify everything I've said—"

"Oh, I don't doubt Aunt Hen would lie for you!" Marianne struck in. "And that's what it would be, wouldn't it? A lie! Blood's thicker than water, after all!"

"That certainly doesn't appear to be true in *your* case," her aunt observed caustically.

Marianne flushed. "I *did* keep quiet, at first. Because I thought you'd taken a lover—the way Uncle Guy had taken a mistress. What had I to say to that? Sauce for the goose, after all."

Lady Charlotte's nostrils flared in distaste. "Don't be vulgar, Marianne." She spoke as if to be vulgar were the worst insult she could confer upon anyone.

The girl lifted her chin defiantly. "I'd rather be vulgar than a murderess!"

Lady Charlotte's hand flashed out in a vicious slap, the force of it almost knocking Marianne off her feet. Daventry sprang from his chair with an incoherent oath, and Sophie found she too was now standing—and staring like everyone else at Lady Charlotte's livid face.

"For that *unpardonable* insult, you are confined to your room until further notice!" Her splendid voice was harsh with rage and the effort to contain it.

"I won't go!" Tears stood in Marianne's eyes, and her cheek burned scarlet from the blow, but still she stood her ground.

Lady Charlotte's hand rose once more, only to be caught and held fast by Thomas.

Daventry strode forward. "You will not strike her again!"

The inspectors had moved as well, now flanking Marianne on either side. "There's to be no intimidation of the witness, Lady Charlotte," Seymore ordered.

"A fine witness!" Lady Charlotte scoffed, raking Marianne with a contemptuous glare. "A foolish, spiteful child, seeking to avenge imagined slights!" She wrested her hand free from Thomas's grip and turned ostentatiously away from her niece. "And hysterical as well," she added. "How can you trust the word of one who leaps from A to Zed as she does?"

"I'm not!" Marianne protested, but fell silent when her uncle held up his hand and approached his wife—warily, as one might approach a coiled serpent or a crouching panther.

Daventry swallowed, not taking his eyes from his wife. "Where were you, Charlotte?"

Her face was set and stony. "I told you. With my sister."

The disbelief in the room was palpable. Seymore cleared his throat. "Lady Charlotte, if you'll just come with us now—"

"Oh, don't be ridiculous!" she exclaimed, rounding on him impatiently. "May I remind you, Inspector, that your own witness described the murderer as a tall, thin *man*? I should say that conclusively rules *me* out."

"But it doesn't," Sophie said. "Not at all."

And seven pairs of shocked eyes turned in her direction.

❧

She could not have said at what point the idea took hold. When Lady Charlotte had spoken so callously of Sara as well as Nathalie, perhaps. Or when she had struck Marianne with such force, her rage stripping her face of any vestige of feminine softness.

A tall, thin man...

A tall lean *woman*, with a deep voice and strong, almost masculine features. In the right clothes, in the right light... she could pass for a man. Glimpsed through a barely open door, in the darkness, a frightened lady's maid would see only what she expected to see.

Nathalie, too, might not have troubled to look closely—if she'd even seen her attacker. Had she known, or guessed what might have happened, when she felt the garrote tightening about her throat?

Seymore was eyeing her speculatively. "Miss Tresilian, would you care to explain that?"

"Certainly," Sophie replied. "I think it's quite possible that, while she was supposedly in Berkshire, Lady Charlotte traveled down to Cornwall, disguised herself as a man, and killed Nathalie Pendarvis."

She infused the words with all the conviction she could muster, knowing how outlandish they would sound once they left the safety of her own head. And indeed, she sensed the doubt emanating from her listeners the moment she'd finished speaking—even Robin. But deep within her soul, she felt increasingly sure that she was right.

Lady Charlotte gave an incredulous laugh. "Disguise myself as a *man*, Miss Tresilian? What an extraordinary idea!"

"Not so extraordinary." Sophie met her gaze squarely. "You played breeches parts when you were younger. Hamlet, Romeo—I heard you were quite good. And you could still pass for a man, in the right clothes. An overcoat. Trousers. A hat, pulled down over your face." She emphasized each item, hoping that at least one person in the room would be able to envision what she described. Thomas, perhaps, if no one else; he must surely remember Lady Charlotte's thespian efforts. "Modern fashions would conceal far more than doublet and hose. And, of course, darkness would help maintain the illusion."

Lady Charlotte was staring at her now—and for the first time, Sophie saw a glimmer of unease in her eyes.

"You stayed at the Pendarvis Hotel at Easter, along with Mr. Daventry," Sophie continued. "Perhaps, thanks to the detective you hired, you already knew that his mistress lived there. And perhaps," she took a breath and ventured into uncharted territory, "perhaps you discovered later that she was with child by him again."

The leaching of color from the older woman's face told her all she needed to know. The quality of the silence, no longer skeptical but crackling with tension, told her the rest.

"My God," Daventry breathed, staring at his wife. "It's—it's true. You killed Nathalie."

"A baby," Marianne choked out. "You killed a woman who was expecting a baby!"

"I rid us all of a worthless little parasite!" Lady Charlotte spat, her control slipping at last, beyond recovery. She rounded on her husband, who recoiled from the naked fury on her face.

"All these years I kept your secret! While your little French trollop tried to bleed us dry, supporting your bastard!"

Daventry flinched at the ugly word. So did Robin. Thomas was staring at his cousin as if he'd never seen her before.

Lady Charlotte swept on, years of pent-up bitterness

spilling from her in a torrent. "I'd thought, when he died, there'd be an end to it. But then," she laughed harshly, "oh, then I intercepted her next letter to you! All tears and Gallic effusions—and a quite blatant demand for money, to support your *newest* by-blow!" Her lips twisted. "She added a few threats to her repertoire as well. It would have started all over again—and I wasn't about to let that happen."

"But an unborn baby…" Daventry said, almost pleadingly.

Lady Charlotte's face hardened, but not before Sophie saw the flash of desolation in her eyes. "Had *we* been blessed with children, would you have been so quick to give away what was rightfully theirs?"

"How did you get her to open the door to you?" Robin's voice was eerily calm, as if he'd gained all the control Lady Charlotte had lost; Sophie could only guess at the storm raging beneath the surface of his composure.

Lady Charlotte glanced at him, almost indifferently, as if she'd forgotten he was there. Perhaps she had; Daventry was the focus of her outrage. "It took little enough. Just a glimpse of all the money I'd brought. She was counting it when I—did what I had come to do." Unconsciously, her hands clenched, twisted, as though stretching the garrote tight between them.

Sophie saw a muscle jerk in Robin's jaw and knew he was picturing Nathalie's last moments. She slipped her hand into his cold one, felt him grasp it like a lifeline.

Lady Charlotte's lips curved in a travesty of a smile. "I thought it fitting that she died fondling what she cherished most in life."

At that last piece of viciousness, Daventry broke.

"Murderess!" He lunged at his wife, hands reaching for her throat, but Thomas and Taunton each seized him by an arm and held him off, still struggling in their grasp.

Seymore began, "Lady Charlotte Daventry, you are under arrest for—"

Marianne, already ghost-pale, moaned and slumped to the floor.

For just a moment, everyone's attention was on her… and Lady Charlotte made her move, launching herself toward the open doorway and freedom.

Seymore reached for her a second too late, before stumbling over the chair she overturned directly in his path. The drawing room doors slammed shut, even as he struggled to his feet, and he and Taunton seized upon the doorknobs, rattling them furiously and to no avail.

"She's wedged the door!" Seymore reported over his shoulder, as Taunton cursed and wrestled still more vigorously with the knob.

"Grimsby!" Daventry roared, coming to pound on the doors as well. "Let us out!"

Sophie looked up from the sofa, on which she had deposited the unconscious Marianne. "Pull the bell rope," she advised tartly.

Thomas, mouth twitching slightly, proceeded to do just that.

Robin, meanwhile, had picked up the fireplace poker and gone to the inspectors' aid. "We might be able to jar the doors loose with this."

A series of thrusts, combined with the forceful application of muscle, breached the doors and sent the Louis Quatorze chair Lady Charlotte had used as a barricade skittering across the floor. Breathless, the men stumbled out into the passage just as an astonished footman arrived on the scene.

"Where's Lady Charlotte?" Daventry rapped out. "Did she pass you coming down?"

"No, sir," the footman began—and was cut short by a chilling scream from above.

Daventry ran for the stairs at top speed, both inspectors at his heels. Robin, Sophie, and Thomas followed only a little more slowly.

They'd reached the second-floor landing when she came

stumbling toward them—a black-clad housemaid, her face as white as her apron, shaking from head to toe.

"Jane!" Daventry caught her about the shoulders. "What's happened?"

She gulped and shuddered, tears spilling down her pale cheeks. "Oh, sir, it's—it's her ladyship! She ran right past me. She… she… straight out the window—" The housemaid gestured shakily back the way she had come.

Toward the stairs leading up to the third floor.

As one, they gazed at the stairs in horrified understanding. Then Daventry uttered an explosive oath, thrust the weeping housemaid at the nearest man—Taunton—and ran for the stairs again, closely followed by Seymore.

Except that there was no need to run now. Just as there could be no doubt of what they would ultimately find. Three stories down to the unforgiving pavement below.

Sophie turned away, swallowing strenuously as she tried to wipe the image from her mind. So Lady Charlotte had taken the matter into her own hands, sparing everyone the cost of a trial in which the outcome was a foregone conclusion. Better than the hangman, or even life in prison or an asylum, but all the same…

Then Robin's arm encircled her, and she leaned into his embrace, grateful for his support and the giving and receiving of comfort.

"Did you know what she meant to do?" she heard him ask Thomas in a low voice.

No question of which "she" he was referring to. Thomas shook his head. "No—but it doesn't surprise me. I knew Charlotte. She wasn't the sort, ever, to let herself be taken…"

Twenty-four

My beloved is mine, and I am his...

—Song of Solomon 2:16

IT WAS SOME TIME BEFORE THEY RETURNED, SOMBER and silent, to Sheridan House. Amy came flying to meet them the moment they stepped through the front door. Her anxious gaze traveled over each of them in turn, settling on her husband's shadowed face. Without a word, Thomas held out his hand, and she took it at once.

Thomas turned to his guests. "Sophie, Pendarvis, will you excuse us? Someone—needs to inform my parents of what's happened."

"Of course," Sophie replied and watched somberly as the Sheridans headed for the library, where they kept the telephone.

So much to come to terms with—all of them. Thomas had lost a relation, not a close one, but still part of his family. And Robin... He now knew the truth of Nathalie's death, but would it bring him the peace he so desperately needed?

She glanced at him, pale and silent beside her. "Come up to my parlor, dear heart," she urged. "It will be quiet and peaceful there."

"That sounds—very welcome, just now," he said on a sigh.

Upstairs, she let them both into the pretty parlor adjoining her chamber, then motioned Robin toward one of the comfortably padded armchairs in front of the fireplace. He sank down upon it without a murmur. Sophie went over to the sideboard, where a crystal decanter of sherry stood, along with a jar of sweet biscuits. She poured out two glasses of sherry, took out a biscuit apiece, and returned to Robin's side.

Much to her amusement, she saw that Tatiana had emerged from whatever hiding place she'd found, and was now draped, purring seductively, across Robin's lap. Some of the grey, haunted look left his face as he stroked her. "And who is this little charmer?" he inquired as he accepted the glass and biscuit Sophie handed him.

Sophie introduced them as she perched on the arm of Robin's chair. "A gift from an admirer—a female admirer," she added hastily. "An older woman who attended a concert I gave during the Little Season."

Robin scratched Tatiana under her chin, and the cat's purr redoubled, making him smile. For that alone, Sophie loved her capricious pet even more.

They sat in companionable silence for a time, sipping sherry and eating their biscuits. Very good ones, flavored with ratafia, Sophie noted idly.

"Better?" she inquired at last, leaning in so that their shoulders touched.

"A little, perhaps." Robin's gaze was a little distant. "God, what a day."

"Difficult for everyone," Sophie agreed.

He sighed. "I don't know how I imagined things would go. Not as they did, that's certain. Watching the Daventrys... I felt like a spear carrier in someone else's tragedy."

"I'd say there was plenty of tragedy to go around. Even if Lady Charlotte hadn't taken that way out. They'd have hanged her, wouldn't they?"

"Possibly. Or consigned her to prison for the rest of her life, if her lawyer was persuasive enough." Robin sighed, raking a hand through his hair. "But I doubt she'd have lasted long in prison. She was too proud to bend, so she'd have broken instead."

Sophie thought of that strong-boned, imperious face, the bred-in-the-bone aristocratic hauteur, and was forced to agree with him. "I know what Lady Charlotte did was terrible—monstrous, even. But I can't help feeling a bit sorry for her. If her husband hadn't betrayed her, twice, with Nathalie—"

"There's no shortage of blame, is there?" Robin remarked. "Lady Charlotte, Daventry, even Nathalie herself. Not that she deserved her fate, but blackmail is a dangerous game."

"I suppose she was desperate," Sophie said. "Perhaps she knew the night you found her with Sir Lucas that it was over, that you were no longer willing to continue in the marriage. And it would be only a matter of time before her pregnancy became apparent. She couldn't be sure you'd claim paternity as you had with Cyril, so she wrote to Daventry instead."

"If truth be told, *I* don't know that I would have done so either," he admitted candidly. "Not this time. But any settlement I gave her would have provided for her and the child."

It just wouldn't have been enough—not for vain, grasping Nathalie. Sophie understood that without a word being said. Some people were just like that, always reaching for more, not caring who might be injured in the process. Moreover, she strongly suspected that it had been power as much as money that Nathalie craved. Power over all the men in her life—perhaps she had clung so tightly to her marriage to Robin because that was the only power she could assert over him. He'd long since outgrown his boyish passion for her, whereas Guy Daventry… Robin was right: there *was* no shortage of blame.

She wondered, fleetingly, what would become of that

family, especially young Marianne. Just after Lady Charlotte's remains had been removed from the scene, the girl had emerged from the drawing room to stand silently beside her shattered uncle. Not for the first time, Sophie thought how convenient the timing of that swoon had been. Had Marianne guessed her aunt's likely intent and, in her own way, tried to aid and abet her? One could resent, even hate, one's oppressive guardian without wanting to see her hanged or imprisoned. Impossible to know for certain, and Sophie had no intention of ever asking. Best to leave it all be, and concentrate on what truly mattered: Robin and Sara.

She studied her lover as he passed a weary hand over his face. "I hardly know what to tell Sara. That someone hated her mama enough to commit murder."

Sophie shivered, her heart aching for that little girl. "Sara's old for her years, but I agree—this will take careful handling. But we'll think of something."

"We." He exhaled. "I'm still getting accustomed to the sound of that."

She smiled, set a hand upon his shoulder. "You'll have a lifetime to do so, I promise."

"A lifetime," Robin echoed. "That reminds me…" He set Tatiana on the floor and stood up. "Wait here, love. I'll be back shortly."

"Of course," Sophie replied, puzzled but agreeable. Tatiana strolled away, sat down before the fireplace, and ostentatiously began to wash.

Robin returned within a few minutes, striding purposefully to Sophie's side. She caught her breath when he opened his right hand to reveal a small velvet box.

"This was—this was my mother's engagement ring," he told her, his eyes dark with emotion. "I've kept it, along with your pearls, in my bank vault for years. I have never offered it to anyone else—or wanted to." He opened the box, turned it to reveal the contents.

The single cabochon ruby shone with a steady radiance in its delicate setting of yellow gold. Sophie gazed at it until her vision blurred with tears. "Robin…"

"The stone isn't very large, I know," he began. "And if you'd prefer something else—"

Sophie shook her head, smiling tremulously. "It's beautiful. Perfect. I would be proud to wear it." The ring of a woman who had loved a man enough to leave her comfortable existence and follow him to the ends of the earth. Who had known great sorrow and loss, but also great joy. What better legacy could there possibly be?

Robin's eyes glowed like twin sapphires. "My dear, these last few weeks have put us through the fire. We're not unscathed, God knows, but we're intact. I shall be sorry to the end of my days that Nathalie died as she did, but I can't regret that you and I are free to be together now. The two of us—and Sara."

She caressed his face. "I can't regret that either. I never could. And I want the same thing you want, with all my heart—you and I and Sara. Being a family."

His smile was almost boyish in its exuberance. "Well, then—let me do this properly. It's high time we followed the rules on *something*!" He knelt before her, holding up the ring box like a votive offering. "Sophia Catherine Tresilian, will you do me the honor of becoming my wife?"

Joy welled within her, so intense and overwhelming she could barely breathe, much less speak. It seemed that she'd waited all her life to hear him ask that question. She wasted no time in giving her answer. "Yes. Robin Lovell Pendarvis, I will happily become your wife."

The ring slid onto her finger as though sized just for her. And when Robin rose and drew her into his arms, she flung her own about his neck, burying her tears and her laughter alike in his shoulder.

They made love by lamplight, savoring each moment leisurely. The ruby shone crimson on Sophie's finger, but no more brilliant than her eyes, storm-tossed green with arousal.

Robin kissed and stroked his way down her beautiful body, reveling in the soft swell of her breasts, the curve of her hips, the long tapering lines of waist and legs. "*Behold, thou art fair, my love,*" he quoted, resting his hand on the gentle rise of her mound. "*Behold, thou art fair…*" He sought her mouth hungrily, the kiss an affirmation of a bond forged in fire and all the stronger for it. She tasted of sherry and sweet almonds—*thy love is better than wine…*

"*Thou art all fair, my love; there is no spot in thee,*" he whispered, positioning himself above her. Sophie shifted as well, her hips tilting to accommodate his entrance, then gasped as he slid into her like a key into a lock.

Robin captured her lips again, and she moaned into his mouth as he began to move within her, slowly at first, then with increasing speed and vigor. Sophie tossed her head from side to side, her breath coming in rough pants, as sensations built and built between their joined bodies. Robin's vision swam, his whole frame shaking with the effort to restrain himself just a few moments more.

"*Let me hear thy voice,*" he urged, feeling the release coming upon them both. "*For thy voice is sweet, and thy countenance is comely…*"

She climaxed then, trembling all over, head thrown back, and he heard her voice, soaring in a triumphant descant. He let go then, his own cry of fulfillment tearing itself loose, and followed her into bliss.

Some time later, when speech and rational thought were possible again, he asked her softly, "So—better than Oxfordshire?"

Sophie gave a husky laugh. "Yes, amazingly enough." She snuggled closer to him. "I never suspected you knew so much of *The Song of Solomon.*"

"How better to woo a singer than with the Song of

Songs?" He dropped a kiss on her hair, the loosened waves of it faintly redolent of violets. The scent, and all its attendant memories, lightened his heart. In that moment, he felt— almost like a boy again, at the beginning of everything: love and life, alike.

Sophie made a contented sound low in her throat. "This is the true start of things, isn't it?" she remarked, as though reading his mind. "Oxfordshire was wonderful, but even then we were preparing to part—"

"And now we don't have to," Robin finished for her. "The future, and what we make of it, is before us now." He paused, trailing his fingers through her fragrant hair. "Sophie, you're—you're not planning to give up your career, are you? Because you don't have to, you know. We can find a way to work around it, accommodate your schedule somehow—"

"Hush!" Sophie caressed his face. "I'm not giving up music, or even performing, dear heart. I just plan to be a bit more… selective about which engagements I accept, in future. Besides, even if I did choose to retire as a touring *artiste*, I daresay I'd find scope for my talents in Cornwall. Truro isn't a cultural wasteland, you know. And there are always those summer concerts at the hotel—if you'll have me."

"*If* I'll have you?" Robin shook his head and kissed her again. "What a question. You can sing for our guests as often as you want, anytime you want. I'm sure they'll flock to hear you. I just… I don't want you to have to give up anything for me."

Her eyes shone, luminous as a sunlit sea. "I won't be giving up a thing. I'll be gaining you and Sara—a whole new world." She stroked a hand lingeringly down the expanse of his bare chest. "Make love to me again, Robin?"

He considered the matter with the utmost gravity. "Yes, I do believe I will," he remarked judiciously, and was rewarded by her laughter as he rolled over and pinned her to the mattress.

Sophie smiled up at him, wrapping her arms about his neck. "*I found him whom my soul loveth,*" she quoted in her turn. "*I held him, and would not let him go...*"

Epilogue

Love, all alike, no season knows nor clime,
Nor hours, days, months, which are the rags of time.

—John Donne, "The Sun Rising"

Cornwall, December 1896

"Perfect," said Sophie, stepping back to admire the lavishly decorated Christmas tree in the grand ballroom.

"As I recall, my love, you once said that this room was made for a big Christmas tree," Robin observed, slipping an arm around his wife's crimson-clad waist.

His wife. It filled him with delight and wonder that he could call her that at last. They had married just a fortnight ago: a simple ceremony here in Cornwall, attended only by their families and closest friends. They'd have a honeymoon in the spring, but for now they were settling in at the hotel as a married couple, preparing for their first Christmas together and planning entertainments for their holiday guests. Much to his relief, Sophie appeared to be enjoying her new role as proprietress and featured performer. She would be giving a concert tonight in this very room, and several others would be performing as well.

"It's beautiful," Sara breathed, coming up to gaze at the tree.

Robin smiled at his daughter, dressed for the occasion in a blue velvet frock that complemented her eyes. "I'm delighted that you approve, sweetheart." He scooped her up into his arms for a closer look. "Do you see that angel on the top branch? Sophie and I chose it especially because we thought it looked like you."

"A dark-haired angel," Sophie put in, smiling.

"But angels are blond," Sara protested, even as she flushed with pleasure.

"Who says?" Sophie inquired, reaching out to stroke her stepdaughter's hair. "*I* think angels may be dark, fair, and even redheaded."

Sara giggled at the thought of a red-haired angel. "With freckles too?"

"Freckles too," Sophie told her solemnly. "It's the goodness within that makes an angel."

Sara's face grew wistful. "Cyril was good too—and he loved Christmas," she murmured.

"I know, sweetheart." Robin dropped a kiss on top of her head. "And we put his favorite ornament on the tree, just below the angel."

He would never forget the boy he'd called his son. Even if, God willing, he and Sophie were blessed with children of their own in the fullness of time.

He looked from one to the other of his two most-loved ladies. They'd got to know each other better over the autumn, and had become the best of friends by the time of the wedding, in which Sara had participated. His daughter seemed more confident too, less shy than she had been. She called Sophie by her first name, but Robin thought he'd seen "Mama" trembling on his daughter's lips a few times and wondered if, in the fullness of time, Sara would decide to use that name instead. He knew Sophie would be deeply moved—and honored—by such a change.

"Papa?" Sara was tugging at his collar, a tacit request to be set down. He complied, and she began to circle the Christmas tree, studying every bauble, candle, and strand of tinsel as if committing each to memory.

Apropos of which… He glanced again at Sophie. "We met at Christmas, remember?"

"New Year's Eve, actually," she corrected, a dimple quivering at the corner of her mouth.

"Yes, but your Christmas tree was still up," he countered. "I remember watching you from behind it, dancing with and captivating half the men in the county—myself most of all."

"You hid it remarkably well," she teased. "It was months before I learned your secret."

"And I was never more glad than when you did." *Exposed his secrets, breached his defenses, changed his entire life…*

She studied him closely, hearing—as was her wont—so much more than he ever said. "Truly, dear heart?"

"Truly, my love." The man he'd been, the old, secretive Robin Pendarvis who'd brooded over his youthful mistakes and believed himself unworthy of love, had finally gone. In his place, Robin hoped, was a man brave enough to seize his second chance, generous enough to love without reserve, and wise enough to cherish his newfound happiness. A happiness that was all the sweeter for the obstacles he and Sophie had faced and overcome.

Sophie smiled, leaning against his shoulder as they gazed up at their Christmas tree, around which Sara was now twirling like a pantomime fairy. After a moment, his wife began to sing, low and sweet, her voice pitched for his ears alone: *"Tomorrow shall be my dancing day…"*

Author's Note

Until 1857, divorces that preserved the legitimacy of children born within the marriage *and* permitted both parties to remarry were rare, expensive, and obtainable only through a special act of Parliament. The Divorce and Matrimonial Causes Act of 1857 established a new civil divorce court in London that granted judicial separations and divorce decrees. Nonetheless, dissolving a marriage remained difficult, especially for women. A man could divorce his wife on grounds of adultery, while a wife had to provide additional evidence of physical cruelty, bigamy, incest, bestiality, or two years' desertion before she could divorce an unfaithful husband. English law also favored fathers when it came to granting custody of the children, although the Custody Acts of 1883 made it possible for mothers to obtain custody until their children were sixteen years old.

Whoever was seeking the divorce, proof of adultery still had to be provided, a process that was not always easy or straightforward. Critic and philosopher George Henry Lewes was unable to obtain a divorce and marry his soulmate, Mary Anne Evans (the author, George Eliot), because he had made himself complicit in his wife's adultery by accepting her children conceived by another man as his own. Much to the shock of Victorian society, Lewes and Evans lived together openly until his death.

Acknowledgments

Writing the sophomore novel is a challenge in its own right. So I'd like to thank some of the people who made the process easier.

My agent, Stephany Evans, for believing that I *could* get the hang of writing under deadline.

My editor, Leah Hultenschmidt, for pinpointing exactly what was needed to make the first third of the book stronger.

The rest of the Sourcebooks team for their attention to detail in every aspect of my work.

My family, for giving me support when I needed it—and space when I needed it even more.

Angela, Queen Beta, for faithful critiquing and useful information about what it's like to be a performing musician.

Wolfgang Amadeus Mozart and Henry Purcell, for existing and being so good at what they did.

Elfrida Vipont and Winston Graham, whose novels provided an invaluable insider's view of a professional singer's career.

Readers everywhere, especially those who told me they were looking forward to the second book—a surefire remedy for sophomoritis!

In case you missed it, read on for an excerpt
from Pamela Sherwood's debut,

Waltz with a Stranger

Available now from Sourcebooks Casablanca

She was a Phantom of delight,
When first she gleamed upon my sight…
A dancing shape, an image gay
To haunt, to startle, and waylay.

—William Wordsworth,
"She Was a Phantom of Delight"

London, May 1890

IF SOCIAL SUCCESS WAS MEASURED BY THE NUMBER OF
guests the hostess could cram into a limited amount of space,
then Lady Talbot's ball honoring her daughter's betrothal to
Viscount Maitland's heir was an unqualified triumph. James
Trelawney wished he could be properly appreciative of such
an achievement, instead of counting the minutes until he
could make his escape. Another half hour or so before the
break for supper—perhaps he could slip away then.

"I see you made it after all," a familiar voice remarked at
his shoulder.

"Thomas." Despite the crowd hemming them in, James
managed to turn his head to smile at his closest friend. "Well,
Jess is my cousin, and my aunt can be very persuasive."

"So she can. Pity the army doesn't recruit women. Lady Talbot would make a formidable general. Here." Thomas Sheridan held out a brimming champagne flute. "This should help."

"Do I look that uncomfortable?" James took a sip of the excellent wine.

"Like the proverbial fish out of water. Wishing yourself back in Cornwall?"

"When am I not?" James sipped his champagne again, thinking longingly of the open spaces and crisp, salty air of his home county. "I only come up to London when I must. Frankly, I don't know how you stand it, Thomas. You're an artist, for God's sake!"

His friend's eyes glinted. "There's beauty and grace to be found even here, James. Or perhaps I should say *especially* here."

He meant women, of course—being something of a connoisseur. Amused, James surveyed the ladies gracing the ballroom. Most were attractive, he supposed, but there were lovely women to be found in Cornwall too. He was just about to point that out to Thomas when the musicians struck up a waltz. The couples assembled on the floor began to move, the ladies' jewels glittering beneath the radiance of the gas-lit chandelier, their pastel skirts belling out behind them with each whirling turn. He glimpsed his cousin Jessica, all in white, floating rapturously in the arms of her betrothed.

A flash of vivid blue among the preponderance of white and pink caught his eye. Idly, his gaze followed the motion of that swirling gown, traveled upward to the wearer's face...

He ceased to breathe, as if a fist had driven the air from his lungs. Beauty. Grace. *Oh, yes.*

Eyes as blue as her gown, the color of sunlit summer skies; a creamy complexion blushed with rose; smiling lips of a deeper rose hue; and a glory of spun-gold hair, bright as any coronet.

"Thomas." His voice sounded husky, even far away. "Thomas, who's that—in blue?"

His friend followed the line of his gaze, stilled abruptly. "Ah. *La Belle Américaine.*"

An odd note in that cool, cultured voice, like the faintest crack in a bell. James glanced at his friend but saw only Thomas's habitual expression of ironic detachment.

"Miss Amelia Newbold," Sheridan continued. "Amy, to her closest friends. The latest heiress to cross the Atlantic and lay siege to our damp, foggy island."

"An heiress. From America?" That might explain her vivacity; English misses tended to carry themselves more demurely, with downcast eyes and half smiles reminiscent of *La Giaconda.* Miss Newbold looked as though she was on the verge of laughter—enchantingly so.

"New York, to be precise. The father's in shipping, I understand. Miss Newbold arrived in London with her mother and sister about two months ago and proceeded to cut a swathe through our susceptible young—and not so young—aristocrats. I've heard she'll accept nothing less than a peer. They don't lack for ambition, these Americans! And as you see," Thomas nodded toward the waltzing couples, "she already has Kelmswood in her toils."

James glanced at Miss Newbold's partner, noticing him for the first time: a tall, athletically built young man whose dark good looks seemed the perfect foil for the American girl's golden beauty. The thought gave him no pleasure whatsoever. "An earl, isn't he? I suppose they're as good as betrothed, then."

"I wouldn't bet on that." Thomas's mouth crooked. "Glyndon's entered the lists as well."

James's brows rose. "Good God, really?" Viscount Glyndon, Thomas's cousin, was heir to the Duke of Harford. "How do their graces feel about that?"

"My uncle and aunt are maintaining a well-bred silence

on the subject. However, I doubt their plans for my cousin's future include an American bride."

Having met the duke and duchess, James was inclined to agree with his friend. Not that it mattered—could matter—to him; the likes of Amelia Newbold were out of his humble star. He made himself look away from her and her handsome, eligible partner. "I think I'll go and get some air. If you'll excuse me?"

Thomas relieved him of his now-empty flute. "Of course, old fellow."

James threaded his way through the crowd toward the French windows, standing open to the warm spring night. Just as he was about to step onto the terrace, a raucous male laugh assailed his ears. A raucous, all-too-familiar male laugh.

Damn, and damn again. Gritting his teeth, James ventured a glance onto the terrace and saw several men leaning against the balustrade in a haze of cigar smoke. In their midst he spotted a familiar blond head, a heavy profile: his cousin Gerald, Viscount Alston.

He ought to have expected this; Aunt Judith was the family peacemaker. If she'd invited one of her nephews to attend Jessica's betrothal ball, she would certainly invite the other, despite knowing that he and Gerald met as seldom as possible. They both preferred it that way.

Memories stirred, a dark tide with a deadly undertow. James forced them away, turned from the doors. The conservatory—he'd go there instead. Even if other guests had sought refuge in the same place, they could hardly be less congenial company than Gerald and his cronies.

But at first glance, the conservatory appeared to be deserted. Moonlight poured in through the glass-paneled walls, bathing the plants and stone benches in an otherworldly glow. Loosening his collar, James inhaled the warm, jasmine-scented air and felt himself relax for the first time that evening.

Hands clasped behind him, he strolled along the nearest

walkway. Feathery ferns, sinuous vines, potted palms...
he could not identify more than a few of the more exotic
species, but it scarcely mattered. Here, at last, were peace and
tranquility. Then he rounded a corner, came to a halt at the
sight of the figure standing in the middle of the conservatory,
the moonlight frosting her golden hair and casting a silvery
sheen upon the skirts of her blue ball gown. Her eyes were
closed, her slim form swaying gently in time to the waltz
music drifting in from the ballroom.

James wondered if he'd lost his mind. Hadn't he just seen
her mere moments ago, dancing in the arms of an earl? Then,
looking more closely, he saw that the shade of her gown was
closer to turquoise than azure, her hair dressed a touch less
elaborately—subtle differences but telling nonetheless. What
had Thomas said? "She and her mother and her sister..."

He must have made some sound, some movement,
because the girl suddenly froze like a deer scenting a hunter,
apprehension radiating from every inch of her.

James spoke quickly, seeking to reassure her. "Pardon me,
Miss Newbold. It is Miss Newbold, is it not?"

⸙

Aurelia fought down a rush of panic and an irrational urge to
flee—for all the good it would do her. The stranger's voice
was deep and pleasant, with a faint burr she could not place.
She wondered if he was as attractive as he sounded; the
thought made her even more reluctant to turn around.

But it would be rude not to acknowledge his presence.
Keeping her face averted, she nodded. "I am Aurelia Newbold."

"Miss Aurelia," he amended. "My name's Trelawney.
Again, I ask your pardon. I could not help but stare—no one
told me that you and your sister were identical twins."

Aurelia swallowed, knowing she could no longer delay
the inevitable. Best to get it over with, as quickly as possible.
"We are twins, sir. But—no longer identical."

She turned around, letting him see the whole of her face now—thinner and paler than Amy's, despite their maid's skilled application of cosmetics. But no amount of paint or powder could disguise the scar that ran along the left side of her hairline before curving sharply across her cheekbone like a reversed letter *J*. She forced herself to meet Mr. Trelawney's eyes, even as her stomach knotted in dread over what she would see.

And there it was—that flash of pity in his eyes; dark eyes, in a strongly handsome face that recalled portraits of dashing adventurers and soldiers of fortune. At least they held no distaste or revulsion: a small mercy. Or perhaps he was simply better at hiding them.

"A riding accident," she said tersely, anticipating the question he was trying not to ask. "Three years ago. It's left me with a limp as well."

"I am sorry." His voice was kind. "That must be difficult to bear. Do you need to sit down? I could escort you back to the ballroom, find you a chair."

Aurelia shook her head. "That won't be necessary, sir. I just—came to admire the conservatory." And to escape all the stares, whether curious or pitying. She'd have preferred to stay behind in their suite at Claridge's tonight, but Amy had refused to attend this ball without her. Beautiful Amy, who looked the way *she* had used to look.

"I see." And as his dark eyes continued to study her, Aurelia had the uncomfortable feeling that Mr. Trelawney did indeed see.

"They fade, you know," he said, almost abruptly. "Scars. When I was a boy, I knew a man who'd served in the Crimea and had a saber cut down one side of his face. Many saw it as a badge of honor. In later years, some even thought it made him look distinguished."

"Scars on a man may be distinguished, Mr. Trelawney," Aurelia said, more sharply than she intended. "On a woman, they're merely ugly. And there was nothing—honorable or heroic about the way I acquired mine." *Merely stupid*.

His brows drew together. "Surely you need not be defined by your scars, Miss Newbold."

She felt her lips twist in a brittle smile. "It's hard not to be, when they're the first things about me that people notice."

"But you are under no obligation to accept their valuation of you. And would *you* judge another solely on the basis of injury or illness?"

He spoke mildly, but she heard the faint rebuke in his voice, nonetheless. Flushing, she looked away, ashamed of her outburst. She'd thought herself resigned, if not reconciled, to her disfigurement; what was it about this man that unsettled her so? "I would hope not, especially now. Pardon me, sir, I let my—disappointment get the best of me. A graceless thing to do, and I'm sorry for it. If you'll excuse me, I'll return to the ballroom." Still not looking at him, she turned toward the conservatory doors.

"Wait." The urgency in his voice stopped her in her tracks. "Miss Newbold, may I have this dance?"

Aurelia whipped her head around, astonished. "Dance? Pray do not mock me, sir."

Dark eyes gazed steadily into hers. "I have never been more serious in my life. You have a fine sense of rhythm—I noticed that when I first saw you. Are you fond of the waltz?"

"Well, yes," she admitted, after a moment; there'd been a time when she loved nothing better than to whirl about the floor in her partner's arms. "That is, I was before. But my limp—"

"A limp is surely no worse than two left feet—and the latter affliction has not prevented quite a number of people from dancing tonight."

A breath of unwilling laughter escaped her. Mr. Trelawney's eyes seemed to warm at the sound. He held out his hand. "I do not ask this out of mockery—or pity," he added with a perception that surprised her. "Will you not indulge me? We need not return to the ballroom. We can have our dance here, unseen, among the flowers. Unless you find it too physically taxing?"

He'd just handed her the perfect excuse. All she had to do was plead fatigue or discomfort, and Mr. Trelawney, gentleman that he was, would surely let her retire and not importune her further. Instead, she stepped forward—and placed her hand in his.

He smiled at her and her knees wanted to buckle; she made herself stand fast and look him in the eye. She could feel the warmth of his hand through the evening gloves they both wore, and smell his cologne, an appealing blend of citrus and clove. Then he drew her to him, his hand resting lightly on the small of her back, and led her into their dance.

Her first steps were halting, hesitant, and she felt her face flaming anew, but Mr. Trelawney took her clumsiness in stride, adjusting his movements to hers. A few more bars and Aurelia found herself dancing more easily, as if some purely physical memory had taken over, leaving her mind free to concentrate on the beauty of the moonlit conservatory and the light pressure of Mr. Trelawney's arms enfolding her as gently as if she were made of porcelain.

Together, they waltzed along the paved walkways, around benches and garden beds, beneath the light of the moon and stars. With each circling turn, Aurelia felt her spirits rise, a sensation that had become as alien to her as a man's touch. Mr. Trelawney danced with an easy assurance that seemed in keeping with his forthright manner and confident air. No other man she'd waltzed with had ever made her feel this safe—not Papa, not Andrew…not even Charlie.

That last realization was so startling that she almost stumbled; Mr. Trelawney steadied her at once, concern in his eyes. Aurelia summoned a smile that surprised her as much as it did her partner, and they waltzed on, whirling back toward the center of the conservatory and the pool of moonlight on the tiled floor.

The music ended, the last chords quavering into silence, and Mr. Trelawney swirled them both to a stop. Aurelia stifled a pang of regret at how quickly the time had passed.

"Thank you," she said, and meant it. She was slightly breathless, and her bad leg twinged after the unaccustomed exercise; it would be worse in the morning, but she felt not even a particle of regret.

He gave her that knee-weakening smile again. "The pleasure was mine, Miss Newbold."

The sound of a throat being discreetly cleared drew their attention to the doorway, where a liveried footman now stood. "Mr. Trelawney?"

His brows rose inquiringly. "Yes?"

"Lady Talbot wishes to speak with you, sir. In the supper room."

"Ah. Tell her I'll be along straightaway."

"Very good, sir." The footman withdrew at once.

Mr. Trelawney turned back to Aurelia. "Pardon me, Miss Newbold, but I must wait upon my aunt. May I escort you back to the ballroom now?"

She shook her head. "No, thank you. I'd like to remain in the conservatory a while longer." Solitude would give her the chance to recover her poise—and invisibility.

"As you wish." But he lingered a moment longer. "Thank you for the waltz. Perhaps we might attempt it again sometime?"

Aurelia swallowed, deliberately not allowing herself to dwell on that possibility. "Perhaps we might, at that. Good evening, Mr. Trelawney."

He raised her hand briefly to his lips. "And to you, Miss Newbold."

He bowed and strode from the conservatory. Much to Aurelia's vexation, her traitorous gaze followed him, long after he had disappeared into the crowded ballroom.

New York Times and *USA Today* bestselling author

Lady Jenny's Christmas Portrait

by Grace Burrowes

They share a dream…

Elijah Harrison is working on the commission that could finally gain him a place at the Royal Academy of Artists when he meets Jenny Windham. She is both a talented artist and an inspiring muse, but if Elijah supports Jenny's career at the cost of his own, he could lose her forever.

…but can only one achieve it?

Jenny Windham is thrilled to assist Elijah with his portraits for a holiday open house. Working with an artist of Elijah's stature is her greatest desire…until chemistry develops between them and other desires begin to burn. Jenny isn't sure which path her life should take, but Christmas with Elijah might be just the thing to light the way.

Praise for Grace Burrowes:

"Burrowes brings to life a deeply moving romance that's sure to be remembered and treasured."—RT Book Reviews

For more Grace Burrowes, visit:

www.sourcebooks.com

Love on a
Midsummer Night

by Christy English

How to avoid an unwanted marriage:

1. Track down your first love
2. Slap his face when he propositions you to become his mistress
3. Flee to the countryside with aforementioned scoundrel
4. Join a traveling troupe of Shakespearean actors
5. Don't fall under the enchantment of a magical midsummer moon...

To escape the scheming, pawing clutches of her late husband's nephew, Arabella Darlington turns to Raymond Olivier, the only man she's ever loved, for help. But the sweet Raymond she knew as a girl is now the dissolute Earl of Pembroke—the most notorious rake in London.

When the situation turns deadly, Arabella and Raymond are forced to hide in the country. As she finds herself succumbing to Raymond's puckish charm, Arabella starts formulating a new plan: how to persuade a rake to propose.

"With its quick and engaging characters, here's a pleasurable evening's escape."—RT Book Reviews

"The theater details add interest... Fans of Grace Burrowes will enjoy English's smart series."—Booklist

For more Christy English, visit:

www.sourcebooks.com

Lady Mercy Danforthe Flirts with Scandal

by Jayne Fresina

--- ❦ ---

Lady Mercy likes her life neat and tidy. She prides herself on being practical—like her engagement to Viscount Grey, whose dark coloring coordinates very well with her favorite furnishings. But things start to get messy when her best friend abandons her fiancé at the altar, leaving it up to Mercy to help the couple. There's just one problem. The jilted man is Rafe Hartley—Mercy's former husband.

Rafe has not forgiven Mercy for deserting him when they were seventeen. Their hasty marriage was declared void by law, but in his eyes the bossy little vixen is still his wife, even if the marriage lasted only a few hours. And Mercy "Silky Drawers" Danforthe still owes him a wedding night.

--- ❦ ---

For more Jayne Fresina, visit:

www.sourcebooks.com

One Night with a Rake

by Connie Mason and Mia Marlowe

— ❧ —

For King and Country, three notorious rakes will put all their seductive skills to work.

After all, the fate of England's monarchy is in their hands.

Since the death of his fiancée, Nathaniel Colton's polished boots have rested beneath the beds of countless wayward wives and widows of the ton. He's careful to leave each lady smiling, and equally careful to guard his heart. So seducing Lady Georgette should pose no problem. But the beautiful reformist is no easy conquest, and Nate's considerable charm fails to entice Georgette to his bed. To woo her, Nate will have to make her believe he cares about someone besides himself—and no one is more surprised than Nate when he realizes he actually does.

— ❧ —

Lady Vivian Defies a Duke

by Samantha Grace

The Naked Truth

Lady Vivian Worth knows perfectly well how to behave like a lady. But observing proper manners when there's no one around to impress is just silly. Why shouldn't she strip down to her chemise for a swim? When her betrothed arrives to finally meet her, Vivi will act every inch the lady—demure, polite, compliant. Everything her brother has promised the man. But until then, she's going to enjoy her freedom…

A Revealing Discovery

Luke Forest, the newly named Duke of Foxhaven, wants nothing to do with his inheritance—or the bride who comes with it. He wants adventure and excitement, like the enchanting water nymph he's just stumbled across. When he discovers the skinny-dipping minx is his intended, he reconsiders his plan to find Lady Vivian another husband. Because the idea of this vivacious woman in the arms of another man might be enough to drive him insane—or to the altar.

"An ideal choice for readers who relish smartly written, splendidly sensual Regency historicals." —Booklist

For more Samantha Grace, visit:

www.sourcebooks.com

If You Give a Rake a Ruby

by Shana Galen

—— ❧ ——

Her mysterious past is the best revenge…

Fallon, the Marchioness of Mystery, is a celebrated courtesan with her finger on the pulse of high society. She's adored by men, hated by their wives. No one knows anything about her past, and she plans to keep it that way.

Only he can offer her a dazzling future…

Warrick Fitzhugh will do anything to protect his compatriots in the Foreign Office, including seduce Fallon, who he thinks can lead him to the deadliest crime lord in London. He knows he's putting his life on the line…

To Warrick's shock, Fallon is not who he thinks she is, and the secrets she's keeping are exactly what make her his heart's desire…

—— ❧ ——

For more Shana Galen, visit:

www.sourcebooks.com

About the Author

Pamela Sherwood grew up in a family of teachers and taught college-level literature and writing courses for several years before turning to writing full time. She holds a doctorate in English literature, specializing in the Romantic and Victorian periods, eras that continue to fascinate her and provide her with countless opportunities for virtual time travel. She lives in Southern California, where she continues to write the kind of books she loves to read. Visit her on the web at www.pamelasherwood.com.